CW01371611

RE-READING
A GAME OF
THRONES

An unauthorized critical response
George R.R. Martin's
fantasy classic

BY REMY J. VERHOEVE

NIMBLE BOOKS LLC

NIMBLE BOOKS LLC

> Nimble Books LLC
> 1521 Martha Avenue
> Ann Arbor, MI, USA 48103
> http://www.NimbleBooks.com
> wfz@nimblebooks.com
> +1.734-330-2593
> Copyright 2011 by Remy Verhoeve
> Version 1.0; last saved 2011-04-20.
> Printed in the United States of America
> ISBN-13: 978-1-60888-115-4
>
> The paper used in this publication meets the minimum requirements of the American National Standard for Information Sciences—Permanence of Paper for Printed Library Materials, ANSI Z39.48-1992. The paper is acid-free and lignin-free.

DEDICATION

A shoutout to my friends on *Is Winter Coming?*, the Ice & Fire message board that does not censor readers for asking questions about *A Dance with Dragons:* Scorpiknox, Oliveira8, Iblis, Lori_Petty, Rex, JJH (thanks for helping out), fish, darkway, aussiechris, RolandofGilead1, robotosaur, Annan, khen r.r. nymous, silent_majority, KrKreuk, Splitter, flodros, flowered, scottishtroy and all the rest of you.

A hearty thank you to Sogge for introducing me to the series way back when. Had I known how long these books were going to take after *A Storm of Swords* maybe I wouldn't have listened to you. Still glad I did.

"Obviously, this book would not exist if George R.R. Martin hadn't been such a terrific spinner of yarns. I salute you, Ser."

And, of course, warm thanks for putting up with me blogging about geek stuff at all times of the day, my sweet lady Slynt.

NIMBLE BOOKS LLC

Contents

Dedication iii
A Prologue Before The Prologue 1
Prologue 4
Ice Meets Throat 6
The Quiet Of The Godswood 9
Dressed Up And Rhaegal 11
What The King Dreams 14
A Bastard And A Dwarf 17
An Instrument To Help Us See 21
Horseface 24
The Things He Does For Love 28
The Waddler In The Courtyard 32
Sadly Short 35
How I Learned To Stop Worrying And Love The Naughty-Naughty 37
Snowfall On The Borderlands 39
The North Went On Forever 41
A Dagger In His Hand 43
The Prince That Wasn't Promising 45
I Wish I Could Step Into This Novel And Kick Eddard In The Nuts 48
Make Him Fly! 51

The Whispering Of Little Birds 56
The Song Of Swords 61
Flatterers And Fools 64
I'll Be There For You 69
Vayon Poole, Escort Duty 74
Preggers And Beggars 76
Old Nan, New Saddle 78
His So-Called Father 82
Bumping Into The Fat Wall 85
Slynt's In The House Baby 88
She-Who-Thinks-In-Italics And The Mexican Stand-Off 92
Hounded 95
Private Investigator Eddard Vii 98
My Name Is Bronn. Prepare To Die 102
Chasing Cats And Shadows 106
Mercy Is For Dumbheads 109
Into The Vale Of Arryns 111
"Yay, Me!" Eddard Thought ... But It Was "Jai, me!" 115
Deaf, Dead Or Down In Dorne (An Excursion into Dunk & Egg)118
Beyond The Horse Gate 121
Totally Out There In The Woods 125
The Awesome Concept That Is The Sky Cell 127
Promise Me 129

The Vale Of Arryn Goes On And On 135
Attack Of The Mysterious Mummer Monkey 138
The Early Adventures Of The Unlikely Duo 141
The Hand Of Justice 145
Evil Anne Of Black Gables 149
Return Of A Con Man 154
Spoonfeeding Lord Clueless 156
A Crown For A King 161
The Boar Did It! 165
How To Become A Black Brother 171
Is There More Shit Left With Which To Hit The Fan? 175
Fear Cuts Deeper Than Swords (But Swords Kind Of Cut Deep Too) 180
Losing Fans Fast? 185
Disengage Slynt Rage 192
A Bird Of Betrayal 194
Let It Burn 198
The One Thing Hodor Had Going For Him 203
Whine And Wine 211
The Beard-Grower 218
Hear Me Roar And Watch Me Waddle 225
The Promise Of Mercy 233
Dungeon Lord 238

A Flurry Of Freys	247
The Price of Honor	255
More Salt In The Wound, Please	265
Imp Into The Fray	274
A Wood For Whispering In	283
Blood Sugar Sex Magik	291
A Bitter Pigeon To Swallow	299
Cryptic Aha!	307
Weeping And Sleeping	316
Eeew Dragondew	323
No Time For Mercy	330
Deal Or No Deal	338
The King In The North	345
Summing Up	353
Enter The Coal Chamber	356

NIMBLE BOOKS LLC

A Prologue Before The Prologue

Most people I know obsess over one thing or the other, be it football, knitting, geology, music, astrology, art, what have you. I have also noticed that if your particular obsession involves fantasy—be it in literature, computer games or movies—you are almost automatically considered a "nerd" or a "geek." Personally, I don't mind. But I must admit that it feels a bit unfair. Why is it more geeky to discuss the plot of, say, *The Lord of the Rings* than to discuss points gained by various football teams during the season? To me, it is all the same. We like some stuff *a lot*, it is just the stuff itself that differs.

The last ten years I have been obsessing over George R.R. Martin's *A Song of Ice and Fire* novels. Before that, I was an obsessive roleplayer and avid *Star Wars* fan. I don't know, I just think that imaginary worlds appeal to me more than, say, sweating hairy men running after a leather ball. I respect those who prefer that kind of entertainment, however (though I have yet to meet an ardent football fan who's *not* snorting when I say I love to read fantasy novels).

A friend of mine introduced me to the world of Westeros way back in 2000 or 2001. *A Storm of Swords*, the third book in the series, had just been published and I devoured those books, realizing that what I had been given wasn't your usual standard-fare fantasy. This was something more, this was something that grew on me. This was the kind of powerful narrative that changed my way of thinking, just like *Star Wars* did when I was a child, and *The Lord of the Rings* did when I finally got out of that teenager period. It had that kind of impact.

Soon I was collecting *A Song of Ice and Fire* cards, buying different editions of the books just to have the different covers, spending money on comic books and calendars. The world created by George R.R. Martin was so appealing, I wanted to *stay* there, live it ... much like I felt when I was collecting *Star Wars* merchandise. I became a fan boy.

When *A Feast for Crows*, the fourth book in the series, was finally—finally!—published in 2005, I devoured it the moment the pre-order arrived in the house. And that is, I guess, the moment when things began to change. We had been waiting five years for *this*? The author himself promised that the second half of the book, to be called *A Dance with Dragons*, would come in 2006. Finally, there is a publication date. In this long interval, the author treated his fans to everything else but *A Song of Ice and Fire*, which has resulted in a growing disappointment in the author and his promises. It is a long and sad story that will come to a break this year—but there are still (at least) two huge volumes to complete the series, and Martin is a not terribly healthy procrastinator who was 62 years old in 2011.

Checking in on Martin's blog *every day for five years* to see the magical "It's done" message was tiring. Yes, it became an obsession. But it is no longer a positive obsession. I, and many other readers, have grown disillusioned with the author and the franchise, and have spent many an hour on the Internet arguing with those who defend the author's behavior towards his readership, without ever reaching an agreement.

So what can one do as an obsessive fan of the series? I chose to re-read the first book in the series, *A Game of Thrones*, for the tenth time. And blog about it. The result of this is *this* book, written while waiting for *A Dance with Dragons*. I wrote the blog's entries using my Internet nickname of "Slynt," taken from the very series—which I refer to a few times.

For a longer and more detailed history of how George R.R. Martin's fan base became increasingly divided after 2005, there are several websites dedicated to the subject that you can visit to read more about it and get a clearer picture. Meanwhile, I'm still waiting for dragons.—*Slynt*.

Prologue

So, a few days ago I started reading *A Game of Thrones*. Again. For the *tenth* time. Usually, I am able to read a few other books in between re-reads, but with all the news about HBO's upcoming TV production, the increasingly long wait for *A Dance with Dragons*, and a yearning for returning to Westeros, I felt it was about time to get back into this wonderful 1996 novel by George R.R. Martin. Also, I recently bought three *A Song of Ice and Fire* role-playing products, rekindling my devotion to what I deem the greatest story ever told.

Upon opening the book again, I perused the maps (as if I don't know them by heart), then went straight into the prologue.

It strikes me for the tenth time, that even though it's just a short prologue, Martin manages to sneak into it quite a lot of detail regarding stuff that will be coming up much later in the series.

I feared that on my tenth re-read of the series, it would finally grow stale. I already knew what Gared was going to say once I opened the book; "We should start back," Gared urged—or something like that, and yet—and yet—the moment I am reading, I am swallowed heart and soul into the cold darkness beyond the Wall, following poor Will and Gared with his ears frozen off (and a finger), and Ser Waymar Royce. The prologue does a good job at describing, although it doesn't really give a good first impression of the series as a whole. The first time I read it I remember being disappointed that I was reading another "standard" tome of fantasy, well except for the dialogue which seemed razor-sharp and realistic instead of vague and unrealistic.

Best line of the prologue is undoubtedly, "Never believe what you hear at a woman's tit", which serves as the first indication that this novel is not gonna stay in the bogs of high fantasy for very long.

It's interesting to see a phrase such as "For Robert!" long before the Robert Baratheon character is properly introduced; I wonder how many such small pieces I missed on my first read. I do remember the second re-read being full of "Wows!" and "Ooohs!" and "Of course!."

Martin is a master at puzzling together small pieces of his setting and characters. Only much later did I think of Ser Waymar Royce as a Royce of the Vale of Arryn, for example.

The spooky mood of the prologue is perfectly paced, and the Others' appearance reminds me of *Predator*, but more ghostly.

What I don't understand is why Gared didn't flee back to Castle Black; why did he flee into the lands north of Winterfell, he was a veteran and most likely knew that doing this could lead to him being executed for desertion. There's a chapter later on where Ned Stark muses on the fact that Gared seemed half-mad with fear, but still ...

ICE MEETS THROAT

Sometimes I wish the chapters in *A Game of Thrones* c had actual titles, because that would make it a bit easier to refer to different chapters, and also they would provide more interesting titles for these posts. Not that I know what I'd call this chapter. *At Summers End? Of the Finding of the Pups? Theon Kicks a Head? After two ears and a finger, Gared also loses his head? Justice in the North? Ice Meets Throat?* I don't know.

What I *do* know, however, is that this chapter has a beautiful, haunting, evocative beginning.

The first sentences are very evocative—very visual, and there is so much going on in these sentences alone. We learn that summer is soon coming to an end, "they" are going to behead someone (which makes us want to continue to read to see what the hell is going on), and Bran rides among them and is excited about it. Who would want to put down the book after such a wondrous composition of beauty contrasted with a fearful anticipation?

I'm pretty sure I didn't catch the fact that the man to be beheaded is, in fact, Gared from the Prologue, and I am still wondering about his motivations (as indicated in the first post). Reaching the small holdfast, we are introduced to many of the characters come to see the man beheaded, if not all twenty. The first small steps of characterization are taken; we learn that Jon Snow cares about his siblings and is dutiful; Theon Greyjoy is, in the words of Jon Snow, an ass, kicking Gared's head away after it has been cut off his body. I was like "Wtf?" the first time I read that. With the hindsight of nine previous readings, it is pretty much consistent with his character. It seems a little strange that Lord Eddard Stark allows Theon Greyjoy to behave like this, though.

This is, of course, a vital chapter in that it sets up so many characters, and of course it is the chapter where Robb finds the dead direwolf and its living pups. Reading this it all seems so innocent and "high fantasy" compared to how things go down the drain for the Starks later—it almost seems like a whole different story, the dialogue a little more rough around the edges, certain character traits never seen again later in the series, but at the same time it is beautifully told. I get a feeling the story went a wildly different way from here than what George R.R. Martin may have originally intended; I believe the focus, initially, was more on the Starks, but who knows.

A small cast of tertiary characters are introduced as well; Hullen, the master of horse, Jory Casell, and Harwin, who returns later in the story in a larger role, which is something that definitely went over my head the first time I read the novels.

On my tenth re-read there are few surprises left in this chapter, but there is one sentence that I believe I have overlooked earlier, and which I find quite amusing now: Jon Snow tells Lord Eddard how he should be taking the finding of the pups as a sign, and that there are five pups, one for each of the lord's children. Jon Snow then says that he is no Stark, so no pup for him.

Now I can really imagine George R.R. Martin at his DOS computer, chuckling as he spells it out for all the world to read—Jon Snow is not a Stark—and as Lord Eddard thinks about it, I am wondering what goes on in his mind? "Maybe: *If only you knew, Jon. You are the son of Rhaegar Targaryen. Yet your mother was a Stark, and I thank the old gods you got her looks,"* Ned thought solemnly. **Technically that *does* make Jon a Stark, and it must be painful for Lord Eddard to not to be able to say so to him.**

Of course, if you doubt this decade-old theory of Rhaegar and Lyanna being the parents of Jon, there is no irony in Jon Snow calling himself "not a Stark."

THE QUIET OF THE GODSWOOD

I guess I'd call this chapter "The Quiet of the Godswood"; the Michael Kormack art print depicting Lord Eddard Stark polishing the greatsword Ice from this very chapter is called "The Quiet of the Godswood" as well. It fits the chapter, as it is kind of quiet—two characters alone, having a discussion. Of course, the things they are discussing are far from quiet—the tone is ominous and hints at things to come.

Catelyn Stark is one of my favorite POVs (point-of-view character) in A Song of Ice and Fire. I was surprised I was reading a fantasy where we got to see the world from the view of a noblewoman, and her inner monologues and motherly actions make her a fairly realistic character I can empathize with. Not that I am a noblewoman, or a mother. I am a father, though.

I love this little chapter; once again Martin creates strong visuals—this time the Godswood—in a perfect, somber manner, and we get to know more about two of the book's main characters, the lord and the lady of the North. We are given insight into the difference between the old gods of the North and the Seven worshiped in the South; and we learn the house motto of the Starks—*Winter is Coming*. When Catelyn tells Eddard that Jon Arryn is dead, we get some insight into Eddard's past and how he and Robert Baratheon were wards at the Eyrie. The number of characters mentioned grows, and Martin easily draws me deeper into his world by mentioning characters offhand who will become important later (Benjen Stark, Tommen Baratheon, and Maester Luwin, to mention a few).

Two things that run through my mind when I read these chapters again.. Since I last read *A Game of Thrones*, news about the HBO TV series has been spilling out, and I notice that I am now "seeing" / visualizing Catelyn Stark as the actress who is going to play her in the pilot; that's kinda weird, cause I always had a very defined Catelyn in my mind's eye who looks more slender. However, I have a really hard time picturing Sean Bean as Ned Stark, even though Sean is a favorite actor of mine. I wonder if his role as Boromir will make it harder for him to truly become Eddard Stark in my eyes.

The other thing I notice that I also mentioned in my previous post is that some of the dialogue seems a little "rough" as if the characters aren't yet as well-defined as they become later. For example, Eddard's comment about Rickon being three years old and needs to learn to face his fears seems a little out of character for Eddard, or maybe it's just me.

The chapter ends with an appropriate warning about the ruling Queen of Westeros, Cersei Lannister, of whom it said that she is growing more and more prideful. I really dig the Cersei character at this point; just by this reference I know we have a bitch on our hands in the Lannister queen.

When I wrote this post, it was still actress Jennifer Ehle who was cast as Catelyn Stark; when HBO green-lit the series and reshot the pilot episode, a new actress was hired to portray the character.

DRESSED UP AND RHAEGAL

I remember vividly coming to this chapter the first time I was reading *A Game of Thrones*. First of all, I struggled with the character's name, thinking it was too different from the other characters (Bran, Jon, Robb ... Daenerys?). Of course, I didn't know that this was the point—Daenerys is, of course, a scion of Targaryen bloodline, and these people weren't Westerosi, and her story takes place on the other side of the world (well maybe not that far). The jump to the Free Cities was a bit jarring at the time, and I felt I was being taken out of a good story in the North, and I know some people still feel that way, as if the Daenerys storyline is merely a plastered-on additional story. But with time, I grew to appreciate this rather original way of telling the whole story, and with *A Feast for Crows* we got even more of this kind of storytelling with chapters jumping all over Westeros, but that is far ahead as of yet.

Of course, on my tenth re-read I know that the Daenerys character is more closely linked to the Westeros characters anyway; there are many links in her storyline, such as her protector knight Ser Jorah Mormont, and her supporter Illyrio Mopatis, who is given screen time in this chapter.

Viserys Targaryen, her older brother, is characterized as a stereotypical villain, and I love to hate the character for it. He is not far off from Joffrey Baratheon whom we meet later in that he lacks a number of social antennae, pinching his sister's nipples and threatening with gang rape (by horses, even), but Martin also manages to let it shine through that this character is, in actuality, a coward. He is angry yes—but he takes it out on his little sister.

One little thing I noticed which I like is when Daenerys is dressed up (before her meeting with her groom to be), Viserys enters the room and looks her over, trying to find the word to describe how she looks in her wedding attire. It is the magister, Ilyrio, who calls her "regal."

It is probably not intended, but Illyrio's 'regal' fits so nicely, the word having some Targaryen connotation ("Rhaegar", "Rhaegal").

I have to say, I didn't really like the Daenerys chapters the first few times around, but now I have grown to love most of them. They are full of interesting tidbits of recent history of Westeros; there is some serious drama going on between the siblings (and later, Daenerys and her followers); and Magister Illyrio is certainly a slime ball whose importance to the story is not revealed in the beginning, making him an interesting character to re-read to pick out motivations.

Another interesting thing is how early Martin manages to establish a plot point that isn't really touched upon before *A Feast for Crows*, literally thousands of pages later: the fact that many nobles in Westeros still secretly hold with the Targaryens. While Viserys is probably exaggerating, his boast that many prominent Westeros lords (among them the Tyrells, Greyjoys and Martells) support a Targaryen re-conquest of the Iron Throne is very interesting, especially after *Feast* where it is revealed that at least one of these lords indeed has such a motivation.

Notice how Viserys looks to Illyrio to confirm his boast. Viserys, and thus House Targaryen, are dependent on this fat spice merchant. This is a hint of Illyrio's importance, but not too obvious. Also shows Viserys' weak character. This is awesome writing, again.

Anyway, reading this part with *A Feast for Crows* in mind, it becomes clear that Viserys is speaking, at least partially, a truth: The Martells of Dorne are hankering for a union with the Targaryens, and the Greyjoys of the Iron Islands are also travelling in her direction; the Tyrells are making a mess in King's Landing and may this be motivated by a hope for the return of the Dragon Kings? How about the Redwynes? I can't say I know too much about them at the moment, but is there a link between them and the Waters bastard and the fleet moving east? I am looking forward to re-reading *A Feast for Crows* to refresh my memory.

If you blink you might miss it, but the Unsullied are also introduced in this first chapter of Daenerys' story, and they are also going to become pretty important later on.

All in all, a good chapter, showing what a bastard Viserys really is, and setting up the marriage between Daenerys and the horse lord, Khal Drogo.

After publishing this post, I received a comment that pointed out a possible connection between Ilyrio Mopatis and House Martell of Dorne, because among the wedding guests we glimpse the brother of the Archon of Tyrosh. Keep it in mind when you read the Arianne Martell-chapters in *A Feast for Crows*.

What The King Dreams

A Game of Thrones for me is a real page-turner. Few books are that alluring to me; if I am tired, I put the book away and go to sleep. But *A Game of Thrones* ... it beckons me, urges me to read just a little more. And so, while I really should have stopped at "Daenerys I" last night, I plunged headlong into "Eddard I" and a number of chapters after that. So I have read a little too far compared to where I am on this blog. Oh well. Maybe if I am able to let the book rest tonight, maybe try and read something else ... but few books keep my attention. Only *The Lord of the Rings* (although that one is easy enough to put down), Joe Abercrombie's marvelous *Best Served Cold*, and a few other titles here and there. Usually, I read a number of chapters from any given book recommended over at the Westeros forum, then give up and go back to *A Song of Ice and Fire*. However, the last couple of years I have been able to distance myself a little more and get into other novels, so I have actually finished novels such as *Gardens of the Moon*, *The Name of the Wind*, and Abercrombie's *The First Law* trilogy. But at the same time, there are far more books lying about that I have started, but haven't finished. Books from all kinds of genres, from historical (a number of Penman novels including *The Sunne in Splendour*), to popular (*The Shadow of the Wind*), fantasies (*The Lies of Locke Lamora*, and a veritable host of others), to dry prose.

I guess what I am trying to say is that no book shares the superb, eloquently paced style of *A Song of Ice and Fire*; no other books have the kind of characterization I love (though *Best Served Cold* comes very close).

Anyway, into the first of Lord Eddard Stark's chapters!

This is a chapter with a lot of exposition. From the opening paragraph describing the visitors pouring through the castle gates to the silence of the crypts of the Winter Kings, there is a lot of interesting detail here. I'm going to pick out a few.

I think Robert Baratheon, the king visiting his old friend Eddard, is superbly characterized. Even though the character concept could be seen as a little worn, cliché even, Martin keeps Robert a real person through his dialogue, which fits the character so well. Lines like "Ned! Ah, but it is good to see that frozen face of yours" effectively demonstrate the difference between the two friends—where one is stern and concerned, the other speaks more plainly, and is more open. The contrast between the two makes the chapter work well, a simple dynamic on which Martin can build their relation—and what a relationship it is—Robert loved Eddard's younger sister, but is married to Cersei Lannister, who will turn out to become a major adversary of Eddard.

The trip down to the crypts of the Winter Kings is a great sequence. The talk between the two—the mystery surrounding Lyanna Stark, Robert's obvious loathing of his wife, Cersei Lannister—things becoming more complicated ... yet a clearly visible plot line has yet to emerge from all these relationships.

Of course, the main point of the chapter is Robert giving Eddard the title of "Hand of the King," which sets off a long chain of events that will shape so many of the situations ahead. Being the Hand means that you are effectively the king's second in command, reminiscent of the relationship between King Edward of York and Richard Warwick the Kingmaker in the historical Wars of the Roses, conflicts that without doubt have influenced George R.R. Martin's series (the most obvious example being the names of the two Houses who fought for control of the English throne being the Yorks and Lancasters, turned into the two Houses fighting for the Iron Throne being the Starks and Lannisters).

My favorite part in this chapter is when Ned talks about what the king dreams, the Hand builds; which is countered by Robert's "the king eats, and the Hand takes the shit."

And, as Hand, our friend Lord Eddard will indeed have to take some shit.

In addition, Robert suggests marrying his son Joffrey to Eddard's daughter Sansa.

On my tenth re-read, I still envision Robert as looking a lot like the actor Brian Blessed.

A Bastard And A Dwarf

All right, it's been a few days since I blogged about my tenth re-read and I am still a few chapters ahead of myself. As I've mentioned before, this book is hard to put down. I realize I haven't mentioned which edition I am reading, so here goes: It's the Bantam Spectra hardcover edition, published in September 1996, with the cover illustration by Stephen Youll. I do have a few other versions of the novel as well, but I won't refer to specific pages so it doesn't really matter which one I have at hand.

So we have already met the bastard of Winterfell, Jon Snow (that's such a cool name by the way), seen him through the eyes of Catelyn in her first chapter, and through the eyes of Bran at the holdfast where poor old Gared was executed. I remember how cool and novel it was at the time of the first reading, with all these different POVs, and I am sure that George R.R. Martin's brilliant use of POVs for different chapters has influenced more than one budding author since. In fact, I find it hard reading books that are not somehow changing between POVs the way it is done in *A Game of Thrones*! This particular chapter is a nice read, grounding the characters even more into the setting; and when seen from Jon's point of view, we begin to see that this novel will be quite different in the way that the setting is not static, and different characters will see things in different light.

It is the fourth hour of the welcoming feast for King Robert Baratheon, and the Great Hall of Winterfell is hazy with smoke. Jon, not seated with his siblings or lord father, tells himself that being a bastard ain't that bad after all—in fact, being "hidden" on a bench far from the true nobles gives him the opportunity to drink as much wine as he wants, and he can keep his direwolf Ghost at his feet. Reflecting on the visitors as they enter the Great Hall, we get our first proper descriptions of the Lannister siblings—Jaime, Cersei, and Tyrion.

This is what a king should look like, Jon thinks of Ser Jaime, and that is so awesome a thought in hindsight, for we all know Ser Jaime isn't among the most honorable men in Westeros.

We are introduced to Jon's uncle Benjen Stark, and through him we get more information about the Night's Watch introduced in the prologue. There is the small but probably important description of Theon Greyjoy ignoring Jon completely (this could be foreshadowing actually, or not at all—it may be just to drive the point home that bastards aren't regarded as nobles; could also be a reflection of the greater problem of the realm—the nobility of Westeros ignoring the importance and dedication of the Night's Watch).

Jon tells his uncle that he wants to become a member of the Night's Watch and it does look like that is what is going to happen.

Jon leaves the Great Hall, takes a stroll outside and we get our first proper meeting with Tyrion Lannister, stunted dwarf lord with a sarcastic streak, one of the truly great characters of fantasy ... nay, *literature*, and his introduction seems ... wildly different from how the character is written throughout the rest of the series. Tyrion is sitting on a ledge like a gargoyle before spinning around in the air and landing onto his legs before Jon. This acrobatic stunt will probably be handy should Tyrion

WAITING FOR DRAGONS

"need" these skills later, but for the rest of *A Game of Thrones*, it feels that his first appearance here is a bit awkward. For a comparison, it makes me feel a bit like I felt when I saw Yoda back flipping and somersaulting his way through a light saber duel with Count Dooku in that dreadful turd of a movie, *Star Wars: Attack of the Clones*. Completely out of character, and not really believable. It's not *that* bad with Tyrion's scene here, though, because Tyrion's defining personality does shine through in his dialogue already here (and besides, him being acrobatic lends some credibility to his skills in warfare);

"Generations of capering fools in motley have won me the right to dress badly and say any damn thing that comes into my head."

Another interesting thing with this meeting is that George R.R. Martin is clearly setting up something between the two characters Jon Snow and Tyrion Lannister, even to the point I feel it's a bit too bluntly written. As if the characters *have* to meet and talk, because the author wants them to have known each other for a later point in the story. I get this feeling in a later chapter too. Not that it bothers me too much—the series as a whole is still the bestest thing I have ever read—but the last part of this chapter... I feel it is a bit weak compared to the rest. It seems somewhat contrived—more on that when Tyrion decides to travel north with Jon to see the Wall for himself.

Finally, there's been some discussion regarding Tyrion's heritage and whether he may be a bastard just like Jon: Could this be another bit of straight information from George R.R. Martin, like Jon Snow's line about his parentage in the first Bran chapter? After all the dragon needs three heads, and if Jon and Ty-

19

rion both are half-Targaryens that may be just enough ... but I am getting ahead of myself, deep into speculation territory, where I really shouldn't be hanging. At least not here and now, pretending not to know how it all unfolds.

Of the revealed actors in the HBO TV series, I think Kit Harrington is the one actor coming closest in looks to how I envisioned the character in the books. I hope he totally nails the role of Jon Snow.

An Instrument To Help Us See

On page 49 in my edition, we get our first returning Point-of-View character, Catelyn Tully Stark. I remember thinking "This is it" in the sense that I had now been introduced to all the PoV characters of the novel. Little did I know at the time that there would, in due time, exist PoVs for Arya, Sansa, Jaime, Brienne, Davos and I am sure I'm forgetting someone too (not counting *A Feast for Crows* here)..

The whole chapter is one scene, taking place in Catelyn's bedchambers, which are the hottest of all the rooms in Winterfell's Great Keep. I wonder about the phrasing here—does she have her own room or does she share the room with her husband, Lord Eddard? Anyhoo, we learn that the noble couple have just had some quick sex (and little did I know there would be plenty more of it later on, more explicit than I could have ever thought doable in fantasy literature—and in some cases, *doable at all*).

Lord Eddard stands by the window, seemingly unaffected by the cold, and they have a short, heated discussion, and we learn that something—someone—is still a bit of an obstacle between the two: Lord Eddard's dead brother, Brandon Stark, whom Catelyn was supposed to marry. Complex gets more complex.

They are interrupted by Maester Luwin, who brings a hidden message from Catelyn's sister Lysa. There is an awkward moment where Catelyn drops the sheets she's been covering herself with, to stand naked before the poor, old man. It is one of those few moments in the saga where it feels a bit awkward, as if the author just *wanted* to have her naked. Now, I'm all for nudity, especially female nudity, but in this case I am thinking

"Why can't she just keep those sheets on and get dressed?" Maester Luwin could've had a heart attack, poor guy.

The message from Lysa Tully Arryn is a warning, and it seems that Queen Cersei Lannister was somehow involved in the death of Jon Arryn, Lysa's husband. Oh, how confused I was by all these names and family relations on my first read! And oh, how wonderful it is to read this thing for the tenth time, and have no trouble keeping straight who's who! So, the letter says "Jon Arryn was murdered by the Lannisters, by the Queen" (to paraphrase Catelyn), the very same golden-haired people visiting Winterfell.

Acting on this new information, the Starks conclude that Eddard must go south with Robert the King to become the Hand of the King. If Eddard's former foster father Jon Arryn was indeed murdered by Queen Cersei Lannister, he actually has the murderer in his own castle—why don't they go down and arrest her, or at least interrogate her? I am not quite sure I feel convinced by this plot point; the author needs Lord Eddard to go south and become the Hand for the rest of the plot to follow, but is this hidden message really strong enough a plot device? I am unsure. As I have said in a previous post, I feel that *A Game of Thrones'* first half is a tad weaker than the rest of the series in that it seems a bit unpolished, a bit rough, as if the greater concepts and ideas haven't been hammered out properly, but it remains a very satisfying read nonetheless—some plot devices may seem weak, but on the other hand we can't really *feel* all the things that happened before the story actually starts: it is hard to get into Eddard's emotions regarding Jon Arryn, for example. Or maybe I have read this book too much. Could be.

A harder decision is, of course, the splitting of the children. Eddard will take the girls south, to marry Sansa off to Prince Joffrey, and teach Arya some ladylike manners. Through their discussion about the children, we learn that Bran is Catelyn's special boy (can't help but think of Marge Simpson and her special boy Bart here), and that she displays anger even at the mention of Jon Snow. The mystery surrounding Jon's parentage is touched upon here, with the mention of Ashara Dayne, but the way it is described it is most certainly a red herring. Catelyn wishes Jon to be sent to the Wall with Benjen Stark, and gets her wish. That left me thinking, wait a minute, these characters aren't as black and white as I thought; she actually wants to get rid of him.

Another sign of the greatness to come; these characters have depth.

Horseface

What? Another POV? I remember thinking something like that when I came to the page with the heading "Arya." I also remember thinking something along the lines of *How interesting can a POV from the point of view of a little girl be?* Oh, how deliciously prejudiced I was in those early days of what is now called "medieval fantasy" (or at least, that's what I call it; has it become a proper subgenre now?), and boy was I in for a surprise—Arya Stark's storyline is perhaps the most gripping of all the POVs, the one most fraught with darkness and tragedies, and George R.R. Martin writes her POV remarkably well. Arya is one of the more distinct voices in the saga. Perhaps the most distinct one, in fact—at least to me: When I think of the series, Arya's trials and tribulations come to mind quickly.

The chapter begins by contrasting Arya with her older sister, Sansa. Where Sansa is the perfect lady, her needlework exquisite, her hands delicate—Arya is the opposite; a tomboy of sorts, her stitches crooked, with the "hands of a blacksmith." Poor thing.

We are introduced to the character Septa Mordane, a fairly stereotypical "strict school miss", who is instructing the ladies in the arts of sewing. Doesn't sound much like fantasy, but when we see it through the eyes of Arya, we get a fairly humorous look at it all. Lord Eddard's two girls are not alone; the Princess Myrcella, daughter of the king, is with them, as are several other girls whose fathers serve the lord of Winterfell. The girls are talking about how handsome Prince Joffrey is. This part is written nicely, it is easy to imagine the stars in their eyes as they, in hushed voices, talk about how Sansa is going to become the Queen of the Realm. Arya, however, doesn't care, and through her dialogue we learn that she is closest to her bastard brother Jon Snow. Eventually, Arya can't take it anymore and leaves them. And as a reader, I feel for her.

There is one line here which I would like to point out, because I don't think I have caught it before now, proving that *A Game of Thrones* can still hold a surprise thirteen years after its publication. When Arya reflects on the situation between herself and Sansa, this little gem shows up:

> Sansa could sew and dance and sing. She wrote poetry. She knew how to dress. She played the high harp and the bells. Worse, she was beautiful. Sansa had gotten their mother's fine high cheekbones and the thick auburn hair of the Tullys. Arya took after their lord father. Her hair was a lusterless brown, and her face was long and solemn. Jeyne used to call her Arya Horseface, and neigh whenever she came near.

First, this paragraph makes it so clear how Arya feels about the difference between Sansa and herself; and it is a way of thinking I guess many readers can recognize—there's a bit of envy in there. Second, that last line is nothing less than hilariously ironic considering later events regarding Jeyne Poole and Arya Stark.

Seeing the young actress who is going to portray Arya Stark in HBO's upcoming pilot episode I am thinking that the actress is too cute compared to how Arya is described here, but I don't really mind. Arya *is* cute in her own way, at least through this first novel. Before winter ...

Escaping the noble girls, Arya finds herself on a window sill next to her bastard brother Jon, watching boys drilling in the courtyard below. A very nice scene, showing more of Jon and Arya's bonds (which I guess will have some sort of outcome in the future—maybe not even a good outcome; note Jon's later comment about finding her frozen in the snow with a needle in her hand); we are told once more that Theon Greyjoy is a bad boy ("a look of wry contempt on his face," ."he said derisively"). Arya is sure she's a better fighter than the young boys in the courtyard (Bran and Prince Tommen), and we get to watch, over the shoulders of Jon and Arya so to speak, an exchange between Prince Joffrey and Robb Stark, which gives us our first hints of just what an idiot Joffrey is and that Robb may be a tad proud.

And, we get our first proper glimpse of yet another important character—Sandor Clegane, the burned man, the Hound. What GRRM does brilliantly here is to give the character just a few lines as if to warm us up, not revealing anything that can't be surmised from what Arya actually sees. She doesn't know the guy, so we don't learn more about him than what she sees: " ... A tall knight with black hair and burn scars on his face." Notice how deftly our favorite author works here: even though *he* knows Sandor isn't a knight at this point, he still writes it " ... A tall *knight*", because that is what Arya thinks he is. Brilliant, and but one of many examples of this technique that suits the story so well. I sure didn't catch it on my first read, neither the words spoken between Sandor and the master-at-arms Ser Rodrik Casell, which I now of course notice drive home the very point that Sandor isn't a knight.

So, through Arya we get some exposition on her relation to both Sansa and Jon, and we learn a little bit more about some of the secondary and tertiary characters. A good chapter, well written, but I am a bit confused about a few lines at the very end of it, and what they signify:

He messed up her hair again and walked away from her, Ghost moving silently beside him. Nymeria started to follow too, then stopped and came back when she saw that Arya was not coming.

So what is GRRM trying to tell us here? Those wolves seem to have some sixth sense; is Nymeria trying to say Arya should follow Jon, and not go south with her lord father? Am I reading too much into this? Probably.

Of course, we get Jon's aforementioned line here at the end as well, where he talks about her lying in the snow, her fingers frozen around a needle.

So gloomy! Is this foreshadowing? After all, Arya does get a sword called "Needle" in the next chapter with her POV. Will Jon be the one finding her? Once again, am I reading too much into this? I believe it is proper foreshadowing. Martin has spoken of ending his series on a bittersweet note, and wouldn't it be bittersweet if Jon finds Arya frozen in the snow, clutching her sword Needle ...

|

THE THINGS HE DOES FOR LOVE

... And so I return once more to the chapter that, more than any of the early *A Game of Thrones* chapters, shows just how different this ride is going to be from the traditional fantasy yarns steeped in the legacy of J.R.R Tolkien. I have absolutely nothing against the professor, of course, but it was and is absolutely refreshing to read a fantasy that has its own uniqueness. This chapter is a good example of just how well George R.R. Martin can write. The prose is almost *music*; building to a crescendo, quite literally, with Bran climbing the walls and towers of Winterfell, going higher and higher until he can see everything below him, the music of the words swelling with each description, and we are *inside* Bran's mind, enjoying the thrill of climbing like I guess we all did as children, and then ... bam! The music stops, a break of sorts, before the instruments produce a sorrowful, spiraling sound ... We learn through Bran's thoughts that he wished to become a renowned knight, and we are treated to the names of some legends of chivalry, such as Serwyn of the Mirror Shield, Prince Aemon the Dragonknight, and Ser Arthur Dayne, the Sword of the Morning. Such names! I love George R.R. Martin's ability to come up with these great nicknames for his characters. Bran is still deciding on a name for his wolf, and while excited about leaving Winterfell with his father to see the city of King's Landing in the south, he now has his doubts and wants to stay at home. Throughout the chapter we are witness to Bran's inner thoughts, which are surprisingly mature for his age, but somehow written in a way that still makes the character believable.

Waiting for Dragons

And, of course, this is the chapter where Bran climbs to the very tower where he overhears a conversation he shouldn't. Ser Jaime Lannister, and his sister the Queen Cersei, naked, giving us a tantalizing glimpse at the intrigues and plots being hatched; and our first little shock in the chapter—what? They are twins—what are they doing together *nekkid*?? (Unlike Catelyn in her first chapter, their nakedness has a very real function in the story here). Listening in, Bran doesn't understand everything they are saying, but as a reader on his tenth time with this fabulous masterpiece of literature, it is fun to read the scattered dialogue between the Lannister twins. The first thing Bran hears is Queen Cersei saying "I do not like it," followed by Ser Jaime's reply, "Gods forbid, it's not an honor I'd want. There's far too much work involved."

Queen Cersei doesn't like that Lord Eddard will become the Hand of the King; Ser Jaime's reply is lazy, giving us a first impression of his lack of chivalry. Jon's thoughts from the Great Hall of Winterfell echo in my mind; "That is what a true knight should look like."

"Robert loves the man like a brother," Cersei says, and confirms what we've seen already, but then we learn that "Robert can barely stomach his brothers ...", so we learn that the king has more than one brother (interesting too, that Ned is the "brother" he loves while his true brothers aren't loved by him), and the cast is once again expanded, and little did I know the first time that it would swell to epic proportions. This must be the fantasy series with the most characters ever. And I love it. Where Tolkien's greatness is in his ability to convey a fantasy setting, Martin's greatness is in his characters and his characterizations.

Bran overhears more; there is talk of a character named Littlefinger, and Cersei mentions Bran's dead aunt, Lyanna Stark, and I guess at first read most of this went completely over my head. But each line uttered by the Lannisters is a deftly placed hint, a piece of the puzzle, and everything they say comes together later in some form. I still don't see a distinct, red thread between the various elements that make the plot move forward, however; what does Cersei care about Lyanna? She doesn't love Robert anyway; and Lyanna's dead; why would Cersei use Lord Eddard betraying a king as an argument to Ser Jaime, the Kingslayer?

Oh well.

The chapter ends dramatically with Bran being discovered by the twins, and Ser Jaime giving the seven-year old a shove. Screaming, Bran went backward out the window into the empty air.

And that is the point where many readers have become hooked. Like me. I no longer care whether the motivations and plot devices used to get Lord Eddard and his children to King's Landing are contrived, not properly set up or whatever. With Ser Jaime's classic line "The things I do for love", Martin adds another layer to the story, takes us further away from the standards of fantasy literature, and ... sigh, I could go on and on gushing about this.

Incidentally, when Lord Eddard later insists on that he now *must* go to King's Landing, I am not sure I follow; wouldn't having his son hover between life and death be a good reason to at least delay the journey? Maybe not. Where the king goes, the realm follows. But it's a bit heartless of Robert, if he loves Eddard like a brother, to not allow Lord Eddard to at least temporarily remain at Winterfell.

The Waddler In The Courtyard

If I was surprised when Arya got her own chapter, I was even more surprised that we suddenly got a POV from someone not in the Stark family. What I believed to be a (fantasy) family saga turned out to include more than one family—and **Tyrion Lannister** made an impression from the moment we got into his head. Undoubtedly the number one fan favorite, Tyrion is a great read for many reasons: He is witty, sarcastic, and has a background even more twisted than his physical appearance.

The chapter itself is, perhaps, a little unremarkable compared to many other chapters in the novel: it is an easy chapter to overlook, for it does not really contain much at first sight—Tyrion's been reading all night, then waddles out onto the courtyard to teach his nephew Joffrey a lesson in humility before going to eat breakfast with his siblings. Really, that's it.

Of course, master of storytelling that George R.R. Martin is growing into with this book, there's a lot more going on beneath the surface; and through Tyrion's eyes, we are given a rare glimpse of how a person with severe physical deficiencies sees himself and others in a fantasy setting (I do believe Tyrion will become a hero, eventually, but that's another matter). I remember when first reading this, how hard it was to imagine a dwarf. And by dwarf, I mean a real dwarf. I was so tainted by high fantasy that it took me a while to shake off the fact that Tyrion was not an axe-wielding, bearded barrel shouting "Khazad!" or what have you. It also took me a good while to visualize him as he is actually described—with blonde hair, differently colored eyes, uneven beard...for the longest time he looked more like Frodo than Tyrion.

It is strange to reflect on this now, on my tenth re-read, when the characters are so ingrained in my conscious: that at one time, *"A Game of Thrones"* was shockingly different; and indeed, it seems that this book started a whole new trend in fantasy literature—one where more realism was infused, where characters were no superheroes. This is the most important book in the genre since, well, *"The Lord of the Rings."* I have no doubts about that. To me personally, it's the most important book regardless of genre. It's the book that changed my view on writing fantasy, it changed how I play role-playing games, and it fueled my interest in British medieval history to the point I began buying history books and historical novels (which made the wait for *"A Feast for Crows"*, and now *"A Dance with Dragons"* somewhat more bearable).

But I digress. I thought this short chapter wouldn't give me any new insights but reading through it I notice one thing I don't believe I have noticed before: another ironic line of dialogue (like Jeyne's in the first Arya chapter), this time from Ser Jaime Lannister who says he doesn't want to be crippled. George sure does like to sneak them in. This made me think of Ser Jaime's line of dialogue in the chapter where Bran is thrown off the tower by his hand—Ser Jaime says he rather wants to fight an honorable man than a sneaky one—could this also end up becoming a heavily ironic line, if you assume that Brienne of Tarth will face him, sword in hand? I refer to Brienne's last chapter in *"A Feast for Crows"* now... it does look like it is going that way—Brienne going after Ser Jaime for Lady Stoneheart. But I am far ahead of both myself and the series now. Something to think about though!

Two other things: George is clearly setting Tyrion up for some interaction with Daenerys' dragons, and Tyrion teaching Joffrey a lesson gives us a valuable insight into his character—he has honor where his knightly brother Ser Jaime has none—it is also the first of many incidents where we see the injustice of life through Tyrion's eyes. He sees himself as the "good guy", but receives no credit for it.

The character of Tyrion Lannister is still not as well characterized here as he is later in the saga (the highpoint being each and every of his chapters in "*A Clash of Kings*"—wow those are amazing), but I believe that once the story is complete (or closer to completion) some of the aspects he shows in the beginning and then are "forgotten" will come full circle (his fascination for dragons, him building a saddle for Bran, his acrobatic skills). It is impossible not to see that the story at some point will have Tyrion riding a dragon, or building saddles for the dragons' riders.

Sadly Short

A sad (and sadly short) chapter this is, giving us a rare glimpse of a different Catelyn Stark, a cold and spiteful Catelyn, which adds to her character and gives us some insight into Jon's problems.

He reached the landing, and stood for a long moment, afraid.

Here we are shown that Jon Snow, for all his later heroics, really was *afraid* of Catelyn Tully Stark. Beautifully written, we get a conversation between the two characters that makes us feel empathy for Jon from the get-go; who can forget Catelyn's scathing remark, *"It should have been you"*? We are also shown just how emotionally distressed Catelyn is here, with Bran not waking up from his coma. Jon comes to say goodbye to Bran, because Jon is definitely joining his uncle Benjen for a journey up to the Wall, to become a member of the Night's Watch.

Supporting my earlier notion of Jon possibly facing Arya (or another Stark) later in the story, Jon has the line *"You Starks are hard to kill"*, but of course it could also be just a nod and a wink to the fact that so many Starks later will face ze grim reaper.

Finally, Jon gives Arya the sword Needle, and we get another glimpse of their friendship. Damn, I am *sure* Jon and Arya will face each other as enemies somewhere down the line! All these little details spread across these opening chapters of *A Game of Thrones*, all these subtle hints ... I haven't seen this crackpot theory on the Westeros forums yet, but I am convincing myself as I write that GRRM is setting up this confrontation. Maybe Arya is hired to kill Jon?

Beautiful and sad chapter, 'nuff said.

How I Learned To Stop Worrying And Love The Naughty-Naughty

> Daenerys Targaryen wed Khal Drogo with fear and barbaric splendor in a field beyond the walls of Pentos, for the Dothraki believed that all things of importance in a man's life must be done beneath the open sky.

Daenerys' second chapter begins with the wedding between her and barbaric Khal Drogo, and the opening paragraph shows us how efficient the author is with words; just look at how much he is actually telling us here: Dany did indeed marry the Khal; it was splendid, yet barbaric (as the chapter will detail later); she married in fear; it happened outside of Pentos; the Dothraki is a male-dominated society (".. in a man's life ..."), and the Dothraki are a people of the open, flat world. Re-reading *A Game of Thrones* is a rewarding experience, even on the tenth time, since there is so much information in every sentence; Martin is a master of dishing out atmosphere, and with this chapter we get a very stark (no pun intended) contrast to the chapters taking place in the cold north of Westeros. The Dothraki culture is at once both interesting and disgusting, with rape and murder apparently necessary for a wedding to be really successful.

We are given more reasons to hate the foul Viserys Targaryen: his contempt for his sister is a hook to make his later 'crowning' all the more fulfilling.

Ser Jorah Mormont's role expands as he becomes part of the Targaryen retinue, and Daenerys is given three handmaidens. In a particularly disgusting reveal, we learn that both Viscrys and the absolutely grotesque obesity that is Ilyrio Mopatis both have enjoyed Doreah, the handmaiden who is going to teach

Daenerys "the arts of womanly love." The whole vibe from this chapter is one of sexual abuse and violence, and gives the Daenerys story arc a sense of the "sword & sorcery" style, reminding me of *Conan the Barbarian* and similar fare, with scantily clad women (and young girls, even), big warriors etc.

The last half of the chapter is a quiet, yet terrifying, moment where Daenerys and Khal Drogo are alone, and she has to have sex with him. In the end, it seems she is quite all right with it, after all.

I like this chapter, and I don't like it. I feel almost guilty about liking it, LOL.

SNOWFALL ON THE BORDERLANDS

In the hour before dawn, Lord Eddard is summoned by King Robert.

"Up, Stark! Up, up! We have matters of state to discuss."

Together they set out on their horses, away from the eyes and ears of the entourage, just the two of them, and we get a short but vividly described chapter where we learn a little more about the relation between the two characters. Through their dialogue we get a little insight into a few tertiary characters— Ser Jorah Mormont is mentioned, Varys the Eunuch, and we get to see Daenerys Targaryen through the eyes of King Robert— which is quite different from reading about her in her own point of view. I am surprised to see that Ser Jorah Mormont is revealed to be a spy already now—can't say I remember that from earlier readings.

Mmm ... maybe I did notice it. It's right there. The interesting thing here, of course, is that Varys is the one controlling Ser Jorah's destiny, and Varys is the one who tells the king what is a good thing to do and not. So, the author pretty much confirms what we've witnessed so far—King Robert isn't really the ruler of the realm. He's a figurehead for his councilors.

Another interesting bit here is of course the talk about Wylla, whom Robert calls the mother of Jon Snow. Eddard does not confirm this, however, keeping his silence on who Jon's mother is; however, with Eddard's honor being so thoroughly rigid, it is obvious that Wylla is a red herring—that Robert *believes* her to be the mother, and Eddard is content with that lie—and that the identity of Jon's mother is a mystery that will continue throughout the series. I used to love this mystery—with five years between books, it has become hard to hold on to that passion.

The last part of the chapter gives us a glimpse of the past, and this is a strong point with *A Game of Thrones*; that there's always something behind the current events: Personal relationships from the past, events of conflict and intrigue, a lot of things that help shape the motivations and actions of the current cast. We get that fantastic image of Ser Jaime on the Iron Throne, and Eddard's account of what exactly happened on that fateful day when King Aerys opened the gates of King's Landing to Lord Tywin Lannister.

The hints of the past really make me want to read these events as a prequel book!

THE NORTH WENT ON FOREVER

Yay, wawaweewah and woo-hoo! Another Tyrion chapter—although, in hindsight, his chapters are infinitely more entertaining and well written in *A Clash of Kings* and *A Storm of Swords* ... Here, he is still a character in development (or so I read him), and I don't really see the Tyrion of the later books here; I may be wrong, but it does seem to me (as I have mentioned before) that the character does things in these first chapters that don't really gel with the way he acts and thinks later, and that his first chapters are setting him up for events that have yet to come to pass in the saga. In this particular chapter, it is his decision to go to the Wall. The character doesn't really have a strong motivation beyond "always wanting to see it"—which, of course, is fine, but doesn't fly in the context of a tightly plotted fantasy novel. I do accept it however, and once Tyrion gets into his stride with his quips at Castle Black, I am laughing along with the men of the Night's Watch. What I am trying to convey here is that his decision to go north seems a bit contrived.

The chapter details Tyrion's (and Jon's) journey from Winterfell to the Wall, providing us with some beautiful descriptions of landscape, some of the aforementioned setup for Tyrion (*"Tyrion had a morbid fascination with dragons"*), more history is laid out before us about the Targaryens and their dragons (quick digression: When I was in the habit of playing *World of Warcraft*, my Blood Elf hunter had a pet tiger called Meraxes), and the beginning of the friendship between Tyrion and Jon that I suspect will get an outcome (one way or the other) later in the series, possibly in the final book.

The dialogue between Jon Snow and Tyrion Lannister is pretty good. When I, on my tenth re-read, see the line *"When I was your age, I used to dream of having a dragon of my own"*, it pretty much nails my suspicion that Tyrion will ride a dragon in the future. Tyrion compares his physical disability with Jon's problem of being a bastard, making Jon think about things in a new light, and some of this will shine through in Jon's character later, which is a nice touch. I am very curious to know how all this setup between the two characters will end up—after the next Tyrion chapter (getting ahead of myself here I know) there is, after all, 3000 pages or so with no interaction between the two characters. It only seems to confirm my suspicions that Jon Snow and Tyrion Lannister are two of the three heads of the dragon (if you don't know about this theory, do visit Westeros—the website that is, not the actual continent because it doesn't exist you know).

I am wondering, and this is idle speculation at best, if GRRM has put a little hint of Jon meeting another character in here as well. I am not going into detail on this as it touches on *A Dance with Dragons* spoiler material, but consider the following:

> *The boy stood near the fire, his face still and hard, looking deep into the flames.*

I received a comment on this particular post that I shouldn't be too sure about my predictions regarding Jon Snow, Tyrion Lannister, and the dragons. Of course, everything is up for speculation until we actually get Martin's resolution. He may even have changed his mind in the ten years since *A Storm of Swords* was published. Is he trying to write his way out of his fans' predictions?

A Dagger In His Hand

This is going to be a quick post, as befits a quick read of a chapter. In this one, a pivotal event shapes the entire chapter— an idiot puts the Winterfell library on fire to divert attention from the rest of the castle, so he can go about killing poor comatose Bran Stark without the hassle of guards or, indeed, Bran's mother Catelyn Stark, who sits by him night and day.

The assassin has been hiding out in the stables, waiting for his chance. It seems to me that he finally got sick of waiting for Catelyn to leave Bran's side, hence putting the library to the torch.

Only that makes his line, *"You weren't s'posed to be here"* a bit of a strange thing to say, as he would be, or should be, expecting that, maybe she wouldn't come. Or even notice the fire. A strange thing to say, anyway, upon entering the room. Catelyn is rescued by Bran's direwolf, Summer, which is convenient as that allows the direwolf to remain at Bran's side as his canine bodyguard, thus keeping the poor boy alive and nurturing his story arc to come.

Catelyn decides to go to King's Landing, because now she knows the Starks are deeper in trouble than they had realized, not only because of Jon Arryn's murder but because she believes Ser Jaime Lannister threw Bran Stark out the window.

The awesome thing is that Catelyn suspects it already this early, and we know it's true. Of course, it wouldn't make sense for George R.R. Martin to have Catelyn trying to figure out who pushed Bran; since we already saw it happen first-hand ourselves. But wait a minute, doesn't a certain Maid of Tarth spend an entire volume of ice and fire searching for someone we know she won't find? Another point in favor of this first volume—yes, I have some grievances with the fourth book. Back to Catelyn, I admit I find this business with Ser Jaime and Bran far more interesting than the whole deal with Jon Arryn's death.

We get a few insights into Robb's character and how he is changed by being the commanding lord of Winterfell, but Theon Greyjoy seems to me a bit undefined yet; in one chapter he laughs while kicking a recently decapitated (or shall I impress you even more with "obtruncated") head, and in this one he draws his sword like some hero (but that could be, of course, him feeling heroic in the heat of the moment). When we get Theon's own chapters in *A Clash of Kings*, we'll get to see the character for what he really is, and I really can't wait cause I love to hate the idiot.

So, another mystery is given to us with the dagger, but then I guess we agree with Lady Catelyn that the killer was hired by either Ser Jaime or his sister, Queen Cersei—at least at this point in the story.

THE PRINCE THAT WASN'T PROMISING

And we're at Sansa's first chapter. As if George hadn't surprised me enough already, he suddenly throws at me a chapter from the point of view of a spoiled princess, the opposite of Arya and Jon. Yet it is written just as vividly as the other chapters, and the book would have been poorer without Sansa's hopelessly deluded point of view.

The chapter itself has a fairly simple structure, with a fairly simple plot progression; Sansa and Prince Joffrey go riding, meet Arya and Mycah, the butcher's boy, there is conflict, and Joffrey is wounded by Arya's direwolf Nymeria.

This is, of course, the exterior action of the chapter—we are treated to much more in the course of the few pages. More of Westeros' history is told through the characters' dialogue.

This chapter gives us a geographical pinpoint to the exciting, legendary confrontation between Robert and Rhaegar; it gives us insight into the relationship between Arya and Sansa (."..like she was so stupid", it's so well-written, as if Sansa herself told George to write it this way), and it tells us that Arya has paid attention to quite different things than Sansa.

In fact, a lot of this chapter is all about contrasting the two sisters. Arya doesn't want to ride in the Queen's wheelhouse because it doesn't have windows so she can see the world; Sansa can't understand why that would be interesting. Sansa shudders at the thought of the black bogs of the Neck, while Arya relishes exploring that area. Arya is careless, Sansa is prim. They are night and day, yet sisters. I hope this contrasting will get a huge and satisfying payoff later in the series.

The most important contrast between the two, however, may be that Arya sees through the false pretenses and behaviors of the nobles, whereas Sansa is enamored by the gold and glitter and courtly talk. This particular point is well addressed at several instances, but maybe the following utterance from Sansa seals the deal:

"Gods be true, Arya, sometimes you act like such a *child*."

The third major character in the scene is Joffrey, and we are getting to see more of his true personality: a spoiled, wicked child, the archetypical elitist noble.

Then there's the scene where Sansa returns to the wheelhouse, and we are introduced to three more important characters—Ser Barristan Selmy, commander of the Kingsguard, Renly Baratheon, the king's youngest brother, and the mute Ser Ilyn Payne.

Ser Ilyn Payne is given a thorough description, but is it for effect or will George make him more and more important as the story progresses? He does get a bit of a sidekick role in *A Feast for Crows*, but I suspect there's still more to come of Ser Ilyn. Of course, setting him up as George does in this chapter also makes it more painful at the end of the book, when Ser Ilyn swings the sword ... but I am getting behead ... I mean, ahead of myself again.

We have already been introduced to The Hound, but we get more of him in this chapter, his rasping voice and black humor, and I think around this time he became a favorite of mine.

When Joffrey is assaulted by Arya's direwolf, I can't help but think "Yes! Get him!" but *damn*, the boy is, what, thirteen years old? He should've been sent away as a ward long before

Cersei could turn him into this monstrous little prince (although we only get glimpses of his wickedness in this chapter, most notably his last line of dialogue, where it becomes clear that he doesn't have any love in him for Sansa).

I'm not sure what I expected the consequences of this scene would be. Arya's wolf attacking the prince, Arya playing with a boy who smells of the slaughter block, Prince Joffrey being such a prick. But I sure as hell didn't expect the outcome to be Lady—Sansa's direwolf tied up back at the royal camp—taking the blame, so to speak.

Maybe I didn't expect anything. First time I read it I was still expecting things to follow the traditional fantasy pattern, with everyone living happily ever after (well, except for the Lannisters and their retinue, of course). So one of the big surprises in the book, for me at least, is actually Lady's death.

NIMBLE BOOKS LLC

I Wish I Could Step Into This Novel And Kick Eddard In The Nuts

All right, four days have passed in the story but I just flipped to the next chapter. Arya's been gone for four days (I wonder what she was doing all these days—would be nice to have an Arya chapter squeezed in between here, just to get to see her survival instincts for the first time—she certainly needs them for later), when Vayon Poole tells Eddard that his rascally daughter has been found.

Now, George is a master at portraying minor characters in a broad stroke or two, but steward Vayon Poole strikes me as a very anonymous character—what's his "hook" which I haven't caught even on my tenth re-read? I mean, characters with less "screentime" and dialogue, such as Jhalabar Xho or Stygg, are more vivid in my mind's eye than poor Poole. Maybe because Xho and Stygg are represented in the *A Game of Thrones: Collectible Card Game* with their own art? I haven't seen Poole depicted in any art, but I quit collecting the cards a few years ago, so who knows, maybe Vayon's in the pool of cards by now.

Well that was a digression if ever there was one. At least Vayon Poole gets some screentime here in this blog.

Stops writing to use google-fu on Vayon Poole

[Found 4,500 matches for 'Vayon Poole]

* Clicks 'Images' button*

No heroic poses from our Winterfell steward there.

* Goes back to blogging*

WAITING FOR DRAGONS

All right, I am coming straight out with this: *Eddard III* is probably one of my **least** favorite *A Game of Thrones* chapters! How's that for shock and horror.

Why? I hear Mormont's crow caw, *Why? Why?* (Not because of corn, that's why).

Well, I find this chapter to be a bit ... I'm not sure how to put it ... well, it is an *annoying* chapter. I'm like, "Ned! Open your eyes, man. Surely you realize one of your daughters is a [explicit deleted] *liar?*" I'm like, "Sansa! What the [explicit deleted] are you doing? This is your *sister!*" I'm like, "Renly, why are you laughing instead of standing up against the Queen?" I'm like "Robert! Did you leave your wits on the bottom of a wine barrel? Why do you let Cersei decide on the matter? Why can't you see Joffrey can't possibly be of your loins? And how can you allow such a weird decision to be made?"

Aggravating chapter, to say the least. I find the chapter a little bit strange, too. I mean, why kill Lady? What is the point? How did it benefit anyone? If the point is to show us how Cersei has control over Robert, why not something more ... believable? I guess I just find it hard to believe that the royal family bothers to make such a farce out of it; these kids are only *kids*; why does punishing Lady (and thus, Sansa) make for a better narrative choice than having Arya punished somehow? Or Mycah, for that matter?

If George wants to have Lady killed to make a point of Sansa "leaving" the Stark family, why in such a blunt manner? Am I missing something?

The ending of the chapter is also eyebrow-raising. Sandor Clegane returns with Mycah's corpse in a bag—there's an interesting discussion regarding this very scene online, do check it out, the Hound's glittering eyes which I always took for some sort of blood fever may just be tears shed (!). I like the thoughts behind this possibly surprising interpretation of an otherwise grim and gory ending to an annoying chapter.

Ned is so helpless in the situation in this chapter, and it just bugs the [explicit deleted] out of me. Heh. I do think, however, that the Cersei character is further fleshed out here, as is Robert's weakness towards the Lannister family, and as I got deeper into the series Cersei became a favorite love-to-hate character of mine. Up until book four, where I find her less interesting.

I'm glad I finished this chapter (for the tenth time, LOL), 'cause few chapters irk me the way this one does. Now there's gonna be a whole lot of time before I have to read it again. It would be interesting to hear other people's thoughts on this chapter. Maybe enlighten me to the whole deal around Cersei ordering Lady dead on behalf of her wicked son. Is there a plot here that I fail to see? Or do I just, after all, only want Lady to live?

MAKE HIM FLY!

This is one of those short, but intensely interesting chapters spread throughout *A Game of Thrones* in which George R.R. Martin plays with (prophetic) visions, uses a dreamy, surreal language to kind of mask his foreshadowing (another good example is the chapter where Ned dreams of the Tower of Joy). As such, it's an interesting short piece of text, even though there is little external action. If the guys making the HBO series need to save money, they only need the actor and a bed and a few seconds of film where we see Bran twist and turn in his bed

(As long as it doesn't look the way it did when Anakin Skywalker was dreaming about his mother in that wreck of a movie, *Attack of the Clones*. It did definitely look like Anakin was doing something quite different under the sheets.)

So, we have a crow spiraling down with Bran, as Bran dreams he is falling towards the ground far, far below. What is this crow? *Who* is this crow? One of the many mysteries of this chapter. Some people believe it is the voice of the Old Gods (or one of them); others believe it to be a Greenseer; yet others think it may be a Child of the Forest, that legendary vanished race of beings. Yet others believe it may be a combination of these; and I think I am in that camp—that, maybe, just maybe, the Old Gods and the Children of the Forest are the same, a bit like some people today believe God may have been an alien, and things got mixed up.

Who knows what George is thinking—but he *does* have a background in science fiction. Even more options exist as to who or what this crow is—an agent of the Others? Someone who's skin-changed ("warged") him or herself into the crow? Later in the series we do get evidence that in the world of Westeros, it is quite possible to change into the skin of a beast (or even man), and so that's also a possibility. To think that this book was published in frickin' 1996 and we still don't know about this crow!

Could the crow actually be Old Bear Mormont's crow? It has a knack for talking and understanding things. Could the crow be a spy placed at Castle Black? There's another theory to chew on. Maybe not one most people will fall for, but it's a theory nonetheless. It *is* rather fond of corn, though, but so were the crows atop the Great Keep, and it does look like Bran mixes some of his experiences into his dreams (he hears and sees Jaime Lannister as he pushes Bran out of the window, for example).

As Bran falls, we get a beautiful description of what he sees as he plunges through the air.

I'm probably reading too much into this, but is this a way of saying that once you have the crow's abilities, you can spy on everyone across the realm? Or, once Bran becomes some sort of "magician" (for lack of a better word), that he may see everything, possibly seeing how everyone is fighting each other and not the real threat?

What does Maester Luwin see that makes him frown? Is this a foreshadowing of the Red Comet?

Is this a foreshadowing of Robb becoming Lord of Winterfell in the nearby future?

WAITING FOR DRAGONS

Is there foreshadowing of Hodor carrying Bran on his back through the North?

He sees his mother on a galley racing across the waters of the Bite; Ser Rodrik leaning across a rail, shaking and heaving, these two visions are clearly "true" in the sense that Bran sees something that is actually happening (or is about to happen?), which would make this a Green Dream, no? He also sees Lord Eddard pleading with King Robert, Sansa crying herself to sleep, Arya watching in silence—referring to the previous chapter.

The interesting thing is that Bran sees that *"there were shadows all around them."* Threats.

One is dark as ash with the terrible face of a hound—without a doubt, Sandor Clegane.

Another was *armored like the sun, golden and beautiful.* Could be Cersei, could be Ser Jaime, and could be Joffrey. The "armored" part makes me sure its Ser Jaime Lannister, he's got gilded armor if I remember correctly.

Over them both looms a giant figure in stone armor, but when the apparition opens its visor, there is nothing inside but darkness and thick black blood.

Now who is looming over both Ser Jaime and Sandor Clegane? The obvious interpretation is Ser Gregor Clegane, the Mountain that Rides, brother of Sandor. He's gigantic, he's the Mountain (."... made of stone"), and in *A Feast for Crows*, we get the impression that he's gonna lose his head, or has lost his head ("nothing inside"). Now, Ser Gregor definitely looms over Sandor as the big, evil brother, but how does Gregor loom over Ser Jaime, a member of the Kingsguard, the Kingslayer?

Will Ser Jaime and Ser Gregor face each other in a dramatic trial by battle in the future? I am beginning to think so; based on *A Feast for Crows*' final Jaime and Cersei chapters I speculate that Ser Jaime will return to King's Landing to defend Margaery Tyrell, while whatever remains of Ser Gregor Clegane will champion Cersei's cause. Quite a twist, and I am looking forward to it (whether it happens or no, LOL).

... And there is even more mystery in this chapter. It's short, but it sure is filled with interesting descriptions and hints. George is a master of this storytelling technique in my opinion. I am amazed at how he is able to put in something so early in his work, and then have the payoff so much later. It definitely makes re-reading these books a worthwhile pastime (besides, I have yet to find anything remotely as engaging).

Bran looks to the east, and to Asshai by the Shadow, "where dragons stirred beneath the sunrise." What do you mean, awesome? Does Bran see actual living, breathing dragons over there? Is it meant as a foreshadowing of the birth of Daenerys' dragons? Who knows—we haven't seen one inch of Asshai yet, so we can only speculate. Sigh.

Finally, Bran looks north. And here we get a memorable, beautifully written passage.

It is good stuff. What does it all mean, though? The curtain of light sounds like Northern Lights to me (Aurora Borealis) and that is all I get out of it, LOL. Is the "heart of winter" simply the farthest north, where darkness could be eternal (since we got these crazy long summers/winters, maybe the poles of the world are in continual cold night)? Only George knows. I hope he knows.

The chapter ends on a pretty upbeat tone for being part of *A Game of Thrones*. Where the previous chapter ended with Sandor Clegane riding down the poor butcher's boy, this one ends with Bran waking up in his bedchamber at Winterfell. Okay, he's lame from his waist down, but still. He *does* awake. And his direwolf is right by his side, happy as a pup (so to speak). And then it ends so beautifully with Bran's line:

"His name is Summer."

Even this line can be dissected for meanings and/or symbolism but I think Bran came up with the name because he now has learned through his (Green?) dreams that the true enemy is Winter (aka the Others), and he is gonna fight this enemy—with Summer. I wonder if Bran briefly considered calling his direwolf pup Spring, which I guess would be appropriate too. I mean, why Summer and not Spring? Why *do* they talk so little of spring and fall in Westeros? Yes I know, the seasons are skewed (as is the planetary axis I assume), but ... oh well, that's a really minor question considering the many awesome mysteries to ponder from this chapter alone.

Interestingly, the casting of Bran Stark for HBO's pilot episode of *A Game of Thrones* is now official, and I think the young lucky boy who got the role looks *precisely* the way I'd like to see Bran Stark. If he can act, well that's a bonus. My excitometer regarding the TV pilot is about to burst into flame by now. After putting up this post, I received a few comments from fellow fans of the series. They pointed out that I should be interpreting the titan as Littlefinger, and not Ser Gregor—and I guess with hindsight that is a more valid interpretation.

THE WHISPERING OF LITTLE BIRDS

I have always felt that there should be (could be) a Catelyn chapter between this one and the previous one; her voyage, together with Ser Rodrik Cassel from Winterfell to King's Landing, it transpires so fast compared to other voyages during the series (Samwell Tarly spends a whole *book* travelling from Eastwatch-by-the-Sea to Oldtown), but on the other hand it is also nice to get our first proper view of King's Landing. Still, I wouldn't mind a Special Edition of *A Game of Thrones* where there's a bonus Catelyn chapter, describing the unexpected storm off Dragonstone referred to in this chapter.

Poor Ser Rodrik has shaven off his whiskers, and with his seasickness and all, Ser Rodrik becomes a pitiful, sad character instead of a knight. I don't know if this is intentional or not, but I think it does add to the impact once Ser Rodrik bites the dust a few books down the line.

An interesting aspect in this chapter is how many places, persons, and cultures are only mentioned in passing, but which will be further explored at a later point; there's the Tyroshi accent (maybe an attentive reader would quickly realize Captain Moreo Tumitis and Magister Ilyrio Mopatis are characters from the same place; me, I needed more than one read to be sure). We hear of White Harbor (which we still wait to "see", hopefully the place will feature in *A Dance with Dragons*). There's the mention of the Bite, confirming the vision Bran had in the previous chapter; the Fingers are mentioned which of course is the holding of Petyr Baelish, Dragonstone is mentioned but we have yet to experience it; we hear of Ser Aron Santagar, the king's master-at-arms, who like steward Vayon Poole is a horribly underused character—with a great name nonetheless—Ser Aron Santagar. I wouldn't mind bearing that name. There's more of Westeros' history nestled in the chapter as well, but not so much as in some of the previous chapters.

Then we get the great description of King's Landing as the *Storm Dancer*, the galley with Catelyn and Ser Rodrik aboard, slides into the harbor.

My point is that George R.R. Martin here shows just how skilled he is at describing places with quick, broad strokes; by putting many commas into the paragraph to separate a large number of different buildings he gives the impression of a bustling city; all very good, but he manages to top it off by adding two named buildings that make me as a reader very curious about these places—especially the Dragonpit with its closed doors is a very alluring place, and by not describing everything in detail, GRRM allows us to "see" into it what we want. Wonderful, and King's Landing becomes a place alive in our minds.

Before long, Catelyn is taken by the City Watch to the castle on the authority of Petyr Baelish, and we get to the meat of the chapter.

Now I have to ask this, just to be 100% sure. Check out the following:

The men who pushed into the room wore the black ring mail and golden cloaks of the City Watch. Their leader smiled at the dagger in her hand and said, "No need for that, m'lady. We're to escort you to the castle."

We're not given more than this about the leader, but this is Janos Slynt right? Why does he smile at the dagger? Did it smile to him first? Did he recognize it? Was he expecting it? I wonder. There's so much mystery when Slynt is involved.

The meeting between Catelyn and Littlefinger is very interesting, more so on the tenth read than the first, because now I am well aware of their back-story and how it fits into the larger story, with Petyr's love for Catelyn and all.

They talk about Lord Varys, the *other* mischievous councilor of the king, and it seems to me that Petyr is trying to set Varys up as someone Catelyn (and the reader) shouldn't trust, which is very Petyrish, no? When Varys arrives onto the scene, GRRM takes care to describe him as a somewhat obnoxious character too, almost reinforcing Petyr's hints that Varys is as slippery as an eel.

Of all the wonderful characters in *A Song of Ice and Fire*, Varys is one of the best portrayed/described non-POVs, I think. He comes across so vividly, maybe because he is surrounded by mystery, maybe because he is overly different from the other characters. And maybe because he is somewhat stereotypical, too. GRRM takes care to give him a number of mannerisms, such as bobbing his head, smelling of lilacs, soft and moist flesh, giggling ... and so forth.

I remember reading this the first time, and I remember that I was sure Littlefinger and Varys were in cahoots; the way they kind of complimented each other in this scene made it look (and still does, to be honest) as if they were working together. Only later surfaced the idea that these guys are bitter enemies, mayhap without even realizing it, because their agendas haven't yet forced them to a confrontation. The sly smiles are sly because they are trying to outwit each other, not because they are working for the same cause. Or do they? ...

Finally, the chapter reveals that Petyr owned the dagger Catelyn has brought to King's Landing, the weapon that was used to scar her hands and was intended for her son Bran's throat. But Petyr also tells her the dagger belonged to Tyrion Lannister, and that is of course crucial to remember, to understand why Catelyn is so intent on taking Tyrion captive a few chapters later.

I was neither surprised nor shocked by this reveal; I don't think I was concentrating enough on the story to actually see that it could not have been Tyrion; he was far away, at the Wall, but I do remember thinking that the Catelyn-chapters were like a murder mystery, and that this murder mystery was the main plotline of the saga, and that the true murderer wouldn't be found until the final book. Only I had no clue where to fit in the Others, and all the other storylines, LOL. Good I was wrong, though. The plot that emerges from this scene, with Catelyn taking Tyrion to the Eyrie, which results in more and more political turmoil, is far more interesting and epic.

I love these books. I am so impressed with GRRM's writings on so many levels. The details; the characters; the scope; the hidden nuggets of prophecy, history, back stories etc.; and everything else, really.

Flipping the page, I see that the next chapter is Jon Snow. His storyline is, for me, the least interesting, but the chapters do hold many interesting secondary characters, and the mysteries of the lands beyond the Wall are slowly unveiled, so I am looking forward to it nonetheless. But I have noticed that whenever I read *A Song of Ice and Fire*, flipping the page to find a Jon Snow chapter is most often an invitation to put the book away and go to sleep, or do something else. I always wait before reading him. It's not that it is bad or anything, they are just not as interesting or colorful (literally) as the other chapters.

But he's got to wait until the next time. My eyes are almost lazily dropping out of their sockets, I need sleep.

I'll just plug a book that I am reading next to *A Game of Thrones*. If you're like me, you find other books less interesting than *A Song of Ice and Fire*, and have a hard time finding something to sate your literary thirsts while we wait for the *Dance*. My suggestion is to read *When Christ and His Saints Slept*, by Sharon Kay Penman. Set in the early Middle Ages, I would not be surprised if GRRM had read this one and let some of it influence his amazing story. If such a book is too dry for you I can only recommend Joe Abercrombie's *Best Served Cold*, which at times comes quite close to the feel and tone of *A Song of Ice and Fire*, but somehow cartoonier.

Night gathers ...

THE SONG OF SWORDS

The chapter opens with such a simple, yet elegant line:

The courtyard rang to the song of swords.

There's really not much to blog about from this chapter. Of course, that's not true, depending on which angle one takes. One could delve into the early developing friendships at Castle Black, take a look at the various characters here, like Ser Alliser Thorne (the archetypical love-to-hate flawed instructor), or Grenn (the typical big, strong sidekick), or Donal Noye (I must say, I have wondered for the last eight or so re-reads, just *how* does Donal do a smith's work with one hand?). There are a few names strewn about that at this point of the story do not matter, but belong to characters we hear or see more of later in the unfolding saga, such as Cotter Pyke.

For all its importance to the overall story, I still find the other stories of *A Song of Ice and Fire* more interesting; it's not that I don't *like* the Wall, Castle Black, the Lands of Always Winter etc., it's just that the chapters taking place here have characters that are nowhere near as interesting as the chapters taking place in King's Landing (I mean, we've got Eddard, Sansa, and Arya there, Catelyn's been there, Tyrion's going there) while Castle Black has Jon Snow; it becomes more one-dimensional, until Samwell Tarly gets his own POV at any rate. I don't remember, at the moment, just when he gets his own POV.

Jon learns a good lesson in this chapter—he is surprised to hear from Donal Noye that the other recruits look at him as a bully. *"Best you start thinking,"* Noye warns him, *"That, or sleep with a dagger by your bed."*

For all the dreariness of Castle Black, its black-clad inhabitants, and the coldness of the North, at least this chapter has Tyrion Lannister. Jon's somewhat pessimistic introspection pales in comparison to Tyrion's sharp tongue, although we don't really get any sparkling quips in this particular chapter.

While the chapter ends on a relatively cheery note (again, compared to most chapters of the saga), there is a great ending with Ser Alliser Thorne speaking in "the acid tones of an enemy" to Jon, *"That was a grievous error, Lord Snow."*

It sets up all manner of delightful confrontations between Thorne and Snow, but I must admit that the story doesn't really follow up on this promise. In fact, as I write, I can't really remember there ever was a climactic final confrontation between the two, or even if Ser Alliser is alive or not by the end of *A Feast for Crows*. Oh, we'll see.

I hope this post doesn't feel *too* lukewarm; after all, *A Game of Thrones* remains one fine piece of literary magic, but I guess when you're lukewarm about a particular chapter, your blog post will reflect that.

It's hard to pinpoint exactly why this chapter doesn't work for me. There are many things that *do* work; I *love* the setting; the broken down Castle Black, the magnificent, shimmering Wall; the concept of the Night's Watch and their all-black fashion sense (which I happen to share to a certain degree); but at the same time, Ser Alliser Thorne seems too stereotypical a character (although that's changed *somewhat* later), Donal

Noye's preternatural dexterity is unconvincing[1], and Jon, well, Jon remains my least favorite POV. The whole scene in the courtyard too: I've never been fond of "training scenes" for some reason or the other (and no, it's not because I am lazy and reading about training wears me out). The scene reminds me of sports movies, which also leave me rather lukewarm, LOL

Now, a decent fantasy TV series based on, say, *A Game of Thrones*, maybe from HBO, filmed in Ireland and featuring great actors such as Sean Bean ... now *that* would be something I would love to see

---

[1]. Although a fellow enthusiast commented that Donal Noye has apprentices to help him out.

FLATTERERS AND FOOLS

... And so Eddard Stark rides into King's Landing and the Red Keep, and GRRM's description is hauntingly effective as it evokes a certain other time when Eddard rode into the Red Keep. Then, he actually rode all the way into the throne room to confront Ser Jaime Lannister; this time he contents himself with the courtyard, where he is met by the unnamed king's steward (almost as unknown as Vayon Poole? who *is* the king's steward in this chapter? Ser Aron Santagar?). And lo, and behold! Vayon Poole is called upon, he does as he is bid, and remains a background character if there ever was one. He hasn't been cast for *Game of Thrones* as far as I know, either. Vayon, Vayon, what's to become of you?

This chapter is a chapter that I really, really like, and which clearly displays where GRRM excels when it comes to writing: *characters*. Most of the chapter takes place inside one well-decorated room, but the room isn't important—the characters inside are, and through their dialogue we get a closer look—a better picture if thou willst—of some of the important players of that game, you know, of thrones. We also learn more about certain persons that are *not* attending, simply by their lack of presence. I am looking at you, Stannis. You're way too *tight*.

Eddard asks himself an interesting question about the lot gathered; who are the flatterers, and who are the fools? Eddard thinks he knows. But Eddard isn't the best player of the game of, you know, thrones, and so I can only assume that he's got it all wrong; in Eddard's eyes, Varys the Spider and Petyr Baelish aka Littlefinger are probably the flatterers; Varys with his wringing hands and "I am all yours" and "I serve the realm",

WAITING FOR DRAGONS

Littlefinger trying to flatter himself into Ned's good graces, trying to use his past connection with Lady Catelyn ... and he probably thinks Renly Baratheon and Grand Maester Pycelle are the fools; one spending too much money on his clothing and being a tad mischievous, the other old and doddering and ready for pension. Of course, we readers know better; Varys and Littlefinger are neither flatterers nor fools; they just *play* the role, when it suits them. Now Renly *is* a fool, so Ned *really* thinks he's trying to flatter him by dressing flamboyantly, while Grand Maester Pycelle... okay I am confused now. Why did I even write this?

Let's get it right: Renly *is* a fool, so Ned thinks him a flatterer. Varys *is* a mastermind, so uh Ned thinks him whatever. Same with Petyr. Grand Maester Pycelle? I dunno. I have a weird feeling about him. Sometimes I think "he's SOOO in on everything", at other times I think him merely the pawn of Cersei. I know I would have been a pawn of Cersei.

One thing that's certain is that Ned is surrounding himself with intrigues and plots within plots, and that's not good. The chapter is full of great lines of dialogue; there's humor, there's mystery, there's dialogue that gives us a sense of who these people are.

In some quickly exchanged banter, we learn that Littlefinger is indeed a man who likes to make a joke, or quip, at the expense of others, and GRRM also gives us the first hint that Renly is, and we're not gonna beat around the bush here, a butt boy. Or gaylord if you will. He's a lord. And he's gay. Gaylord. Totally missed this one before, but there are more and more obvious hints spread throughout the book later.

Another perfect description of Littlefinger follows;

"No doubt Lady Catelyn has mentioned me to you."

The "sly arrogance" on display is not something Ned likes. No, really.

I rest my case. If "sly arrogance" doesn't cover Littlefinger, nothing will.

What about the Grand Maester then? He tells Ned that he tires easily, is blunt about being so old. Is this a ruse? Does he *want* Ned to think of him as old, doddering, *unable*? Mmm ... I'll try to keep this one in mind and see if we can find more on this later. For a man who tires so easily and is so damnably old, he sure's good at being on top of things. Just a little while later, he adds that if they do not actually start their meeting soon, he'll fall asleep. *Will he?*

The lovely thing is, of course, that GRRM gives nothing away; we have to infer from dialogue what exactly is going on, and hope we're right. It makes for awesome reading, once spellbound by the story. He is a curious character, this Pycelle.

So, what are they meeting about? King Robert wants to throw a tournament in honor of Ned's appointment as Hand of the King. And I'm like, *awright!* Cause I am just a sucker for knightly tournaments. Ever seen *A Knight's Tale* with Heath Ledger in the main role? Say what you will about the movie, but those jousting scenes are brutally awesome. The HBO series ... I hope they can do it just as well. To a lesser extent, I am also charmed by the jousting scenes in series such as *The Tudors* and *Ivanhoe*. But watching such a tournament with the Hound, The Mountain, the Kingslayer ... it's gonna be all the richer.

Ned obviously doesn't feel honored and he isn't reassured by the fact that he learns the Crown has a debt of three million gold dragons to Lord Tywin Lannister, the father of the Lannister brood and lord who is mentioned from time to time, but haven't met yet (and I can't wait to re-read *that* badass again). Interestingly, the Crown also owes money to the Tyrells, the Iron Bank of Braavos, and the Faith; all three factions awaiting a more prominent role in later installments. For now, we know the Crown isn't doing too well, and I know I expected Ned to set things right (though I didn't really consider we're he'd get six million gold from).

The news is too much for our Lord Eddard Stark, so he leaves the council and goes outside, where the rest of the King's retinue are still pouring through the castle gates. There's a brief reflection of the troubles on the road with Arya and Sansa, before Ned is interrupted by Littlefinger who's hurrying to catch up with him. He leads Lord Stark to a brothel, where his Lady Catelyn awaits him.

There's a hilarious line from Littlefinger here, when Ned finally believes that Catelyn is nearby:

> "Follow me, and try to look a shade more lecherous and a shade less like the King's Hand. It would not do to have you recognized. Perhaps you could fondle a breast or two, just in passing."

I can do naught but LOL. What a funny dirtbag he is.

I wonder why Petyr goes through all this trouble, though. Trying to impress Catelyn? He does try to turn the Starks' attention away from the dagger Catelyn brought, though. Littlefinger claims he has Lord Varys' balls in his hands, and (I mentioned this in a thread over at Westeros by the way) in my opinion this is the author telling us that Petyr *believes* he has Varys' balls in his hands, but really doesn't (Varys has no balls, he got *seriously* cut back in the day, as revealed later in the series); of course, it can just be an empty comment, but I feel there's more to it, as mentioned. Littlefinger does say, just a few lines later, that Varys doesn't have balls so there goes my theory before it took flight. Oh well. Another paragraph well spent.

Such great drama unfolds between the two characters in a brothel room. It's interesting the way GRRM chooses to use "Ned promised her"… another promise that went awkward? Or did Ned's promise to Lyanna *not* go awkward? If not, it probably will … poor Ned. All his promises are worth so little, yet he means them with all his heart…

With a silent *"woohoo!"* I realize that the next chapter is Tyrion, which is always great, but the dwarf with the mismatched eyes will have to wait until next time.

I'll Be There For You

Tyrion Lannister. Was there ever a wittier, more sarcastic, more interesting character in the realm of fantasy literature? If there is, I sure haven't discovered it yet. Tyrion carries a lot of the story as the saga unfolds, and his chapters get increasingly more interesting as *A Game of Thrones* progresses, with some truly great chapters to follow in *A Clash of Kings* (like the chapter where he is slapped, slapped, and then slapped by his sweet sister Cersei) and *A Storm of Swords* (who can forget his initial encounter with The Red Viper of Dorne, Oberyn Martell?) *A Feast for Crows* has few Tyrion chapters I find genuinely as good as the first three, but I have high hopes for *A Dance with Dragons*, which is now seriously contending with *A Feast for Crows*, *The Phantom Menace* and *Fellowship of the Ring* for most eagerly anticipated product of the imagination, EVAR.

In this particular chapter, I am still not wholly comfortable with the character—but it's gonna change soon, cause once he gets off the Wall and goes south, the character becomes more firmly established and his motivations and events surrounding him follow a stricter, more well-defined plotting. What I mean is, that there really is no good incentive for the character to travel up and down to the Wall (as I mentioned in an earlier post), it's explained with a vague "he HAS to see it", and of course that is enough for a real person (I mean, I've visited places just to have been there and seen them), but in fiction characters need strong motivations or reasons for the things they do (for love). Of course, having Tyrion at the Wall provides GRRM with all manner of setups for future plot points, reaffirming my belief that Tyrion and Jon will end up together—

now they are friends, but what will they be the next time they meet? (I bet on enemies, in case you wonder; Jon will fight Daenerys, oh yes, and she'll have the Imp by her side; strange thing by the way, how some characters' nicknames become really embedded in the brain, such as Littlefinger, the Red Viper, and the Hound, while others—I am thinking of the Imp in particular, but also Kingslayer, don't—how's that for digression).

Anyhoodidelidoo, Tyrion is at the Wall, and Castle Black, up in the freezing North, but as the first sentence makes clear, he's going back south.

The Lord Commander, Tyrion, and other men of the Night's Watch are eating crabs, arrived from Eastwatch-by-the-Sea the same morning, and we get some delightful quips from Tyrion, mocking Ser Alliser Thorne, the dour man-at-arms of Castle Black.

The way Tyrion provokes Ser Alliser in this chapter is priceless, I can do naught but love it, and think of people just like Ser Alliser, who are so easily provoke and take things too seriously.

After Ser Alliser leaves the group, *"as though he had a dagger up his butt"*, the Lord Commander once again reiterates the point that the Night's Watch is dwindling, getting only thieves and rapers; interestingly, both Ser Alliser Thorne and Ser Jeremy Rykker both fought for the Targaryens and were given the choice of taking the black or getting their heads on pikes. No wonder Ser Alliser has soured.

Some more clues as to Lord Tywin's nature are provided as well, and I like the pieces of the puzzle we are being given as to just how ruthless a character this is: Tyrion explains how his father is very fond of spiked heads.

I chuckle and love the way Tyrion doesn't care what he says, even to anointed knights. Of course, his big mouth will also turn up to become troublesome, and I love how GRRM puts in snide remarks not only for the entertainment, but at the same time building the Tyrion we know and love throughout the series.

... And then we get a more ominous foreshadowing, one that has yet to be fully revealed in the saga, if I am not mistaken: Maester Aemon states that Tyrion is a "giant among men." Didn't he also stand tall as a king (metaphorically speaking, of course) earlier? Two telltale signs of Tyrion becoming something great, perhaps even the King of Westeros.

We know now, with *A Feast for Crows* behind us, that Maester Aemon is something of a the archetypical fantasy type I'd call "the blind seer," or "oracle." Is this prophecy? I am as dumbstruck by Aemon's statement as Tyrion is. Why did Maester Aemon choose to say this? What does he mean? And, "at the end of the world"; is he talking literally, or figuratively? An interesting little section, this.

Afterwards, the Lord Commander shares more of his concerns, about the wildlings and the White Walkers, but Tyrion is bored and drowsy, and on a whim decides to go onto the top of the Wall. Now, for those of you who believe Tyrion might just have a drop of Targaryen blood in him (Maester Aemon's a Targaryen too, could that explain his earlier comments?), check out how GRRM words Tyrion's decision to go up the Wall:

> Suddenly a strange madness took hold of him ...

Guess that's another thing to look into; more hints of "strange madnesses"; could be a subtle hint, could be me looking too deep (again). Tyrion is probably mad in the eyes of many.

Tyrion decides to use the convenient lift up to the top. GRRM describes the "journey" so vividly, I can almost smell the icy wall, the cold dark night, I can almost hear the creaking of the wheels that bring him upward. An excellent piece of description right there.

Atop the Wall, Tyrion stumbles into Jon Snow, who is patrolling the gravelly, wide top of the Wall. Another meeting between them to further establish relationship for a foreseen future plot point? It seems obvious to me.

Where else in the saga do we get such a charmingly naive, almost Middle-earthly exchange between two important characters? Why does GRRM go through the trouble of setting up this friendship? No matter how this unfolds, I am looking forward to it. Finally, we get to see through Tyrion's eyes the darkness of the woods north of the Wall; and we are reminded of the prologue, where poor Will, Ser Waymar Royce, and Gared met these silent, deadly creatures ... GRRM is really good at setting the mood, and the lands beyond the Wall are perfectly described in broad strokes here. Gotta love it. Sounds like he describes the landscape outside my house. If I were a location scout for HBO's Game of Thrones I would definitely consider Norway as a shooting location. But of course, it's so expensive to film here, that few big US films are filmed here. Well, *The Empire Strikes Back*'s Hoth scenes were filmed in

Norway, but from what I've gathered cast & crew didn't particularly like filming up in the cold, isolated parts of the country).

A fellow fan of the series asked me what I meant by Tyrion's chapters in *A Feast for Crows*. I was being sarcastic about the distinct lack of said favorite character in that volume.

Vayon Poole, Escort Duty

Back in King's Landing, Arya is in a dark mood, which she has been since the incident at the Trident when her friend Mycah, the butcher's boy, was killed by the Hound and Sansa's wolf pup Lady was executed. We learn that Arya had to chase off her own wolf pup Nymeria with rocks, so that the Queen wouldn't decide to kill her wolf as well. All in all, things are pretty dismal for our young friend. She fights with Sansa, and as a reader I certainly feel compelled to give Sansa a proper clout to the ear, for she is not exactly lovable from Arya's point of view. GRRM's description of Arya and Sansa's bitter quarrels is quite good, and quite unusual for a fantasy series as far as I know.

Yesterday I accidentally hit upon a site called "Good Read" and out of boredom I searched for *A Game of Thrones*. Naturally, it had a pretty high score but there was one review that caught my eye, as the reviewer gave it one out of five stars.

First I thought it had to be a joke. Then I noticed the review had attracted 70+ comments. I chuckled and clicked myself into the review and comments to see a torrent of arguments against the review. I was shocked to see that there were people agreeing with the review—agreeing that *A Game of Thrones* is a bad novel which doesn't bring anything new to the genre, a novel with boring, flat characters. Arya was mentioned as a one-dimensional character. Naturally, my eyebrows did a somersault upon reading, for surely there are few characters in fantasy literature as engaging, interesting and three-dimensional as those who inhabit the world of George R.R. Martin? Frankly, I am astonished.

This Arya chapter alone has more characterization than entire series of other fantasy authors. Well, the reviewer may think whatever she wants about *A Game of Thrones*, but calling the characters flat and one-dimensional seems to me to be more than a bit unfair. Then I noticed the reviewer preferred, among other authors, Terry Goodkind. I sighed; LOL'd, and closed the browser window. I felt like I've been reading a creationist's attempt at convincing me that the Earth is 4000 years old (someone corrected me to 6000—not that it really matters; point being that some people choose to remain blind, which incidentally is a bit ironic considering where we leave Arya in *A Feast for Crows*).

The end of this Arya chapter is of course one of those "kewl" moments in the saga, almost like Boba Fett's appearance in *The Empire Strikes Back*, only in this book it is the appearance of one Syrio Forel, a Braavosi blademaster whom Arya's father hires to teach her to use the sword she was given by Jon Snow, *Needle*. Just so.

Some interesting points about Lyanna Stark are raised as well, about her having the "wolf's blood", and Arya having it too. Could Daenerys' vision in the House of the Undying, with the blue flower in the wall of ice, refer to Arya? Or is it, as common theory suggests, a vision of Jon Snow? Interesting stuff. Oh, and Vayon Poole is still around ... escorting.

PREGGERS AND BEGGARS

This chapter has few action-scenes, but has a very important confrontation between Daenerys and her vile brother Viserys. She is finally finding the guts to speak up against him, and as they travel with the Dothraki across a sea of grass, Viserys is properly infuriated by her new, more regal way of handling him.

It is clear that he is no longer respected (or ever was), and when Ser Jorah Mormont sides with Daenerys, we know that something really ugly's gonna happen to either of the Targaryens. I guess no one really roots for Viserys but I remember thinking, and still think, that it would be cool if he was around a little longer in the story, it's always fun to read about characters you love to hate.

Anyway, the main thing in this chapter aside from setting up Viserys' fall is of course that there is still warmth in the dragon eggs, and that Daenerys has become pregnant with Khal Drogo.

Which is kind of *eew* but also cool. I remember wondering what this child was gonna be like, whether this was the Prince that was Promised (which I thought it was at the time of my first reading of the series).

I imagined that this son would be the great star of the series once he came of age. Like a cross between Rhaegar Targaryen and the Terminator, with braids. At one point I believed the whole story was leading up to this son of Daenerys, that everything was being set up for his birth.

Now, of course, I know better. Or so I tell myself.

It's interesting to read Ser Jorah Mormont while keeping in mind that he is paid by King Robert Baratheon to spy on Daenerys' doings. It makes it a bit more confusing until you realized the old dirtbag is attracted to the beautiful, silver-haired young Targaryen princess.

I hate "Dany" by the way so I usually write her full name "Daenerys." Another wondrous and needless bit of geek info; but perhaps not as nerdy as dressing up as Dr. Spock. I believe it's a subconscious thing. When they began calling Darth Vader "Ani" I stopped liking shortened names. I really should do a *Star Wars* blog sometime, shouldn't I?

Old Nan, New Saddle

... And so I have arrived at the twenty-fifth chapter of *A Game of Thrones*, and it is another **Bran Stark** chapter. I really like Bran's point of view, even though it isn't always consistent with the character's young age (but it doesn't really bother me—the fact that he doesn't always sound or think like a seven year old—after all, this is a story that also has dragons and they are not consistent with reality either as far as I know).

The character of Bran Stark is wildly different from the other POVs in that it is the story arc with most of the mystical elements of the saga; it is Bran who listens to tales of the Others, it is Bran who dreams of flying and meets the Three-Eyed Crow; his story has many of the traditional elements of a typical high fantasy yarn—the story of the young wizard's apprentice. Knowing that Martin was partially inspired by Tad Williams' *Memory, Sorrow, Thorn* or whatever that fantasy trilogy is called, this makes sense. Of course, Bran Stark is anything *but* the typical wizard apprentice—but the core of his story seems eerily similar. He's even on a mysterious quest fueled by dreams.

Couple of interesting things going on in this chapter; I better start at the beginning.

So we start out with poor Bran, having lost the feeling in his legs, watching his little brother Rickon running outside in the courtyard with the wolves. Now I can only imagine how painful that must be to Bran. Not only is his little brother running outside, he's having fun with *wolves*. Reminds me a bit of that episode of "The Simpsons" where Bart has to stay inside because he faked illness, and can do naught but watch all the kids having fun outside. But poor Bran, he doesn't fake it. He was pushed out of a tower window by Ser Jaime Lannister. GRRM does a great job of describing Bran's sadness.

At once a small, sad boy and a boy who wants to be brave. It's beautiful and morose.

Bran's not alone in his room however. Old Nan is sitting in a chair doing her needlework, and she is described so perfectly as the quintessential old and toothless, yet wise lady.

I can almost *smell* her. And it doesn't smell good. Of course, Old Nan's appearance isn't really important, but she's like *really* old, and that is of course of interest to the reader, because it means she has a lot of things to say, and she does. Through her, we are given glimpses of the evils of the far North; the Others. Through her, we get glimpses of the previous Lords of Winterfell, whom she has served. The crone is an interesting, albeit archetypical character, but she is also the relative of one of the most mysterious characters of the saga: Hodor, the simple-minded stableboy who will play a crucial role in Bran's quest—as a packhorse.

Since the first time I read *A Game of Thrones* I have always wondered about Hodor. I simply just can't let go of him—I do not accept him as *just* a simple-minded stableboy who can only say "Hodor." I've given it some thought from time to time: He *could* of course be a simple-minded stableboy, and the story works fine like that—Bran needs a strong companion later in the story, one who doesn't mind carrying around the young prince of Winterfell on his shoulders. But at the same time GRRM gives us some additional information that makes it easy to speculate. Apparently, Hodor's real name is Walder. And who else but the Freys call their children Walder? There are a *lot* of Walder Freys. Is GRRM beating us over the head with this? Is Hodor a Frey? If so, what's the point?

What I personally think however, is that Hodor in his childhood got really fucking scared of something. He was so scared he stopped talking and all that. It has happened in fiction before. Which begs the question, why does he only say "Hodor"? Is it the only word he can remember from before the traumatic event that turned him into a simple-minded man? Could "Hodor" be ... "Other"?

Bran doesn't really wanna listen to Old Nan's stories, but he agrees to listen when she proposes a dark tale of the Others (incidentally, Hodor barges into the room during the story and announces "Hodor!"), giving us some interesting tidbits:

The children still lived in their wooden cities and hollow hills sounds almost like the Elves of Lórien and the Hobbits of the Shire at first; but in the world of Westeros, could Old Nan be talking about the swamps of the Neck where Howland Reed makes his home, and could this line indicate that the old, little wrinkled lady atop the High Hill or whatever it's called in *A Storm of Swords* mean she's a Child of the Forest?

Then, Old Nan talks about something that doesn't come up later in the series so far as I remember. So the cities are up in the North; the "dead lands"? Is there a reference to "dead lands" elsewhere? Does she mean the lands of always winter? Or the lands beyond the edge of the world, which Bran saw in his dream? It reads as if GRRM was on a bit of a Tolkien binge when he wrote this chapter. Sounds like Mordor, or Jordan's The Blight.

Or is this part foreshadowing Bran's own quest? Is he going to find the Children of the Forest up there in the cold north? Interesting. It definitely gets Tolkienish (or "high fantasist") with the mention of pale white spiders big as hounds ... Bran's chapters are definitely the closest to vanilla fantasy literature in my opinion.

Hodor's arrival is convenient because we are interrupted and hear no more of the Others for now; instead, Tyrion Lannister has returned from the Wall and has come to Winterfell. Once again Tyrion is kind to a Stark, and again it feels a bit forced as if setting up future events. He presents an idea for a saddle that Bran could use to ride a horse even without his legs. A setup for Tyrion riding a dragon, or maybe Bran? Sure sounds like it (but then, I am pretty convinced Tyrion *will* be riding a dragon in the future, provided that the books are actually published; GRRM tells us that Tyrion is capable of fabricating saddles for special people like cripples and dwarfs—there may just come a scene where he fashions a saddle for one of Dany's dragons).

Finally, the chapter gives us a hint that the line between life and death may be blurred up in the North, beyond the Wall ...

Next up is Bran's lordly father, Eddard, in the far-more-medieval-than-fantasy setting of King's Landing. I really dig the juxtaposition of Bran's eerie, high fantasy-ish chapters and Eddard's down-to-earth dealings in politics going all wrong.

HIS SO-CALLED FATHER

Wow, nearly two months since my last post. Time to catch up; I guess we can call it a New Year's resolution. Or maybe I should learn from GRRM and not promise anything. I guess 2010 is a make-or-break year for our dear author, because if he waits any longer with *A Dance with Dragons*, I believe (even) more and more people will pick up on the current negativity backlash. Imagine George Lucas waiting and postponing *Return of the Jedi* a few more years than expected. I'd be in a white shirt in an instant.

Anyway, I'm back into the *game*, and reopening my book I see I have come to an Eddard chapter, his fifth to be exact, and he is still stumbling about in that viper's nest of a city called King's Landing, being presented with a number of obvious clues as to the motivations for murdering Lord Jon Arryn, without him becoming the wiser.

Lord Eddard is chatting with Grand Maester Pycelle, perhaps the character in the king's council with the least easily discernible motivations. Is he Cersei's pawn? Is he beholden to the Maesters of the Citadel? Part of the plots and counterplots of Varys or Littlefinger—or *their* pawn? Personally I believe he serves whoever rules the realm, but that he has a weak spot for Cersei because, you know, she is sexy. Yes, he is old, frail, seemingly dozing off numerous times during the day, but he's still a man. And men, regardless of age, like hot sexy ladies, no? I haven't met one who hasn't at any rate.

Pycelle spends some time yada-yadaing about the good old days, specifically King Maekar's summer. Is this a way for Pycelle to try and talk Eddard away from the more pressing matters at hand? Or is he really just an old, sad man the way GRRM portrays him (*"Forgive an old man his wanderings if you would"* is a line that doesn't really make sense if Pycelle was trying to steer Eddard away from the topic of Jon Arryn's death). Is GRRM trying to *make* us suspect Pycelle while he is, after all, a good-hearted old man? The mind starts boggling again. Damn.

The Grand Maester tells Eddard that Jon had been healthy but the day after he came to fetch a particular book, he became ill. After a long interrogation, in which we get a classic line about poison being a woman's weapon, Ned finally asks to examine the book and I'm happy he got the clue even though Pycelle didn't use clamoring sirens to tell him about it.

After the meeting, Ned talks to Arya who is working on her water dancing and they speak of Bran who's woken up. But it's sad because they have learned he will never walk again. *Or will he?*

Finally, Littlefinger takes time out from his busy schedule to have a chat with Eddard, telling him he's found four people who may or may not have information regarding Lord Jon's death. The last paragraphs of the meeting are very interesting as they set up a fantastic payoff later in the book, with Littlefinger essentially yelling into Ned's ears, *"don't the fuck trust me!"*

Poor Ned. In this chapter, we really get the feeling he's lost in this city of intrigues; he's at a loss.

Not the most memorable or interesting of Ned's chapters, but a good chapter nonetheless. I guess I am jaded as to the whole murder mystery. It's not like I am reading it for the first time...but then again, the murder mystery was never the most interesting plotline of the novel. Next post, we're back at the Wall with Jon Snow. Let's see if he fares any better than his, er, so-called father.

BUMPING INTO THE FAT WALL

Happy New Year 2011. May this be that rare year when we are all delighted with a new book in the saga. The wait is really getting on my nerves, and yes I do read other books and no they can't captivate me the way GRRM's saga does.

Anyway, I'm back in the world of Westeros with *A Game of Thrones*, and today's chapter is short and dripping with fat and grease. Figuratively speaking.

Jon Snow is showing Dareon (I never remembered him when I came to *A Feast for Crows*, but now that I am re-reading the series I see "more" of the character; the fact that it is Dareon being trained is a miniscule but wise choice, since Dareon is a character who *needs* the training; I am, as always, impressed by Mr. Martin's attention to detail) how to fight when a new major character enters the saga—and the practice yard at Castle Black—Samwell Tarly.

Having spent too much time over at the blog Finish the Book, George![2] (don't worry, I'm not hateful towards GRRM for not delivering *A Dance with Dragons*, though resentful may cover my feelings), I can't help but think of Samwell as, at least partially, George R.R. Martin's alter-ego within his fictional setting; I believe he loves to write Tyrion cause that's what he'd perhaps like to be—sarcastic, funny, intelligent ... And he probably is—but Samwell may just be young GRRM incarnate; inept, afraid, good with letters but no masculinity ... heh, I may be reading too much into this, and I don't want to affront any

---

[2] http://grrrm.livejournal.com/ (that's three "rs" in "grrrm").

fans so I won't go into this anymore. Just a thought, really, based on Martin's own description of himself as a youngster.

The plot of the chapter is rather straightforward, with an archetypical situation—new recruit gets the shit, but one recruit can't deal with it and helps out—but GRRM is so honest and straightforward in his characterizations that although it could have been the plot of a teen movie, harsh language is used to humiliate Samwell, giving it a sense of reality in the fantasy. I mean, "Ser Piggy is starting to grasp the notion" and "Cut us off a ham!" are but two cruel lines thrown at poor Samwell, yet this is what fat kids around the world hear, maybe even harsher. The nasty part is that even the arms master, Ser Alliser Thorne, is cruel to Samwell, making it a bleak and dismal day for our new character.

The unlikeable knight Ser Alliser has one great line in there, though: "The Bastard speaks and the peasants tremble." You can practically *hear* the sarcasm dripping. Much like I can practically *see* Samwell's fat rolling as he walks.

The whole exercise of setting up Jon to help Samwell is of course carefully constructed plotting: Much later these two will be the saga's Frodo and Sam (even the character's name hints at this), although in a vividly darker way. And it helps sharpen the conflict between Jon and Ser Alliser, without a doubt.

In light of my first paragraph the following section is quite interesting:

> (Jon) could think there, and he found himself thinking of Samwell Tarly...and, oddly, of Tyrion Lannister.

Waiting for Dragons

Jon wonders what Tyrion would make of Samwell, and I am once again thinking, hey, GRRM is living it out here.

We're given some insight into Samwell's past, not too much, and a friendship between him and Jon begins to develop, giving the last half of the chapter a lighter tone, with the exception of Samwell's stories of how he was treated by his own father, Lord Randyll Tarly, a bannerman to Mace Tyrell, the Warden of the South (another name thrown into the mix, to become more crucial later—I *love* how this story has so many characters, but I remember that I was rather confused during the first read-throughs). The way Lord Randyll treated Samwell is cruel, and we have yet another character to love to hate. A shame (in my opinion) that his cameo in *A Feast for Crows* didn't live up to the setup here, in fact it was a bit of a letdown, mainly because it feels as if GRRM put him in that Brienne chapter just for the sake of showing the character without him really being needed.

The chapter ends with Jon wondering if he will ever see Benjen Stark again. And we wonder the same, a decade after last reading a Jon Snow chapter...Gaaaaah!

SLYNT'S IN THE HOUSE BABY

This chapter starts with a line of dialogue from the Commander of the City Watch, the one and only Janos Slynt, whose surname I've used as my Internet nickname for many years now. Seen a Slynt over at Westeros.org? That's me. Ever seen a Slynt post at 'Finish the Book, George'? That was me too. Perhaps you've seen a Slynt post at the Green Ronin forums for the *A Song of Ice and Fire Role-playing* game. That's me too. And the Slynt who used to harass the Fantasy Flight forums for the *A Game of Thrones* collectible card game? That was me too. I won't forget the thread about shuffling cards with the ass. Long story.

I've been calling myself Slynt for so long that people *call* me Slynt, even in real life. Should you encounter a Slynt on non-ASOIAF related websites the chances are, that's me too.

So why did I choose Slynt as a nickname? There was a thread over at Westeros where the poster actually wondered who, in their right mind, would choose *Slynt* when making a nickname based on the series. I never said I *am* in my right mind, though. But it seems that fans of the series, who instantly recognize the nick, can't detach the character from the Internet anonymous geek (or in this case, blogger). I didn't choose Slynt because I find Janos Slynt a particularly appealing or interesting character. I simply chose "Slynt" because it is short and simple, easy to remember. And it has a certain sound to it ... "Slynt." Sounds like a bad guy, kind of. Now of course I know most English speakers pronounce the name "slint", but pronounce it the way Scandinavians and Germans (among others) do it, and the name gets an extra aura of naughtiness; you gotta use the German "ü" (or Norwegian "y") sound—*Slünt*. Bad-ass name. Perhaps my favorite name in the series, although I wish it had been used on a better (read, cooler) character—Bronn, for example.

Bronn is a Slynt, if you know what I mean. Ser Jaime is a Slynt. Janos Slynt ...well, he's more of a Ser Harys Swyft. But I have digressed even more than usual.

"It's the Hand's tourney that's the cause of all the trouble, my lords", Slynt announces to the king's council. A really cool way of starting the chapter, it is immediately interesting because, you know, you wonder *what trouble?* And, *oooooh a tourney!* I do love medieval tournaments. Having one in *A Game of Thrones* was an awesome bonus for me. The clash of swords, lances splintering upon impact, the heraldry ...

Lord Eddard keeps iterating that he wants no tourney in his name, yet the city of King's Landing is filling up with people from all walks of life, from all over Westeros. And, King Robert Baratheon I is not present at the council. He sure doesn't seem like a good king.

When Slynt leaves, the council discusses the Hand's tourney further. Ned (again) complains, Littlefinger has a comic line (*"The whores are walking bowlegged and jingling..."*, LOLety!). There is doubt about Stannis' absence (or rather, the why of it). Once the council is over with, Ned returns to his chambers, sitting for a moment with the book he's found. Ponderous reading, yet Jon Arryn had asked for it.

/slapface

Don't you get it, Ned? Aw come on. Ned does finally connect Jon Arryn with Stannis Baratheon, however. That's a step in the right direction. So why do you think Stannis ain't present at the council meetings, Mr. Warden of the North?

Ned decides to go seek out an armorer, Tobho Mott, who supposedly had made a fine piece of armor for Jon Arryn (accompanied by Stannis). In between the investigation and the visit at the armory, GRRM throws a few new names into the mix—Margaery Tyrell, Lord Beric Dondarrion—I wonder at times whether he put in those lines *after* having written most of the book or did he, at the time, already have the basics of these characters? I mean, with such a large cast of characters I am really impressed how GRRM keeps it all together; Renly showing Ned a locket with the picture of Margaery doesn't seem to serve a purpose here and now, but it foreshadows events to transpire much later in the series. This specific example isn't the most masterful of GRRM's "putting stuff between stuff" stuff, but still. Amazing how, when re-reading, there is always something to discover, another vaguely visible line drawn between characters in the story, connections that make sense later. Impressive. More impressive than opinionated blog posts about American football, anyway.

The chapter ends with Ned getting a look at Mott's apprentice, whom we later learn is named Gendry, and who is obviously a king's bastard. So, Ned, what do you think? All of Robert's bastards have his dark, nay, super-black, hair. His three royal children are as golden as wheat in the sunrise (sorry, recently saw the beginning of *Gladiator* again).

Connect. Dots.

Come on, Ned, you can *do* it!

(I propose a new word in the English vocabulary to describe a person who fails to connect dots—a *nedhead*). The copyright's mine!)

SHE-WHO-THINKS-IN-ITALICS AND THE MEXICAN STAND-OFF

And so I have come to the 29th chapter of *A Game of Thrones*, the fifth Catelyn Stark chapter, and a fairly interesting one too. I remember thinking after I first had finished this book that the main scene in this chapter, the confrontation between Lady Catelyn and Lord Tyrion, was a standout. You know, it's such a simple scene yet so strong because of these characters—both POVs—meeting each other.

The chapter begins with Ser Rodrik Casell and Lady Catelyn Stark riding north through a soft and warm rain, making Catelyn remember her youth which was spent in this very region—the riverlands. From here on, we get a number of little insights into Catelyn's youth, at the same time shedding light on the pasts of a number of secondary characters, mainly Lysa and Littlefinger.

The opening paragraphs tell us that Ser Rodrik likes to whine ("You will take a chill", "I am soaked through", "Even my bones are wet"), and that the woods press close around them (hang on, it gets important later!). They encounter a group of Mallisters, including Lord Jason Mallister and his son Patrek. I am not quite sure why George adds this little encounter, but it could be as simple as adding a little spice; to show how her father is a major lord with many vassals (including Lord Jason of Seagard), or to add in the exposition of many travelers on the muddy road. Or, as is revealed as I read the next paragraph, to convince Ser Rodrik that it will be safe to visit the Inn at the Crossroads, just ahead. /faceslap

The sourleaf-chewing innkeeper is a woman called Masha Heddle, but the character isn't really that interesting, just a dash of ghastly red color (her "ghastly red smile" could be considered a little touch of ye olde foreshadowing). I like the inn at the crossroads. With a few sentences, George makes me visualize this dank place with its cramped narrow staircase and low, dusty garrets. From the crossroads, Catelyn considers going west to seek out her father at Riverrun, or go east and seek out Lysa in the Vale of Arryn. She decides instead to go north, back to Winterfell.

Sitting by a window, Catelyn sees the fields beyond the crossroads, and knows there's a marketplace, and a village nearby. Aha! I thought she was riding in a forest pressing close to the road! Got ya. Unless the woods suddenly stopped before they reached the inn, of course. This is perfectly plausible, but never mentioned. Heheheh. Her thoughts drift from fields and farms to her father's bannermen, a bit more fleshing out of the feudal system in the riverlands, and more hints that it may come to war.

Finally finished with the thinking on this and that, she joins Rodrik for supper downstairs, and the stage is set for the confrontation.

Marillion, the minstrel, appears for the first time in this chapter as one of the guests in the taproom. This character's name rips me straight out of the story, to be honest. "Marillion." I mean, either you think of the British prog/pop/rock band, or you think of Tolkien's *Silmarillion*. I hope the name was meant as a nod to Tolkien. But I can't be sure. But I can't help but imagine the character singing old Marillion songs while at the tavern. This is not good, as I can't stand that band's music.

And then they enter.

There were four of them, Catelyn saw. An old man in the black of the Night's Watch [Yoren], two servants...and him, standing there small and bold as life.

That's funny. So how will it go? I think I'd bet on Tyrion winning the day, with more men and a sharper tongue, but George is ever a surprising one, and the victory goes to Catelyn who, by revealing herself as the daughter of the Lord of the Riverlands, gets the support of most men in the crowded room. They do as she bids them—which is to take Tyrion captive for her.

At this point, one could argue that Catelyn is being a bit unfair towards our little lord of Lannister. She accuses him of attempted murder [on Bran], without a shred of evidence. Oh well, it is the middle ages and considering his reputation, not at all a surprising act. But *maybe* she should have considered the implications. But boy do the consequences of this little scene make for some astounding bits later in the story. Can't wait.

Oh, and back in the "real" world there's a new discussion forum up and running. Do we need another *A Song of Ice and Fire* forum? Maybe not, but *this* particular forum allows you to vent about the wait for *A Dance with Dragons* without fear of reprisal. Come on over and vote for the usefulness of posts about American football, among other things ;-)

HOUNDED

It used to be hard to like Sansa Stark. Her first chapter showed her off as a bit of a spoiled-princess type of character, and encountering another Sansa chapter wasn't the most inspiring development. Now, however, I know better. Sansa is a well-realized character (in the genre of fantasy, at least), who has an interesting story arc. Some of her chapters are also the windows through which we see some of the more important secondary characters—such as the Hound, Joffrey Baratheon, and Cersei Lannister—and also the windows through which we witness some of the crucial events of *A Game of Thrones*.

One such event is, of course, the Tourney of the Hand, a grand tournament ordered by King Robert Baratheon to honor his old friend Lord Eddard Stark's appointment as the new Hand of the King. For this event alone, the chapter is a must-read for fans of the series. Numerous characters of varying importance are mentioned, and GRRM describes the knights clashing in an efficient, yet evocative manner. This chapter awoke in me a keener interest in all things knightly, all things tournaments. Because of this chapter, I have watched the jousting scenes in the *A Knight's Tale* film (featuring deceased actor Heath Ledger) over and over again; because of this chapter, I bought and read Chaucer's *Canterbury Tales*. Because of this chapter, I ran a role-playing game where knights and tournaments were central—which again led me to research the subject more thoroughly, to present it in the game much like Martin does it in his novels. Because of this chapter (okay, not this chapter alone—but you get what I mean, I am talking about the novel's overall influence on my life), I have visited renaissance fairs (those are a bit creepy though). And so on, and so forth.

Choosing to present the Tourney of the Hand through Sansa's eyes was a good choice; she is the perfect character to witness the splendor, but also the blood. Had we seen the tournament through the eyes of, say, Lord Eddard Stark her father, it could've become an event more focused on the excesses—a more negative approach. In Sansa's own words, *"it is better than the songs."*

So while on first read many of the names thrown at me were confusing the reading experience, on the tenth re-read it is a joy to read, as I know where most of the participants come from, what kind of character they are, or some other snippet of information giving the Hand's Tourney an extra edge of realism and color. We get our first close look at Ser Gregor, the Mountain That Rides, but in this chapter he seems a bit childish, methinks:

All the knights are arrayed in their finest armor, and then he comes thundering before them, no doubt kicking up dust and being an annoyance—a bully.

What kind of childish behavior is this? When the splendorous Kingsguard comes forth, you know, the most epic warrior-heroes of the time, you thunder past them, leaving them in the dust? He really doesn't care a fig, does he? But however rude an act, it does nothing to prepare the poor reader for some of Ser Gregor's later ... adventures.

There is a quick foreshadowing of Littlefinger's relation to Sansa, with him comparing her to Lady Catelyn Stark her mother, and a longer first encounter and dialogue between Sansa and Ser Gregor's younger brother, the terribly scarred Sandor Clegane, aka the Hound. The writing is pretty much straight forward, but I certainly didn't notice the seeds GRRM was planting here until much later. It is a cool juxtaposition of characters—the nasty Hound versus the halfway uptight young noble lady. Ice and fire?

In case you haven't seen it yet on any of the numerous Westeros-related websites around cyberspace, there's an excerpt from the upcoming third Dunk & Egg short story, *The Mystery Knight*, available for your reading pleasure over at Pat's Fantasy Hotlist.[3] Now I yearn even more for a return to Westeros.

---

[3] Now available in the anthology *Warriors*. http://amzn.to/f7ehZo

NIMBLE BOOKS LLC

PRIVATE INVESTIGATOR EDDARD VII

It strikes me again that it is, in fact, quite hard to blog about a tenth re-read. It's not like I have a fresh perspective on things.

Perhaps it doesn't matter. One of the best things about *A Game of Thrones* is precisely the fact that it still feels relatively fresh on re-read ten. That's high praise, indeed. Imagine reading, say, *The Sword of Truth* for the tenth time. It is still exciting to read certain paragraphs in *Thrones* which I've forgotten, or see them in a new light (often those that link to *A Feast for Crows*, which I've only read thrice).

A few things, however, are sadly becoming a bit less interesting. Yes, I am looking at you, my lord of Winterfell. Your mad detective skillz are getting on my nerves.

> Slain by a Lannister bannerman before Ned could speak to him; could that be mere happenstance? He supposed he would never know.

Are you shitting me, Lord Eddard? Of course, to Mr. Stark's defense, this is the tenth time I am reading about him fumbling about in the mired webs of King's Landing intrigue. And the first time I read this book I certainly didn't register just how blindly Lord Eddard is stumbling. Then again, I am not a native speaker of the English language and am allowed a few re-reads before catching it all.

Lord Eddard and Ser Barristan Selmy, Lord Commander of the Kingsguard, are shipping off the body of Ser Hugh of the Vale with the rather intriguing Silent Sisters. Ser Hugh was knighted in Jon Arryn's memory by King Robert. Now there's a character with little screentime, HBO can give me a call anytime and I'll play the role of Ser Hugh. I can play dead; I did so at work today when the boss came to present us with more work.

Fortunately, this seventh Eddard chapter is more interesting than just being a bit slow on the uptake. There is a great scene between him and King Robert, where GRRM also slyly adds the character of Lancel Lannister, squire to the king and soon to be his murderer as well. Did I catch this character's importance on the first read? Definitely not. Now that I know the story pretty much inside-out, it's great fun to see how GRRM adds these minor characters into the circumstances, and how it all plays out. It's fun knowing who the bad guy is when the good characters don't.

He ain't the wittiest of characters, but Lord Eddard's agreement with the squires who try to get the king in his armor is pretty funny, when he simply states that the king is too fat for his own armor.

Great stuff, simple and effective. Ned is worried about the squires being Lannister boys, correctly identifying the Lannisters as ambitious. Reminds me of the Boleyn family, if you know your medieval history (or *The Tudors* on the TV).

Lyanna Stark once again crops up. I have come to like this character more and more for each read; whenever her name shows up I try to add the information to "complete" her character. She's been dead for years when the book begins, yet she is given a fair amount of description, making her fairly pivotal after all. Could the song of ice and fire be about—Lyanna and Rhaegar? Or does GRRM use this title for several such juxtapositions? Jon Snow and Daenerys Targaryen? House Stark and House Lannister? The Others and R'hlorr, the Lord of Light?

Sansa and Sandor? Loras and Renly? I guess it is too early to say. But the more I think about it, Lyanna and Rhaegar as the titular Ice and Fire makes sense. After all, a lot of the things that transpire in *A Game of Thrones* go back to them.

Once Eddard convinces King Robert not to participate in the jousts (the Tourney of the Hand is still going on; as a side note, I find it an amusing name for a tournament as it sounds like a masturbation competition), they go to the field to watch the spectacle, where the Hound and his brother Ser Gregor take center stage. The latter is once again shown to be a somewhat unintelligent (but extremely strong) brute, killing his own horse with a single blow in anger at having been unhorsed by the Knight of Flowers, Ser Loras Tyrell. Ser Loras is lucky not to be obliterated by the Mountain that Rides. The scene further establishes the Clegane brothers as bitter enemies, a plot we have yet to see the resolution of (my suspicion is that they will fight each other in some sort of trial by combat—Ser Gregor championing the Queen and the Hound championing the Faith perhaps—but this speculation is based on *A Feast for Crows*).

GRRM sneaks in yet another new character that we'll see more of later (a whole book later, in fact)—Anguy the Archer, while Jalabor Xho remains a splash of color but (not yet) fleshed out. I am convinced the exiled prince from the Summer Isles will be pivotal in a later book. Perhaps as an ally of Daenerys Targaryen? GRRM has so far not been able to resist taking obscure characters to the forefront at a later time. Same goes for Thoros of Myr, also fighting in the Tourney of the Hand (hee hee) and winning the melee. At the evening feast following the melee, Eddard senses hope. Rub it in, George.

"*I'm sore all over,*" Arya reports happily, talking about her training with Syrio Forel. "*You must be a terrible dancer,*" Sansa says doubtfully. I giggle at Sansa's ignorant comment.

Finally, Lord Eddard has a little chitchat with our friend and eunuch Varys the Spider. He is once again described as something of a slippery eel, and it's not hard to believe Eddard when he instinctively distrusts the man. Trying to figure out exactly what Varys is up to makes my head hurt. There are many theories and speculations, but we won't know for sure ... ever, it seems. Anyhow, Varys reveals how Jon Arryn died—by the Tears of Lys—and he also hints—nay, *spells it out for Ned*—that Ser Hugh's accident on the field wasn't an accident, but an assassination, because Ser Hugh knew stuff that the Lannisters don't want Eddard to know.

Whether a veiled threat or no, it seems that Varys wants Ned to either a) stop asking questions and thus not interfere with the royal couple anymore or b) nudge him on to finally get it right and accuse Cersei of incest ["twincest" among fans] and thus save the realm from Lannister rule.

... or is there an option c) there somewhere? I suspect Varys of having Targaryen sympathies (obvious, if you choose to believe he's the one talking with Ilyrio Mopatis in that Arya chapter), but how do these sympathies tie in here? Does Varys just want to weaken the realm politically, no matter who stays alive and who dies? In that case, if he is the cunning Spider he seems to be, why not ... damn, now my head hurts. Again.

MY NAME IS BRONN. PREPARE TO DIE

Back in the day, I guess four or five years ago, when I decided to baptize myself with a permanent Internet nickname, my first thought was to call myself Bronn. The reasoning behind this is simple; he's a favorite character from *A Game of Thrones*, and at the time I was thoroughly in love with the series, waiting for *A Feast for Crows* to be published. I was on the Internet before this time too, of course, but I used different names depending on where I was (in cyberspace). Usually, my usernames were based on *Star Wars* characters, especially in the beginning of both my Internet adventures and the announced new films. When that franchise crashed, burned and was immolated, I lost the obsession somewhat and this was gradually replaced by my new, searing obsession: *A Song of Ice and Fire*. Choosing a character from that series of books would be a little more obscure than calling myself, say, Boba Fett.

Then I realized Bronn was quite popular among other readers too; he was despicable in an enjoyable way, the mercenary with his notched sword and his attitude. He's not the first mercenary to become popular, so I decided to find a more obscure name from the series. At the time, I hadn't read the books ten times and so did not memorize the *truly* obscure characters. There are people within the thousands (!) of pages of story that are mentioned once and nothing more. As discussed earlier, I settled on "Slynt"; but Bronn "coulda been a contenda," as Marlon Brando says at the end of *On The Waterfront*. Anyway, it was Bronn that sparked this post, and that is of course because from this chapter—Tyrion IV—the character Bronn comes into his own (he was in the previous chapter, but from here on he begins to *shine* with his dark gleam).

To put it bluntly: the banter between Tyrion and Bronn is among my *favoritest* parts of the whole saga of ice and fire. There you have it. I just love their quips. I really enjoy re-reading their story up until *that* point in *A Storm of Swords*, which frankly disappointed me but was very well written by George R.R. Martin. But that point is still someways into the future, innit. I wonder how long it will be until the next time there is a new scene between Tyrion and Bronn..

... and so Tyrion is taken into the Mountains of the Moon, as a prisoner of Lady Catelyn Stark. This chapter opens with a typical GRRM description of casual violence (and I'm lovin' it):

"As he stood in the predawn chill watching Chiggen butcher his horse, Tyrion Lannister chalked up one more debt owed the Starks."

Using this "casual violence" (for lack of a better term) is one of the saga's strong points and immediately throws me into the "mood" of Westeros. And just a few sentences on we get the first humorous, snarky comment from Tyrion:

"I am not fond of eating horse. Particularly *my* horse."

The chapter is pure storytelling, but has one important purpose—to show how Tyrion eventually manages to impose his will upon the Lady Catelyn, and how he, through the lure of Lannister gold and his wit, gets Bronn on his side in the matter.

Tyrion has a few *classic* lines in here; "Why does a bear shit in the woods?" comes to mind. His brutal honesty about Littlefinger is well placed too. I admit, I wouldn't mind having Catelyn by my side after reading that description. But this blog is not naughty, so the fantasy within the fantasy remains a fantasy ... I wonder whether Tyrion is right about this, though? *Did Littlefinger utter sexual boasts? Or is Tyrion fanning the flames so to speak? Whether right or not, it is essential stuff.* Cleverly, GRRM gives us a quick additional characterization of someone far, far away from the actual events of the chapter that helps us build the image of this character for later chapters.

The group is attacked by clan members and we get an exciting action sequence in which Tyrion shows himself to be quite adept at fighting. It feels strange, but so does it feel to Tyrion—indeed, it is revealed that this is Tyrion's first battle. So how come he's so good at it? Of course, if he sucked and was killed off *now*, we'd lose an insane amount of great story. But story-wise, that's another question. Why is Tyrion an acrobat in the early Jon Snow chapters? Why is he successful in this battle (and later battles, too)? Does he have dragon's blood, as some people seem to think? Or does he need this setup because he's gonna do some incredible fighting in the last half of the saga? I wonder.

Go Tyrion, go Tyrion! It is hard not to root for him after his unlucky entry at Masha Heddle's tavern. It is hard not to root for a witty, funny, clever, sarcastic dwarf. I can only hope HBO gets the TV series into gear and that we will be able to *see* this chapter (and Jennifer Ehle's ripe breasts).

The chapter ends with another classic line, Tyrion's *"I never bet against my family."* We'll see about that Tyrion, we'll see about that.

I like the whole journey of Lady Catelyn and Tyrion up to the Vale. It has a sense of "classic high fantasy" (after all, wasn't the *journey* the great thing about *The Lord of the Rings?*) and yet it is so grim and grey, with more than half the fellowship slaughtered before even reaching the Bloody Gate, with suspicions and grievances, calm and cool mercenaries who *really* don't have good hearts but *really* just want coin ... can't wait 'til the next Tyrion chapter.

The next chapter being Arya isn't too bad, though. Her story is also one of a journey, but of a different kind, and even more brutal once it gets going.

CHASING CATS AND SHADOWS

Damn but this book has many chapters. I have come to the 33rd of them, featuring our favorite wildcat Arya. The chapter is placed near the middle of the book, and rightfully so—it features a sequence that could be viewed as the "heart" of the book, a centerpiece—in my opinion, at least. I am in no way a professional literary analyst although I have studied such things at university and probably know how to analyze a story at least a little better than, say, a sailor. Har. Go prejudice.

The centerpiece I am talking about is also slotted nicely in the middle of the chapter, with a build-up and a denouement: First, we have Arya chasing the Red Keep's tomcat (which I'm confident is a survivor of the Targaryen dynasty), which leads her down into the dungeons where she finds the hidden dragon skulls Robert Baratheon removed from the throne room after usurping the Iron Throne. Here, she overhears a more than interesting conversation—the centerpiece, if you will—before returning to her father the Lord Eddard to tell him what she overheard down in the darkness of the Red Keep. A simple structure then, making for a well-paced chapter, where I as the reader follow Arya around like a ghost. Well written and dripping with atmosphere, the chapter gives us a brief glimpse of Princess Myrcella and Prince Tommen (I find the two characters rather underdeveloped at this point, although Prince Tommen gets time to shine in a later volume. Actually, he has one of my favorite lines of dialogue from *A Feast for Crows*. I don't remember the exact wording, but it had to do with outlawing beets. Agreed, Prince Tommen! Getting a couple of thousand pages ahead of myself, though—one of my fatal flaws.

Reading this chapter the first time was a bit confusing. Who were the two guys Arya overhears? What were they talking about? Okay, I figured out *some* of it, but still. One must needs cling to the Internet's more devout readers to figure it all out properly I think. It is obvious now, on the tenth re-read, that the two men having their secret little talk are Varys and Ilyrio Mopatis, the latter somehow having found a ship strong enough to carry him across the Narrow Sea just to have a chat with Varys. The novel doesn't give us any other information as to why the fat magister has come to Westeros—could he have magical powers allowing him to teleport back and forth? If he is some kind of undercover sorcerer, that is ... So, they are in cahoots. That's good to remember, but also confusing considering how Varys acts in the King's council. Is he working *for* Daenerys Targaryen? If yes, why does he (seem to) agree on assassinating her in a later chapter?

Wait a minute—Varys has his little birds—could a little bird tell him that Arya had overheard him talking with Ilyrio? I wonder ...

The chapter has some nice foreshadowing pointing all the way to the end of *A Feast for Crows*, with Arya feeling blind in the darkness of the Red Keep's unlit chambers below ground. It makes me wonder once again—did GRRM have this in mind (the blindness) when he wrote this little foreshadowing detail, or did he later when writing *A Feast for Crows* go back through Arya's chapters and retroactively apply it—or is it coincidental? Only GRRM himself knows the truth, I guess. Makes for enjoyable re-reading, though, finding all those small nuggets that connect here and there. I would be very interested in reading or hearing anything about the process of writing this masterpiece of fiction, but the author doesn't really come off as someone who likes to share much about his story. Basing this on his blog which is not a blog but really is a blog when push comes to shove.

Mercy Is For Dumbheads

An interesting chapter. I am not going to make a long, rambling post this time, however. I live in the fear of repeating myself. Basically, the chapter is one of exposition—told through the eyes of Lord Eddard Stark, at a meeting with the council members of King's Landing. This means a heap of interesting, intriguing and mysterious characters all playing their game of thrones, with poor Ned in the middle of it, none the wiser.

It is interesting that Ned should make an example of Ser Barristan Selmy, telling Robert that mercy can be useful. The interesting thing being, of course, that Ser Barristan later returns to those who King Robert defeated—the Targaryens. Another interesting thing is that as a reader I still don't have a clue as to what Grand Maester Pycelle is up to. *Is* he just an old doddering maester? Is he completely loyal to the Lannisters? He frowns when Varys mentions the Tears of Lys—an indication that Pycelle connects Varys to the murder of Jon Arryn? Possibly ... speaking of repeating myself, I guess I have made it clear that I am confused about Pycelle now, right?

The discussion at Hand is the assassination of Daenerys Targaryen. The council has learned that she is pregnant (from Varys through Ilyrio Mopatis I guess—see previous chapter), and Robert sees her as a threat. The session ends with Lord Eddard resigning as Hand of the King, a powerful scene and I love the dialogue. Mind you, I am paraphrasing as this is my first post without the novel at hand—Robert says he will need to find a Hand who will listen to him, and Lord Eddard retorts with something like "good luck with that." It's a great exchange, which can be seen as the breaking of the two characters' friendship, and as such it is quietly powerful. Imagine having read the twosome's adventures during Robert's Rebellion and Greyjoy's Rebellion first—then this scene would be resonating even more.

What's more, my good friend Vayon Poole appears on the scene! Seriously, what an understated character. I still don't know what he looks like, though, but he certainly is dutiful. Eddard tells Poole to prepare for leaving the city, and it's like a breath of relief to read that Eddard finally decides to give up. Unfortunately, I know that he won't get out of this viper's nest, and I feel sorry for him. His fate is sealed when Petyr Baelish, Littlefinger, makes an appearance and tells Eddard he'll bring him to a certain brothel. Eddard is unable to say no to a chance at solving the murder of Jon Arryn, and so he allows himself to be pulled back into the webs of intrigue. It is interesting that Petyr chooses *this* moment to tell Eddard about the brothel, no? Just when Eddard resigns as Hand of the King. I wonder why Petyr wants Eddard to continue his search. Is it to destroy House Lannister?

INTO THE VALE OF ARRYNS

Now here's a chapter I really like, because it features two well-written characters (Lady Catelyn herself and Tyrion Lannister) in one of my favorite locations of Westeros, the Vale of the Arryns. I can totally see this place come alive, with its holdfasts and homesteads scattered about a fertile land encircled by jagged, snow-capped mountains—and of course, the Eyrie—the fortress of the Arryns—is well described and an adventurous location closer to the high fantasy spectrum of the genre than the grittier fantasy *A Game of Thrones* finds itself in most of the time. I remember a thread over at westeros.org where I started, a questionnaire of sorts where fans could answer a few questions just for fun. One of the questions was "How old is Ser Donnel Waynwood?" The question was meant to gauge just how geeky you are about the series. I didn't know the answer back then, but rest assured I remember his age now—twenty if you insist on prying. It is Ser Donnel's voice that opens the chapter, and he's worried about Catelyn's safety.

Don't worry, young man. I think Catelyn knows all about the safety of the high road by now. She has just travelled through them to the Gates of the Moon, Ser Donnel. Throughout the chapter we learn that Catelyn is beginning to doubt Tyrion's guilt. Could he be innocent after all? Her pride and suspicions—and perhaps prejudice—doesn't allow her to think it through though, and so she transports the Lannister dwarf across the Vale to the great mountain where her sister, Lady Lysa, awaits.

Lots of new characters here, including Ser Brynden Tully, her uncle. I always envision him as much younger than he is, but whenever I re-read this chapter I remember that the guy is an old dude, just a few years younger than his brother, Lord Hoster Tully of Riverrun. The most interesting new characters, however, are Lady Lysa and her shaky son, Robert, the Lord of the Vale since the death of Lord Jon Arryn—whose ghost continues to linger in every page of Catelyn and Eddard's chapters. I like these two characters for all their weaknesses—they show a different type of character in the series, cowardly, afraid, doing things to protect themselves that to other characters seems unwise. The chapter is dense with details; in these pages, we learn the layout of the Vale, we learn that Bronn was largely responsible for the survival of the party this far, we get glimpses of Catelyn's childhood, we learn of Lord Robert the six-year old's disease, we learn of Lysa's plays at courtship, we learn more about the relationship between Lysa and Jon Arryn, we learn of the three way castles up to the Eyrie and how they are connected (I assume this is important later on—we're told quite often how impregnable the Eyrie is; at one point there's got to be an army landing in the Vale; or more interesting, we see how the characters enter the Gates of the Moon and are taken up to the Eyrie—maybe an army will never be able to seize the castle, but a single character could slip inside—which is exactly what happens in *A Feast for Crows*). Interesting, no? We meet yet another bastard of Robert Baratheon in the form of Mya Stone, we learn about bastard surnames, we have Catelyn's journey alone the last leg up the mountainside, which is a few pages of excellent description (we get almost overexposed to the layout—did we ever get such detailed descriptions of, say, Storm's End, or Riverrun? Maybe Riverrun—but this kind of shows that knowing the layout of the Eyrie is more important than the layout of Storm's End). When Catelyn finally stands before her sister, we get some really good dialogue that gives life to the relationship between the characters; the way Lysa is overprotective of little Robert is so well done, with strokes of realistic characterization meshed with some over-the-top moments. I love it. It is a bit creepy, in fact:

> "Is he a bad man?" the Lord of the Eyrie asked, his mother's breast popping from his mouth, the nipple wet and red.

We all know Martin's fondness for nipples, but in this instance it's gross. This sentence tells us just how screwed the relationship between Lysa and her son is. Breastfeeding a six year old. I guess there's no milk for him to be had, but it is the intimate action before the eyes of Lady Catelyn that tells us that things are ... wrong in the Eyrie. On a tenth re-read I can't say I'm having trouble keeping all the strands of story separate. I can view them as a whole; Catelyn's past—which includes Lysa and Littlefinger—makes perfect sense as a background to current events; her actions and way of thinking are perfect in this regard. She remains one of the more well-rounded and satisfying characters in the series. Doesn't mean it's her POV I enjoy the most, of course—it is through Catelyn's POV, however, that some of the series' most excellent set pieces are witnessed, in this case we get to see the Vale of Arryn, the Eyrie, the relationships between Lysa and Robert, and Tyrion and Bronn.

As a side note, this chapter is one of those chapters where I clearly see the influence of Prof. J.R.R. Tolkien, the grand master of high fantasy. The Eyrie would easily fit into Middle-earth; the descriptions provided by Martin here have some of that same ethereal quality. Of course, he contrasts this with the actual inhabitants of the Eyrie being more than a little disturbed, as further chapters will explore.

For now, I am pleased to say that this is one of my favorite, albeit a bit slow-moving, chapters of *A Game of Thrones* so far.

What I meant with the reference above to a "single character could slip inside", was Petyr Baelish being able to take control of the Eyrie without needing any army, so yes, in a way I was also referring to the Moon Door's use in Sansa's final chapter in *A Storm of Swords*. (That is to say, Lysa's exit ramp.) It's interesting to read people's ideas of how a huge army will invade and take the Eyrie (because it is always mentioned how impossible it is to take), but maybe the point has already been made—that an army was not needed to take the Eyrie, just an especially sly man named Petyr Baelish.

"Yay, Me!" Eddard Thought ... But It Was "Jai, Me!"

Ok that's a ridiculous suggestion for a title for this chapter, but I couldn't resist. Sorry. It's been a long hard day. If you don't pronounce Ser Jaime's name as "jay-me" it doesn't even make sense.

So. Back to *A Game of Thrones*. We're at chapter 36 already (where does the time go?), and once more we get to see Westeros through the eyes of Lord Eddard Stark.

It's quite interesting, really, how the one honorable, dutiful and all around *good* character in this book is the one who causes all the shit that's about to hit the fan. And that shit hitting the fan—well, it really happens in this very chapter. Now, don't misunderstand me—characters like Lysa Arryn and Joffrey Baratheon are certainly responsible for much of said shit hitting said fan, but Lord Eddard is the POV that really, *really* messes things up—and the interesting thing is of course the fact that it his stoic sense of *justice* that causes his downfall in the game of thrones.

The first half of the chapter is relatively uninteresting (in the greater scheme), but once Lord Eddard gets moving from the brothel we get a serious confrontation when Ser Jaime Lannister appears. I can only drool as I await this scene to be part of HBO's *Game of Thrones* TV series. How can it not become a pivotal scene? Well, to be honest, it *could* fall flat., depending on a lot of factors of course. Why am I thinking this? Because I don't really feel that the confrontation sits well. It doesn't work 100% for me. Why?

It's because I can't see the motivation behind Ser Jaime's actions in this chapter. It certainly doesn't gel with how he is portrayed later in the series. It's all a bit weird; he shows up, has his men hack down Eddard's men, then leaves. It's not a threat, it's violence. He *kills* Eddard's men. It's an act of war, considering Eddard is the Hand of the King, the Warden of the North. Why did Ser Jaime do this?

Is Catelyn having captured Tyrion enough motivation for Ser Jaime to do such a rash action?

Why didn't he let a band of hired thugs handle this? He must have *wanted* Eddard to see that it was Ser Jaime who did this. A message saying, "If you fuck with my family again..."

But shortly afterwards we learn that Ser Jaime has left the city, presumably fearing retribution?

In short, I don't understand the sum of this chapter's parts. If anyone wants to enlighten me, feel free to go nuts in the Comments section on Is Winter Coming?

The scene itself is course very cool, and a bit disheartening (on behalf of Eddard) to read. The rain, the clatter of horses' hooves on the cobbled streets, the short, ill-tempered dialogue ... as a stand-alone scene I'd say it works great. It's just ... I can't quite put my finger on it ... but it's like there's something askew here; I love how Littlefinger hurries off on the first chance he gets—a little detail that paints the character as something of a coward when it comes to actual fighting.

On my tenth re-read, I find this chapter to be a bit like a piece of the puzzle that doesn't quite fit, in the same way that Tyrion's acrobatics in the beginning of the book don't really fit.

That being said, Ser Jaime throwing Bran out the window is also a bit out of character compared to how the Kingslayer is described in the remainder of the series.

It's a minor nitpick, this, but if you have any thoughts you'd like to share about Ser Jaime's motivations in this chapter, as I said, feel free to comment.

I did get a few comments on this post, trying to rectify my impression of Ser Jaime in this chapter, but I still don't understand the character's motivation here. Of course, it is a fantasy story so anything can happen and characters can be bolder than what would be realistic but I really don't see why Ser Jaime would take the lives of Ned's men like this.

DEAF, DEAD OR DOWN IN DORNE (AN EXCURSION INTO DUNK & EGG)

Dutiful nerd that I am, I've had the new *Warriors* anthology on pre-order for some time, and to my surprise it came early (as in, yesterday. or was it the day before. anyway); I'd rush straight through the newest Dunk & Egg novella, if not I had more pressing demands on my time ... But this evening I found time to read it, and here is a short but honest assessment of the latest work set in the world of Westeros:

Pros:

- ❖ It has the same atmosphere and mood as *The Hedge Knight* and *The Sworn Sword*, with more of the former than the latter.
- ❖ It has a few great new lines. My favorite was already spoiled in the excerpt on Pat's Fantasy Hotlist:"Deaf, dead or down in Dorne." It just rolls off the tongue, and is funny too.
- ❖ It has the best pace and flow of the three novellas, in my opinion. It moves forward in a perfect pitch, each section leaving you wanting to go on to the next immediately (it is the only of the three I've read from start to finish without taking a break).
- ❖ A few surprises aren't that surprising, but at least one *is*.
- ❖ Some fun new characters, including The Knight of Pussywillows (!), Gormond Peake & I-forget-his-name-but-his-squire's-name-is-Will.
- ❖ I like most of the plot and how it unravels.

Cons:

- It strays a little too close to *The Hedge Knight* with regards to content, character types, and situations (what I liked about *The Sworn Sword* was that it was a loose episode, kind of how *Temple of Doom* works in the Indiana Jones-trilogy; the first and third have Nazis, and well, the first and third Dunk & Egg have ... Targaryens); but then again, it seems that most people find *Temple of Doom* the weakest link in the Indy trilogy. But not I! Oh no.
- A few (not many) glaring typos. In a story that's been worked on since before *A Feast for Crows* though ...
- I'm not a sucker for cameo appearances and nudge-wink tactics; in *The Mystery Knight*, we get to meet a character from *A Song of Ice and Fire* and it was unnecessary, much the same way we didn't need to see Chewbacca carry around Yoda in *Revenge of the Sith*.
- There is a certain plot point I found unnecessary (not contrived, well maybe a bit contrived too), because it is already revealed in *A Storm of Swords*. To one who has not read *that* particular tome of magic, this point may be moot.
- I feel that the main characters Dunk and Egg have stagnated a little; don't feel they are *changed*, if you know what I mean, by the end of the tale. Can't say I remember if their arcs changed them in *The Sworn Sword*, I don't remember.

Most of these cons are minor grievances, and I would perhaps not pay them any mind if I were not so overzealous in my wait for more Westerosi stories. Overall, I loved being back in Westeros, and GRRM's voice is unmistakable.

A solid effort, about the same overall quality as the two previous novellas, but then there's the law of diminishing returns ...

Now, for the rest of the *Warriors*...and the next chapter of *A Game of Thrones*.

Beyond The Horse Gate

Something I really like about the series is Martin's inventiveness when it comes to naming locations and giving characters nicknames; I know some of it is lifted wholesale or partially from medieval history, but still—it was a stroke of genius (or luck) that he combined fantasy literature with medieval history (particularly English history) in many ways, and using nicknames/heroic names is one of them. "The Horse Gate" is perhaps not the most inspired name in the series as such, but the structure itself—*two gigantic bronze stallions, rearing, their hooves meeting a hundred feet above the roadway to form a pointed arch*—is a cool location, and the "design" of it—wide open spaces littered with loot from other cultures—I find inspired. In this chapter, Viserys Targaryen does earn himself two nicknames -*Khal Rhaggat*—the Cart King, and *Khal Rhae Mar*—the Sorefoot King. Now those are great nicknames. The sound of them, the implications of their meaning ... The Cart King. The Sorefoot King... Awesome. *Books* could have those titles and be alluring. Do the Dothraki have some Valyrian in their language? I just realized that the "rhae" in that second nickname could be the "rhae" in Rhaegar and Rhaegal. If so, "rhae" means either 'sore' or 'foot'. LOL. What does '-gar' or '-gal' mean? Could the great, legendary Rhaegar Targaryen's name actually mean "Foot-something"?? Footsweat Targaryen?

Amazingly, I have digressed before I even got started. We're pretty close to the middle of the novel, and the chapter's POV is Daenerys, who we haven't seen for twenty chapters or so. I remember during my first read that Daenerys was kind of an anomaly in the structure of the story; I found it hard to get into her story, because it was so separate from the other storylines (with hindsight, it is easier to discover the little details that tie her storyline more closely to the whole), and I found her a difficult character to like for some reason. In this book, she goes from rather weak to ... sorcerous and her development from *A Clash of Kings* onward is more interesting. Since my first read, I have read a lot of other contemporary fantasy and realize now that Daenerys is a pretty strongly realized character compared to the competition.

The chapter has, in my opinion, two important functions: It sets up the end of Daenerys' arc in this book (or, for a first time reader, sets up the possibility of the return of dragons), and it goes some way to give the reader a little insight into the Dothraki culture. I can't say I *like* their culture—it's far too hostile for my tastes—but it is well realized and I guess some of this information could be relevant if Daenerys ever brings Dothraki across the Narrow Sea.

Ser Jorah Mormont's disdain towards Viserys becomes evident in this chapter: *"Viserys could not sweep a stable with ten thousand brooms."* It is a line I seldom see referred in those ever-popular quote threads that pop up from time to time over at westeros.org and other assorted hives, so here I drag it forth into the light. It's a funny and sad line at the same time. The exile knight and Daenerys discuss Westeros for a bit, we learn about the crones of the *dosh kaleen*.

There are a few small details nestled within the words of this chapter that I like:

Waiting for Dragons

- ❖ *The water was scalding hot, as she liked it.*—'Cause she's the blood of the dragon. Obvious, but cool.

- ❖ *"The dragons speaks as he likes," Viserys said...in the Common Tongue.*—I love the cowardliness of the character, how he's mean and cruel towards Dany yet soiling his pants before the Dothraki; I like how GRRM has no qualms showing such characters that are easy to loathe, yet I feel a tiny bit sorry for him. He's a bit similar to Joffrey Baratheon in a way; a bit delusional.

- ❖ *" ... and yet King Aerys had been murdered by one of them, the handsome boy they now called the Kingslayer, and a second, Ser Barristan the Bold, had gone over to the Usurper."*—Nice little touch there with regards to a certain character showing up later in the series to advise Daenerys. It makes me wonder whether we'll have a fateful meeting between the Mother of Dragons and the Kingslayer, as well.

Daenerys has prepared a gift for Viserys. Does she still not see his worthlessness? Oh, the ties that bind. Of course, fool that he is, he doesn't accept the gift, instead cruelly sneering at her.

Where did he learn this behavior? I mean, the two have been together since they were born, yet they are dramatically different. The only answer I see is that Viserys has a fair bit of the Targaryen madness in his blood. Dragon blood, sorry. To call your sister a slut, twisting your sister's nipples ... Viserys is a complete failure, and I do root for Dany at this point.

The chapter ends with Daenerys curling up on her side, cradling one of the dragon eggs she was presented at her wedding. The conclusion is vague, but leaves a satisfying hint that there is more to these dragon eggs than just fossiziled stone.

See you next time, in the North...

TOTALLY OUT THERE IN THE WOODS

This particular chapter is one that I remember more strongly than many other chapters, for one simple reason. When Bran is surrounded by the wildlings in the woods outside of Winterfell, one of them suggests "cutting off his little cock" in Bran's presence. The sheer cruelty of that comment made me a little sick the first time around, and further positioned *A Game of Thrones* as a different, nay wildly different, fantasy novel. The grit, the grime, and the cruelty of the most despicable of characters ... also, one of the wildings in this chapter is named Stiv, which sounds very odd to Norwegian ears as the word is associated with having a hard one (the word "stiv" literally translates to stiff, but not as in dead but as in aroused). How could I not remember this chapter more strongly than others? It is full of references to the mighty penis. Oh!

The chapter's structure is similar to a typical short story, with exposition followed by a few events, a few complications arise, and a climax where Robb Stark rescues Bran from the wildlings in the nick of time. Fairly straightforward, then, but also a good chapter. It flows from Winterfell, through the Wintertown outside its walls, to the woods ... and gives us a first, close look at Wildlings; of particular interest is of course the gaunt, flat-breasted woman Osha, who becomes a major character as she is taken back to Winterfell as a prisoner. Strangely, I don't often think of the Osha character, nor does she often figure in discussions around the interwebs (as far as I know; I'm banned from the places where I used to discuss the series because I run a website where you are allowed to be negative towards Martin's lack of progress).

Still, Osha is a cool character and she is rather important to Bran's story arc; she is a bit like Aragorn to Frodo; a rugged warrior used to living out in the wilds, leading a hero towards his destiny—this description fits both Aragorn and Osha, doesn't it?

THE AWESOME CONCEPT THAT IS THE SKY CELL

Wow, where do the days go? It feels like a year since last I blogged a chapter from *A Game of Thrones*. Not that this sense of time crawling is anything new to a fan of *A Song of Ice and Fire*. There was a time, oh in February 2010 or thereabouts, when excitement was (re-)growing as George R.R. Martin suddenly gave us all hope with a slew of minor updates about *A Dance with Dragons*, and then once HBO green-lit the TV series, the updates disappeared *completely*. It's a bit *too* obvious, Mr. Martin. You are hurting your fans, and even the most sycophantic of your followers are beginning to see the problem of arrogance that permeates Not a Blog.

But I have already digressed before starting; I guess that's just me wanting to get out some steam before delving into Tyrion's cold adventures. Maybe I vent so that I don't have all the bad feelings related to the saga affect my re-reading; for no matter how angrily I await *A Dance with Dragons*, *A Game of Thrones* is, was, and remains a masterpiece. So here we are, and Tyrion has been thrown into a sky cell, an awesome concept in itself; reading it was quite exhilarating and the threat of the open space really hit home with me, but then I have a fear of heights. The Mord character is a bit *meh* perhaps—a stereotypical gaoler if ever there was one—interestingly, his name is the Norwegian word for "murder."

Of interest is Tyrion wondering about someone setting up a feud between the Starks and Lannisters, but the real meat of this chapter is of course the very end where Tyrion manages to free himself of the sky cell by demanding a trial by battle. The whole sequence, with the dialogue between Tyrion and Lysa

Arryn is *awesome*, and I love the description of the Eyrie's great hall. Blue-white marble gives it that lofty, cool sense that fits the setting.

When Bronn steps forward to champion Tyrion, I'm all *OH Hell's Yeah*. Gotta love that Internet meme.

Not much more to say of this chapter. It's a winner. But so are most Tyrion chapters.

Promise Me

There is, and has been, a lot of geeking out on this particular chapter, because of Lord Eddard Stark's ethereal dream, the opening passage of the chapter that so looms like a (small) shadow over the character and his chapters. 'Cause it's in this dream that we get some juicy information on what happened to Lord Eddard's sister, Lyanna. Reading it the first time, I don't think I really grasped this somewhat symbolic piece of writing. Or I didn't care; in fact, I'm not sure I *do* care that much. Lyanna is a nice character and all, but she's but a minor piece of a gigantic (some would even dare say *bloated*) story. I wonder whether the character of Lyanna has been reduced in importance, what with the growing cast of characters and plot threads from *A Clash of Kings* onwards. I guess we will *still* have to wait and see, no?

Now, to the dream. It is an old dream; Eddard has dreamt this many times before, which I guess explains how vividly detailed his dream is. There are the three knights in white cloaks, a tower long fallen, and Lyanna in her bed of blood; there are Lord Eddard's friends; Martyn Cassel, Theo Wull, Ethan Glover, Ser Mark Ryswell, Howland Reed and Lord Dustin. Seven in total, then—not an insignificant number in this series. But did George choose seven companions on purpose? Where do the seven gods of the Andals come into the picture of *ice* and *fire*?

The seven face the three knights in their white cloaks—Kingsguard—Ser Arthur Dayne, the Sword of the Morning; Ser Oswell Whent, and Ser Gerold Hightower. If seven companions is significant, then I assume the number three is significant too—the dragon has three heads ... So is this a clue that the

Seven gods of the Andals are in fact, siding with *ice* (the Old Gods of the North) against *fire* (the Targaryens); and does this mean that R'hlorr sides with the Targaryens, you know, to even things out? Two pantheons on either side? I am tempted to follow this line of thought, but until the grand master reveals it all, it's just another theory in the cracked pot. The numbers used seem symbolic enough in this perspective, at any rate.

The dialogue in the dream is pretty cool and straightforward, giving us useful information on the end of the War of the Usurper, and of course the final exchange of words between Lord Eddard and Ser Arthur has become a favorite among fans and will probably rock hard once spoken in HBO's *Game of Thrones*. Maybe it's bordering on cliché, this exchange, but it does work, doesn't it? I think George has put in a pretty blunt hint as to the properties of Ser Arthur's sword too. Pale as milkglass? Alive with light? Called *Dawn*? Surely this *must* be the weapon that Melisandre keeps bugging us about come *A Clash of Kings*: the sword Lightbringer (dawn brings light, as a general rule). So, through this short description George actually ties together several seemingly disparate plot lines, the fall of the Targaryen dynasty, the war between shadow and light (ice and fire?), Lyanna Stark's death, Lord Eddard taking home Jon Snow ... or maybe, just maybe, I did follow that line of thought further than I expected. In the immortal words of Han Solo, captain of the Millennium Falcon: *"Sometimes I amaze even myself."*

Damn, I managed to put in something related to *Star Wars* again. Go me!

Waiting for Dragons

A totally cool last description of the dream is Lyanna *screaming* while they fight it out, swords clashing together. What is she screaming? I am not in doubt. She's screaming with the pain of birthing a certain bastard. On a tenth re-read, the secrets surrounding Jon Snow seem almost painfully obvious. I wonder, with the massive delays of *A Feast for Crows* and *A Dance with Dragons* (surely the latter must be the most-talked about never published book ever), whether George is actually going to change his initial plan concerning Jon. You know, since everybody and their grandmothers have kind of figured it out by now. I hope not, because while it's obvious, it does *work*.

Dreams don't last forever, and Lord Eddard finally wakes up, back in the Tower of the Hand. I must admit, it's been so long since I last read the novel that I at first couldn't remember how he got in this position in the first place. Then I remembered; Ser Jaime, the rain pouring down on the cobbled streets of King's Landing. My good friend Vayon Poole appears on the scene to tell Lord Eddard he's been sleeping for six days and seven nights. A line of dialogue that never fails to make me think of the film with the same name, starring Harrison Ford. What a crappy film that was. Harrison's cool, though. He's Han Solo *and* Indiana Jones.

Ah, since I can't seem to shake the *Star Wars* fever ... the popularity of the aforementioned dream sequence reminds me of that scene in *The Empire Strikes Back* with the bounty hunters lined up, chatting with Darth Vader. It was a great scene because it was short, gave us a glimpse of some cool characters, and that was it. The bounty hunters became incredibly popular precisely because they looked cool and had little screen

131

time; I figure it's the same kind of phenomenon with Ser Arthur Dayne and the other characters present in Eddard's dream—little screen time, but cool as really cold milk. glass. Dawn *is* Lightbringer. You heard it here ... well, probably not first.

Digression complete. Back to Vayon Poole. I want a Vayon Poole action figure. Sir George, you are peddling miniatures, calendars, replica swords ... *where are the Ice and Fire action figures?*

Poole explains to Lord Eddard what's been going on the past six days—that Ser Jaime Lannister has fled King's Landing is the most important event. I still don't understand Ser Jaime's motivations, as mentioned in the previous Lord Eddard post. I understand that he flees, though. I think. Do I? I don't know. What?

Eddard reflects on Martyn Cassel being buried down at the tower in his dream, which Rhaegar apparently called the Tower of Joy. One might wonder why he called it the Tower of Joy. Anyway, the deaths of everybody except Eddard and Howland Reed are confirmed, so Ser Arthur went down, which is good. We don't want an army of cloned Ser Arthur Daynes in the series.

ANYWAY (boy do I bleat today), Lord Eddard is visited by none other than King Robert Baratheon I and his lovely (at least visually) Queen, Cersei Lannister. The two of them are bickering, but the point they've come to make is clear—Catelyn shouldn't have taken Tyrion prisoner. It doesn't make sense to me, but oh well. Wait a minute, are they setting this up? Did Ser Jaime and Cersei concoct the attack on Lord Eddard's men to *start* a war? 'Cause I can't really see Cersei caring about Tyrion's fate. They use his capture as an excuse ... /slaphead. LOL, now I get it. On my *tenth* re-read.

Another nice little detail I noticed during this re-read is how Eddard and Ser Arthur's exchange from the dream quoted above return—Lord Eddard tells Alyn, the captain of his guard, *"I want my daughters kept safe. I fear this is only the beginning"* and then later Robert says *"I want no more of this. Jaime slew three of your men and you five of his. Now it ends."*

Neat little trick, poetic in its repetition. I'm jotting it down as inspiration for my own feeble attempts at crafting stories.

Finally Cersei has gotten Robert's nerves all worked up and he slaps her. I cheer. *"Wear it in silence, or I'll honor you again."* Another classic line right there. Cersei wearing a black bruise as a badge of honor? Sick burn, baby, sick burn.

With Cersei out of the way, we get a short glimpse of a fact I often forget when reading this series—that there was something going on between Robert and Lyanna, at least from Robert's point of view. To his mind, Prince Rhaegar abducted Lyanna; Robert believes she loved *him*, and of course as more back-story is revealed, we learn that the War of the Usurper, at its heart was about Robert, Lyanna, and Rhaegar. A classic tale reworked for Westeros? Do I sense some ... Shakespearian tragedy? I kind of love how George doesn't lay it all out for us—in fact, that may be the one strength of the series that keeps disheartened fans like me coming back, waiting impatiently and eagerly for the next volume.

The chapter ends with Robert forcing the office of the Hand of the King back upon Lord Eddard; quite unexpected the first time, frustrating on the tenth. Throw it in his bearded face, Ned! Go home! Dammit.

THE VALE OF ARRYN GOES ON AND ON

GRRM uses several different techniques when writing his chapters' opening paragraphs. However they come out, it is important to kind of *hook* the reader, to draw the reader into the chapter. He often uses the technique of starting with dialogue, to immediately give you a sense of character. The very prologue begins like this. Another useful one is to have some kind of action going on as the chapter opens—the classic *in media res*—which he actually doesn't use that much. A third technique is to describe a piece of the world of Westeros through the eyes of a character—which is exactly what he does when he opens this particular chapter. Now, if you've read any advice on writing stories you may have noticed that starting a chapter with such a description—also called *exposition*—isn't a smart thing to do, because your readers' eyes will glaze for lack of something more immediately grabbing. Of course, when you have come this far into *A Game of Thrones*—past the halfway point, the author may relax this "literary urgency" and take some time to give the reader more sense of place and time.

And so starts Catelyn's seventh chapter, with her viewing the Vale of the Eyrie from a balcony, and the description is, simply put, *beautiful*. I mentioned it in an earlier post—that the descriptions of the Vale are the most reminiscent of Tolkien's classic work *The Lord of the Rings*—this is where he throws in a little extra color, as if GRRM himself imagines the Vale more vividly than other areas of Westeros; the Vale itself is visually a stark contrast to the more "realistic" / "medieval" places of King's Landing, Pentos, or Winterfell Castle. It has this dream-like quality, which is perfectly conveyed through the first paragraph of this chapter.

But let not the languid description fool you—this chapter *rocks* and is a cornerstone of the novel, and a setup for several things to come later down the line.

The chapter centers on the trial by combat—between Ser Vardis Egen, champion for Lady Lysa Arryn—and Bronn, championing for Tyrion Lannister ... well, Tyrion's purse of gold, at any rate. A compelling chapter that takes us through Catelyn's thoughts as she witnesses the duel. I remember reading it for the first time that I wasn't quite sure about this whole "trial by combat"—business. It was one of those things that lead me to research medieval history a little closer, and when I realized that this "trial"-thingy wasn't just something GRRM came up with, but that it fits the world of Westeros nicely, the whole concept became better to re-read; after all, it does seem like some sort of *deus ex machina* to a reader who doesn't know that much about the Middle Ages. Of course, the duel also sets up a duel in the third book, which is *also* a trial by combat where one duelist is championing Tyrion (again), and by then we buy into the concept immediately. Sometimes I think of these two duel scenes (Bronn vs Ser Vardis / Ser Gregor vs Oberyn) quite often when thinking about the series—they are interesting, cool, and memorable. GRRM describes the way the characters move in and out of each other's reach efficiently. The coolest thing is that the two duels each teach us the opposite lesson—in one, it's not good to be slow and heavily armored, in the other it's the opposite, which is way cooler than yet another lesson of fantasy literature in which the "good guy always wins"; there are heroics on display here, but not necesarily performed by *heroes*, if you know what I mean. I guess you do.

We are treated to yet another *"no, now it begins"*-like line of dialogue (see last post), but by now I feel it has overstayed its welcome. What I really like about this chapter besides the duel itself is the characterization of Lady Lysa and her son with his shaking sickness. Through their dialogue we get a great glimpse of just what makes these characters tick (lots of anxiety, mainly); they are cleverly written villains in that there is a *reason* for them being like they are, and as the story unfolds we'll learn that there's even more to Lysa than just her coldness. If I were working on HBO's *Game of Thrones* I'd make sure that whoever got the role as Lysa be an actress who can play the character to the hilt—a character you love to hate. And little Sweetrobin, so tough as long as mommy's around ... interesting character and fairly untypical of the genre I would say ... bring it on, HBO!

Attack Of The Mysterious Mummer Monkey

It seems that most fans of *A Song of Ice and Fire* have one, maybe two, point-of-view characters that they don't appreciate as much as the others; when their names show up for chapter headings it is easier to put away the book and get some sleep already. I have seen Catelyn and Daenerys been mentioned as such POVs more often than not; but in my case, the least interesting POV remains Jon Snow. So far, Jon Snow's story arc is closest to the traditional fantasy / fairy tale archetype—the boy of low rank rising to become a leader and hero. Fortunately, George R.R. Martin has enough twists to the formula to make it more interesting than, say, yet another Frodo or Luke Skywalker rip-off, but at its heart, the Jon Snow arc contains a fairly predictable development. Reading *A Game of Thrones* for the first time, this wasn't as evident as it is to me now, of course. But even then I found his chapters less interesting, mainly because the Wall is so far away from the intrigues and more interesting plot developments in the south.

I personally prefer the medieval setting to the (high) fantasy one, but as a whole I do have to admit I love the juxtaposition of high and low fantasy, with Jon and Dany on the high end of the scale, and poor Lord Eddard and his lady wife Catelyn on the other end; and the rest somewhere between (although Catelyn's story takes on a decidedly high fantasy twist much later in the story..) Another factor is that Jon isn't surrounded by characters as intriguing as, for example, those surrounding Lord Eddard, through whose eyes we meet Varys, Littlefinger and King Robert, to name a few. The menagerie at Castle Black consists of more typical characters of the genre, like the dour

WAITING FOR DRAGONS

trainer Ser Allister Thorne, clumsy Samwell, envious Chett, and the classic "blind seer" type in Maester Aemon—I mean, these characters are painted in broader strokes while some of the characters in other chapters seem more complex ... And as usual I have digressed.

So, *Jon V*. Ser Alliser Thorne is his usual grumpy self, but he is forced to tell Jon and his friends that they are no longer recruits and will become true Men of the Night's Watch (also called the black brothers, which is kind of funny). Addressing the boys, Ser Alliser mentions "the Mummer's Monkey." Can't say I remember noticing this before, but what *is* the Mummer's Monkey? Gotta keep my eye out for more references to this mysterious entity; maybe it's a huge Chthonian monkey monster? It is referred to with capital letters. Who's the Mummer? A god? A god mentioned here never to resurface in the story? Something from the Free Cities perhaps?

Anyway, Ser Alliser's speech which introduces the chapter (here GRRM uses the "start with dialogue" option to hook the reader) is in fact one of two main points of the chapter—to move Jon's arc forward from recruit to soldier.

The one character not chosen by Thorne is, of course, Samwell Tarly. Jon feels that he needs to do something about this, and decides to talk to Maester Aemon, to convince the old blind man that Samwell would be a useful aide for him as he can read and do other geeky stuff. An empathic move from our Jon, and, unlike his father who would accept that rules are rules, Jon tries to bend the rules to help his friend. This gives us a look at Jon as a compassionate friend, which contrasts with Lord Eddard; a hint that maybe Lord Eddard isn't Jon's father after all?

In Aemon's chamber we get a little glimpse of Chett, it's fun "seeing" him this early in the story considering the prologue in *A Storm of Swords*. How Maester Aemon could hold up with such a prick is anybody's guess. The opposite of "blind seer" is "blind guy has to put up with a lot of crap."

So, a very short chapter with two important plot developments—Jon becomes a Night's Watch man, and he shows compassion for his friends.

There are a few small, perhaps unimportant hints in here as well. Animals seem to like Sam (maybe this one has already had bearing on the story, considering Sam takes care of the ravens later on, I don't remember at the moment), and we get some more exposition on the order of the maesters and the chains they wear around their neck.

Now while turning the page to see "Jon" wasn't very motivating, the next chapter's heading reads "Tyrion", and I am excited even though it's the tenth re-read. Tyrion is such a fun character, and he's travelling with Bronn to boot. I wonder who they'll have playing Bronn's part in the TV series.

A reader of the blog informed me of the existence of the archaic word "mummer"—"a masked or costumed merrymaker, especially at a festival"—but I knew that already—my point was that the Mummer Monkey is given capital letters as in a name, hence me pointing it out it the way I did. Not a "mummer's monkey" but the Mummer Monkey.

THE EARLY ADVENTURES OF THE UNLIKELY DUO

And here's the reward for patiently getting through another Jon Snow chapter (all right, I don't think Jon's chapters are *that* uninteresting; the character just pales a bit compared to the others, as if he is *too* conventional—but at the same time I guess Jon serves as a character for readers to easily identify with).

Ah, Tyrion Lannister, the Imp ... what a great character he is shaping up to be at this point in the story; and you know, I think I've found out just what makes him great. It's not just that he's a misshapen dwarf lord, and it's not just his quick wit; his chapters are generally the most entertaining because of how *other* characters react around him. You know, one of my favorite scenes in the entire story is a simple, but effective, discussion between Tyrion and his sister, Cersei. I grin just at the thought of her *slapping* him every time he opens his mouth. Yeah, I'm a book ahead of myself. But whereas Cersei loathes her little brother, other characters react in other ways to him, and the interaction with this unusual character makes the other characters—and the story itself—that more vivid.

In the case of this particular chapter, it is Bronn who shares the limelight with Tyrion, and his reaction to the dwarf is perhaps my favorite. Where most characters instinctively distrust and/or dislike Tyrion, Bronn *likes* Tyrion for being the smartass he is. Bronn sees the worth of Tyrion Lannister, and although Bronn in these first chapters together mainly is interested in Tyrion's gold, there is a distinct notion of respect from the hardened mercenary, as evidenced in some of his lines of dialogue already in this chapter.

Bronn's grin here says it all, doesn't it? Incidentally, Bronn taking a liking to the cunning Lannister lord is perhaps the *only* instance where we see Bronn have an empathic side. I may be wrong, though.

So, Tyrion and Bronn have been freed from the Eyrie and sent down the road through the Mountains of the Moon, and like Tyrion noted in his previous chapter, this is just another death sentence. The two are gathering firewood in a copse of aspens just off the high road, a scene vividly described by George R.R. Martin, really taking the reader into the scene to get a closer look at the two characters—Tyrion promises Bronn more gold than he can dream of, in exchange for his protection. An unlikely duo—a lord and, what Tyrion refers to as scum—but don't all the great stories have unlikely duos? It's my favorite pairing in *A Song of Ice and Fire*, with Arya and the Hound a distant second.

The chapter has two main parts—the first being the two travelers bantering back and forth, the second being the arrival of several threatening wild men from the Mountains, who have come to kill the two for trespassing. I remember that the first time I read this I envisioned these characters as *Conan*-types with bear hides, skull helmets and stone weapons. And some artists who have painted these characters also seem to have that impression. So every time I "meet" them again I force myself to readjust my mental perception of the mountain clans—'cause if I'm not mistaken these people wear stolen armor and carry stolen weaponry, making them look much closer to soldiers from the lowlands, only with their equipment being mismatched. A minor point this, I know. On a related note, I don't think I envisioned Tyrion the way he's supposed to look for the first five or six re-reads. The first time he looked like Gimli. It was a time when reading a fantasy novel with a dwarf automatically set off the "beard/axe/underground mining city" image. Weird, that.

Anyway, Bronn realizes that Tyrion is actually trying to draw the men of the mountains down to them; where Bronn believes it's best to try and ride for their lives, Tyrion is gambling again—another great aspect of the character is the way he takes chances and I think Bronn likes that as well. Now, the men of the mountain clans appear at their campfire, and while I didn't notice it the first times I read the novels, they are clearly meant to be not only a threat but also something of comic relief. Yes, they are deadly. Yes, they are sneaky. Yes, they are hard. But they also have a sense of humor and, just as with Bronn, they become fond of the little Imp's sarcasm. Shagga son of Dolf roars when Tyrion utters his classic line about how he wants to die—and in this moment I knew that Tyrion would get out of this just fine. Foolishly courageous in the face of the enemy, Tyrion manages to promise them steel weaponry (mmm... did they have stone weapons after all?) if they will let him live, and they agree.

More interestingly perhaps, Tyrion offers them the Vale of Arryn, something we have yet to see happen—will it happen? Considering some of the theories I have presented earlier on how this story might go, it is not unlikely that Daenerys lands on Arryn land when she returns to Westeros—and she will probably bring Tyrion with him ... Will there be a scene where he invites the mountain clans into the Vale, perhaps letting them go ahead and rape, pillage, and plunder? Seems Daenerys has allies up on the highroad ... unless proven otherwise in the remaining novels, that is.

There is one other interesting possible foreshadowing in this chapter—Bronn, incredulously, thinking Tyrion a fool if he believes he can outlive Bronn. Will we experience a time in the novels where Tyrion lives and Bronn is dead? Only the author knows... but seeing how deftly George R.R. Martin weaves irony into his saga, I wouldn't be surprised if this particular line from Bronn will come back to slap him in the face. *Slap!*

Oy, I thought that slap was a nice way to finish this post, but I forgot to mention the whole Tysha story that Tyrion tells to Bronn. Not that the story he tells is the *exact* version of how things happened...so it can wait until the little lord finds out the truth.

The Hand Of Justice

The first time I read *A Game of Thrones*, it was a confusing read at times. There were so many names, so many characters; the background events were never explained fully ... of course, on later re-reads this only served to make reading the story again an even better experience. It was the first book where re-reading, for me, wasn't just about getting back to a great feeling or experience (like *The Lord of the Rings*); it was about discovering new details, it was about solving clues and putting together pieces of the puzzle. Now that I am deep into Steven Erikson's *The Malazan Books of the Fallen*, I find it amusing that I once found *A Game of Thrones* so dense and complicated. Trust me, it's a breeze compared to Erikson's writing. Of course, I am also ten years older—the first time I read *A Game of Thrones* I was still a student. Since then, I've spent eight years working as an English teacher.

So why am I mentioning this? Well, because this particular chapter I've read today is tied to those initial feelings of bewilderment as to the number of characters, names and events in *A Game of Thrones*. Because this short chapter with Lord Eddard Stark sitting on King Robert Baratheon's throne is basically a short interlude in which we get a fair amount of exposition on the state of the kingdom of Westeros, and we meet some new characters at the same time.

The chapter starts with a short, colorful description of the throne room itself, before we learn that Eddard is seated, as the King's Hand, on the Iron Throne itself. We get a short description of the forging of said throne, which is a neat idea I think. But it is hard to imagine the thing as real; I mean a throne forged of razor-sharp sword blades? I wonder how it will look in the TV series. Below Eddard, the Small Council is seated—the slimy Varys, the frail Pycelle, the dubious Littlefinger. We learn that the King has gone hunting. So, the hall before Eddard's eyes is filled with petitioners, and through his interaction with them we learn a little bit about what exactly is going on in the lands north of King's Landing as a result of Catelyn's kidnapping of Tyrion, and Lord Eddard's confrontation with Ser Jaime Lannister; in the west, both Riverrun and Casterly Rock are calling their banners, massing armies, and villages have already been destroyed. Lord Eddard is forced to hear of cruel acts perpetrated in the riverlands, giving us a terrific yet terrible glimpse of medieval brutality. "'Oh, dreadful'," murmured Varys. "'How cruel can men be?'" As it turns out, *very* cruel: and there is one character more cruel than all the others, bestiality incarnated—his name is Ser Gregor Clegane, also known as The Mountain that Rides. Here we get our first glimpse of his terror, and later on as we get a closer look at his adventures, these glimpses confirm how bad he really is. Re-reading the dialogue as the characters come to the conclusion that Ser Gregor Clegane is responsible for massacres and pillaging is quite rewarding, because once you've read the entire series you better understand the villagers' fear of him. From a political point of view, the fact makes war even more likely, as Ser Gregor belongs to Lord Tywin Lannister. It seems at this point that a war between Lannister and Stark is unavoidable.

Much of the chapter deals with setting up the political and military strategies and preparations, and I love reading it. I love maps, I love battles, I love medieval times, and in this chapter the "medieval" aspect of Westeros is layered thick. The villagers believing Ned is the king, because they have never actually seen the king; small details like these give the world of Westeros that extra touch of realism—in the Middle Ages, peasants never ventured far from their homesteads, and so it is in Westeros.

Lord Eddard decides to set up a company of soldiers to track down and capture Ser Gregor. The villagers want him dead, obviously, but Eddard remains level-headed and his honor bids him to instead take Ser Gregor alive, so he can stand trial for his crimes. As Lord Eddard proclaims his decision, the Knight of Flowers, Ser Loras Tyrell, steps forward and we get our first proper look at this particular character. I am not sure what George R.R. Martin tries to achieve here by having Ser Loras want to hunt down Ser Gregor, only to be turned down by Lord Eddard. Does he try to show that Ser Loras is confident? That he is fearless? Lord Eddard seems to think Ser Loras wants the mission only for revenge, not justice. But what would Ser Loras, in this case, want revenge for? What I am trying to say is I do not understand Ser Loras' motivation in this particular instance. Maybe this is what is supposed to set up Ser Loras' taking charge for the siege of a certain location in *A Feast for Crows*, that he wants to be recognized? But he is already recognized ... he is known as a great knight, even at his young age. Now on my tenth re-read it also somewhat surprises me to see Ser Loras here in the throne room; wouldn't he want to go hunting with King Robert Baratheon, and more specifically, Robert's brother, Renly? In the end we get a few minor characters sent on the particular mission, under the leadership of one Lord Beric Dondarrion (great name). Little does a first-time reader know that him being sent off to catch the Mountain that

Rides will spawn several plot arcs involving other characters reaching all the way into and beyond *A Feast for Crows*. But it is satisfying to read on a tenth re-read, when you know who Dondarrion is, and don't have to flip back to the appendix to find out who was this guy and who is that guy?

The chapter ends with Varys suggesting that Ser Ilyn Payne, the physical manifestation of the King's Justice, could take it as a slight that he's not sent to fetch Ser Gregor. A slight nudge to Eddard's last chapter in *A Game of Thrones*?

A reader pointed out Ser Loras' motivation for killing Ser Gregor: it goes back to the tournament where Ser Gregor unhorsed the Knight of Flowers. How could I have missed that having read the book ten times?

EVIL ANNE OF BLACK GABLES

What would a reader think if he or she was presented with *A Game of Thrones* as this epic, gritty fantasy tale and then read this particular chapter? As I re-read "Sansa III" for the tenth time, it strikes me that the character of Sansa Stark—particularly in this chapter—may be seen as a fairly stereotypical, dare I say clichéd, character. In this particular chapter she displays a few traits that can be considered unsympathetic, which most stories tend to let the bad guys have. Consider the exchange between Sansa and Jeyne Poole, the daughter of the steward of Winterfell, the much overlooked (but not on this blog) Vayon Poole. Jeyne dreams of Lord Beric Dondarrion, yet Sansa thinks Jeyne is silly because Beric is way above Jeyne's station. Here, we see Sansa thinking politically (which is cool, because she is growing into a politically savvy character) but also that she has no empathy for Jeyne in the sense that she doesn't seem to understand that Jeyne can dream of Lord Beric regardless of her station. Yet she is a dreamer herself, dreaming of Ser Loras Tyrell, the Knight of Flowers. She does tell herself that it would be unkind to say what she thinks, though. But even then, the way she tells herself that makes Sansa seem aloof. The chapter also shows us that Sansa, at least in this book, puts too much value on looks—she can't understand how her father could refuse Ser Loras since he looks like a hero. So what we have here is a silly little girl who thinks highly of herself; how does George R.R. Martin make this work? There are many answers—she contrasts pretty well with her tomboy sister Arya; at this moment she is but starting on her story arc, one that will indeed change all of her notions; and, of course, through her we witness important events at King's Landing not covered by the Eddard chapters.

To get back to my original question—would a potential reader decide to read the series if this was the first chapter read? I don't think so. As a stand-alone chapter, I think the character Sansa is easy to dislike (which may influence a reader's decision) and the chapter itself doesn't really glimmer with the gold that is all over the series elsewhere. However, and I'm finally getting to a point here, I think this may be a reason why Sansa Stark is a fairly unpopular character among the many fans of *A Song of Ice and Fire*. She's like a surly version of Anne of Green Gables; reading her lines of dialogue I almost hear her speaking Oxford English as she sips her tea and nibbles "delicately at a chicken leg." Try it. Read this in your best British English and see if that doesn't reinforce the negative image of Sansa:

> "Father's leg, silly. It hurts him ever so much, it makes him cross."

Put some extra pressure on *ever* while you're at it and there she is. I wonder if that is how young actress Sophie Turner is going to sound in HBO's *Game of Thrones* TV series—I mean, not just British-sounding but also with an intonation that shows us how stuck-up Sansa is at this point. As I've said before, I like the character when you consider her entire arc so far, but in this chapter she is almost insufferable. George R.R. Martin is really layering it here, but it does pay off in the end when she is thrown into terrifying and humiliating situations. But she does remain stupid for some time to come, so let's see what bits of plot we can get out of this chapter.

Waiting for Dragons

The first interesting bit comes about three paragraphs in when Sansa remembers a conversation with Lord Petyr Baelish, also known as Littlefinger. Here we get our first (I think it's the first) foreshadowing of the pairing Littlefinger/Sansa, with Sansa feeling uneasy about it, Littlefinger's exaggerated bow, and him thinking Sansa cleverer than she actually is (he thinks she has a good answer for why sending Ser Loras to catch Ser Gregor would be a good idea—to keep the Lannisters from the Tyrells). She explains about heroes and monsters; it would be funny to see that meeting play out instead of seeing it through Sansa's memory; I totally see her trying to explain to this devious master of the game about heroes and monsters.

All right, what else have we got. There's (yet) another comment on Ser Ilyn Payne; I feel he's being referred to very often and I wonder—is it to make the impact of a certain beheading later in the book stronger? Did George R.R. Martin intend to make Ser Ilyn a more important character than he has been so far? Has Ser Ilyn Payne been dead and resurrected? (He is described almost like an undead.)

There's also the notion that "everyone knows dreams are prophetic," which is a sneaky way to tell the reader to pay attention to any dreams the characters have—they may just come true. And many dreams have come true—makes me wonder about Ser Jaime's dream in *A Feast for Crows* though. That dream is *really* bugging me because I don't know what it's supposed to tell me—feel free to educate me on this one). And of course Sansa thinks of her prince, Prince Joffrey. Most of the realm knows by now that he's a bit of a scumbag (to put it mildly) but Sansa still fawns over this pitiful excuse for a human being. Maybe she's forcing herself to think positively of

151

him. I mean, when you tell yourself that your dream prince likes hunting—but *especially the killing part*—you got to be a bit delusional, no? Jeyne and Sansa keep talking, discussing Arya's strange antics in the stables (she's training with Syrio Forel, remember), the Night's Watch, Ser Gregor ... and Sansa has few nice things to say about any of them; they're all smelly and stinking. Giggling and gossiping and eating cake, the two girls are definitely starting to bore me, but fortunately things start to happen the morning after; Sansa sees Lord Beric leave the Red Keep to take up pursuit of Ser Gregor Clegane and bring him to justice, followed by another quarrel between Sansa and Arya, which is entertaining, with Arya's line *"You have juice on your face, Your Grace"* making me laugh. Arya is as easy to like as it is difficult to like Sansa here. Also, she's a poet but does she know it?

Finally we get to this chapter's important plot development, which is Lord Eddard telling his daughters that they are going home. For Sansa, this is a tragedy. Unlike Arya, she revels in the luxuries of the Red Keep, loving the lifestyle and being around gallant knights and Prince Joffrey. As Sansa and Arya begin to argue, Lord Eddard finally realizes that Joffrey Baratheon isn't a Baratheon at all—he's a Lannister, through and through—the product of incest. Congratulations, Lord Eddard, but you're not a master of the game of thrones yet. Sansa is heartbroken knowing that she will have to leave King's Landing behind. When Arya tries to console her, she only makes matters worse and the rift between the sisters deepens. I wonder if the characters will come to some kind of confrontation—or reconciliation—somewhere down the road. I would like to see that. But I'd also like to see Jon and Arya meet up again. Or

Jon and Tyrion. Or Ser Jaime and Bran. Or Sam and his father. Or Tyrion and Tysha .... More urgently, I would very much like to read *A Dance with Dragons*. How much longer can we be tortured?

RETURN OF A CON MAN

So as I write today's blog entry, George R.R. Martin has returned from yet another con(vention), complaining about all the work he has to do, before telling everyone visiting his website that he is soon off to another con. How *hard* can it be to see what the problem really is? Fortunately, the grand master spent some time giving us some juicy insights into the everlasting creation of *A Dance with Dragons*. Oh, wait a minute, I just dreamed up that last bit. He did, of course, not mention the one thing everyone and their cats are waiting for—but no longer with bated breath, which is good as it would deprive the author of 99.99% of his readers. Only the 00.01% *Wild Cards* fans would live to see the fifth novel published. Maybe.

Yup, I had to get a little rant out of my system. What to do, what to do while waiting. *Read other books, you idiot!* I do read other books. I'm deep into the *Malazan book of the Fallen* saga by Steven Erikson, which along with Abercrombie's novels are the closest to give me some sense of literary satisfaction—but honestly, I am not sure I would have bothered if it wasn't for the fact that I am waiting for dragons.

Then be happy, George made you read other novels! Yes, this is a fact. Without the long wait, I would most likely not have been ensnared by the strange, yet alluring Malazan Empire, and I may not have discovered the rich, black humor in a novel like *Best Served Cold*. But on the other hand, I am not quite sure these books would've existed without *A Song of Ice and Fire*, which let's face it, was the book that kind of heralded a darker side of fantasy to come. George also made me read more on medieval history and history in general. In fact, *A*

Song of Ice and Fire is responsible for many changes in my life—it inspired me to start writing some shit myself, it reinforced my love for the Middle Ages; it was a definite painkiller once the *Star Wars* saga which I loved with all of my heart was flushed down the toilet by its creator; through George R.R. Martin's works, I have discovered other fantasy novels that I can like.

But nothing of this changes the fact that the author of *A Song of Ice and Fire* is screwing with our heads in a mean way, belittling those who ask about the next novel, censoring or outright banning those who try to make him see that we're waiting for *A Dance with Dragons*, not *Fort Freak* or a comic book adaptation of *Fevre Dream*, or a replica, or a signed (!) but damaged copy of an RPG book. Sigh.

Then shut up, the book will be finished when it is finished. True. It will probably be (though I am not sure; *A Feast for Crows* sure doesn't feel finished to me). So I should really be shutting up about waiting for the fifth book. But that doesn't take away from the fact that the author is coming off as a supremely arrogant person, and has been showing less appealing sides of his personality for the last five years. Anyone who refuses to see that he treats his fans like *utter shit* is blind.

GRRM is not your bitch! Indeed; you must have misunderstood. Or heard this phrase somewhere else, perhaps from some author who has worked for Martin. I don't know. The correct phrase, at any rate, is *GRRM behaves like a bitch!*

SPOONFEEDING LORD CLUELESS

... And so we have come to the twelfth chapter featuring Lord Eddard Stark, Hand of the King. Eddard is the character with the most chapters in *A Game of Thrones* (fifteen), and one can argue that this makes him the book's main character. The hero, if you will. He is, after all, a good guy (though, if you remember, the first thing he does in the series is to decapitate Gared). So even as each Eddard chapter is part of a downward spiral, with the character barely keeping his head above water in the political climate of King's Landing, I think we all rooted for him and thought of him as the book's hero. And before *A Game of Thrones*, I think it is safe to say that we didn't expect our heroes to *fail*. Yes, this book was different—it wasn't about the farm boy seeking out a great destiny as a warrior or magician—it was about a feudal lord investigating crimes—but in I believe most of us who read the book didn't see that Lord Eddard was, slowly but surely, digging his own grave. And in this chapter, he chisels his headstone.

So count me among those who didn't see the signs on my first read! On my tenth re-read, the story of Eddard becomes a different beast altogether. I know where things are (be)headed. I have already mentioned, a few months back, that re-reading Eddard is a bit irritating because I now see so clearly his mistakes. But re-reading Eddard is also interesting in the sense that his story arc becomes more of a *tragedy*. And like watching a train crash, it is fascinating to read about Eddard.

The chapter opens with Grand Maester Pycelle—perhaps the most ambiguous character of them all—treating Eddard's wounds. The old, doddering man tells Lord Eddard that there

Waiting for Dragons

has been a message from Lord Tywin Lannister to his daughter, Queen Cersei. Which is sufficient to raise my eyebrows; isn't Grand Maester Pycelle totally and utterly a Lannister supporter? Has he been *ordered* to reveal this to Lord Eddard Stark—an attempt to threaten Lord Eddard, perhaps? Pycelle tells Eddard that Lord Tywin is angry about Eddard's decision to send knights out to find and bring Ser Gregor Clegane to justice; yeah, it does sound like a barely veiled threat. I can totally see Cersei telling Pycelle to tell Eddard this, hoping that he would back off. Instead, Eddard feels he has done the right thing. Another nail in the coffin?

> The old man hurriedly gathered up his things and took his leave. Ned had little doubt that he was bound straight for the royal apartments, to whisper at the queen.

This pretty much confirms my suspicion, but as we all know Eddard is a bit of a mule when it comes to intrigue, so if we are to remember that the chapter is from his point of view, we can never be certain that Pycelle is indeed going straight back to Cersei.

An hour later, Littlefinger comes knocking on Eddard's door, and he gives Eddard a similar warning that free riders and sellswords are flocking to Casterly Rock, seat of Lord Tywin Lannister. We also get a quick reminder of Sandor Clegane's hatred for his brother Ser Gregor, with Littlefinger suggesting another reason why it was dumb to send Lord Beric Dondarrion into the field. An interesting little bit of info that almost passed me by even on the tenth re-read is when Littlefinger comments on Robert Baratheon's hunt:

> "They found the white hart, it seems ... or rather, what remained of it. Some wolves found it first, and left His Grace scarcely more than a hoof and a horn."

Not only is this, as far as I can tell, the first time we hear about wolves roaming about—and as the story progresses it becomes clear that it is Arya's wolf Nymeria who is leading a pack to terrorize the countryside—but it is also an omen as far as I am concerned—eerily similar to the omen in the first chapter of the book, but mirrored. Eddard's boys found a dead direwolf in the snow, an antler lodged in its throat; and now Robert has found a hart ripped apart by wolves. Not only is House Stark going under because of House Baratheon; House Baratheon is going under because of House Stark. At least, that's the way I read this. I haven't taken any courses in prophetic revelations, so who knows.

Once Littlefinger leaves, Eddard reflects on what to do next. He has finally understood that Cersei's children are not Robert's—but her brother Jaime's—and he knows that he cannot keep quiet about it—his duty requires him to tell Robert.

The last part of the chapter takes place in the Red Keep's godswood, and is a conversation between Lord Eddard Stark and his enemy, Queen Cersei Lannister Baratheon. It is a great and memorable scene, and I remember the first time I read this I was ... aroused by Cersei Lannister. Great character; cold yet sexual, aloof yet a bitch; I loved to hate her ...until *A Feast for Crows*—but that's another matter entirely.

> She came to him at sunset, as the clouds reddened above the walls and towers.

How's that for ominous? Another (perhaps not so) subtle foreshadowing of Eddard's destiny?

"Almost angelic in her beauty," no wonder I was aroused. Of course, once she begins talking and shows her true demeanor, she isn't quite that interesting anymore, but physically, at this point in the saga, she's the hottest female character in the series for me, and her cruelty is kind of alluring in its own way. I hope you understand me correctly. I am talking about a fictional character. A real-life Cersei would appeal to me physically but her personality is a turn-off, obviously.

Anyway, what is really cool about this scene between Lord Eddard and Cersei Lannister is that it is so atypical of fantasy, because here we have what can arguably be perceived as the main hero and main villain facing off. But lo! This is not the peasant-turned-hero against the Dark Lord; these are two people, one of them stoic to a fault and the other a whole bundle of psychological trouble, and they meet to *talk*. This is one of those scenes that I feel really helped turn the genre around, because it is simplicity itself yet also a powerful confrontation—and it is basically the scene that seals Lord Eddard's fate.

At this point, Cersei's character is given some extra depth as she confirms her love for Ser Jaime, and she comes across as well constructed, a defined and icy woman with everything to win *and* everything to lose, depending on how you look at it. I wish *A Feast for Crows* didn't introduce the *valonquar* prophecy of Cersei's doom ... it really ruined what used to be one of my favorite characters. But more on that should I ever venture as far with my blogging as the fourth novel in the series

The dialogue isn't entirely believable all the way through, but that is mostly because of the plot point being discussed—that Cersei's three children were never Robert's and that nobody figured this out before Jon Arryn—I mean, *A Song of Ice and Fire* is an incredibly well-written story but this central plot point never sat that well with me since it should be / would be so obvious for other characters to discover. On the other hand, later novels may just introduce us to more characters who knew all along and have kept shut about it; I can't say I remember reading any of those but I may have forgotten.

A Crown For A King

Unlike Eddard, Daenerys's chapters are few. This one is only the fifth chapter featuring the young girl with the silver hair, and it is still strangely disconnected from the other elements of the story; but it doesn't feel that way on the tenth re-read. It is an essential part of the overall story, and once her storyline is drawn closer to the others, I hope to be delighted by a transition in the unfolding plot where her story merges with the others towards the end. That's what I am assuming will happen, at any rate. Of course, there are some minor elements that connect the ongoing plot threads, at this point most obviously the character of Ser Jorah Mormont, who (secretly) works for King Robert Baratheon and has something of an enmity going on with Lord Eddard Stark.

In this particular chapter, we are treated to more of Khal Drogo's culture, and I love how George R.R. Martin manages to convey this culture in a manner that is dissimilar to the medieval European feel of Westeros; the author does not shy away from describing cultural traits that we enlightened westerners (and I am saying this tongue firmly in cheek) find somewhat ... politically incorrect. But hey, I am pretty sure part of *A Song of Ice and Fire*'s appeal is the fact that it shows violence, decadence and depravity without flinching. I am all for it. Made it stand out all those years ago when it was first published. These days, fantasy readers will barely frown should there be some depravity in *A Dance with Dragons*—so many fantasy novels have been published while we've been waiting, that George R.R. Martin has been equaled and at times surpassed in sheer political incorrectness (I am looking at you, Mr. Abercrombie, and looking forward to *The Heroes*—the title probably being hilariously ironic).

The chapter's very first line is politically incorrect, so Martin draws me in, reading as Daenerys is forced to eat a raw and bloody horse's heart. He then proceeds to describe how she plunges her teeth into the tough, stringy flesh, the warm blood running down her chin ... you get the point. A visually grotesque, yet symbolic, act to hook the reader onto the next chapter, bringing you straight back into Daenerys' point of view, and on hindsight George R.R. Martin couldn't have started off the chapter better than by giving the reader such a visually disturbing introduction, ensuring that even though Daenerys has been active for just four chapters, you are right back with her.

There is an interesting bit where a crone of the *dosh khaleen,* as part of the ritual, peers into the "smoke of the future", which is quite similar to how Melisandre looks into the flames in *A Clash of Kings.* Are they using the same techniques? Do their faiths have a common, ancient birthing ground? Who knows? Of all the things that make *A Song of Ice and Fire* feel so realistic and medieval, religion is perhaps portrayed with the least detail, a part of the overall saga that George R.R. Martin began exploring later down the line. The crone proceeds to tell Dany how her son shall ride swift as the wind, a *khalasar* behind him. On the tenth re-read I can obviously give the crone a stamp of "epic fail," but on the other hand, she may just see things right—only it is not Dany's son who is the stallion who mounts the world—it is Dany herself (as far as I am concerned; I could be wrong though). After the ceremony there's a procession, followed by a feast at Vaes Dothrak where Daenerys has a chat with Ser Jorah which serves as exposition, giving us more

Waiting for Dragons

details about the Dothraki customs, particularly those concerning the holy Vaes Dothrak.

That scene builds up atmosphere for the real meat of the chapter, which is the fate Dany's brother Viserys, who still hasn't repaired his social antennae: refusing to be like the Dothraki, he dresses—or tries to dress—as a king or lord of Westeros, making him stand out—and he carries a sword, which is forbidden in Vaes Dothrak as Daenerys has learned from Ser Jorah. Drunk with wine, Viserys is making a fool out of himself, calling his sister a whore and going on even more foolishly. Soon, thousands of Dothraki are laughing at him, leading to Viserys pulling his sword. Dany, now obviously fearing for her brother's life, tells him he can even have the dragon eggs.

What if he had taken them? Now that would make an interesting "what if?" line of questioning. He doesn't, of course.

Viserys is tired of waiting for the crown Khal Drogo has promised him, and finally Khal Drogo gives him a crown. Drogo throws golden medallions in a heavy iron stew pot. The medallions melt, and Drogo upends the pot over Viserys' head, drowning and burning him in liquid gold. No blood is spilled by Drogo, so it is a fair kill according to the Dothraki tradition. And Viserys, a mean and easy-to-hate character for the five chapters he's in, gets his comeuppance. It is not as satisfying as the comeuppances that certain other characters will get later in the saga, but still ... it is a moment of terror, of pure horror. Try to visualize the event—now try being Viserys whose patience was at an end, who all his life harbored dreams of being a king, only to die in this horrible and gruesome manner.

Again, George R.R. Martin does not shy away from grim violence, instead showing us that Khal Drogo is indeed a cruel and hard man, and of course this opens up the story for Daenerys, as an important obstacle has been taken away. Whoops, I meant, it opens up the story for her son Rhaego, of course. Viserys will not be a Targaryen conqueror like Aegon, after all.

It's a short and (bitter) sweet chapter; I like it, although I wished Viserys' comeuppance had come later as I enjoy reading about characters like him. Fortunately there are replacements for him, with both Theon Greyjoy and Joffrey Baratheon sharing some of the negative character traits of Viserys Targaryen. A great thing about Viserys's demise, by the way, is that we can be pretty sure he'll stay dead. As the story develops and more supernatural elements are thrown in, certain characters continue to exist beyond death—a minor niggle I have with this otherwise excellent series. I certainly do not hope to see a golden-helmed resurrected Viserys gurgling about the countryside in search of vengeance.

The Boar Did It!

Since my favorite author finds it more prudent to blog about how he's been watching actresses audition for the role of the harlot Shae and needing to take a cold shower after that, and also telling the world that he didn't particularly like *Iron Man 2*, I guess it's up to his readers to blog about that which interests his readership in the first place: *A Song of Ice and Fire*. Apologies to the *Wild Cards* fan out there. But *A Song of Ice and Fire* is the masterwork we're all hooked on, right? I'm not saying Martin *shouldn't* be allowed to blog about the casting of whores or about going to cinemas to watch superhero movies. By all means. It's not like I'm blogging about my work either (but then, nobody visits this place to hear about my workday).

The simplest solution would of course be for GRRM to use his update page for *A Dance with Dragons*-related news, or even better, have *two* blogs: one for *Ice & Fire* and one where he can blog about all the things that he wants to blog about. Why do I suggest this? The answer is that I think Martin is making himself look and sound quite ridiculous in some of his non-*Ice and Fire* blog posts. I mean, "Mood: Horny"? I didn't need to know that.

On a related note, I find it disappointing that he tries to sell us miniatures and busts and whatnot but doesn't mention the release of Green Ronin Publishing's *A Song of Ice and Fire Roleplaying: Campaign Guide*, the first worthwhile franchise product since the third Dunk & Egg novella appeared in the *Warriors* anthology. Oh well, enough about the man—it's the story that matters, and *A Game of Thrones* is a fantastic story full of vivid characters, a novel that deserves even more attention than it already has.

Once again we are back to Lord Eddard Stark—also called Ned among friends—and his investigations in the city of King's Landing. Last time he was dismissing Queen Cersei Lannister, a chapter that ended on a dark note, with the two characters threatening each other. For a first-time reader, a virgin of thrones so to speak, I speculate that one naturally expects Lord Eddard to win through in the end and ruin Queen Cersei. Why not? He's the main character of the novel, as I suggested in my previous Ned post. Yes, things have been going downhill lately, but surely as we move into the story's final act, things will be set right and Lord Eddard will win. But as any fan of the series knows, Martin is quite able to ... make dark things *darker*.

Eddard is summoned to the royal bedchamber. Unfortunately we are not treated to a hot scene of seduction courtesy of the Queen, whose looks and shape I greatly admire (well, for a fictional character that is)—no, GRRM turns the grit up (down?) a notch, with King Robert Baratheon, that easy-going, fun-loving, reckless friend who became master of all Westeros, lying on his bed, bleeding to death. To death! Is no one safe in this novel? I chuckle with glee. The king is surrounded by many of the important characters of King's Landing and the Red Keep—Grand Maester Pycelle, that wily old fox, Queen Cersei, the king's brother Renly ... it is a delicious twist in the story, to be honest. Maybe a virgin of thrones expected the king to come around and see his folly and so deal with his lady wife to the satisfaction of the readers. Instead, he lies dying, gored by a boar while out hunting. Which, of course, is way more cool and fits the setting's tone perfectly; after all, much of the King's

Landing plotline is inspired by medieval history, and medieval history tells us that kings usually didn't die of old age.

The scene where Eddard enters the royal bedchambers is written in a very vivid way; I can practically *see* the characters discussing, voices lowered, and the fat king bleeding on his bed. Don't know if I visualized it as well the first time I read it (I struggled a lot keeping all of the characters separate in my admittedly unimpressive brain).

> Fires blazed in the twin hearths at either end of the bedchamber, filling the room with a sullen glare.

This description is short yet so effective. It sets the mood of the scene perfectly.

Ned is told what happened. There is a sly hint in there as well, from the mouth of the king himself: *"My own fault. Too much wine, damn me to hell. Missed my thrust."* As we'll discover, the king may just have survived his encounter with the fierce boar in the woods had not someone poisoned that wine.

The king commands everyone to leave the room; when Cersei objects we get this little gem:

> Cersei gathered up her skirts and her dignity and led the way to the door.

I chuckle at that one. Skirts and dignity.

What follows is a critical plot point—the king wants Ned to rule the realm until his son comes of age; Ned writes down the king's will, but instead of *Prince Joffrey* he scribbles down *heir* before having Robert sign it. Knowing that Joffrey isn't Robert's son, Ned now sees an opportunity to use this letter to give the throne to the true heir, which is Robert's brother Stannis, still brooding on Dragonstone. The king also has a last minute regret about sending assassins after Daenerys, and so he is kind of redeemed before his death; his arc is at an end, and so Ned can only watch, grieving, as his old friend takes his last breaths. I hope the actors nail this scene in HBO's show; it has so much potential in raw emotion.

Pycelle gives the king the milk of the poppy, and Ned leaves the chamber. Outside, Varys hints to Ned that the king's wine was poisoned; and we get a scene where Renly offers Ned the chance to seize Queen Cersei and end the conflict immediately. Honorable to a fault, Eddard refuses—and once again he digs deeper his own grave.

Next, he summons Littlefinger and has a chat with him. Ned has decided to write a letter to Stannis summoning, him to King's Landing to take the Iron Throne. Littlefinger thinks it unwise, and suggests that with Stannis on the throne, the realm will surely go to war.

Littlefinger is right that Eddard's honor is making things difficult for himself; but Lord Eddard doesn't think it keeps him safe; it's just that he values honor above his own life, and Petyr fails to see this—or so I read it. Petyr promises to bribe the City Watch to support Lord Eddard—the Hand of the King—and not Prince Joffrey and his mother.

It is certainly an exciting chapter, even though all that's happening is characters talking—but there is this undercurrent of threat throughout it, the promise of war. Lord Eddard tries his best to keep to his honor, and as readers we are wondering who is trying to gain advantages here—Petyr, Renly, Varys—

Waiting for Dragons

and who is genuinely interested in removing Prince Joffrey and let Ned rule the kingdom for a time.

I can't help but love the intrigue, the dealings...the medieval fantasy aspect of *A Game of Thrones*. Hell, Martin could have left out the whole Daenerys story as well as Jon Snow's chapters, and it would still be the greatest thing I've read. Makes it that much harder to change perspective when the next chapter up is Jon. Suddenly, there's this whole other story which isn't nearly as interesting. Fortunately, Jon Snow's chapters are still miles ahead in terms of entertaining me than most other fantasy novels so I don't want to complain anymore about that.

Before *A Game of Thrones*, I was used to what I call "linear fantasy": there's a plot, there's heroes, they move towards their desired goals, mission accomplished—with few frills. With this book, however, I had to learn to keep track of wildly different characters, many of them often appearing in the same scene (as in this chapter), and for each re-read I began to read more between the lines, trying to gauge character motivations. This is one of the factors that make re-reading the novel such a worthwhile experience. There's always something more to speculate about. There is no clear-cut good side and evil side; I mean, who should Ned trust in this chapter? Should he have gone with Renly? Listen to Littlefinger and abandon summoning Stannis? Characters have more choices—more *moral* choices at any rate—than is usual in the genre, and it makes them stand out that much more, and this is of course also a reason why I believe HBO's TV adaptation will become a genuine success. It has characters to root for, characters to hate, they are all interesting in various ways,, the dialogue is both entertaining and often realistic ... characterization made *A Game of Thrones* such a strong novel, and characterization will make the TV series great. Or so I hope.

How To Become A Black Brother

A fine day to blog a little about *A Game of Thrones*: after all, HBO gave us a tantalizing teaser of their upcoming show based on the very novel I am blogging about. Will they do it justice? I believe so. Will I most likely be annoyed at certain decisions and nitpick those? Certainly. Am I giddy about the project anyway? Yes.

Unlike some of my fellow "detractor" brethren, I have no real complaints about the teaser. It seems some people expected a huge trailer, showing off the main characters, letting us hear some dialogue, what have you. But that is way too early—the show is still in production and the pilot itself will be (or already is) most likely reshot due to the two new actresses. So, all in all, the teaser does just what it is meant to do—tease us. I think it an interesting gesture of HBO to give us this glimpse; maybe it is more to gauge interest. Anyway, it has been a while since we've had some actually interesting news on *A Song of Ice and Fire*. I am happy with HBO's little teaser. From now on, there's something to be excited about that *does* seem to have a fixed release date. Grrumble ...

So, we're back at the Wall, and Castle Black, and of course Jon Snow and Samwell Tarly, who is so fat that the very first action he takes in the chapter is to *plop* himself down on a bench. I can almost *hear* his massive layers of fat flopping about as he sits down. Jon and Sam, and the other young recruits at Castle Black, assemble in a small sept where they are forced to listen to a rambling speech from Lord Commander Mormont—they are going to become actual men of the Night's Watch. The organization itself is a fairly interesting concept, so seeing how this is done makes the chapter more interesting than the preceding chapters in the practice yard with sour-faced Ser Alliser Thorne. By the way, Alliser's last name is an anagram of 'throne'. Guess who will eventually win the game of thrones?

Jon Snow does not want to say his vows in the sept, as he belongs to the Old Gods of the North; Samwell, although from the fertile southern lands of the Reach, also wants to say his vows before a heart tree. The fat boy seems to have little faith in the Seven, and he is clinging to Jon and his friendship, so off the two go. My guess here is that by saying the vow to the Old Gods, the author ties Sam closer to the story of the North, and him being vowed to the Old Gods may just be a setup for a certain encounter late in *A Storm of Swords*. But who knows? We've been waiting for that particular plotline's continuation for a decade. Sorry, eleven years. Time flies. But why? asked Bran. Why does it fly? *Because winter is coming.* I'll believe it when the first flake of snow falls on Daenerys Targaryen's pretty head.

The main plot of the chapter isn't the two taking their vows, however. It is the fact that Jon has been requested to become the personal steward for the Lord Commander. At first, Jon is pretty disappointed. He wanted to become a ranger, like his uncle. Don't ask me why he'd rather want to follow in the footsteps of an uncle who's been lost in the woods since 1996. Anyway, it is a classic moment— dare I say "mythological," in the spirit of Joseph. Campbell? When Jon exclaims, "It's not *fair!*" we have the typical lowborn character who one day will become a great hero, the world being unfair until he rises above himself and becomes the hero of the story. If I remember correctly, Luke Skywalker said the same thing when he was sweltering beneath the twin suns of Tatooine, working for his grumpy uncle and not doing what he wanted to do: "Biggs is right; I'll never get out of here. It's just not *fair!*" Excuse me if I am misquoting here. It's been a while since last I watched the holy trilogy. The middle episodes of *Star Wars* have been forever tainted by prequelitis.

It is fat Sam who finally puts Jon in his place, and together they march off to the heartwood tree, somewhere beyond the Wall itself, in the creepy dark forest which we now can watch on repeat in the HBO teaser.

"They're watching us," Sam exclaims as they reach the grove. Does he genuinely feel a divine presence watching them, or is he just commenting on the fact that someone carved faces in the trunks? *Is* there some connection between Samwell Tarly and the Old Gods that we'll see explored later? If yes, how will it play out considering Sam isn't near the Wall at the end of *A Feast for Crows*? Will he be the Old Gods' eyes in the south? Quite interesting. Well, kind of interesting. A little bit interesting. Want. New. Novel. Now.

When they speak the oath of the Night's Watch, author George R.R. Martin weaves a little literary magic. Yes, it may sound corny if you read it aloud, but *wow* does the Night's Watch oath ooze with atmosphere and solemnity. I love it. Obviously, it is the greatest piece of dialogue (monologue) in the chapter; it is such a haunting little piece of coolness.

Finally, there's a little hint (ok, it's hammered home) that there's a connection between Ghost, Jon's direwolf, and the Old Gods. Ghost comes padding with a hand in his jaw. Nasty—and setting the stage for things to come, involving more body parts.

IS THERE MORE SHIT LEFT WITH WHICH TO HIT THE FAN?

It's Sunday, the sun is shining, and I've read through another chapter of *A Game of Thrones*, this time outside, in the garden. Blissful it may sound, but the plot unfolding isn't quite as idyllic.

Whereas other characters can linger in memory for many chapters, we always come quickly back to our main character, Lord Eddard Stark. There is a point to me mentioning him as a main character so often these last posts, bear with me. You can probably guess it, anyway.

The poor lord of the North started out as a brave and wise leader. Our first glimpse was him being the executioner of a deserter from the Night's Watch, calmly chopping off a man's head with that nasty sword of his, *Ice*. Now as the noose is tightening around his throat, Lord Eddard is no longer that man—he has essentially been broken by the intrigues of King's Landing, and at this point in the plot, it all finally comes crashing down. And *still* I am rooting for him, the poor soul. I am not sure whether I am thinking of Eddard or myself as a poor soul in this instance; not only have I waited for a decade for resolutions to certain plotlines from *A Storm of Swords*, but I also still root for Lord Eddard, ten years after the first time I followed him through *A Game of Thrones*. Yeah, it's sad. All of it.

Anyway, the "grey light of dawn" is streaming through Eddard's window as he is awakened when he hears horses outside. He's been sleeping at the table. Down in the courtyard he watches Sandor Clegane practicing, and our friend Eddard wonders whether the scarred knight has been ordered to practice by Cersei, as a not-so-subtle warning. Interestingly, when good people are going down, it seems that the weather is miserable in Westeros, just as it is raining in every sad scene in every movie ever made. Does anything bad ever happen when the sun is shining? In this chapter, the morning is overcast and grim; giving it a sense of foreboding, though during my first read I hadn't the slightest clue things could go that bad for the hero.

Eddard allows Arya to go practice her sword-play one final time with Syrio Forel, but doesn't allow Sansa to visit Prince Joffrey. How unfair the world is, Sansa. And how enjoyable that you don't get what you want, heheh. It's still really easy to dislike her at this point in the story.

An hour later doddering old Pycelle comes along, telling Ned that yes, Robert is now pushing daisies. So, this author isn't afraid of killing off secondary characters. Robert's is a very important demise as it leaves the Iron Throne vacant* and thus sets up many of the plots to come, and irrevocably changes the already existing plotlines. A bit of a shame though, I liked the Robert Baratheon character, both as the young, fearsome warrior and the fat, drunken king.

(Well, not exactly vacant; after all, the realm thinks Prince Joffrey the true heir and son of Robert, but that boy's head *is* pretty vacant though.)

Eddard immediately summons the council to his solar (an odd touch of Martin's science fictional past shining through here?) though Pycelle tries to postpone the meeting for some reason I wish I knew. Arf, how Pycelle annoys me. I just can't get a grip on this fossil. Martin is careful to show us in which order the council members arrive: Ser Barristan Selmy immediately displays his allegiance to the "young king" thus referring to Prince Joffrey Baratheon as the new king. Next up is Lord Petyr Baelish—Littlefinger—and Martin slips in a hint that he's been busy, his boots dusty from riding—he says he's done what he has been asked to do. He is followed by Varys, the slimiest eel of Westeros. What a disgusting guy he is with his lack of genitalia and overperfumed bald head. Ugh. And that's it. Stannis sits on Dragonstone, and Ned is informed that Renly has left the city. No support for you there, Ned. Maybe you shouldn't have brushed him off so quickly.

The letter from Robert is opened and read, and Ned asks the council to confirm his as the Lord Protector of the realm until Prince Joffrey is old enough. They are interrupted by a summons to the throne room by Prince Joffrey—Ned suspects that this is Cersei's work, which it of course is. Outside the throne room we get a little glimpse of the saga's tragic hero Janos Slynt before Ned is ushered into the throne room; he is relieved that he sees no Lannister crimson around, but a number of gold cloaks—the very soldiers he now counts on, as he thinks Littlefinger was going to bribe them to fight for the Lord Protector, and not the boy king.

Martin gives us a lengthy description of who's in the throne room, including a number of Lannister guards, and he properly instills the sense that now everything is going to hell.

Still Eddard does not relent (or buy a vowel). He proclaims loudly that Joffrey is not the heir of the Iron Throne, and Joffrey's face reddens with anger. He's such a spoiled brat, a shitty snotty kid you just want to give him a good beating (though as you may or may not know, it wouldn't help the kid at all. Am I speaking from a modern enlightened view of parenting here, or simply acknowledging that Joffrey is already a conscienceless sociopath?

And then it comes: Ned tells Slynt to take Cersei and her son into custody, and for a moment we were all thinking be thinking, hey, Ned came through after all. Then the gold cloaks he relies on begin killing off his men around him, right there in the throne room.

There are many so-called painful scenes in *A Song of Ice and Fire*. For me, this is one of them. I didn't see it coming, although Martin does build up to it (specifically going into detail as to what Ned is up against); yes, characters are thrown off towers, and yes, characters die—but this one stings a lot, because the betrayal is so rotten. One moment you are right there with Ned, walking up to the dais and the Iron Throne, thinking *go get 'em Ned*, then Martin just slaps you in the face (a bit like adding spoiler policies to his blog, then) with this shitty turn of events. And I love it while I loathe it.

To drive it home, Littlefinger comes up with his dagger to Ned's throat, giving us a great memorable quote that ends the chapter at its climax; no resolution here, Ned's left dangling, and of course we just *have* to read on, 'cause we wanna see how is he gonna get out of this one. Chapters like this, where characters are left in a dire situation—let's call them cliffhangers—I must say, Martin excels at writing them. He really makes me want to continue.

I am not a particularly fast reader, but *A Song of Ice and Fire* is always a breeze, partially because of these cliffhanger chapters. I mean, when I got my hands on *A Feast for Crows* oh, about half a decade ago, that is the fastest I've ever read a book. I *devoured* it. I wonder if I will be able to show more restraint come *A Dance with Dragons*. Maybe I'll try reading one page a month to ease the wait for *The Winds of Winter* or whatever the hell the next book is called.

So, we have Eddard in a really tricky situation. We all wonder what's gonna happen next. But first, we have to see what happens with Arya, one of my favorite characters. Will Martin be able to hold my attention, to keep up the suspense built in this chapter? Only time will tell.

Today I woke up and then went through my normal morning ritual. Included in said ritual is checking for updates on *Not a Blog*. It is more out of habit than actual (morbid) curiosity, but yeah I always have to go get disappointed. I'm like an abused wife who keeps returning to her violent husband.

Lo, and behold! There is an actual post about *A Dance with Dragons*, and it even has some insight into the process, and that was all I wanted. Thank you, finally.

As to what the contents of the update bode for the quality of the fifth *A Song of Ice and Fire* novel, now that's another matter entirely. Arianne Martell is back? It sounds like this novel will suffer the same structural problems as *A Feast for Crows*. Too many characters we do not relate to crammed in. But if that's what it takes to get things in repair before the resolution, so be it. I am going to devour it anyway.

And hopefully, *hopefully*, it will be good. But I'm not betting on it.

FEAR CUTS DEEPER THAN SWORDS (BUT SWORDS KIND OF CUT DEEP TOO)

Incredibly, it's July already. Still no *A Dance with Dragons*, but as many like to point out, I can always read something else. And boy am I reading something else. Just started *The Bonehunters*, the sixth volume of Steven Erikson's *The Malazan Book of the Fallen*, and this work is definitely the best to make the wait for *A Dance with Dragons* a little less painful. With Joe Abercrombie's works a good second choice. But even as I am overwhelmed by Erikson's high fantasy epic, trying to absorb the details (of which there are very, very many), I find myself waiting for the continued adventures of Tyrion Lannister, Bran Stark and the rest of the crew of Westeros. GRRM certainly hit a lot of us—*hard*—with his works. They have this hard-to-describe quality that lifts at least the three first novels in the saga head and shoulders above everything else, to stand tall and proud alongside *The Lord of the Rings*—classics, not mere enjoyable fantasy romps. After all, there's got to be a reason why new *A Song of Ice and Fire* blogs keep popping up, as well as sites dedicated to specific parts of the franchise. The saga has become a force on its own, and it's a shame the author himself perhaps—*perhaps*—doesn't have the same enthusiasm and interest in his world anymore.

With that little digression out of the way, it is time to delve into another chapter of *A Game of Thrones*. Last time, we left Lord Eddard Stark with a dagger at his throat, and it would of course be very exciting to see what happens next. But first, we need to read about Arya Stark, one of his daughters, and that is not a bad thing at all. I find Arya one of GRRM's best characters. He writes her into a realistic character (well, realistic in the sense of a realistic character in a fantasy setting), and he gives her certain qualities that make her easy to like and want to follow. Her sometimes childish answers, the way she chews her lip when thinking about something, these small details help her come alive on the paper.

Arya is training with Syrio Forel, a fan favorite among the secondary/tertiary characters. He's a bit of a caricature as a stereotype mentor but I do love the way he speaks of himself in third person, and his words of wisdom are small nuggets of gold. His teachings have become favorite lines for many fans, perhaps especially *fear cuts deeper than swords*, a line which has become the title of a card for the fantastic *A Game of Thrones: Collectible Card Game* by Fantasy Flight Games. Really, it's a great game.

For a change, I didn't actually re-read this chapter—in fact, I listened to the audio book's chapter, read by the guy who got the role as Grand Maester Pycelle in HBO's TV series. What listening to this chapter did was make me realize just how intense and exciting it really is. Reading it for the umpteenth time becomes more of a "been there, read that" kind of exercise but Roy Dotrice's narration really grabbed me and I "saw" everything happening: the excitement as Arya escapes Ser Meryn Trant who interrupts the training and attacks Syrio, the intensity when she considers crossing the courtyard ... wow! Roy really grabbed me, the way he utters the sentences in rapid succession: it made me appreciate the chapter more. Maybe more re-*listenings* are in order?

Anyway. So we know Lord Eddard is being held in the throne room, and now that we read about Arya's misadventure, we begin to see that things are finally *really* going down the drain for the Starks. Ser Meryn Trant arrives with Lannister guards to fetch Arya, but as Syrio is trying to teach her, there is a difference between seeing and … you know, really *seeing*. It kind of reminds me a little bit of Yoda's teachings to Luke Skywalker in that film you may have heard of, *The Empire Strikes Back*. It's eloquent, easy to grasp, rooted in wisdom, Syrio Forel is the man. And then he gets into a fight with the guards and Ser Meryn, and Arya is forced to back off; and what does GRRM do? He *doesn't* let us know how the fight went. He does tell us how it *ends*; because later we see Ser Meryn Trant, and we do not see Syrio Forel. The Kingsguard knight won. But how? And where is Syrio? Deaf, dead or down in Dorne? Thrown in a dungeon? Could Syrio Forel be Jaqen H'ghar (if you don't know what I am talking about, just bear with me 'til we get into book two). *No explanation.* Ten years on, it is a bit annoying. At the time, I found it awesome. Usually you are spoon-fed everything, right? But Syrio's fate remains shrouded in secrecy. It *can* be a hint that he'll be back. But he can just as easily be dead as the dodo. Whatever his fate is, it gives the dancing master from Braavos that extra coolness factor that makes him into a fan favorite (or at least, I believe he is; I am not exactly mingling with "fans" in the adoring sense of the word anymore).

Oh well. The main plot of the chapter isn't even about Syrio Forel. It's just that his scene in the beginning of the chapter is so damn cool. The real meat lies in Arya's escape; the excitement as she decides to walk as slow as she can across the courtyard, knowing she's got Lannister eyes on her, pretending to be just a servant or whatever, now there's magic there that I simply cannot find in *A Feast for Crows* or the cage match fan fiction GRRM wrote on his blog. It is *intense*. I'm *right there*, urging Arya on. Come on girl, you can do it. Don't look back. *Fear cuts deeper than swords.*

Awesome is a word that adequately describes my feelings about this chapter. Once across the courtyard, we get a tense scene where she enters the stables, finds one of her father's guards dying, and finds her suitcase ready for travel. They were about to leave King's Landing remember? But Lord Eddard kept getting reeled back in by the plotters in the council. And the Bitch Queen. Here she finds her sword, *Needle*, and her finding the blade is the chapter's brightest moment, in the positive sense. It's not like the people we cheer for are going through good times, so I am happy GRRM at least allows her to keep the blade (though I must say, it's quite miraculous how she is able to not lose it later down the line). Now, reunited with her blade, she continues her escape. As we remember from an earlier chapter where she was chasing cats across the Red Keep, she has some knowledge of the many areas of the castle and so she finds herself en route to the scary room with the dragon skulls ...

... and Arya's story begins in earnest. With her bastard brother's gift—*Needle*—and Syrio Forel's words echoing in her mind, she is off. I kinda wish I didn't know what's going to happen. It is such an exciting and dramatic turning point in her story so far. Well-crafted, Mr. Martin, impressive. I hope the young actress who is going to portray her will really inhabit this role. It is a crucial role.

That was the 51st chapter of *A Game of Thrones*. To be honest, I didn't think I'd last this long, my attention span being what it is and all. But I do so enjoy this novel that I automagically also love writing about it. I call it The Therapy of the Long Wait.

That new game from Fantasy Flight Games, *Battles of Westeros*, looks quite like therapy too. Oh oh oh I know the wait is slow oh oh.

Losing Fans Fast?

Moderating policies at westeros.org, the official fan site of a speculative fiction author: Could this be an interesting topic to write about? I mean, moderating policies. Taste those words. They are almost meaningless, and in a sense they are. For 99% of the inhabitants of planet Earth, "moderating policies" means nothing. Lest we feel too important about ourselves, remember that relatively few care about Internet forums, and even fewer care about they are moderated. Most of us are geeks discussing stuff most people in our real lives don't care about at all.

Still, some message board and Internet forums generate more interest than others, and there can be no doubt that the one provided by Elio Garcia (Ran) at westeros.org is an active place with many members. Their "Literature" sub-forum is almost a message board on its own. Hell, even respected genre authors visit this place. As such, it is quite interesting that the way the place is moderated is somewhat different than what you normally expect from a message board on the Internet.

I have been a member of westeros.org's message boards since they were still using EZboards. And that's a while ago. While there, I enjoyed reading threads and discussing the upcoming novel, *A Dance with Dragons* (!). Of course, what we were really discussing was *A Feast for Crows*. When westeros.org was reborn, I became member # 600-something. Like many other fans of George R.R. Martin's ultimate work, I became more and more distressed with the way the author used his blog; the way he treated his readership—in short, his arrogance.

I soon realized that there was no place for discussing Martin's procrastination at westeros.org. I was told to understand this—it is, after all, his official fan forum. Or whatever they call it. For the first few years I complied. There were still nuggets from *A Feast for Crows* to discuss. But I think I had been ... noticed.

I think I made an off-hand remark once about George being either lazy or procrastinating or something to that effect, and I was sent a warning.

All well and good; so far, you may be thinking, "why is this guy complaining? The moderating policies seem fair enough.". And it was fair; in the beginning.

Because during the year of 2009, all things George R.R. Martin began to intensify; more and more people became disgruntled, and I noticed I wasn't alone in my sentiment. Hey, I'm not being an ass alone anymore.

Still, whenever someone posted a vaguely critical or questioning post or thread, it was soon deleted.

And what happens when enough people feel they are being forced to keep their opinions to themselves? Yup, you get a problem if you're moderating the boards.

Instead of trying to do something about this, the moderators at westeros.org just kept on deleting comments, censoring dissent, and pretend that all was well in wonderland. Which of course made disgruntled fans even more agitated: To make a long story short, we got such sites as *Finish the Book, George*, and in January this year I set up a message board where people are actually allowed to discuss Martin's shortcomings this last decade without fear of being banned, perma-banned, shunned, or ridiculed by moderators or fans who see nothing wrong with George R.R. Martin's treatment of his readership.

When I set up the message boards where criticism was allowed, I didn't expect it to take off at all. But soon there were many members, and some drifted off from westeros.org too; George R.R. Martin himself said, and I believe it was in his embarrassing "To My Detractors" post, that those who didn't like the way he was doing things could run off and start their own forum or blog. Which is what happened—and is still happening. Now we have more excellent sites, too, and I'm sure we'll have many more.

Now, back to moderating policies and where things got interesting. A member of the message board I set up turned out to be a raving lunatic. Not my fault, nor any other regulars' fault. But there he was. The guy who spam-bombed Pat's Fantasy Hotlist with, among other things, the link to my forum (the old forum, anyway; we made a move to the current Is Winter Coming? Boards in an attempt to get rid of said sociopath).

Next thing I knew, I was banned from westeros.org.

Do you see what doesn't make sense here?

A weirdo spams Pat's Fantasy Hotlist, and I get banned from westeros.org. Not just me, either. Another member of *Is Winter Coming?* was searched out by the moderators over there and was banned, too.

We received no e-mail or message or anything. We logged onto westeros.org (in my case, I liked to hang out in the Literature forum most of the time) and found a message stating that we were not allowed to visit the site anymore.

Now, how's that for moderating policy? Banned because someone else did something on another site. It is quite baffling, actually. I guess they were monitoring us all along, and probably other members who used the same usernames at *Finish the Book, George* or *Is Winter Coming?* and then decided to simply shut out the detractors. Fans of GRRM, some of us, I'm sure, who are *at least* as big fans of his works as those who monitor, are *being watched*. Hell, I just heard that two known so-called "detractors" were banned immediately upon joining Ran of westeros.org's twitter channel. They were banned on being recognized! They are actively shutting out members of the fan community—there is a *split*—and I have lived this experience before; I, and many others, were shut out from the once global *Star Wars* community for not adori ng *The Phantom Menace*.

Back to Westeros ... that galaxy far, far away is no longer what it used to be ... and I fear this is happening to Westeros too ... ruined by its creator. More on that later.

Censorship, banning, monitoring. Are we back in the sixties? The eighteen-sixties? The fact that they didn't even bother sending us a confirmation that, yes, you're banned, speaks volumes. They tried to keep it all under cover, to keep their place clean so to speak, and what did they gain? I'll go out on a limb and state that the way they so bluntly moderated westeros.org was the underlying cause for all that happened since in the tiny corner of the interwebz dedicated to *A Song of Ice and Fire* (another factor is of course GRRM's own comments, of course—his "To My Detractors" masterpiece ultimately led to the *Finish the Book* site which spawned *Is Winter Coming?*... which lead to two bright heads meeting and setting up, you guessed it, *GRRumblers*—who knows what is next? I had this idea of starting *Another Not a Blog* mirroring the GRReat man's posts).

I had a fairly successful thread or two at Westeros (I remember I had three on the front page of the General forum on the day I was kicked out): a thread which moderator Werthead promptly closed off, then restarted as "Part II" under his own name. There's a "Part III" now, I have noticed. The same Werthead admitted in a post over at sffworld.com that he wasn't comfortable with the way westeros.org was run. *Oh?*

How did I notice there's a third version of my thread? Well, for some automagical reason I was suddenly allowed back the other day. After six months. I don't know why. I have not received any message stating anything; no "we're giving you a last chance," or "try to behave this time"—nothing. What are they trying to tell me? "Please sneak back in; we don't want to cause uproar so we're doing this quiet-like?" You tell me. Are they now trying to stop a rift in Martin's fanbase? Or did someone write over the "banned" data table during an update?

All I know is that the day we were banned simply for having a different opinion than the mainstream GRRiMlin (as we so lovingly call the loyal fans who dare nothing but grovel) was the day I lost all respect for those guys at Westeros and I haven't really found any reason to go back there. Why post on a message board that is actively censoring my input, when I can just kick back on at least three other GRRM-related sites with witty, intelligent posters who dare post their opinions—and aren't ridiculed for it?

Now I'll probably get banned all over again. I don't care. All I've been caring about in this context is to crack open *A Dance with Dragons*. I understand that these guys have to run the site according to Mr. Martin's wishes, or else they'd have to close shop. So in the end this is another grief laid at Mr. Martin's door. He is the one getting it all wrong on his blog—he is the one who does not want to hear any dissent. Had the moderators acknowledged this and given a warning instead of simply banning people and censoring posts ... but, in fact, this is exactly how Mr. Martin (and his assistant) runs his own blog. I made one post over there saying I was looking forward to *A Dance with Dragons* winning awards in 2041, and was instantly banned forever without further ado.. And I know of quite a few other fellows being insta-banned from the great author. He comes across as the grumpiest guy since, well, Grumpy. He desperately needs someone to coordinate his PR. Really. **He is losing fans** *fast*.

So, moderating policies at westeros.org and *Not A Blog* are practically the same and can be summed up like this:

If you have any opinions that aren't entirely positive, you are banned forever or at least for half a year. (More than a year later I am still banned).

Read people's posts at N*ot A Blog* for good examples of how to behave (also called 'suck up'); and, of course, if you are the Man himself you can write whatever pleases you. Even to the point where you compare the genocide in World War II with...oh, I won't even go there.

In conclusion, I hope you have been enlightened by this rather-quickly-hammered down rant and now know a little more about how things don't really work at westeros.org.

Next post is back to *A Game of Thrones*. It's just that I forgot to bring my book when I went on a holiday and I have not, at least not yet, memorized the entire novel. Maybe I will once I am waiting for *Winds of Winter*?

I know this post may cause some emotion—feel free to comment! The only one I censor is the porn-spamming guy. And I don't censor him for his opinions, I can tell you that.

One final note:

Just a thought, really. I called this post 'Is GRRM losing fans—fast?' mostly because I needed an interesting title. More interesting than "Moderating Policies" anyway. But is he? Losing fans fast? What do you think?

Is an author like Steven Erikson *gaining* those fans? Why do people accept the author plugging his side-projects? Does the header of his website say "Author of *Wild Cards*"? No. It says "Author of *A Song of Ice and Fire*." Then why are people banned for asking for *A Dance with Dragons*?

DISENGAGE SLYNT RAGE

The last months I've been thinking more and more about the whole debacle regarding George R.R. Martin and the continued delays of *A Dance with Dragons,* and of course his horribly maintained *Not a Blog.* I guess it is no surprise I have been thinking about all this, since I run a blog dedicated to the re-reading of *A Song of Ice and Fire* as well as a forum dedicated to the painful wait.

But what I am trying to say here is that I have been ... *reconsidering.* Reconsidering my admittedly harsh accusations, reconsidering whether a forum such as *Is Winter Coming?* deserves the right to exist, reconsidering whether I and many others have taken the backlash against George R.R. Martin too far. I have been feeling guilty for initiating flame wars, feeling guilty for (directly or indirectly) verbally attacking people who defend Martin and his blog ... in short—I've been feeling bad about letting negativity rule the day, painting everything black and not really listening to different opinions.

No, I'm not all mushy all of a sudden. I am still mad as hell for Martin's attempts at selling water-damaged books, for misleading his fans countless times as to the publication of *A Dance with Dragons,* for his "To my Detractors"-post; and as a previous, recent post shows I also have my opinions of Martin's "thought police." This is all beside the point. What I have discovered is that by fueling negative emotions with regards to all things Westeros, by giving in to what has been dubbed "the Slynt Rage" whenever there is something to get aggravated about, I am only fooling myself. *A Dance with Dragons* won't come any sooner. Martin won't automagically gain those much-needed PR skills. His official fan forum will not suddenly allow dissenters to, well, dissent.

So I have decided to just mellow out a bit. And that's it.

Yes, I do think such places have the right to exist. Freedom of speech and all that. I still think the backlash against George R.R. Martin is well deserved. I will still post vitriol when I feel the urge, but I'll keep it at *Is Winter Coming?* and not clutter up this blog with too much off-topic blogging. This one is all about reading *A Game of Thrones* for the tenth time. And waiting for dragons ... If only the author could be clearer about his motivations instead of constantly baiting us with promises. If he has writer's block, why not tell us?

A BIRD OF BETRAYAL

Chapter 52. Sansa. For the tenth time. No *A Dance with Dragons* in sight as of yet. Fortunately, at the moment the Fourteenth of the Malazan Army is taking a lot of heat (pun intended) at Y'Ghatan, a great set piece full of action and excitement (and grisly violence), in Steven Erikson's sixth Malazan Book of the Fallen, *The Bonehunters*. What a series! Interesting how radically different two series within the same broad genre (fantasy) can be. Erikson's novels are brimming with (somewhat absurd) imagination, a sense of time and place ... but I am never *there* the way I am when reading *A Game of Thrones*. For one of Martin's greatest strengths are the characters. His choice to write his chapters from the POV of one specific character helps us relate even more to that character and see the world of Westeros through his or her eyes, making the experience that bit deeper, and for a fantasy type novel, more immersive and realistic.

After two intense chapters depicting what happens in King's Landing once the tables are turned—first with Lord Eddard being betrayed and then Arya fleeing from Ser Meryn Trant—Sansa's chapter is altogether different. She is in no immediate danger (or, to be more precise, *she* doesn't notice the danger she's in), locked up within the Red Keep in the custody of the Queen Cersei Lannister, yet this chapter too oozes with threat to the Starks. The chapter opens with a simple, but effective sentence.

> They came for Sansa on the third day.

The threat is inherent in the way it's written. There's a conflict—*they* and *Sansa*. They control her—decide when she's to be picked up—and she's effectively a prisoner. A prisoner in richly embroidered clothes, but a prisoner none the less. I am curious as to why Martin chose "third day," whether it was a conscious decision. The "third day" in theology is considered the time when promises are fulfilled (by God) and in this chapter Queen Cersei does promise Sansa that she'll get to wed Joffrey if only she does as the Queen orders. How's that for looking too deep into things?

It's easy to dislike Sansa in this chapter. *Very* easy, in fact. She thinks of her friend Jeyne Poole as "such a *child*," thinking herself oh-so-grown-up and ladylike. Seeing the chapter through her eyes, it is easy for us to read between the lines that she's just as childish herself, and it makes for interesting reading. It is fun to read Sansa because she doesn't see herself realistically, so her POV is kind of skewed, and in how many fantasy novels do you get skewed POVs? Not that many. (The "unreliable narrator" is a familiar device in mystery fiction, though, dating at least back to Agatha Christie's *The Murder of Roger Ackroyd*). But there is more to it; what Martin does is imbue his unreliable viewpoints with life in a way few other fantasy writers manage.

Anyway, I wrote at length about characterization when I blogged the previous Sansa chapter, didn't I? So let's have a look at the plot of the chapter instead. It's fairly simple, really. Queen Cersei confronts Sansa and, using Sansa's self-imposed love for Prince Joffrey, the queen makes her write letters to her family in which she lies about the events that have just happened—she writes that her father Lord Eddard *betrayed* King Robert, now dead. What an act! But when reading it through her POV, it makes sense. She is desperate, and let's be honest she's a bit dumb at this point in the story, and Queen Cersei is charming *and* the prince's mother. She is so infatuated with Joffrey that *"nothing else mattered,"* and so she is really fooled into betraying her family. It's quite dramatic, and as mentioned above, *different* from the two previous chapters dealing with the aftermath of King Robert's death.

Aided by Varys and Grand Maester Pycelle, Queen Cersei ensnares Sansa, and she falls for it. This is a very interesting bit when you have read *A Feast for Crows*, the fourth novel, in which Sansa begins to develop into a player of the game of thrones. Here, in *A Game of Thrones*, she still has everything to learn (and everything to lose)—I wouldn't be surprised if a scene in a future novel will give us Sansa playing a similar trick upon someone else, kind of mirroring this scene. For now, she is enamored with the thought of becoming a queen herself, and it is obvious she is egoistical in a childish, dreamish way. There's some great irony in this chapter too, especially when Sansa thinks of Prince Joffrey as *good and kind, she knew it in her heart*. Great heart you got there, Sansa. You are an awesome judge of character. Sansa's insight is followed closely by another heavily ironic scene where Queen Cersei's smile is "as warm as the sunrise". Sansa really doesn't see Cersei for what she is. It almost makes me think that Sansa's story arc (in which she is becoming a player, as mentioned above) isn't really that well constructed, considering how blind she is here. But then you have the "love makes blind" adage, and that's what Martin is using here to make it work—Sansa's blind love for all things chivalrous and royal—her imagined love for Prince Joffrey (speaking of characters that are easy to dislike ...)

The final sentence of this chapter is perhaps the most important one, because it tells us so much about Sansa's character at this stage of her arc: She suddenly remembers that she didn't ask about Arya, her own sister.

That really says a lot, doesn't it? Sansa is rather different from her father and her brothers, but there is an echo of Catelyn, Sansa's mother, here. Just like Catelyn has no love for Jon Snow, it seems that Sansa hasn't for Arya. On the other hand, at least Sansa notices her own shortcomings ... there is some movement on her arc.

I wonder the surely obligatory scene with the sisters meeting again will play out!

LET IT BURN

It is apparently snowing where GRRM lives. *Ohwaitaminute*, he's just telling us that he's working on a Jon Snow chapter for *A Dance with Dragons*. *Butwaitaminute*, wasn't it just the Meereeneese knot and some polishing that was left to do? Regardless of the wait made so much more painful by Martin's obvious lack of communicative skillz, it is only fitting that it is Snowing on this here blog as well. Wink and nudge.

So, we return once more to the Wall, that icy thing that shuts the utmost north off from the rest of Westeros. It is one of many cool concepts from *A Game of Thrones*, it is high fantasy yet Martin makes it seem so real anyway, because he gives it—literally —some grit, too. People fall off and die, people try to climb it and slide down, there are elaborate winches and wooden walkways built along its side, gravel and boulders are embedded in it, know what I mean? It's not just some amazing ice wall, it is a defensive structure and Martin explains how the Night's Watch makes use of it, so even though there are stories of spells being used to raise it, there is also this everyday feel to it for the men of the Watch, blurring the line between the obviously impossible and the mundane. Is the Wall *the* landmark of the series? I believe so.

In this seventh Jon Snow chapter, we are treated to some interesting information linking all the way back to the prologue. So, when the Others slay people, those people become wights, undead minions of ... the Others, we can only presume, though it isn't stated very clearly if you ask me. Now, that is interesting. Imagine the size of the army of undeath should the Others break through the Wall and begin killing left and right. Talk about reinforcing success! The more casualties they cause, the bigger their army gets. No wonder they built the Wall so tall and thick (though I admit I'm a bit lost to as exactly why the Wall had to be *that* ridiculously high; the Others are no taller than Ser Gregor Clegane, I suspect, probably smaller). Of course, a really tall Wall also gives a really great view of the surroundings.

Enough about the Wall already. This is about Jon Snow, the most archetypical character of Westeros—until proven otherwise in a future volume of the saga (I do hope GRRM has a nice twist going for Jon—at a whim, allow me to suggest that Jon Snow…

BREAKING NEWS!

In an update from George R.R. Martin, he wishes to share with us the frustration of having to work on that same Jon Snow chapter instead of being at some comic convention. I don't know about you, but Martin whining about having to work on a book that's five years late is neither making me happy or appreciative. His hint about Jon meeting people from the Iron Islands is interesting, though. Vaguely. But sympathy? Not from this guy.

Back to Jon Snow. Hey, see what I've been doing in this post? I've been procrastinating. Jon bores me. The glistening grey-white Wall of ice is more interesting. But sometimes one simply has to cut the knot and get on with it.

The chapter opens with Ser Jeremy Rykker announcing the identity of two found corpses—Othor and Jafer Flowers and through Jon's thoughts we learn that they were his Uncle Benjen Stark's men. For a chapter in *A Game of Thrones*, I think its opening paragraph is a little weak. It feels a bit detached. Martin uses the same adjective twice—the corpses' blue blue eyes. I don't know, it's just a bit weak in my opinion (which you must know by now is not that humble).

A few paragraphs later, Martin more properly instills the right "feeling" when he describes how the horses and the dogs are frightened and skittish around the corpses, and that Jafer's right hand is torn off and lays floating in a bottle of vinegar over at Maester Aemon's pad. Yum!

Next paragraph Jon reflects on having dreamed of Winterfell—again. Hey, now this is interesting considering Martin's Snow/squid comment (see **BREAKING NEWS** above). The dream is dreadful, instilling terror in him, and he dreams of the dead king stumbling forth. It could simply be a dream—a haunting nightmare to reflect his experiences during the day—or it could be a foreshadowing of certain characters hiding down in the Winterfell crypts later in the series—or this sense of foreboding can be connected to Jon Snow coming to Winterfell in *A Dance with Dragons* ... would be cool to see him find Winterfell in ruins ....

There is some discussion about the grisly find—where is Benjen and the rest of his crew? Why didn't Othor and Jafer sound the horn? How could they have been killed so close to the Wall without anyone noticing? The mysteries beyond the Wall are certainly a tad more horror-influenced than the rest of the story, and I can't help but love it—the atmosphere and mood is perfectly described most of the time by Martin.

Jon Snow continually tells himself that he is no longer a boy, but a man of the Night's Watch—these ugly corpses

WAITING FOR DRAGONS

shouldn't frighten him, yet they do. Maybe if he'd not been so introverted and he'd notice that the grown men are just as uneasy as himself. Only Samwell Tarly is finding it more difficult. However, it is Sam who has to point out that the corpses are *old* and not fresh; his father Lord Randyll apparently enjoyed stuffing animals and the seasoned commanders of Castle Black ... well, apparently they don't know that fresh wounds bleed and old wounds don't. What I am trying to say here is that it is kinda weak the way Sam is the one to bring up this point. It is so obviously a way to make Sam more respected/needed by the Lord Commander Jeor Mormont, when it should be quite clear to all these guys that the corpses are old. However, Martin throws in a few arguments *against* Sam's suggestions, with Ser Jeremy pointing out that there is no stink. Sam tells them that these corpses aren't rotting, and everybody can see that. Mmm, not a very good argument then, Ser Jeremy. In the end, the Night's Watch men gathered around the corpses come to the realization that neither Othor nor Jafer are supposed to have blue eyes. The Lord Commander decides to bring the corpses back to Castle Black for examination (though someone whispers *"burn them")* which sets up the end of the chapter).

Returning to Castle Black without incident, there is a growing chill in the tale as Jon begins thinking of the Others and Old Nan's tales about said supernatural beings. One-armed Donal Noye makes an appearance, and I am still impressed he's able to be a blacksmith with just one arm. Jon learns that King Robert Baratheon is dead, and is told by the Lord Commander that Robert was betrayed by Lord Eddard Stark, his father. Jon doesn't believe this. I like how the news about the king's death travels through the chapters of the various characters, coming here—at the end of the world—the last. It also shows how it affects everyone, everywhere. The Lord Commander seems to test Jon as they discuss these latest events, to gauge Jon's feelings. Mormont probably understands that it will be very hard for Jon *not* to react, somehow, to this.

The last section of the chapter gives us a little action with Jon Snow and his direwolf Ghost saving the Lord Commander's life when one of the wights—Othor—comes knocking. There is a fight between Jon and the walking dead man, there's a hand crawling across the floor, in short—we have a pure zombie scene and it works, it's exciting and haunting. Finally, Jon thinks of fire, and the chapter ends with Jon's haunting thoughts, *Let it burn, gods, please, please, let it burn.*

In conclusion, I'd say this is one of the weaker chapters of *A Game of Thrones*, although the ending is pitch-perfect and we are given a lot of exposition on the Others and their ability to raise the dead into wights. Questions remain, however. Foremost is the question as to why Othor and Jafer were lying around in the forest being wights, why Othor didn't wake up until inside Castle Black—was it on purpose—are the wights basically being possessed by Others, a little bit like the warging going on in this series? The Children warg into animals, the Others into the dead?). Oh, and why only Othor and not Jafer? Maybe it's revealed later, it's been a while since I've read the series. But if I were an Other, I'd send both wights to take out the Lord Commander, double the chance of great success. Assuming the wights are controlled, of course. Maybe they are not.

The One Thing Hodor Had Going For Him

August already. Sigh. Still no *A Dance with Dragons*, of course. Some vague updates, they are usually more frequent before George R.R. Martin is going away somewhere, you know, to keep us motivated. Lots of people have lost their motivation, though. The book really, *really*, has to be announced done soon, Mr. Martin, for your own reputation's sake.

Once more into the fray then, diving into *A Game of Thrones*, that fantastic novel from 1996 (!) that is written so eloquently that I lose myself in it each and every time I crack it open. We're back with little Bran. It is only his sixth chapter in the novel which is kinda weird, since he's the first POV character to appear in the first chapter, and it simply doesn't feel that way—he's part of the tapestry, so it feels as if I've been reading Bran a lot more than six chapters. It is a really strange and somewhat surprising experience, this. Bran Stark, I know ye so little. How does George R.R. Martin do it? Make me feel so much about a character, a young crippled boy with a wolf for a pet, in just six—no wait, I've just read *five* so far—chapters? The magic lies, as I have stated (too) many times before, in his characterization skills, deft descriptions and dialogue that offers us insight into his characters. Bran's a special case, being the youngest character in the series with a POV, and I know that Martin has admitted writing such a young character has been difficult for him, and I guess it kind of shows in that Bran doesn't really feel like a seven year old. Then again, who are we to know how the mind of a seven year old—*in a brutal medieval fantasy world*—should or could work? Indeed, how are we to know that years are 365 days each? If Westeros years are longer than our Earth years, then all the characters are more mature than they would be if their ages were expressed in Earth years.

In a story that features the Others, mystical powers that actually work, and more, why get hung up on whether Bran is a realistically portrayed little boy? He's a cool little dude. So maybe some of his inner monologue is a bit too mature for his age, especially compared to the children in the real world. I know seven year olds in my street, and none of them have Bran's emotional and intellectual capacities, nor do they really deal with, and think about, consequences. However, they also don't have fathers who tell them to be brave when they are afraid, or tell them when they are three years old that it is time to grow up 'cause, you know, winter is coming (I guess in our world, that would be something like telling your three-year old to grow up, it's almost 2012 dammit).

Note the following remarkl in this very chapter from Robb Stark, aged 15, to Bran Stark, aged seven:

> "Don't act the boy with me, Bran," Robb said. "You know better than that."

There are other things in the series that deserve more to be criticized than the character of Bran. *cough*A Feast for Crows.*

Karstarks. They are coming in great numbers to Winterfell, and Bran is watching their troops ride towards the gates from the wall, together with Hodor! and Maester Luwin. I love this scene; it has this surreal mixture of beauty (in the vivid descriptions) and harsh reality (the fact that these guys are soldiers, preparing for war). Once again I catch myself thinking how this scene will translate to the screen next year. Many scenes in *A Game of Thrones* are practically begging for a film adaptation, this one among them. You can play with angles (Bran high up on the wall, the army arriving down on the road), you can have this real character moment between Luwin and Bran, the cold surrounding landscapes, the majesty of Winterfell itself ... yeah I admit it, I'd love to be a cinematographer or set designer or matte painter or some such on HBO's *Game of Thrones*If I helped out with the writing of the script, I'd make sure Janos Slynt would be given his deserved time in the spotlight, perhaps as the prince who was promised. Prince Piggly-Wiggly *rocks!*

There is something wondrous about Bran's chapters that I feel the other chapters don't have, at least not in the same amount. This quality, which I find hard to describe, is all over this chapter and I will refer back to it a few times in this post. It is the almost ethereal use of color and other adjectives to give Bran's chapters a viscerally :magical: quality more reminiscent of *The Lord of the Rings* than the more hard-boiled medieval trappings of, say, the Lord Eddard chapters: *Ned noir.*

In the first few paragraphs of this chapter we get pikes winking in pale sunlight, deep-throated marching rhythms—reminding me of Treebeard in this instance. Martin is using onomatopoeia—*boom, boom, boom* just like Tolkien did. Summer's eyes smolder like liquid gold. Not just regular gold, but liquid, melty, magical gold.

You get the point: Bran's chapters feel, prose-wise, more colorful, richer in its descriptions, than other chapters. Maybe I'm wrong. I guess I have to make a mental note of this and see whether I am right or not.

At the same time, Martin manages to put in some more realistic bits, as well, to make the whole feel complete. A good example of this is Maester Luwin's considerations of medieval army logistics. Just a quick note to the reader that, yes, this is a fantasy, but remember in the world of Westeros more rules of medieval history apply than in other fantasies. Hood squeeze my balls, I like it! (Yes, I am still engrossed in Erikson's books as well.)

Still, of all the POVs in *A Game of Thrones* Bran's are the most magical, with Three-Eyed Crows, wolf dreams, and all that. Where will it lead? Will Bran become a sorcerer of some sort to combat the Others? Will he be this age's incarnation of the Night King? Okay, ahead of myself again.

After the Karstarks arrive at Winterfell as the chapter opens,; we learn that the other lords have already arrived. There is a short exposition where Bran remembers the banners of the various lords, at once giving us more "medievally realistic" details—the importance of heraldry in such a society—and a few more names in the brew. And somehow, even though Martin is just bluntly giving us some exposition, even the mention of the various northern lords' heraldry is *magical*:

> ."..the mailed fist of the Glovers, silver on scarlet; Lady Mormont's black bear; the hideous flayed man that went before Roose Bolton of the Dreadfort; a bull moose for the Hornwoods..."

It's really cool, isn't it? Probably a bit geeky to think this is cool, but damn. It's cool. Note how mister Bolton is given a little more exposition than the others—full name and the name of his keep in addition to the heraldry—in fact, there are several subtle or not-so-subtle hints about mister Bolton, neatly dispersed throughout the chapter: not only do they have a grotesque coat-of-arms; there is Old Nan's story about the Boltons hanging the skins of their enemies in a room in the Dreadfort; there is the very name of that keep; and Lord Roose is scary according to Bran. Re-reading this chapter now, it is easy to see that Martin is setting up the Boltons as bad guys, but I am sure I only thought of them as cool, bad-ass throwaway characters. After all, they are allies of House Stark, so they have to be cool even though they are somewhat disturbing, right?

Along with Bolton, there is a second bannerman who is given a little more exposition, the Greatjon. He's a walking cliché of a character, vaguely reminiscent of Little John from *Robin Hood* (even the name, in fact), boisterous and loud, staunchly loyal ... clichéd, yes, but *very* easy to like. He gets his hand maimed by Summer, which turns him into a loyal defender of Robb Stark's honor. When a giant wolf chews *my* hand, *I* certainly feel more loyal to its owner! It *has* happened before in literature, but it works so wonderfully well here.

HBO are apparently changing around some character names to avoid confusion among the audience for their 2011 *Game of Thrones* series; Martin mentioned this in one of his *Not A Blog* updates; he wrote that he liked to have characters with the same names for realism. And I agree. First time I read *A Game of Thrones* I was certainly confused with all the Jons in particular, but on re-read # 10 it's a breeze. Seeing characters with the same name usually implies some connection or relation, and the best example is Jon Snow who was probably named for the late Lord Jon Arryn. In this chapter, we learn that Lord Rickard Karstark's sons are named Harrion, Eddard and Torrhen. Another Eddard! Not confusing anymore; it further develops the realism, and thus immersion—in the series.

Heraldry is not the only important piece of exposition in this chapter. Luwin gives us a look into the way knighthood works differently in the northern lands of Westeros, while one can read between the lines that knighthood as we know it from medieval history is how it works in the southern lands. So many glimpses and details to absorb. No wonder these books lend themselves well to a re-read or ten.

The humor in Bran's chapters is more subdued than in other chapters (particularly compared to the Lannister boys), but there is one moment where I had to chuckle: the way that Hodor keeps forgetting about low doorways. Bran is now being carried around in a wicker basket on Hodor's back, repeatedly knocking his head when Hodor forgets to crouch. It is not hilarious or anything; it is a more innocent kind of humor, more fitting the character of Bran. I like. The sweet humor in the relationship between the mysterious Hodor and Bran is contrasted immediately with a description of the ferocity of the Stark direwolves and how they affect the horses of the Karstark riders. I wonder exactly *how* bad-ass they will be when they are sent forth to do battle with dragons..

Hodor (!) takes Bran to the godswood, and here we get some intriguing stuff. Bran feels himself drawn more and more to the godswood, and he takes comfort from being watched over by the Old Gods of his father. He even *talks*, literally, to them. Among his prayers, he wants Rickon to understand why Father—that is Lord Eddard—is gone. Rickon is just three, so I am quite impressed with the young boy's understanding of things by the way, but the reason we get this prayer is for Martin to give us a little insight into what Rickon probably will become—some dark avenger of the North; "his baby brother had been wild as a winter storm ... cried and screamed for most of a night ... Shaggydog had come slavering out of the darkness like a green-eyed demon. The wolf was near as wild as Rickon ... "

Just sayin'. We'll get more of Rickon. Maybe. If the series ever sees a finale. Where is *A Dance with Dragons*, George? Please!

Robb is changing, and we read this through Bran's POV. He is no longer the fifteen year old racing with Jon—he is Robb the Lord now, and he is doing his best to emulate his Lord Father in this. And he does it well, aided by Grey Wind, striving to be as bad-ass as Ned. We get to see some of Robb's interactions with his father's bannermen and it is obvious by now that he is going to actually lead a host south to fight the Lannisters. Things are shaping up pretty cool, in other words. Ah, I remember the first time I read this. Little did I know just *how* fricking cool things were gonna get.

Finally, we get a long scene between Osha, who appears before Bran in the godswood, and Bran. Osha is the wildling woman they captured in Bran's previous chapter. That's about 30 chapters ago, so I thought a little reminder would be in place. Through Osha, we get some more exposition, but it is handled deftly through their dialogue, so it's all good. Except for this one sentence snuck in there, about Hodor's manhood. I didn't need to envision that. So *big*—HOWEVER! I believe there's a reason why Martin snuck in that description of Hodor's manhood. Because it's described right when Osha talks about giants. Is this a hint that Hodor is a half-giant? And will this be important if Hodor should end up meeting one? I have a feeling he's going to end up beyond the Wall, you see ... I wink and I nudge.

We also get some more info on Mance Rayder and the threat of the Other. Martin reinforces the notion that the high lords wage their wars while the real enemy hides north, beyond the Wall of the Night's Watch. Chilling stuff.

And then, Robb Stark leaves Bran behind, leading a great army of the North out Winterfell's gates, to war.

The chapter has one of the more annoying endings; not as annoying as Brienne's final chapter in *A Feast for Crows*, but still ... Bran wonders what "hodor" means. That's it. And I'm like, yes George; I have been wondering for a *decade* what in Hood's name Hodor means! Is it "Others" slightly mispronounced like I suggested many moons ago? I am curious. Bah! GRRuMble!

WHINE AND WINE

We move across the Narrow Sea, beyond the Free Cities and into the lands of the Dothraki, in particular their holy city of Vaes Dothrak. The switch from little Bran beneath the Heart Tree to the markets of Vaes Dothrak is pretty brutal, perhaps even a bit jarring, but once I'm a few paragraphs in, Bran has taken a seat in the back of my mind, allowing me to focus on Daenerys Targaryen, her story so very different from Bran's in almost all aspects. Where fate doesn't smile much on Bran, it shines brightly on Daenerys.

Trying to remember what happened last time with Daenerys, I remember her brother Viserys getting a crown of molten gold all over him, killing the bastard dead. Maybe there's been a Dany chapter after that, I really can't remember. Even though I am reading this for the tenth time.

Imagine how hard a time I am having with Steven Erikson's series. Every time there's a new character POV I have to flip back to see what that character was doing the last time. It isn't nearly as hard with *A Game of Thrones*, fortunately. I've read people commenting here and there that they sometimes read the POV chapters of one character in a row. I have not done that before, as I like to include everything and everyone, to keep the grand perspective if you will, but I admit it sounds tempting to read, say, Tyrion's chapters in a row. He's such an easy read. A finely crafted character.

Now, I don't find Daenerys nearly as interesting, though I hold her higher than Jon Snow, the other POV character I don't care all that much about. The reason may be as simple as the fact that Daenerys is hot, but I also like that she's operating in a completely different environment. Still, when thinking of *A Game of Thrones*, the images that come to mind are those of the city of King's Landing, Winterfell, and the Starks and Lannisters; seldom, if at all, do I think of the oriental/Middle-Eastern look and feel of the eastern lands. It's quite logical, though. Westeros is featured in all chapters other than Dany's.

The first section of the chapter gives us yet another glimpse of a "manhood." Where in the previous chapter Hodor's manhood was immense, Khal Drogo's glistens wetly. Yes, he's just been sexing it up with Daenerys, poor little thing. Oh wait. She enjoys it now. She's come to love him, it seems! The real point of the scene is not the fact that they are sexing it up, though. It introduces Khal Drogo's reluctance to commit to Daenerys' cause—which is to invade Westeros.

"*The stallion who mounts the world has no need of iron chairs,*" he tells her. I kinda get the feeling Daenerys was giving him a great sexytime to make him reconsider. But once he's "taken his pleasure,", the man is just as resolute. Khal Drogo explains that the Narrow Sea, to the Dothraki, is the "poison water," which they fear to cross. I am not quite sure as to *why* George R.R. Martin introduces this little hindrance, as it is solved actually in this very same chapter. Maybe it will come around in *A Wait for Dragons*, or a later novel. Maybe there will be a tragic irony when the Dothraki all drown. Who knows? Is it just to add flavor to the Dothraki culture? Daenerys tries to convince the Khal that taking ship to Westeros isn't dangerous, but he won't listen. He is superstitious about the sea.

Part two of the chapter is Daenerys summoning her handmaidens, those lovely ladies who will be portrayed by lovely actresses making George R.R. Martin's mood: horny. If they are going to portray Shae's ... *skills* as they are described in the novel, well, hey, then the latest HBO casting is probably a good choice (they've hired a former porn actress—who apparently can act in more than one way). But I don't think she quite *looks* like Shae.

Okay, that was a digression. But it is hard to avoid the topic of dirty sex when talking about *A Game of Thrones*. And the author himself has proven, beyond a doubt, that he himself has quite a dirty mind (as if the novels didn't already reveal that)—some of his blog posts sound like they were written by a twenty-year old guy. But I do not blame him. A man's mind doesn't change when it comes to enjoying the fine looks of a foxy lady. Hot is hot. Though the observer of said hotness may be ancient and FUBAR. This is a universal truth I am sure.

The second part gives us a little insight into the time that has passed since Dany's previous chapter; in fact, at this point, she has become like, *really* pregnant. Fat and ungainly, she admits to herself that now she needs the help of her handmaidens getting washed and dressed up. Dany sends Jhiqui (that's a handmaiden, it is known) to fetch Ser Jorah Mormont. That's the guy who's spying on her for King Robert, but seems to fall more and more under Dany's spell. He's dressing as a Dothraki now.

She wants him to help her convince Khal Drogo to invade Westeros—to reclaim the Iron Throne.

Dany is adamant about going west, which is a nice little detail considering later advice she gets about going east. Ser Jorah doesn't believe he can change the Khal's mind. All in all, it seems that the Khal's set on not going out onto the sea, and therefore the chapter's conclusion is somewhat surprising and/or jarring (you guessed it, he changes his mind).

There is some nice, albeit blunt, symbolism featured in this chapter as well—her memories of the red door, the one thing that she connects with the notion of "home." Will it make a return appearance in her life? Maybe not *that* door, but some red door? Some place to call home? I think so. It seems obvious that at the end of her arc, she'll have a place with a red door. A home. But that's just me thinking. And my thinking is often bad. Could be a door with the blood of her foes (or allies) running off it.

The third, and major, part of the chapter deals with Daenerys and her retinue going to the market. It doesn't sound super-exciting, does it? Like Britney or Lindsay going to shop on Rodeo Drive. There's some more exposition on Dothraki culture told through the witnessing of the marketplace, and as her litter passes beneath the stolen monuments, *"she went from sunlight to shadow and back again"*—now, is this a little hidden gem? Her story in one sentence?

In addition to exposition on Dothraki culture (how the market works, how pregnant women behave) and some strengthening of Dany's motivations (she's the blood of the dragon, she must not forget—she *must* retake the Iron Throne, it is her debt to her bloodline), Martin gives us some tantalizing glimpses of places we probably will never experience through a character's POV—Ashai'i, Yi Ti, Bayasabhad, Shamyriana, Kayakayanaya. Maybe we'll see Ashai'i, it's featured quite prominently compared to the other names. I like those names. They sound very Indian. Could an India-like culture surface later in the series? Why not. I bet you had forgotten these places, though. I don't think there's any mention of, say, Kayakayanaya except for this one time, in this chapter. But it is enough to allow us readers to believe in the vastness and reality of the world.

At the market, Ser Jorah is acting strangely. We know why, of course. It has already been established that he's working for the king of Westeros. But now we get Daenerys suspicious about him. We get a little insight into Dany's feelings developing since the death of her brother—one of the handmaidens comments that here, in the market, is the first time she has seen Dany laugh and smile since Viserys melted. (Eew!)

Then we get to the action. You probably remember this scene. There's this wine dealer. The weird thing is, as I am reading it, I get a bit confused about the wine dealer. At first, it seems he knows who Dany is as she approaches *"A taste for the* khaleesi? *I have a sweet red from Dorne, my lady ... "* The way he talks to her ("my lady," and specifically mentioning a Westerosi kingdom) makes me think he already sees through her. After all, while she looks like a khaleesi in the dressing department, her hair and eyes must give her away, right? But then follows a bit where the wine dealer seems surprised at her speaking in the language of Valyrian. So, either he's lying, or he was oblivious to her identity. Maybe George wrote it this way with intentional ambiguity. He offers her some better wine, a barrel that he's kept specifically for her should he meet her—

with poisoned wine. This one is as an assassin then, trying to collect the bounty King Robert had placed on Dany's head.

Fortunately for Dany, Ser Jorah arrives at just the right moment to avert disaster. When the dealer refuses to taste his own wine (effectively proving that the wine is poisoned), he tries to escape but is caught by Ser Jorah and Dany's bloodrider, whips cracking.

After the incident, we get a denouement where Ser Jorah reveals a folded parchment, which says that King Robert Baratheon offers lands and lordships for the death of Daenerys and her child. So, she gets the message too late, but she survived the murder attempt. In her grief at the fact that the growing son in her belly is already an assassination target, she decides on a whim to heat her three eggs back in her tent, as if hoping that somehow, the eggs could crack and reveal living dragon babies. Poor deluded Dany.

Finally, when Khal Drogo hears of the incident at the market, he gives Ser Jorah gifts for saving Dany, and vows to his unborn son that he shall gift him with the Iron Throne. Just as easy as that, Khal Drogo's entire disposition towards crossing the Narrow Sea has changed. Was it necessary to introduce his reluctance at all? Could the chapter have worked without Drogo complaining about those poison waters? Why is it in there? Yes, I have already wondered about that in this post. But I still wonder. Not a biggie, though. I just feel that first Khal's determined resistance to the idea comes off as really strong, making it harder to swallow his sudden turnaround at the end of the chapter. Oh well.

The chapter ends with the khalasar leaving Vaes Dothrak, striking south and west. The wine dealer is there too, hurrying behind them, tied with chains to Dany's horse, echoing Viserys, the Sorefoot King. And so Daenerys' journey begins in earnest.

Do I like this chapter? It is definitely not the most interesting chapter of *A Game of Thrones* in my opinion. I find Dany's arc to be a bit slow-moving in this particular book of the series (it picks up, though). I am not sure whether I like Daenerys as a character. She's a bit less realistically rendered than the others, methinks, but that comes with her story being more fantastical, of course. I am not enamored by the Dothraki, either, nor Ser Jorah or the handmaidens. These characters are a bit bland compared to what we get in Westeros. But, obviously, Daenerys is vital to the overall story—after all, she's the *fire* in *A Song of Ice and Fire*, no?

Next chapter is Catelyn: now there's a POV I appreciate as she sees so many cool characters and locations. Her POV has that flavor that makes *A Game of Thrones* so memorable. (Fish?) The Riverlands with its distinct castles (Riverrun, The Twins, Harrenhal) and medieval military plotlines, these are the things that come to mind when I think of *A Game of Thrones*.

NIMBLE BOOKS LLC

THE BEARD-GROWER

Here I am again, spending too much time thinking about *A Song of Ice and Fire* and all the woes associated with that series the last decade. Like you (presumably), I'm just dying for *A Dance with Dragons*, and it just isn't forthcoming. Since my previous post, our favorite (he's still our favorite, right?) author has posted about an especially well-painted Cersei Lannister miniature figure—and I mean *miniature*, how small can these things get? Had they been action figure size I'd consider buying them but they are so small you need Maester Luwin's far eye just to enjoy the sculpting—but no, he hasn't made a single post relating to the fifth volume of *the* saga.

There was also post about a comic book series based on *Fevre Dream*—which, incidentally, is not the fifth volume of *the* saga, it's a novel he published in *1982*. And we learn that he's updated his site with a sample about something called *Wild Cards:* a seemingly endless series of "sharecropped" novels and story collections about a geeky collection of superheroes.

Now, *A Dance with Dragons* can be regarded as something of a wild card at this point, but this is not interesting to me. I ain't blaming Martin for posting stuff that doesn't interest me, by the way. Then his blog would be full of extreme underground metal bands, classic *Star Wars*, role-playing stuff, perhaps some interesting thoughts on the subject of teaching, or medieval history, or something about cool early nineties computer RPGs ... no, the point is, as it has been for too many years, that we care so much about *A Song of Ice and Fire*. It is book five we're all waiting to read news about upon visiting the site.

WAITING FOR DRAGONS

It is definitely not fun going there and see an update about Martin going on extended vacations for the rest of the year. Which is him basically admitting that, no, there won't be a big fat Christmas present for us this year either. I'm glad he isn't Santa Claus. The real Santa Claus: Weird to think that the likelihood of *him* dropping by this Christmas is just as realistic as *A Dance with Dragons* dropping. And there have been posts about many of the actors being signed to HBO's *Game of Thrones*. I'm kind of fine with that; after all, it is exciting to actually learn something about a forthcoming *A Song of Ice and Fire-* product. Take that, Mr. Martin.

(By the way, HBO's *Game of Thrones* website would be infinitely more interesting if *they* actually did the news on each actor, that way their site wouldn't be in suspended animation as it has been since launch; they kind of miss the actual interest from many fans this way, but that's my opinion, and it's neither humble nor anything anyone should care about).

With that out of the way, let's dive back in and see where we are in that classic novel *A Game of Thrones*. Let's see. I have many editions of the novel (yes I suck). Today's version is a Bantam paperback, published in 2005.

I'm on page 595 in this edition, which brings us to the eighth chapter starring Lady Catelyn Stark, one of my favorite characters. I've already mentioned why she's my favorite, but to reiterate—she is a fleshed-out, well-realized character with real emotions, possibly the most realistic character thrown into this brutal fantasy world. And she meets interesting people and visits interesting locations (all the kewl castles and stuff). So, here we go.

Thing is, this is one of my favorite chapters in the series. And it doesn't even have a great plot twist, or some central scene that makes you jump around feverishly. It's basically a quiet scene between Lady Catelyn and her eldest son, Robb Stark, and the chapter is much about Robb's development from a young noble boy to a leader of hard men. I love this chapter because Martin has some very nice and evocative descriptions of location, and because he draws us so easily into Catelyn's point of view, and finally because the chapter sets up Robb Stark in a clear manner, making him grow more as a character to remember (I think he's a bit ... vague ... before this chapter).

Martin has a talent for drawing me in, right there into the scene, looking over Cat's shoulders. That immersion isn't always as strong throughout the series (for example, I feel detached when reading about Euron Crow's Eye, but the whys and hows of *that* is for a much later post), but it is remarkably often there when reading Catelyn's chapters. Maybe precisely because she is so well-defined that her POV becomes easier to identify with. For the record, I am not a middle-aged fairly hot woman with five children and a tendency to think in italic sentences. Now, Martin grabs me right away with the chapter's introductory paragraph.

Don't you just *see* it? I know I do. Lovely, isn't it. And the fog, could it symbolize the uncertainty ahead, not just in this chapter, but for the Starks themselves? After all, Robb is torn among his bannermen, not knowing whom to trust, and Catelyn is torn by basically everything. Not delving deeper here, because to be honest I believe the fog is just fog. Added to enhance the atmosphere of the scene in question. Oh, if only the

Not A Blog had just a tiny bit of the atmosphere in this chapter!

Catelyn is headed towards Moat Cailin, after having left White Harbor. She is escorted by the two sons of Lord Manderly, and they are described as gross overeaters. I think I have a suggestion for that HBO *Game of Thrones* cameo. Just by the off-hand mention of White Harbor, I am intrigued. I want to 'see' that place, but that's a problem I have, I always get curious about the stuff casually mentioned in books and films, like when I was younger, I always wanted to see the "spice mines of Kessel" in *Star Wars*.

It is clear that Catelyn is very adamant about reaching Robb, in fact "nothing else mattered"—not even the fact that she has to be escorted by these overweight walrus-mustached weirdos from White Harbor. I wonder why it's *White* Harbor. Because of snow? Do they use white bricks for their buildings? (I wonder if Martin was making a sly reference to the greasy US hamburger chain immortalized in *Harold & Kumar Go To White Castle?*) Dammit, thinking about unimportant stuff again. But the main reason for Martin starting the chapter before she reaches Robb is so that he can tell us a little bit about this place called Moat Cailin (sounds quite a bit like Moat Catelyn, doesn't it?) Riding there, we get to see it through Catelyn's eyes, and learn an important plot point—how an army can defend virtually anything trying to cross the Neck, that is, the boglands which Moat Cailin defends.

Again, Martin uses broad strokes to evoke a haunted quality to the location. Catelyn reflects upon one tower that looks as if some great beast has taken a bite out of it—mere atmospheric description, or has there been a dragon hungry for stonework here?

When Catelyn finally enters the drafty hall of the Gatehouse Tower and faces her son, we get to the meat of the chapter. The pivotal scene, if you will. The direwolf food. Through their dialogue, we feel Catelyn's conflicted feelings—both pride and fear. At first, Catelyn wants to run over to Robb, but she doesn't want to shame her boy in front of the bannermen. This is cool.

Then, moments later, she comments on him trying to grow a beard. In front of his bearded bannermen. Not cool, Cat (see what I did there?). Now he feels awkward, m'lady. I like the way it's written though I am not sure whether it was intentional. First she thinks I'm not gonna embarrass him, and then she does. It kinda feels *real* you know.

Anyway, Catelyn explains what's been going on around her, and then Robb explains the situation in the Riverlands. She tells Robb that she's sent Ser Rodrik home to Winterfell to command the keep until her return. The Greatjon seems to think it an unnecessary precaution because "Winterfell is safe"—the northmen will break Lord Tywin Lannister. If you've read *A Clash of Kings*, you may be feeling something when reading that line. I like it.

We get to read a little bit about Robb's bannermen, basically some short characterization padding, before everyone leaves the hall to Catelyn and Robb alone, and we get a sincere, emotional scene between the two, a scene I very much hope will come out pretty much unaltered in the TV series.

Catelyn wished Robb had given the command of the northern host to someone else, because she fears for him; yet she realizes it is too late, and her son must prove his worth. He presents to her the letter from Sansa, and Catelyn immediately sees Cersei's hand in it. Not literally.

Robb learns that he cannot hope for aid from the Vale of Arryn, where Cat's sister Lysa resides. In the scene, Robb shows that he is afraid, that he is, after all, still a young boy/man, so, dear actor in HBO's series, please pull it off. The vulnerable Robb in front of his ma versus the cool Robb in front of his men. This is characterization at its finest, and I have still to read a fantasy novel with the same kind of grandeur to it.

After showing his softer side, Robb steels himself, and becomes more resolved by the conversation, and we get the wonderfully simple/simply wonderful line from him, *"Then I will not lose."*

During the scene, Robb transforms from the child (*"But mom, what should I dooo?"*) to the boy who is trying to become like his father, the Lord Eddard Stark, and through his dialogue we learn that he has a talent for strategy and tactics, explaining some of his thoughts to Catelyn. Finally, Robb lays before her his actual battle plan—the hope is to capture one of the Lannisters so as to have a prisoner to negotiate the freedom of Sansa down in King's Landing with—and, dammit, I am reading this for the tenth time and I am still all excited about what's coming out of this plan. Heehee.

Concluding the chapter is a short paragraph: Catelyn tells Robb she ain't going home to Winterfell, surprised at her own decision. With tears in her eyes, she tells him she's going to see her father and brother at Riverrun, she must go to them—her lord father's motto is *family, duty, honor*. She must go to her family, as she worries for them. She now feels safe (enough) for Robb. The tears I guess are because she really hates having to leave him, but she feels it's her duty as a family member.

Interestingly, going to Riverrun means going home, her childhood's home. Throughout the series, there are a number of characters trying to get home. Daenerys comes to mind, as does Theon; Arya, of course, her whole plot arc up to *A Feast for Crows* is essentially about going home; Lord Eddard tried to go home with the daughters. Am I discovering something I haven't thought of before, or am I raving?

I'm probably raving.

HEAR ME ROAR AND WATCH ME WADDLE

Weeweewawa and wawaweewa, a new Tyrion chapter! So far, each new Tyrion chapter has been more splendid than the last, maybe because Mr. Martin developed Tyrion's character a little more with each chapter, his sarcasm becoming more caustic, the characters surrounding him more humorous. In this very chapter we get to see Tyrion's father—Lord Tywin Lannister—and boy is it a meeting to remember.

I said the previous chapter was a favorite of mine, and it is, but to make myself clear, it is a favorite chapter when it comes to characterization, it's a chapter with a poignant scene between Catelyn and Robb. As such, *this* chapter beats most chapters so far, because it is just one riveting read from beginning to end, filled with droll humor, biting sarcasm, and powerful new characters. Father Tywin contrasts phenomenally with Tyrion. So does Shagga, son of Dolf, who has just recently been in the news—an actor has been found to play the manhood-cutting mountain clansman, and I have to admit, he looks just how I have always pictured Shagga (sans the wild, unkempt hair, grease, and scars).

Lord Tywin himself has also recently been cast and I am sure any person who bothers to read this already knows that Tywin too has been well-cast by the makers of the upcoming TV series. But Shagga—he's the first actor who is, for me, simply is 100% spot-on. Tywin's a 90%, Robb too—in fact, a lot of actors look a lot like the characters, but there are also some, in my mind, serious miscastings. I'm thinking of the actors who play Theon Greyjoy and perhaps especially Janos Slynt, a shame that—I'm talking looks here, I am sure the actors will do just fine. But, as so often before, I digress.

Okay, so the main thing in this chapter is another meeting between a child and its parent, but the Tyrion/Tywin meeting is something a whole lotta different than Robb/Catelyn. Read those two meetings after another and realize how radically different these two meetings really are.

Hey, maybe that's the point. That these two chapters contrast, kind of. The other main thing about this particular chapter is humor. There are a lot of laughs to be had in this chapter, even for the tenth time (though the laughs have turned into chuckles, mostly). One of my favorite funny lines from the saga can be found in this chapter, you know when Shagga explains what brought the clansmen down from the mountains) ah, it is wonderfully droll. You may note that I am a Lannister supporter. Always have been. Especially in the card game. And it's not because a Lannister always pays his debts. It's more because occasionally you can hear me roar (I've growled in a few extreme metal bands) and because I simply adore the characters in this family, warts and all.

Like in the previous chapter, we don't get right to the meat, however. Catelyn travelled through fog meeting fat Manderlys first before meeting up with Robb, and Tyrion is on his way down the road with his motley band of mountain clansmen, a foul and funny bunch. First time I read about them I saw them more as barbarians, you know the typical fantasy type, with bearskin boxers and huge, double-bladed axes, but in the course of reading this book ten times my perception has been readjusted and I now see them as the proper wild guys wearing stolen armor and weapons, generally mismatched. That is, they aren't that much larger or that more naked than other people. They just don't adhere to fashion. Maybe the size of Shagga made it harder to avoid envisioning them as vanilla barbarians, by Crom! I repeated myself again here, didn't I? At least I am secure in the knowledge that I have told the world how I perceive the clans of the Mountains of the Moon!

So, the chapter starts with Tyrion being informed that his father's army is encamped at the crossroads further south (yes, the tavern where Catelyn captured him), and it is revealed that Tyrion has plans of starting his own army, beginning with these madmen from the mountains. We get a little expo on the names of the various clans, then it is off to meet Tywin. Tyrion initially wants to go alone, but the clansmen do not want to hear it, and so he arrives at the crossroads, with the leaders of the clans at his side—Chella, Shagga, Conn, Ulf, and Timett. Oh, and Bronn. But his limelight has been stolen by Shagga, at least for this chapter. Shagga is the source of much of the droll humor that permeates the chapter. On their way, Tyrion has an interesting reflection on how the clansmen think—that everyone should be heard, even women. The author here lets the main character adhere to "medieval thought' and that I applaud. Anachronisms and all that.

The ongoing joke—Shagga's trademark phrase, "I will cut off your manhood and feed it to the goats' gets a number of variations in this chapter and has me LOLing on the inside (LOLOTI?) each time it appears. Early on, Shagga is about to utter his catchphrase when Tyrion interrupts, with a weary ... *and feed it to the goats, yes.* Funny. Later, when Bronn hears that Timett son of Timett cut out his own eye to be the baddest ass in the clan, Bronn muses, "I wonder what their king cut off." Funnier. Yeah, I know, not directly related to Shagga but the cutting off makes it a worthy addition to this listing of droll comments from the chapter.

The group comes to a barricade and we get a short glimpse of Ser Flement Brax, an answer to a trivia question if there ever was one. Steward Vayon Poole says, "Welcome to the club, Ser." Maybe we'll see more of Ser Flement later. Maybe not. I find that the Lannister bannermen are less involved in the storylines than the Stark bannermen. I mean, "everyone" knows Bolton, the Greatjon, Karstark—but Ser Flement Brax? At the barricades, half a league from the crossroads. Not exactly the center of the action.

Tyrion notes the irony of returning to the Inn at the Crossroads, but I wonder if there is more symbolism involved here. The crossroads—the small village and inn at the crossroad do indeed reappear throughout the series, a repeated motif that is obvious, yet works beautifully.

The innkeeper, Marsha Heddle, is hanging outside. This character has also been recently cast. And that actress looks absolutely *nothing* like the Heddle of my mind. But this is such a minor character I can't be bothered to bother. Inside the inn, Lord Tywin Lannister awaits. And what an introduction he gets from our favorite author. I love to re-read this description of the Lord of Casterly Rock. It just hits right home.

One moment you're reading a fantasy novel, the next you are afraid of this character whose very presence makes you soil your smallclothes. Almost. His brother is seated within the inn as well, Ser Kevan Lannister, and his description pales in comparison to Tywin's, perfectly (and properly) describing their relationship.

Once Tyrion and Tywin start talking, a whole lot about their relationship (or lack thereof) is instantly revealed; not a single line of dialogue is wasted here, and I love re-reading this bit. It is definitely in the top section of my favorite encounters in *A Song of Ice and Fire*. There's actually a somewhat clumsy bit of text here, where Martin tells us more than shows us how comfortable Tyrion becomes under his father's scrutiny (*Whenever his father's eyes were on him, he became uncomfortably aware of all his deformities and shortcomings*)—I am nitpicking, no doubt, but the scene would be stronger if we were shown Tyrion in such an uncomfortable situation. Oh well. For all the gold this book delivers, I am not complaining (*A Dance with Dragons*, on the other hand, has yet to be born, yet alone deliver ...). There's a splendid line from Tywin that is both foreshadowing and irony all at once, when he tells Tyrion that Ser Jaime would never have submitted to capture at the hands of a woman. Not sure if I noticed before. For a tenth re-reader, the line is funny because, you know, it's not true. Ser Jaime has been meek and submitting to Cersei since forever, becomes Catelyn's prisoner and he is also the prisoner of Brienne of Tarth in *A Storm of Swords*. In your lean face, Tywin Lannister.

We get to see more of Tyrion's unsympathetic side in this chapter too—we already read how his mindset is pretty narrow compared to modern standards (which is fine), and he also thinks it a pity that Marsha Heddle is hanged and dead because he'd like better mead. But most of the time, I simply love the character—as do most fans of the series. He's even the big guy's favorite. Tywin continues to boast about his other son—Ser Jaime, that is—and we get a clear picture of how Tywin views his two sons: one a nuisance, the other a great hero.

We also get an early glimpse of Lord Walder Frey's character through Tywin's description, a character we are yet to meet, yet here we get a small morsel which is nice to keep in mind. In the same paragraph, we also learn that Lord Tywin underestimates Robb Stark, which supports the plausibility of certain events that are yet to come (just as the previous chapter showed us Robb quickly turning into a leader).

Then, Tyrion gets the news. He's been out of it for a while, and everybody's having delusions of grandeur, but the news he's getting is really shocking. The Starks are gathering a host in the north, and the king—Robert Baratheon—is dead. Tyrion is the one who immediately realizes what this means. Not that Joffrey, Tywin's grandson and Tyrion's nephew—is the true ruler of the realm, but that it is Cersei Lannister, his sister. Joffrey is too young to be king, and so the rule falls to her as the Queen Regent. Interestingly, Tyrion muses how different the realm will be under Cersei's (mis)rule. To think that this little thought of his has bearing on the story thousands of pages later, that is impressive.

Tyrion demands arms and armor for his clansmen when Shagga crashes into the taproom, the other clansmen following and we get a hilarious moment where Shagga shows his crude character. But Tywin carps the Diem, and effectively makes the clansmen part of his army. So, he's shrewd as well. Man, there are so many great moments when the scene gets to this point. I mean:

Waiting for Dragons

"Who might you be?" Lord Tywin asked, cool as snow.

"They followed me home, Father," Tyrion explained. "May I keep them? They don't eat much."

So droll I LOL.

Or how about Tyrion introducing Bronn to his father:

> And this is Bronn, a sellsword of no particular allegiance. He's already changed sides twice in the short time I've known him, you and he ought to get on famously, Father.

That definitely tickles my funny bone. I hope whathisname from *Prince Caspian* nails Tyrion's wit. There's a small nod to the classic fantasy novel when Tyrion calls his father "once and future Hand of the King." Not funny, but you know, I have to put it in here since this is my tenth re-read and I don't want to come off as too dumb.

And then we get the classic line I so love, which I nominate for best quote of the chapter. First time I read that I was like "WTF LOLZ OMG funny." Okay, not exactly like that. It was more of a quiet chuckle of enjoyment.

"Horses."

And then comes something rather surprising. Call me dense if you will, but I don't think I discovered *this* little gem before:

> Tyrion was about to tell his lord father how he proposed to reduce the Vale of Arryn to a smoking wasteland (...)

If you've finished the fourth book, and perhaps have dabbled with spoilers for the ever elusive fifth book, maybe you too will raise your eyebrows upon reading this, and think what I'm thinking. It involves a head of the dragon.

Finally, a messenger arrives telling Tywin (and us) that the Stark host is moving down the causeway from Moat Cailin. *Oooh* conflict ahead—interest growing even more—followed by some additional characterization of Tywin (another very simple and effective description: *He never smiled*).

Deftly, Tywin talks the clansmen into joining his host against the Stark army, and the chapter ends with Chella daughter of Cheyk demanding Tyrion ride with them.

Pure. Entertainment. Joy.

THE PROMISE OF MERCY

Goodbye for now, Tyrion, and hello Sansa. Yes, we're back in King's Landing and Sansa was not having a good time last we met her, what with her father being imprisoned and accused of murdering his good friend the king Robert Baratheon. This particular chapter is roughly divided into three parts, like Gaul, the first one giving us insight into what has changed since the previous Sansa chapter. The change is, basically, that Sansa has been given the "freedom of the castle": She may move as she pleases as long as she remains within the Red Keep, and she is pretty happy with that, in fact. She doesn't consider herself a (political) prisoner from the way I read her— she tells herself that the Queen Cersei and her son, now King Joffrey Baratheon, love her and that it is okay that they decide what's best for her. Poor delusional thing. Where in the first chapters I found Sansa quite an annoying, somewhat stereotypical character, I now feel a little sorry for her, so that's good writing on George's part (he's quite good at painting characters in different strokes, forcing the reader to reconsider his/her feelings and opinions about a character).

What basically happens in the first part of the chapter is that we are viewing important political events through the eyes of Sansa; much of it is, in a way, pure exposition—primarily to show us the *new* king's council now that Renly Baratheon has fled the city, Eddard Stark stands condemned for treason, the old king is dead, and Stannis remains on Dragonstone, still not having appeared on the grand stage. The first (and maybe second) time I read this chapter I felt a bit at a loss—I guess I didn't know *how* to "properly" decode this stuff (before *A*

Game of Thrones, I had only sporadic encounters with the fantasy literature genre; *The Lord of the Rings* and some *Forgotten Realms*—stuff that never rang true to me)—how was I supposed to see the importance of all these characters and their names, and keep them apart? These days, however, reading this stuff is something I relish; connecting the dots, finding those *aha!* moments, enjoying how vividly everything's become in my mind's eye. But think of it—in this chapter alone the following characters' names appear:

King Robert. Ser Mandon Moore. Sansa Stark. Janos Slynt. Myrcella. Joffrey. Jalabhar Xho. Ser Aron Santagar. Horror and Slobber, the Redwyne twins. Lord Gyles. Ser Dontos. Ser Balon Swann. Grand Maester Pycelle. Lord Varys. Lord Baelish. Queen Cersei. Ser Barristan Selmy. Ser Arys Oakheart. Ser Boros Blount. Lord Stannis Baratheon. Lord Renly Baratheon. Two Lords Royce. Ser Loras Tyrell. Lord Mace Tyrell. Thoros of Myr. Lord Beric Dondarrion. Lady Lysa Arryn. Little Lord Robert. Lord Hoster Tully. Ser Brynden. Ser Edmure. Lord Jason Mallister. Lord Bryce Caron. Lord Tytos Blackwood. Lord Walder Frey. Ser Stevron. Lord Karyl Vance. Lord Jonos Bracken. Lady Shella Whent. Doran Martell. Lady Catelyn Stark. Robb Stark. Brandon Stark. Rickon Stark. Arya Stark. Eddard Stark. Tywin Lannister. Ser Gerold Hightower. Prince Lewyn. Ser Arthur Dayne. King Aerys. Jaehaerys. Sandor Clegane. Ser Meryn.

Forgive me if I didn't catch 'em all. This being pointed out, *A Song of Ice and Fire* is a breeze compared to Erikson's *The Malazan Books of the Fallen*: you have been warned.

But I think it gets my point across—there's a *load* of characters in these novels, and for a first-timer, *A Game of Thrones* sure makes you scratch your head at all those names bandied about. On the tenth re-read it is effective in creating this vivid, *real* world. Did I remember who Beric was the first time I came to this chapter where's he's mentioned for treason against the king? Maybe; maybe I'd forgotten, or just didn't connect the aforementioned dots. Now, of course, it's cool to see how it all fits so nicely together. Of course Beric is sought; he was sent by Lord Eddard to hunt down one of Lord Tywin Lannister's bannermen. There are actions and reactions between characters all the way through the story, and it is, in my opinion, so much more interesting than the usual party-of-dissimilar-heroes-go-on-a-quest-through-mythical-lands story [oh, I know, not all chapters dump so many names in your lap].

So, the first part has a boatload of names, and as I mentioned, exposition is heavy, and it works because we're "watching" over Sansa's shoulders. Now, the second part of the chapter is the direct changes taking place in the king's court. The mighty Janos Slynt is raised to lord of Harrenhal for his services to the Lannisters; well-earned, and he's chosen a cool coat-of-arms for his new House as well—a bloodied spear like the ones that were thrust into the backs of the Stark bannermen. A nod to him being a petty bastard (see: that famous story about Jesus, a spear and stuff)?

In the second part of the chapter, we get the scene where King Joffrey Baratheon gleefully tells the Commander of the Kingsguard, the semi-legendary Ser Barristan Selmy, that his services are no longer required. We are witness to Ser Barristan Selmy's fall from grace, and now that I "know" the character better, the scene where he must step down from his service is more poignant. First time around I was like, whatever, but the more engrossed (read: obsessed) I've become with *A Song of Ice and Fire*, the more such scenes "work" on an emotional level.

Poor Ser Barristan Selmy. Poor Sansa. Go Janos! (The weird thing is, that even though I feel sorry for these characters that lean mostly towards "good," I've always liked the Lannisters and their allies the best—I guess it is the "cool bad guy" syndrome).

There is a whole scene built around Selmy's dismissal, showing us how the Lannisters are changing the political climate to their tastes, with Cersei making her twin brother Ser Jaime the new Commander of the Kingsguard. I don't think I noticed it on the first read, but now it is almost *painfully* obvious how the Lannisters bluntly put their own people in place for the future rule of the kingdom—Ser Jaime Lannister, even though he is the *Kingslayer*, becomes the Commander of the Kingsguard; his sister Cersei becomes the Queen Regent while her son is too young to rule; their father, Tywin, is to become Hand of the King (again); Janos Slynt, who has served the Lannisters so well, gets Harrenhal; Ser Jaime's spot as a knight of the Kingsguard is given to Sandor Clegane, the Hound; this is, basically, the usurpation of the Iron Throne once again: "regime change" at its bluntest. Robert Baratheon took it from the Targaryens first, now the Lannisters take it from the Baratheons—and this short chapter shows it clearly and effectively.

What makes it all doubly (or triply) cool is that the actions performed by the Lannisters here will have repercussions all the way through the series. Won't go into spoilers right now, though, it's late as it is. Reading it for the first time I don't think I caught onto how radically the plotlines of the novel shift during this scene. It's quite interesting to read again.

Finally, the third section of the chapter deals more directly with Sansa. In the first two parts she was merely an observer of, you guessed it, the game of thrones (and maybe in the future we'll see that her witnessing all this will pay off in some plot point), but now she steps forward to plead for her father's life. It is here that I feel pity for Sansa, for the way she so meekly humbles herself before the nobility gathered in the throne room, where she keeps telling herself to believe that Joffrey and Cersei are good people who will listen to her. Is she a fool? Not really, she's merely being foolish.

Martin writes her well in this scene, letting us both understand her motivation, desires, hopes; he lets us get frustrated at her, yet we also know she kind of does not have much choice other than submission. I am confident that once Sansa has learned to play the game of thrones (*A Feast for Crows* sure seems to point that way) these chapters in *A Game of Thrones* will be all the more poignant. I'll go out on a limb and say that Sansa, in this scene, actually *is* playing the game of thrones already—she's made herself look good for Joffrey—using her 'womanly charms' so to speak—in other words, she gives thought to how to get the most out of the situation, perhaps this is her first true lesson in that game of thrones: If you are a woman, use your charms to get ahead. Oink.

Dungeon Lord

I've been playing role-playing games for roughly twenty years, and there is a dividing line, a *before* and *after* if you will, in my gaming experience. There was role-playing before *A Game of Thrones*, and there is role-playing after.

Before, the games I ran were vanilla fantasy games, you know, loosely based on fairy tales, *The Lord of the Rings*, and silly RPG sourcebooks. They were usually played with the *Advanced Dungeons & Dragons* rules, where the cartoony player character fought off hordes of orcs, smashed his way through underground dungeons full of whimsical traps, and should he happen to be imprisoned, languished in nice, 4x4 graph paper squares of prison cell.

After, the games I ran were still fantasy games, but they became more *real*. I had learned that truly powerful stories had great characters with real motivations and flaws made for better gaming, too. Old homebrew campaign settings no longer held my interest, and I wanted stuff in the game to be *realistic* in the sense that everything seemed reasonable in context, with a sense of history. I began studying medieval history and geography to more properly set up a game environment that almost "could have been"; actions would have repercussions; characters would forge more realistic relationships with family members who in turn impacted the stories in their own way.

And it was George R.R. Martin who showed me that way, through the trials and tribulations of his characters in *A Song of Ice and Fire*. Currently, I am running a game on its fifth (or is it sixth) year, a long story involving feudal disputes, the seizing and losing of power, secret cults working to revive their faith, armies that clash, grit and blood and sweat. It is all very *thronesy*, or what I've come to call "mediæval fantasy" for lack of a better term. No longer were characters imprisoned in neat cells where they basically didn't feel worse for the wear—now they were thrown headfirst onto the urine-soaked straw of rat-infested, gloomy cells to rot—*pain* became more realistic; consequences were considered before going into action by the players—and as a result, our game has become so vivid that we've all become doubly addicted to an already highly addictive form of social entertainment (George R.R. Martin was a role-playing gamer too back in the day, by the way).

I felt like mentioning this as an introduction to today's chapter, which begins with Lord Eddard Stark, the proud and honest lord of the North, now suffering in a cell in the Red Keep, King's Landing. Things have been going downhill for the book's main character ever since he chopped off the head of Gared, the deserter from the Night's Watch, and now we are truly going into the abyss with him, through hell—and hopefully back. It's the classic second act of the story, where everything is at its darkest—and, of course, George R.R. Martin will turn this on its head (so to speak) by denying us the longed-for bright third act. Not in *this* book, anyway.

Suffice to say, I'll never enjoy playing a stout Dwarf or an aloof Elf again—but then again, I can't really enjoy any novel as much as *A Song of Ice and Fire* either. This series is like the most appealing thing to my senses ever.

> "There was no window, no bed, not even a slop bucket ... The dark was absolute. He had as well been blind. Or dead. Buried with his king."

There is scant mercy for Lord Eddard here; all by himself, in a dank and dreary cell, all hope seems lost to our dear Ned. Now, in role-playing games, having player characters locked up like this makes for quite an uninteresting game session, 'cause, you know, there's precious little for them *to do*. In this novel, however, Martin can allow us a glimpse into Ned's thoughts, emotions...and memories.

The chapter revolves around a pivotal event, a tourney at Harrenhal, in which George R.R. Martin gives us some tantalizing glimpses into Ned's past, dishing out just enough to keep us hooked, but not enough to settle once and for all the exact unfolding of the tragedy that happened at the Tower of Joy. Hell, we've been debating these scene (or rather, memories- or dreams) for *fourteen years*. Fourteen years, baby.

Before going into that particular sequence, however, we are witness to Ned thinking about other characters, and it is quite realistic in the sense that this is probably how a person would've been thinking in this situation—regret, guilt, and blame.

Robert Baratheon, the Usurper king now dead, is the first to enter Ned's mind. Ned's old friend—it must have been very hard for Eddard to watch him dying. A little later, Ned goes through the list of people who have made his life the hell it has become: Littlefinger is mentioned first, followed by my man Janos Slynt and his gold cloaks, the queen (of whom you *really* should have been more wary, Ned), the Kingslayer Ser Jaime, Pycelle, and Varys, Ser Barristan (a bit unfair of you, Ned—he's just like you, honorable and doing what he thinks is right for the realm), and he damns "even Lord Renly, who had run when he was needed most"—but Ned, my friend, *you* dismissed the guy.

And that's when Ned's thoughts turn, and he blames himself most of all, which I find only fair. I can *so* see Ned sitting there, back to the wall, banging the back of his head over and over gain, crying to the darkness, "You fool, you thrice-damned blind fool." I admit I have a strong disliking to cramped quarters, let's call it a minor claustrophobia, so I really feel for Ned here. The scene is so sad and dark. I love it.

Ned admits to himself that he has played the game of thrones and lost, and Cersei's words seem to whisper in his ears that if you lose *that* particular game, you die. There you have it, the author bluntly stating Ned's fate.

Time crawls in the dungeon cell, and we see Ned drift in and out of maddening nightmares, making futile plans, doing what he can to keep on to his sanity, trying to keep his strength, keeping his sorrow and rage frozen and hard within him, the Stark way. After an undefined amount of time, Ned hears footsteps approaching, and I remember the first time I was like, *yes! help is on the way, get him out of that hellhole*, and then it's just the gaoler throwing Ned a clay jug of water, not telling Ned anything when the lord of Winterfell asks how long he's been down there, when he asks for his daughters ... the gaoler just shuts the door, leaving him in the darkness and his own filth. Now that is harsh, but hey, that's "mediæval fantasy." Things go awry, and they go awry big time, which helps us sympathize with Eddard in a way I have never sympathized with, say, Aragorn son of Arathorn. Man, that ranger of the north never knew how good life was to him—compared to what Ned is going through.

Drinking himself sick, Ned lapses into an old memory—and we have arrived at the famous sequence—the Tourney at Harrenhal where so many of the series' living characters were formed into what they have become. Much has been written of it, and it has been analyzed to death by fans, so I'll try to spend my words sparingly, like the Starks spend their winter stores I guess. Not sure I will be able to, though.

I think I'll just jot down the facts that Ned gives us, though keep in mind that the lord of Winterfell is delirious and he may or may not be re-arranging his memories or even constructing false memories—you see, there is even a hint to be wary of this: *It was the year of the false spring.* The use of the adjective "false" could be taken as an indication that not everything is right. Or I am reading into it too much? Which tends to happen. A lot.

Ned is eighteen years old; he's left the Eyrie for a tourney at Harrenhal, presumably with Robert at his side. His brother Brandon had a good time. Robert fought like a madman in the mêlée. He remembers Jaime becoming a knight of the Kingsguard at fifteen. Crown prince Rhaegar Targaryen was *the* man at the jousting. Even the splendid Ser Arthur Dayne fell to him.

There's a really interesting bit where Rhaegar crowns Lyanna Stark the queen of love and beauty over his own wife...

In an earlier post I mentioned that I found Lyanna something of an underused character, but now she is one of my favorite background characters in the series. What was it about her that could make a public figure—you couldn't get more public than Rhaegar, I believe—do something so shocking? Very interesting, and I dearly hope to read an answer sometime.

George R.R. Martin juxtaposes Robert Baratheon smiling and jesting until *"all the smiles died"*—can you imagine the look on Robert's face as this happens? From smiling to slack-jawed? I wonder how people attending the tourney reacted on this display of ... broken chivalry. Speaking of tantalizing glimpses ... *Promise me, Ned*, Ned remembers Lyanna saying, but now his memory has skipped to the Tower of Joy (where he made this promise to her)—or is the author mixing it up on purpose; did Ned make a promise at the tourney? I don't think so, but who knows but the author himself.

Before Ned drifts back into his delirious state, Varys pays a visit. He is kind enough to tell Ned that Arya has escaped the Red Keep, and that Sansa is still betrothed to Prince Joffrey. I think I know which news Ned likes the most. Varys puts it plainly, telling Ned he's a dead man, another hint of Eddard's fate. And still I didn't trust the author to go through with that on my first read. Or second, for that matter. The most interesting bit between Ned and Varys' conversation is this:

> "Your own ends. What ends are those, Lord Varys?"
> "Peace," Varys replied **without hesitation**.

Emphasis mine; quite interesting. Varys goes on to say he's been protecting King Robert from his enemies for fifteen years, implying that he did this to keep the peace, but then Ned blundered along and with his "madness of mercy" the king was killed. Varys tells Ned that it was indeed Lancel Lannister who poisoned the king's wine, on Queen Cersei's orders. Ned learns that Cersei is working hard to rid herself of her enemies (to keep her son on the Iron Throne), and that she fears Stannis, Robert's brother, the most, for his claim is true. And then there is a ray of hope: Varys says Cersei intends to spare Ned, based on Sansa's plea in her previous chapter. Ned, however, dismisses the notion out of hand. Bah.

Lord Eddard thinks of Jon, and he is filled with shame and a sorrow too deep for words. Interesting, and from the context I can only conclude that this is linked to his memory of the tourney at Harrenhal and the promise he made to Lyanna ...Varys also sharply reminds us that he and Littlefinger are not in league at all, that they are working their own schemes, which is a far cry from the standard Dark Lord type of fantasy story. It is obvious to me that Varys' words are slightly skewed—he does not *lie*, but he doesn't tell the entire truth either. He is clearly a Targaryen loyalist, and he's been keeping Robert out of harm's way because he's been waiting for Viserys to come of age and return to Westeros.

The chapter ends with Varys trying to convince Ned to beg the Queen for mercy, so that he may live, but Ned doesn't want to hear it. Still, I remember hoping that he would some loophole in his own conscience, some excuse to survive. I guess I forgot just how hard and frozen the Starks can be. At least, as Varys reminds him, the choice is *entirely* his.

Speaking of Varys, this is the second time (that I can think of) where he's kind of referred to as a magician. First during his meeting with Ilyrio Mopatis (spied upon by Arya), and now when Ned asks him what kind of magician he is. is Martin subtly setting up Varys as an actual sorcerer of the ancient

Freehold, hence his allegiance to the Targaryens—and a future enemy of a certain Marwyn and a certain Citadel?

A depressing chapter, then, as we move into the final quarter of the story, where chapters get shorter and more intense, the rumor of *A Game of Thrones* being a real page-turner coming to life in all its glory.

There are also a few other tidbits hidden in this chapter: Sansa learns that Arya has fled, though she knows nothing more than that; when Cersei is named Queen Regent the murmurs in the crowd suggest people are surprised and not positively; the displeasure becomes openly obvious when Janos Slynt is named lord (the muttering is louder, angrier); there's this droll line from Littlefinger when Selmy says he's proudly served three kings -*"And all of them dead"*, Littlefinger retorts—*really*, that guy has no shame, but a good point, too!; Joffrey wants Selmy seized when the knight exits and we see the stoic Janos Slynt immediately rise to go do the king's bidding—truly a loyal king's man, Slynt—and, as the chapter ends, Joffrey consents to Sansa's request: Lord Eddard Stark will be spared *if he confesses to his crimes*. Crimes he hasn't committed, of course.

Sansa's heart soars when her noble prince (yech) tells her this. Okay, she *is* a fool. How could Eddard Stark ever do something as dishonorable as confess to something he *didn't* do? That's just not our Ned, is it? But, of course, love and hope makes blind, and Sansa thinks she will save her father from the Lannisters. I admit, upon the first read of this book, at this point I thought that *something* would come out of this, some resolution that would save Ned. I was such a Nedhead. If I had realized just how ingrained Ned's sense of honor is, I'd perhaps more easily foresee the course of events. Even so, on read #10, I keep hoping that Sansa's plea will lead to something good LOL.

A FLURRY OF FREYS

Catelyn Stark is definitely the character who gets the most flak from that geekiest (and most patient) of online communities,*ASoIaF*-fans. Today I browsed the latest comments at *Finish the Book, George* and noticed this lack of warmth once again; there's even a claim that the only good Catelyn did in the series was to die. I am assuming that this particular comment may have a whiff of hyperbole to it, but poor Lady Cat does really irk a lot of fans of the saga. Which makes me wonder, since to me she is a very well realized character (also, she's fictional) and her chapters are more often than not intriguing and interesting. I've defended the character before—so I will try to avoid that for this particular post, and instead highlight some of the arguments *for* Catelyn being a great character among many in *A Song of Ice and Fire*.

Last time we followed Catelyn around, she came to Moat Cailin where she reunited with her oldest son Robb, and she learned that he was growing into the role of commander and that he was becoming much like his father, Lord Eddard (yes, the guy with the urine-soaked straw). In this chapter, the sixtieth of *A Game of Thrones*, we are introduced to more of Robb's development into the leader of the northmen and we're also introduced to that wascally old Walder Frey, one of my favorite secondary characters, who makes his first active appearance.

George R.R. Martin lets us get to know the northern host through some of the generals that Robb Stark consults, giving the reader perhaps a bit more sympathy for them (as opposed to the Lannister generals, whom we do not get so close to); at least, that's what I felt the first time around. Nine times later, I realize there were other reasons to more closely portray the characters surrounding Robb, especially Lord Roose Bolton of the Dreadfort, but also the others—there is this feeling of bonding, a sense of brothers in arms.

What Martin is doing here is, of course, setting up a plot thread that will run through *A Clash of Kings* and half of *A Storm of Swords*, and I am awed at how he manages to juggle all these characters, make them stand out with short, effective descriptions. But I should have known; we never got a chapter where we could indulge in the eccentricities of some of the important characters of the Lannister host; we've briefly met Ser Kevan Lannister, Tywin's brother, and we've so far gotten an inkling as to just how bad Ser Gregor Clegane is, but what about Ser Stafford Lannister, Ser Addam Marbrand, Lord Lewys Lydden, or Ser Forley Prester? I wanna know and read about them too. I guess I am *too* much of a geek.

A Feast for Crows does fulfill my wish somewhat though, with a closer look at a few Lannisters. Did I mention I say yay to the Lannisters?

In typical Catelyn-fashion, the chapter opens with the lady worrying. Now that may not sound like a positive argument for her, but really it is. Because we see this through her eyes, the story becomes more ominous, more uncertain. As Robb's host moves into the riverlands—the lands ruled by her lord father, Hoster—*"her days were anxious, her nights restless, and every raven that flew overhead made her clench her teeth."* Through her apprehension, the reader becomes uncertain of the characters' futures, and the story takes on a darker quality, and the fears that haunt her become real because, you know, she's the mother of Robb, who is heading towards war and death, what *else* should she be pondering? It is quite in character, and thus I am immersed.

Note also that her husband is imprisoned by the Lannisters, her daughter Sansa is a political prisoners of the Lannisters, her other daughter Arya is gone missing and maybe dead, and her son Bran was thrown out of a tower by a Lannister. *And* she believes the Lannisters murdered her sister's husband. It's not hard to believe that Catelyn would spend her day worrying. In fact, she is remarkably strong through it all. That's also why it is so damn cool that she hardens her heart and decides to focus on Robb's campaign and not let all her other worries overshadow her duties to the son she is with. (Did you notice what I did there? "Hardens her heart?" I refer, of course, to Catelyn's future zombie handle, "Lady Stoneheart.")

Robb rides at the front, each day asking one of his lords to join him, which Catelyn notes he has learned from Lord Eddard. From her uncle the Blackfish, Robb learns that Walder Frey has massed a large host but hasn't moved it to reinforce his liege lord, Catelyn's father Hoster Tully. This gives us an early indication as to what kind of man Walder Frey is—the kind of man that waits and abides, not committing until he is sure to be on the winning side. The whole first section of the chapter is, in fact, devoted to preparing us for Walder Frey; and it is Catelyn who seems to know best what kind of a weasel Frey is. However, Robb *must* go to Frey, for he is the Lord of the Crossing, and through him Robb may move his army across the river to engage the Lannister host.

I have to say I love all this military stuff, with river crossings and mustering, and the political underpinnings of Frey having a son married to a Lannister, all the complications that make Westeros come alive. Though there is news that Walder Frey has fought the Lannisters, Catelyn remains suspicious of this man.

The following day, her uncle Brynden Tully, also called the Blackfish, reports that Riverrun, her lord father's castle, is besieged by Ser Jaime Lannister's host. Another cool thing, that stuff can and does happen "off-screen" to complicate matters further. Plotwise, I guess the point is to push Robb into forcing a confrontation with Lord Walder (to keep the plot well-paced), because he's the one who can let them cross the river and relieve Riverrun. Robb gets angry at the bad news, and Catelyn rebukes him, and the scene stands out as a bit odd in that she acts the mother, a bit like in her previous chapter. However, it is perfectly understandable—she's finding it difficult to be *herself* when her son is in charge of a whole lot of northern lords and a whole lot more soldiers. What I guess she's trying to do is to offer him the idea of a diplomatic solution instead of "pulling the Twins down Walder's ears" (paraphrased) but the way it comes out is a bit awkward. Intentional? Only one man knows. He's also the only man who knows what *really* is going on with, you know, *A Dance with Dragons* and the rest of the series.

After the initial introduction of Walder Frey through the eyes of Catelyn, we finally enjoy the dubious pleasure of meeting the man ourselves. Robb's host finally arrives at Frey's castle, the Twins. I've always loved the scenes with Walder Frey, in the love-to-hate sense, that is. He's a disgusting old man with some funny lines of dialogue, and the way he acts is priceless. He comes off the page so very vividly. Outside the Twins, it becomes clear that Catelyn isn't the only one who doesn't trust Lord Walder. In fact, several of the northern lords speak up. Interesting how Martin really pumps up the reader's suspicion, painting Walder black before showing the character at all. It is decided that Catelyn will be the one to enter Lord Walder's fortress and negotiate with him. Upon meeting Walder, we finally get a physical description:

> "Lord Walder was ninety, a wizened pink weasel with a bald spotted head, too gouty to stand unassisted. His newest wife, a pale frail girl of sixteen years, walked beside his litter when they carried him in. She was the eighth Lady Frey."

That sure does tell us a lot about Walder, doesn't it? A little later we get some personality traits exposed too, to complete the picture—he's irascible, sharp of tongue, and blunt of manner. Perhaps Martin wouldn't have needed to *tell* us this through Cat's reflections; the way Walder acts and talks in this chapter makes it clear enough. The exchange between Lord Walder Frey and Lady Catelyn Stark is among my favorite exchanges in the book—they are wildly different, and as Catelyn struggles to keep her dignity and courtesy, Walder is as rude as they come, and the contrast works great. Based on the heavy exposition on Walder earlier in the chapter, I half expected him (talking about my first read here) to imprison her or worse. Of course, now I know better as to why Martin put it in. But that's for another book, thousands of pages later.

Talking Lord Walder into letting Robb cross the river with his army isn't an easy thing, and the exchange takes several entertaining pages of back and forth between the two. Through their dialogue we get inside Walder's mind too, learning that he isn't very fond of Lord Tywin Lannister and that he feels affronted by her lord father, but finally Lady Catelyn sees through the man and she realizes how she can make a deal with Frey.

I'd really like to just quote the entire exchange with Lord Walder but I guess if you're reading this, you have a copy of the novel yourself. I am really entertained by this Lord Walder, *heh*. Anyway, the crossing comes with a price, or rather, several prices. I'll list 'em up here, because you might never know when Walder will show up to claim what Catelyn has promised him:

1) Robb will get House Frey's swords to reinforce his host, but at his mother's suggestion he leaves behind a force of four hundred men to augment Lord Walder's garrison (oh, I do love medieval military logistics, thank you George for reinforcing my nerdiness). Robb decides to have Ser Helman Tallhart oversee these four hundred. So we have Tallhart at the Twins.

2) Two of Lord Walder's grandsons are to be sent north to Winterfell, to become fosterlings of House Stark. We'll see more of those two later. They are basically a (minor) plot device.

3) Lord Walder's son, Olyvar, is to serve as Robb's personal squire, and Walder wants to see him knighted at a later point.

4) If Arya is returned safely, she'll have to wed Lord Walder's youngest son, Elmar. I *do* hope that this little nugget isn't forgotten later on in the series

5) Robb himself must wed one of Walder's daughters.

Now, of the five points, we'll see four of them through in *A Clash of Kings* and *A Storm of Swords*. But #4 is still in the open, *heh*. Not sure if Olyvar got knighted, though, I don't remember at the moment. Anyway, look at how Martin weaves a typical medieval negotiation into the storyline, never making things easy for the characters. Robb consents to marry a Frey "solemnly," the echo of Lord Eddard and his consent to marry Catelyn eerily apparent. From this negotiation we'll get several new strands of story, enlarging the impressive tapestry. Oh, *Dragons*, where art thou! Slynt wants more. Not necessarily more Martells and Greyjoys, but more Freys. More intrigue. Logistics. *This* shit is what is so awesome, not Euron Crow's Eye with his silly horn. Sorry. It just bubbled up.

The chapter ends with Robb's host moving across the river to begin their march south to face Lord Tywin Lannister. The last paragraph is beautifully written, evoking that ominous sense that also began the chapter, with Catelyn not so much worrying this time as *observing*; whereas in the first paragraph of the chapter she was worried as she looked on Robb's host marching south, now she's more detached, noting the makeup of the host (knights, lancers, free riders, bowmen, cavalry), remembering the clatter of hooves across Frey's drawbridge, and

> "the sight of Lord Walder Frey in his litter watching them pass, the glitter of eyes peering down through the slats of the murder holes in the ceiling ... ."

A great passage that, with the juxtaposition of Frey's eyes and the murder holes. A more eloquent way of saying "if looks could kill"? Maybe. I like how the chapter kind of circles—Robb's host moving with Cat worrying, the Twins in the midsection, then Robb's host moving again with Cat observing.

Know what I mean? It is an effective and classic structure, like a play with three acts. I'm convinced anyone reading this chapter comes away with the feeling that Lord Walder Frey is one of the series' villains, where the shade of grey leans close to black.

There's also some quick dialogue about Jon Arryn, Lysa, and the fostering of Sweetrobin, but frankly by this point I have (for the tenth time) forgotten all about the mystery of Jon's death; that particular storyline is pretty weak by now, overshadowed by great characters, interesting larger plot developments, and it seems to me that it kind of faded away a bit, obscured by cooler stuff. Seriously, the whole Jon Arryn murder mystery could have been ditched with some minor changes to the storyline. In fact, even *without* changing that much of the story. Sansa could make the comment that makes Ned realize Joffrey is an abomination of twincest without having this whole elaborate murder mystery leading up to it ...

The Price of Honor

There was an interesting question about Jon Snow that came up in this thread over at SFFworld's Internet website: whether he is more of a clichéd character than other *A Song of Ice and Fire* characters. It didn't evolve into a proper discussion, but it had me thinking. I have complained about Jon Snow being a "boring" character in at least one previous post, but I realize now that what I really mean is that Jon Snow is too close to the "farmboy-turns-hero" archetype for me to really warm up to him. I do like him, I do like his story, but it is just less interesting than many of the other characters—I can say the same for Luke Skywalker in the *Star Wars* films—he is by far the most important character in the original trilogy, and I love his journey, but I enjoy Han Solo a lot more.

Speaking of Luke Skywalker, that character is the perfect example of the type of character I am likening Jon Snow to. If you've read Joseph Campbell's *The Hero with a Thousand Faces* you probably know what I mean. Just for digression's sake let's compare Jon Snow and Luke Skywalker.

- ❖ They both have cool names involving weather (Snow and 'Sky-') that roll easily off the tongue.
- ❖ They both have a dead mother and a bad-ass father who, in the back-story, was both heroic and villainous (This assumes the R+L theory is true, which is obvious, to me anyway.)
- ❖ They both start out living with their family and not feeling at home.
- ❖ They both damage a hand (okay, Luke loses it entirely) during their adventures.

- ❖ They are both on the "edge" of civilization—Luke on Tatooine, Jon first at Winterfell, then at the Wall.
- ❖ Both stories involve mysteries surrounding their parents.
- ❖ Both are given a sword (Jon receives his in the very chapter this blog post will go into below).

... and that's just from the top of my head. There are probably more. Of course, there are *differences* too but I find the similarities striking and they do argue that Jon Snow is, indeed, an archetype of literary fiction.

If GRRM *really* wants to be known as changing the genre or whatever he's credited for, he certainly has to give Jon Snow's fate a thought. Or maybe George *wants* him to follow that classic path from bastard to hero, there's no reason why the series can't contain both typical *and* atypical characters. It does seem that Jon Snow's destiny is to be pivotal once the Others come knocking on the door. His is the song of ice, I guess. I think there will be a comparison or two with Luke Skywalker later in this post if I remember my chapter correctly.

Anyway ... this brings us to today's post, which is the sixty-first chapter of *A Game of Thrones*, and Jon Snow's eighth chapter. Interestingly, most characters in *A Game of Thrones* (I'm talking POVs here) travel extensively throughout the books, while Jon Snow takes a short trip to the Wall and remains there. It makes his story seem more stagnant (and it is), which obviously helps us feeling Jon's plight, having become a man of the Night's Watch, never being able to go anywhere again save to roam about in the dangerous northlands. Compare Catelyn, who travels to King's Landing, then up to the Eyrie, then to Moat Cailin, then to Riverrun. Lord Eddard and the daughters travel to King's Landing (the Big City!) and Tyrion travels all over Westeros. Meanwhile, Jon Snow remains stuck at the Wall, now the steward of Old Bear Mormont, the Lord Commander of the Night's Watch.

Last time, there was this undead attack and Jon Snow saved Lord Commander Mormont's life in a scene more "horror" than "fantasy." I am writing this little digression before reading the chapter; I will return when I have read the chapter to blather on. I honestly can't remember much of this chapter so it will be interesting to see what the main plot development in this one is!

Hours later ... Night has fallen over the southeastern parts of Norway, and in the meantime I have re-read the Jon Snow chapter. Also, and I know I am late to the party; I discovered HBO's new *Game of Thrones* website and became rather stoked upon seeing a new teaser *and* some production stills and interviews. Wow! From the footage it is quite clear that HBO's version won't be able to do justice to the version playing in my brain, but they are damn close and that's quite a feat. It's a small dream coming true. Now give me the "It's done" signal, George, and I am all yours (again). Sigh.

Being excited about the TV series is fun but the excitement diminishes the moment I remember how long I have been waiting for *A Dance with Dragons*. And it disappears completely when I visit GRRM's *Not a Blog* only to see posts about this "NFL"-thingy Americans seem so interested in. He could as well be posting about doing dishes. Oh, and I think I am falling in love with the live action version of Daenerys Targaryen ...

Jon. Jon Snow. Sixty-first chapter. Get on with it, Slynt.

Yes. Sorry. Here we go. Unlike the previous three or four chapters which have my eyes glued to the book in my hands, this one doesn't really take off, though I can imagine it does for fans of the Targaryen dynasty (and, obviously, for fans of Jon Snow). The chapter revolves around one plot point—Lord Commander Mormont, gives Jon Snow a new sword—and one revelation—the identity of Maester Aemon of the Night's Watch. Admittedly, that is a pretty big revelation, although it is less surprising with the benefit of hindsight.

Let's take it from the beginning. The chapter has an obvious theme: the price of honor. The chapter starts right off with dialogue, with the Lord Commander asking Jon if he is well. Jon lies and says he's fine. The Old Bear's raven starts squawking immediately, and the bird doesn't annoy just the characters in the scene, but me as a reader as well. In fact, the damn bird takes me out of the flow of dialogue between the two characters with its shrieks of *Well, well* and *father, father* and whatever else choice words it cares to repeat (the way it is able to emulate so many different words by the way is quite astonishing, and I am tempted to think that *this* particular raven is a tad more special than your run-of-the-mill average Westerosi raven—more on that later).

Jon and the Lord Commander discuss what happened in their previous chapter together, when the wight attacked and Jon managed to stop it by throwing fire at it. (One can only imagine the modern version of this conversation. "Dude, that was one scary wight.") We also learn that Jon's nights are haunted by nightmares of said wight; only in these sleepless "white nights" the wight takes on Lord Eddard Stark's features—does Jon perhaps have a premonition of Lord Eddard's death?

Jon is also troubled by thoughts of honor and whether Lord Eddard truly is honorable, considering he fathered a bastard. One could say it's both psychologically feasible for Jon to dream of Ned and that it serves the plot itself by laying groundwork for the execution to come.

We also learn that in this chapter, first published in 1996, the Night's Watch still does not know the whereabouts of Benjen Stark. Incredibly, it is now 2011 and he is *still* missing, after several thousand pages of new plot developments. This is quite annoying. Will we ever see this particular detail be resolved?

At the same time, I enjoy the fact that George R.R. Martin dares let a character stay off-screen for such a long time (though some theorists will argue that he's in fact showing up again in *A Storm of Swords*; personally, I don't buy that particular theory but that's for a post in the distant future).

Lord Commander Mormont speaks some ominous, chilling words following the discussion about the wight attack:

> "The cold winds are rising. Summer is at an end, and a winter is coming such as this world has never seen."

Pretty grim and dark, and perfectly in line with House Stark's famous motto (which I constantly have to remind myself is *winter is coming*, not *is winter coming*).

As a reader, though, I already I know that winter is coming. The prologue, some six hundred pages back, told us this. I for one think it is about high time winter actually comes. I'm not talking a bit of fluffy nice snow landing on Riverrun in *A Feast for Crows*; I'm talking the Others coming over the Wall to kick some Westerosi *ass*, baby. Give it to us, give it now.

Here we learn that Mormont has sent letters to King's Landing, but the Lord Commander muses that Grand Maester Pycelle most likely doesn't deign to reply, as he has done before. This gives us a hint not only that the Night's Watch is being neglected by the politicians in the south, but also that Pycelle himself is blind to the need of the guardians of the realm. When Mormont has told Jon this, Jon thinks "resentfully" of how he isn't told everything, reminding me of—and here it comes—the resentful and whiny Luke Skywalker we meet early in *Star Wars*. Is whininess a typical trait of the farmboy-turned-hero archetype?

Jon has learned that Robb has marched south with a host, and through his thoughts we see that he is kind of jealous about it; at the same time, though, Jon admits to himself that he has no right to think like this. Robb is of course Ned's true heir and he's just a bastard.

Before Mormont hands Jon the sword, one of two important scenes in the chapter, we get a small exchange which I have graciously rewritten to make it better reflect the current status of the saga:

"(((Soon)))", Jon replied.

See what I did there? Oh yes, the sword. Since I'm in the comparing Jon-to-Luke mood (hey, writing this I see another similarity—both have Biblical names), let's say that, for this chapter at least, the character of Ben Obi-Wan Kenobi is represented by both Mormont and Maester Aemon. Doing this, you see, allows me to claim that Mormont handing Jon the

Waiting for Dragons

sword Longclaw is similar to Ben Kenobi handing Luke his father's light saber. A pretty thin claim, then, but the actual symbolism—handing over a storied weapon—remains the same, whether the sword is the family heirloom of the Mormonts or the light saber once wielded by Anakin Skywalker (bah, writing that name made me see Hayden Christensen in my mind's eye).

The Lord Commander tells Jon that the sword was intended for his son, the treacherous Ser Jorah who accompanies Daenerys in her chapters—so him giving it to Jon is actually quite a statement. Do we see destiny here? The destiny of the farmboy hero? Yeah, I think so. Mormont could have given Jon any decent sword as a thank you for saving his life, or even a gift certificate to Mole Town.

My guess is that Longclaw will be of some great importance later on, hence the time Martin spends describing its appearance and history, to make it stand out among the other named weapons in the series. Jon, whiner that he is, isn't that pleased with the gift but is forced to accept it anyway. The blade is made of mithril, I mean Valyrian steel. A link to that ancient Freehold then. And I like the irony of the fact that the weapon is a bastard sword.

I hope that, in some future novel, Jon Snow meets Ser Jorah Mormont. Will the knight recognize the weapon now that the bear head pommel has been removed and replaced by a wolf's head pommel? Will he be "re-introduced" to his father's sword point-first? Or will he redeem his father's dying wish by bearing Longclaw with honor?

261

Another Luke Skywalker-moment follows when Jon leaves Mormont and he thinks back on how he had used to dream of doing great deeds, just as Luke dreams of doing great deeds while stranded on a remote planet far from the action. Another archetypical trait is having prophetic dreams—Jon dreams of Ned's death, another foreshadowing of the execution to take place in King's Landing.

One thing I am a bit unsure of is the method for killing wights. Mormont states that Jon was smart to put the walking corpse on fire, and muses:

> "Fire! ... We ought to have remembered. The Long Night has come before."

This tells us that during the previous Long Night, *fire* was used to destroy the wights (I assume a wandering army of corpses controlled by the Others)—but later on in the chapter we are told that the other wight was destroyed by being hacked to pieces and no fire was used. Am I reading it wrong? Or *can* wights be "killed" by cold steel, if there are enough people around to hack them to mincemeat? Mormont's musings also reveal to me that "the Long Night" probably is a cyclical thing, maybe something like an Ice Age, and may thus be connected with the Red Comet from *A Clash of Kings*—celestial movements causing the Long Night, beginning with the comet streaking across the sky.

Ser Alliser Thorne has been sent to King's Landing with a wight's chopped-off hand to show the king some evidence of the shit going on in the North, and a new character is on his way to Castle Black, a man named Ser Endrew Tarth, who is to become the new master-at-arms of Castle Black. Don't know if this has any bearing on the future of the story, as I really don't recall Ser Endrew. Will be interesting to see if he shows up. He's like totally faded from my seemingly not-hardcore-geeky-enough *A Song of Ice and Fire* knowledge.

As it turns out, Jon's friends in the Watch—Samwell Tarly, Pyp with the ears, dim Grenn et al—are all really excited about Jon getting the sword Longclaw, but Jon struggles to find his enthusiasm. He's quite the emo, don't you think? He feels so alone in the world, and he comes off as quite self-centered (and I can excuse him that), he's seldom happy, and it makes reading him a little less entertaining than, say, Tyrion.

Finally, Jon is sent to Maester Aemon and here we get a proper lesson, in that typical fairy tale Master-Apprentice fashion. Yoda to Skywalker. Aemon to Snow. Aemon talks to Jon about honor, about choices, and as Jon listens the beans are spilled: Aemon is a Targaryen. A shocking revelation for many readers, maybe, but the first time I read it I shrugged. What was the big deal? Wiser now, I see the impact it has, and like Mormont giving away his family heirloom, Aemon telling Jon this secret is truly a boon; would Aemon have revealed his story to anyone else, or just to Jon cause, you know, he's the Chosen One? I like Aemon's speech about honor—it is woven into the story in a far more fluid way than, say, the blunt speech of that wandering monk in *A Feast for Crows* that many readers seem to hold in high regard. And it gives Jon some new things to mull over, of course—and us, as readers.

In this scene, Jon once again shows his bitter, resentful side much as Luke Skywalker does upon facing some hard truths. Jon and Luke both are cornered into a situation where they must make a choice; remember the scene where Luke decides to go to Bespin to save his friends? It is kind of the same choice Aemon presents to Jon—let's mix up Yoda's wisdom with Aemon's:

> "Go south to help your family in the war you could, but everything you have worked to achieve up here at the Wall destroy you would."

Am I right in this or am I just grasping for comparisons? *Stay or go.*

Speaking of the archetypical mentor or wizard character, Maester Aemon has those scary, white eyes—blind but seeing—a trait I believe he shares with many mentor types in fantasy tales. What I am trying to say—what I have been trying to say all through this long-winded post—is that Jon Snow, and by extension the chapters he is in—are closer to "vanilla" fantasy than the rest of the novel, which are what made *A Game of Thrones* such a breath of fresh air in a stale genre. I'll stop flogging this dead horse now!

In conclusion, not an exhilarating chapter by a long shot. Rather, I find it mildly interesting. In fact, I could probably have blogged fifty words and be done with it, but the aforementioned discussion of how close Jon is to being a cliché made this post a little longer than I initially expected it to be. There just isn't *that* much to write about. I don't really care whether Aemon is a Targaryen or not, it doesn't really impact the plot in any major way except having Jon rethink a bit, and that Aemon's character can be used to finally—in *A Feast for Crows*—determine just who the Prince who was Promised really is.

See you next time when Daenerys brings a visit to the Lamb Men. Ouch, I know I don't like that chapter much either. But for different reasons. Stay tuned.

More Salt In The Wound, Please

(This post was originally called *Daterape Necroparty*, which is the title I am referring to below).

Excuse the lame title of this blog post. But it reflects what I remember upon seeing the first paragraph and remembering what chapter this is. "It's *that* chapter," I think to myself. Reading this chapter was only the second time I was ever revolted by something I read in a book (the first time was, perhaps not surprisingly, in *American Psycho*).

The scene I am talking about is as you can probably guess the one involving a girl being raped on a pile of corpses. More on that later (wow, it looks like I am going for a post without a digression first). George R.R. Martin creates some pretty repulsive scenes later on in the saga as well, but this was the first truly repulsive one—in my humble opinion. Different people react differently to various degrees of violence; I think we can all agree. Of course, this is fictional violence, and that helps a lot. A *live* daterape necroparty would *not* be of interest to me.

Violence and bloodshed in stories is fine by me, but upon rereading this chapter I do feel that George R.R. Martin perhaps oversteps the boundary in places and things turn into what is commonly called "gratuitous violence." However, at the same time, I am glad that it still can be done in the United States—producing works of art that, intentionally or not, are bound to offend. I like a bit of offense. As do the Dothraki, as this chapter clearly shows. In fact, with this particular Daenerys chapter I feel that the tone of her story changes into a more violent one. Yes, we saw Dothraki kill and maim each other at her wedding, but in this chapter we get described some pretty gruesome things being done to the Lhazareen, a people living close to the tall grasses of the Dothraki Sea, a people the Dothraki call the "Lamb Men," for they are meek as lambs in their eyes (can't help but think of Jesus here, he would have a field day with the Dothraki).

Earlier I compared a few chapters with J.R.R. Tolkien's *The Lord of the Rings* (Jon Snow and Bran in particular have chapters with a tone reminiscent, at times, of Middle-earth, perhaps because of the supernatural elements); Daenerys' chapters from here on out are reminiscent, sometimes strongly, of Robert E. Howard's *Conan the Barbarian*. The barbarism displayed by Khal Drogo and his blood riders is quite similar to the barbarism displayed in the *Conan* novels and comic books—blood spraying, limbs hacked off, piles of the slain ... indeed, Khal Drogo is somewhat similar in attitude and nature to the young Conan of Cimmeria. Also, many of Conan's adventures (at least the memorable ones, such as *The Tower of the Elephant* and *The Devil in Iron*) take place in fairly exotic locales not unlike the places Daenerys' journey will take her to.

I have to admit that I do not know whether George R.R. Martin consciously or unconsciously has let himself be inspired by Robert E. Howard's loincloth-wearing (anti-) hero. Perhaps someone reading this can enlighten me? Certainly, Martin, with his long history as a science fiction and fantasy fan, is well aware of both Robert E. Howard and Conan.

Combining the violence with behavior most of us would deem inappropriate is something George R.R. Martin likes to do; there are many examples of this in *A Song of Ice and Fire* (a scene involving two Lannister siblings and their motionless

WAITING FOR DRAGONS

father comes to mind). This chapter, in fact, opens with it: A battle has taken place, and Martin describes dying horses, a harvest of heads, watering the fields with blood, dogs sniffing among moaning and dying men; it is harsh enough to send weaker readers away (and I know some readers have quit on *A Game of Thrones* for this). George ups the ante, however, by contrasting the field of the dead with Daenerys's handmaidens and *khas* smiling and jesting among themselves. It is ridiculously brutal, how can these people be smiling and jesting on such a field of battle? The contrast George paints is baffling. Is the intent to show us how people can behave in a terrifying situation? Or is he just being nasty? I understand people who believe he is writing stuff like this just for the hell of it—and here comes that word again, and I can see why people call the author out on being gratuitous. 'Cause it kind of *is*.

It is a small moment, a few sentences, but it does take me out of the story for a while, but that can be a good thing too—the argument being that Martin is able to make you think, and consider, your own views on violence. More sick violence follows—some of Khal Drogo's riders chase a young boy around, whipping him up good before putting an arrow in him, and here comes the contrast, "when they tired of the sport." The author sure paints Daenerys's allies in a grim light in this chapter, and I can muster no sympathy or liking for the Dothraki—which makes the following sequence, in which Daenerys learns that her husband is grievously wounded, less interesting because I wouldn't mind Khal Drogo dying of those wounds because although Daenerys has influenced him slightly, he is a primitive idiot, bound to his people's moronic traditions, leading brutal men whose worth, in my opinion, is nothing. Bastards.

267

We learn that the battle that has just finished (isn't it great by the way how George can begin a chapter at the *end* of a battle and still entertain us) was, in fact, a battle between two Dothraki factions—Khal Drogo's army and Khal Ogo's—the Lhazareen, or Lamb Men, were merely caught in the middle. Here, Martin once agains rubs some extra salt in the wound by adding the notion that the Lamb Men, under attack from Khal Ogo, maybe found hope when they saw Khal Drogo's army appear. As if the chapter doesn't diminish hope enough. Geez.

More salt in the wound, please. We have arrived at the scene which I mentioned ever so casually in the beginning of this post. The bit where I put the book away (talking the first time I read it now) and had to, you know, take a break. A girl of, what, thirteen, being shoved onto a pile of corpses only to be raped. Did I mention that she is shoved *face down* into the bodies of the dead? As if it isn't bad enough. Did I mention that Khal Drogo's men *form a line* behind her? I was about to write *form a fucking line* to express my angry disgust with the depiction of the scene, but that would make it funny wouldn't it. I don't wanna be funny today. On Wednesdays I am always serious. At least Martin's writing makes me feel something, not many fantasy authors can say the same (except Joe Abercrombie who tickles my funny bone, except on Wednesdays, and Steven Erikson, whose tomes make me feel like I am in a never-ending dream; violent dream, though). At first, Daenerys rides on, but we can sense that she is discomforted by the rape going on upon aforementioned heap of rotting flesh, but first George needs to give us another lesson in how cruel the world is with a short treatise on the usefulness of slavery, with brothels paying double for healthy young girls—here comes another contrast, but this time to make it even more disgusting I guess—and triple for young boys. A bit that makes me think: Do I truly find it *less* disgusting to sell young girls than young boys? I guess not. But Martin, of course, has to add that we are talking about boys under the age of ten. Give me a break, will you?

Be assured I do not recommend this chapter as a teaser to draw in new readers. Speaking of slavery, it seems that the Khal has earned himself ten thousand captives. That is quite a lot! Where did they come from? If the Dothraki are so ruthless, why do cities still exist on the fringe of the Dothraki Sea? Considering all their loot stashed back in Vaes Dothrak, one would think that the Dothraki had conquered and slain the entire continent. How could these Lamb Men have survived so long? The answer is that they aren't as meek as the Dothraki claim them to be, which is revealed when Daenerys finds Khal Drogo somewhere in the city with a Lhazareen arrow through his arm. At least one of them could handle a bow, then.

Back to that poor young girl being stuffed back on them corpses. Daenerys finally decides to do something about it (she's rather quick about it, in fact, only the second man in line is plunging the girl, but when reading the chapter it feels like a large amount of time passes when she rides past the scene of the daterape necroparty). When the girl lets out a "heartrending wail", Daenerys tells the blood riders to stop it. They object, because the girl is a Lhazareen, which equates to nothing in their eyes, but she threatens them and they give it up. I am surprised Martin didn't add that *"sulking and scowling, they went to rape the dogs and the corpses and taking pleasure from the scared, dying horses."*

Daenerys then proceeds to free any women she finds in the process of being surprise-sexed, among them the old, fat woman Mirri Maz Duur (I wonder what kind of hardened Dothraki warrior chose *her*. Can I say that?) who ends up sewing Khal Drogo's wounds and thereby saving his stupid-ass life. Ser Jorah Mormont is perplexed at Daenerys's decision to free the women, which I find passing strange. He's a man from a more civilized part of the world; doesn't he find it at all disgusting what is happening? Yes, I know, in war men rape women yadayada but this is ... ah well I will leave it at that.

No—wait a minute—now George tells us that within the city of the Lamb Men *things are worse*. How much worse can it get? Double-penetration by two Dothraki steeds while forced to eat the testicles of the dead? Okay, that *is* worse. Even worse than the worse happenings in town. Before going into town to check out *worse* Ser Jorah tells Dany that she reminds him of her brother when she goes about being nice.

No, not Viserys you silly girl, he twisted your nipples remember, Ser Jorah is talking Rhaegar. This mysterious character that is so important to the back-story is fascinating to many readers, me included. We want to know more about Rhaegar Targaryen. Now we know that he too would possibly have freed those women.

The interesting thing is, of course, that King Robert Baratheon claims that Rhaegar raped Lyanna Stark but I am not sure if that has been mentioned already or if it comes up later. I am curious as to how Ser Jorah knew Rhaegar; I can't really recall how he knows so much about him. Maybe it comes up later. I guess it does.

WAITING FOR DRAGONS

Daenerys convinces Khal Drogo that freeing those poor female (and maybe a she-male or two) souls is a good thing, and he allows her to keep them as slaves. What a good guy. Yay. He proceeds to boast of how strong and cool he is whenever Mirri Maz Duur warns him the healing will hurt. I hate people who boast of their muscle capacity (maybe because I wish I had the ambition to do some weightlifting instead of just exercising my fingers on the olde keyboard).

The last half of the chapter (it's a short one) is basically a scene between Khal Drogo, Mirri Maz Duur, Daenerys, and Ser Jorah. They are gathered in the city's temple to the Great Shepherd, the god of the Lhazareen, where Mirri Maz Duur patches up Khal Drogo. In the scene, we get a few interesting tidbits, most notably Mirri Maz Duur revealing that she has been to mysterious Asshai by the Shadow, a place I suspect we will see in a later installment of the saga (let's for a moment pretend we'll see the series through to its conclusion), and where she met a certain Marwyn. Marwyn who?

When Marwyn appears in *A Feast for Crows* I had forgotten Mirri's revelation in this chapter. I had to go back and re-read this bit (so in fact this bit is my 11th re-read yay and cheers and hooray). I was astonished at how Martin could add such a little throwaway bit in here, only to have it somewhat culminate thousands of pages later. Now, I am not so sure anymore. Whether Marwyn's story was planned all along, I mean. It's hard to tell unless the author himself gives us the true story behind Mirri and Marwyn's encounter (by the way, I *did* connect Mirri Maz Duur with the Magi mentioned in Cersei's chapters in *A Feast for Crows*). Things are getting a bit too coincidental by that fourth book, by the way.

271

No, give me *A Game of Thrones* any day. It is fresh and can stand on its own, especially compared to *Feast*.

When they are done, Khal Drogo tries to rise but blood begins leaking and he is too weak to stand (ha!). here we get a small nod to J.R.R. Tolkien: Khal Drogo does not want any man to help support him, cause that is weak and stuff, but Daenerys tells him she can support him, for she is no man (the echo of Eowyn versus Darth Ringwraith #1 is clear to me). Maybe intentional, maybe not. Again, only the author knows. Finally, we get a deliciously ironic line from Qotho, one of the bloodriders, telling Mirri that "as the Khal fares, so shall you." Not ironic *right now*, but it will be.

Wiping sweat from my brow, I realize that I have gotten myself through this chapter once more. Do I like it? Kind of. Can it compare to any given Tyrion chapter? Not by a shot so long it orbits the galaxy. The chapter reinforces my dislike of the Dothraki, and not in the "love-to-hate" way of, say, Lord Tywin Lannister or Lord Walder Frey. The contrast between the "Conanesque" (or is it "Onanesque"?) and the more medieval Westeros widens, and I am not all that fond of it being in the same story.

At the same time, I am fascinated, and Martin has definitely taught me how to add some gratuitous violence into my own writing and role-playing. What a valuable skill! Daenerys as a character is becoming more interesting as she develops from abused little sister to *khaleesi*. Now don't think I am a religious zealot out to banish all evil from contemporary literature. Far from it. I am just pointing out stuff. I think the chapter would be just as fine without the necroparty.

I can live with it being in there, but I couldn't have lived with myself if I had walked past an underage girl being raped on a conglomeration of the dead, with guys standing in line to take her from behind. I know the argument: This is medieval, baby, things were different. Perhaps they were (though a lot of *medieval* shit is going down in the world even today). Yes, our views on things change as we (hopefully) evolve into more rational beings (if only we could cast aside the shackles of religion), but this is at the same time a piece of literature, and at times I feel the author takes it too far.

Bah, I am conflicted about this. It's not like I mind when Tyrion crossbows you-know-who later in the story. I love *A Game of Thrones*, and I don't mind 99% of the violence in the novel, as it for the most part suits the story, but this? I don't know.

Looking forward to the next chapter, starring Tyrion and Tywin, my two favorite Mr. T's.

IMP INTO THE FRAY

After last chapter's degenerate Dothraki behavior, flipping to the next chapter to see the heading TYRION is refreshing—instead of the stark brutality of the east, we get the sarcastic, civilized viewpoint of everybody's favorite imp, Tyrion Lannister. It's not like there's no violence in Tyrion's chapters. But Tyrion's slightly askew worldview is a much more entertaining lens through which to see the world of Westeros. Also, his father Lord Tywin Lannister is involved, and I can't get enough of his detached, cold personality. Definitely one of my favorite non-POV characters.

So, where were we? When last we followed Tyrion, he reached his father's army and had a conversation with Lord Tywin inside the Inn on the Crossroads, and we had a quick glimpse of Tyrion's uncle on his father's side, Ser Kevan Lannister. Also, Tyrion surrounded himself with funny characters like Shagga son of Dolf and Bronn. It's almost guaranteed entertainment. Can't wait to see if HBO manage to get across the dark humor that so infuses Tyrion's chapters. Also, *still* can't wait for *A Dance with Dragons*. In case you've forgotten, *A Song of Ice and Fire* isn't finished yet, though you could get that idea when you read all the reactions to HBO's TV series. A lot of people seem to think they are creating the series based on a finished story. They are in for a big surprise! A sigh issues from the depths of my soul (I mean, synapses in the disappointment center of the brain).

The chapter opens with a brief description to set the scene. Upon reading it, George R.R. Martin takes me straight into Westeros and I am all fan boy as I gleefully imagine the hill overlooking the Kingsroad, upon which a long table has been set up, covered with golden cloth, where Lord Tywin and his henchies take their evening meal. It just *looks* so cool ... so medieval ... I am all *there*. I can feel the evening breeze; see the golden standard of the lion flutter, the shine of the lord's armor in the setting sun, the shadows gathering around the base of the hill, the air alive with fireflies ... lovely, isn't it? I have this feeling that the more closely the story resembles "how things were done" in medieval history, the more immersed I become. I have a harder time living some of the events that transpire in, say, *A Feast for Crows*.

Tyrion arrives late and saddle-sore, once again acutely aware of his awkward gait. It *does* haunt him, but the cool thing is that Martin reinforces his low self-esteem when he is around his father, Lord Tywin. He doesn't much think of his waddling when, say, confronting Cersei with his cunning. A sublime touch to heighten the sense of the character being an actual living, breathing ... Imp, more aware of his shortcomings when around his dad.

Upon re-reading, I can't help but notice (again) how often George R.R. Martin expands upon what the characters *eat*. Whenever there's something being served, the author makes sure that we know exactly what the characters are getting. In this case, as Tyrion crests the hill where his father has made his stand, Lannister cooks are serving the meat course: *"five suckling pigs, skin seared and crackling, a different fruit in every mouth."* Now, this is in fact a rather short description compared to many other courses Martin elaborates upon during the telling of his tale, and I have to admit I wonder why. Is it the man's personality shining through? I mean, he's not exactly kept his fondness for food a secret on his blog. Every other post is about the quality of pizza in the various United States. Or is there something more ... literary and profound about the many different courses being described in detail? Throughout *A Game of Thrones* it is quite apparent that the author has a good knowledge of medieval history which he uses to infuse the setting with detail; could he be, among other things, an expert on medieval cuisine and because he simply knows his stuff he adds it to the book? Maybe that's the answer (I know I have researched medieval cuisine myself to make my role-playing game setting more realistic). There's also a saying (in Norway at least) that "you are what you eat." Is he telling us something about the characters when describing the food they eat? Anyway, as soon as Tyrion and Tywin meet, they clash—verbally. I love reading their banter, and the way Tywin treats his disfigured son makes me more empathic towards Tyrion. Maybe that's the point. Or maybe he's setting up abundance now to underline the mass starvation that will ensue when winter comes.

Damn it, now I'm hungry. Me want suckling pig, sizzling.

I lamented in an earlier post that we don't get nearly enough exposition on the high command of the Lannisters (as opposed to the Starks), but what do you know, here we get dialogue from Lord Lefford, one of Tywin's bannermen I suppose. There's not much about him, though. He's a "sour man" and he is charge of stores and supplies. Definitely not in the same league as the Greatjon, or Roose Bolton. Ser Kevan is present too, and we are told that he seldom has a thought Lord Tywin didn't have first. With one sentence, Martin explains the relationship between the two senior Lannister brothers. There is some back and forth about the clansmen Tyrion brought down from the Mountains of the Moon, and Tyrion is told he will be put in the vanguard of the army.

I remember I had to check a dictionary to know what exactly a "vanguard" was. How much I have learned since then. This book *really* made me delve into medieval military history with a zeal I didn't know I possessed. I guess if you don't know your vanguard from your vambraces you might find parts of the writing in *A Game of Thrones* confusing. Throughout the dialogue, Tywin makes Tyrion agree to be in the vanguard. Not as a leader, but serving Ser Gregor Clegane, the Mountain that Rides, a character we've so far been told a little about, but not too much. However, we don't learn much more about him—we just get a glimpse—in this chapter. Instead, two other important characters are introduced in this chapter, Shae and Podrick Payne.

Lord Tywin dismisses Tyrion by an incline of the head— much as he'd dismiss any servant. He is clearly not all that affectionate about his youngest son. This cold detachment from his own son only serves to—in my opinion at least—make Tywin one of the few clear villains in the story. Although, as with many other characters in this saga, one can point to his history to make some excuse for their behavior—unlike typical fantasy yarns, Martin's characters do have a cause-and-effect built into them; in Tywin's case, he both had a weak father and the bad luck to become the dad of a deformed and defiant miscreant.

Leaving his father, Tyrion enters the Lannister camp, and it's not a *small* army we have here—the camp is spread *"for miles between the river and the kingsroad.*" That's a lot of army!

George really makes the camp come alive through Tyrion's eyes as he passes cook fires, pavilions, hears bawdy songs and sees naked camp followers run about. I have to admit, after having started *The Malazan Book of the Fallen* this year, Erikson trumps Martin when it comes to the grit and grime of army stuff, but then again I can't really relate to his characters while I am following Tyrion with all my literary heart. If you know what I mean.

Arriving at his own tent, we are introduced first to his new squire Podrick Payne, a distant cousin to the scary executioner Ser Ilyn Payne, and from the few glimpses here he is quickly established as something of a stumbling sidekick, a bit of comedic relief, but maybe there's something more sinister about him as well? Who knows? Immediately after, we are introduced to Shae, a whore Bronn has found at Tyrion's request. It's a funny scene.

"My mother named me Shae. Men call me ... often."

That certainly gets a chuckle out of me each and every time I read it. I believe Shae's response here is also a favorite in ye olde "What's your favorite quote?" threads on various forums.

Tyrion takes Shae into the tent and to his surprise, she doesn't act repulsed by him. Instead, she plays her part so well, that for the reader it is kind of a surprise too. Tyrion suspects she is feigning interest and thus being a good actress, but he tells himself she's so good at it he doesn't care.

I sympathize with Tyrion. Poor fellow. Interestingly, he remembers the last time he'd had a whore—which was "before he had set out for Winterfell in company with his brother and King Robert." The writers of HBO's *Game of Thrones* seem to have caught this little nugget, as they are said to have filmed a scene where Tyrion is with a whore in King's Landing before leaving for the north. And Robert too? *That* will add something on screen!

After the happy-time, we find Tyrion whistling. A sign that he's in a happy moment, I guess. I guess, because my mother tells me that when she hears me whistle she knows I'm in a good mood.

Later that night he slips out of his tent to find Bronn seated cross-legged outside, sharpening his sword. Tyrion notes that Bronn doesn't sleep nearly as much as other men. Just an offhand remark, or is there something more to Bronn? He was also referred to as a panther in an earlier scene in the novel. They entertain me for a while with their banner, the dialogue setting up the battle to come at dawn.

Tyrion returns to his tent and what do you know; Shae is ready to tackle him one more time. To maximize the effect of rude awakening, the sentence where he falls asleep smiling doesn't really end ... before he wakes to the blare of trumpets. Simple method. Great stuff.

The rest of this fairly long chapter tells the tale of the battle. Robb Stark and his host have marched through the night and are now readying themselves for battle. We follow Tyrion as he is dressed for battle, and I admit I find it a little hard to believe that the dwarf is capable the way he proves to be. But I let it slide because you know, it's Tyrion. And *maybe* there's something in his blood we don't know yet that enhances his prowess. Not a Potion of Heroism +3 or anything like that. I'm thinking more something like ... fire.

The whole sequence from the army waking up until the last word of the chapter is one rollercoaster ride of a read. Riveting, exciting, fast-paced, certainly one of the more exhilarating set pieces of *A Game of Thrones*. Yet, when thinking of the story, this battle seldom comes to mind. I do not have a proper explanation for it—maybe it's because Martin's characters are so great I rather think of *them* instead of great sequences. I am not sure about this. Try to blank your mind for five seconds, then name the five first things you think of when you hear the title *A Game of Thrones*. I see ... Littlefinger, Ned Stark cleaning *Ice*, Arya, Tyrion waddling, and Bran being shoved out a tower window. Okay there was a sequence there. Maybe tomorrow five other things will come to mind. So mysterious, the brain... I wonder why I "saw" Petyr Baelish first?

During the tension to follow, we get to see Lord Tywin in full battle regalia, and he's impressive. We get to see Ser Gregor Clegane doing his butcher's work. Bronn has a few observations about battle that ring true. The mountain clans following Tyrion chant *halfman! halfman!* which is pretty cool. Bronn observes that the vanguard under Ser Gregor's command—including Tyrion—is "crow's food"; war horns blow and, though I know many disagree, I love how Martin simply puts in a *Haroooooooooooooooooooooooooooo* for effect. I buy it. I can "hear" it happen.

The battle is properly medieval, with arrow volleys hissing above the fighting men, followed by the clash of swords. Lovely. In a battle within the battle, Tyrion faces off against northerners, a spear slamming into his shield and for a moment I'm like "how does Tyrion remain standing?" then I choose to forget, frantically reading sentence by sentence, it's every bit as exciting the tenth time; there's a fun bit where Tyrion yields to a knight, but then the situation is reversed, the knight yields and Tyrion still thinks the knight is telling *him* to yield; there is mud and spears and banners flapping, ravens and pikes, murderous fire and in the end, "the remnants of the Stark lines shattered like glass beneath the hammer of their (the Lannisters) charge." Conn son of Coratt, one of the mountain clansmen, loses his life in the battle, while Shagga barely survives. Half the clansmen are dead, in fact. Ouch.

The denouement of the chapter is Tyrion returning to talk to his dad, and as in a previous chapter, there's the shape of a circular plot—it began with Lord Tywin eating, and it ends with Tyrion meeting him again, seated by the river and sipping wine. Lord Tywin tacitly admits that he had planned for the vanguard to be butchered, hoping the clansmen would break against the northerners, to lure them to plunge into the main army of the Lannisters and thereby allow Tywin to gain a decisive victory. In other words, this terrible man so many look up to put his own son where the peril was gravest, and keeps his cool when confronted with the truth by said son. Is it really possible to be so tough-as-nails fucked up? Excuse the language.

Tywin is quite confident of his own command skills, and less sure about Robb Stark's—until Ser Addam Marbrand appears to tell him that the Stark boy has done some strategic thinking himself: he's riding hard for Riverrun. I am assuming here that the northerners whom Tyrion fought were sent down to stall Tywin, and thus they succeeded though they lost the battle.

What I noticed this time at the end of this chapter is Tyrion's gleeful thoughts upon hearing the news of Robb's unexpected move. He would have laughed to spite his father, the first telltale sign of Tyrion's feelings for his father gaining a darker, more spiteful and resentful attitude. I'll be looking for more of those, as I felt that the culmination of their relationship came a bit out of the blue to me. Maybe I was wrong.

A reader pointed out that Martin's focus on food in the series isn't unique to him, and I agree that other authors probably make a habit of over-describing food in their stories; my point was rather that Martin maybe, perhaps subconsciously, is either describing food so lovingly because, well, he loves food, or he has some resources or expertise on the subject. Another reader said that reading the blog eased the wait for *A Dance with Dragons*. Mission accomplished, both ways.

A Wood For Whispering In

Twist my nipples sideways! Here we are, at chapter 64, we're back with Catelyn, and before we've caught our breath reading about Tyrion in the midst of the carnage of the battlefield, we're thrown right into another battle—but written and described in a whole different way. As the chapters are getting more intense with more physical action, Martin still manages to retain that character-specific inner monologue and keep the story grounded in the character's point of view, instead of dishing out a huge battle full of spectacle for spectacle's sake. Admirable. Let's enjoy a different view on a battle. One would think that putting two battles in a row would kind of be bad editing (considering we've been reading for near seven hundred pages without that many large scale battles except for a few references to battles elsewhere, such as Oxcross), but it works because Martin tells the tale from two vastly different points of view—Tyrion's and Catelyn's. Throughout reading this chapter again it strikes me how different the two 'battle chapters' are in *everything* save the fact that lots of people chug it out with pointy things. Tyrion was thrown headlong into battle, *Braveheart*-style (well, almost ...), people fighting and dying around him, whereas Catelyn is protected by thirty soldiers led by underused northern character Hallis Mollen, remaining silent and hidden within the forest, and we are left without the sense of seeing the battle. Instead, we get the build-up, and from then on we have to rely on Catelyn's hearing to gauge the battle at hand. A very interesting and dare I say refreshing take on ye mediæval battle. At the end of the battle, a vital plot point is introduced perhaps unexpectedly. But I am getting ahead of myself.

Because I've been playing the *A Game of Thrones Collectible Card Game* since it was first published in I believe it was 2002, I've thought of the forest in which Catelyn finds herself at the beginning of this chapter as "*the* Whispering Wood", as in a forest having that particular geographical name. But now that I am re-reading it seems to me that this isn't a forest called the Whispering Wood—they just called the *card* "The Whispering Wood." The very first sentence of the chapter is indeed, "*the wood was full of whispers*"—the nervous whispers of the northerner soldiers lying in wait, preparing to ambush Ser Jaime Lannister's host which they hope is approaching. The first paragraph of the chapter is very evocative, and will make a great scene in HBO's series I am sure, what with the dark, ominous trees, rain dripping, nervous horses, armored soldiers and so on.

We learn that Catelyn and her son Robb had something of a dispute about just how many men Catelyn needed to protect her; Robb wanted fifty, Catelyn ten, and they ended up with thirty protectors. A little detail that shows the love between the mother and the son, both ways. A nice touchy touching touch.

In the second paragraph we get an interesting line when viewed in the context of the whole story: *"No one was safe. No life was certain."* Pretty much sums up what people new to the series feel about it. Unexpected deaths, don't get too attached to this or that character 'cause you never know. Having mulled over this series for too long a time, I am not longer sure it really does apply. I mean, sure, some twists and turns came completely out of the blue for me, but I do sense that certain characters *are* in fact protected from the rule of "any character may die." I guess I'll leave it at that, for the time being.

~ *interlude* ~

Ah, back from the French Riviera. I've seen famous cities such as Cannes, Nice, and Montecarlo in Monaco. It was all good. Whereas the Norwegian autumn is cold and rainy, southern France was still clinging to summer, and with a villa with a swimming pool I had a great time with my family. And to be honest, it was refreshing—*good*—to be offline for a week. I almost didn't think of the wait for dragons at all.

Until I by happenstance came upon Bernard Cornwell's novel *Azincourt* (*Agincourt* in the US). A great read, but it brought my mind back to Westeros and made me curious what was happening in Georgeland while I was offline. As it turned out, not much.

Not that I was surprised. If you like *A Game of Thrones* and haven't checked out *Azincourt*, you are missing out on a story that runs quite close to the style, mood and pacing of Mr. Martin. Heck, there's even a character named Melisande. Cornwall's novel is not overly long, nor does it have a multitude of plot strands and POV characters, but somehow it still is the closest thing I have read since getting hooked on Westeros (I've tried other medieval historical novels before, but they didn't have that crisp pacing). Oh, and it has an ending.

I have now returned to *A Game of Thrones* and shall endeavor to finish blogging my thoughts about the events herein, specifically Catelyn's chapter. After all, *A Game of Thrones* is what this blog is *really* about—though I have some plans for this blog once I have finished the first novel of ice and fire. Expansionist plans, so to speak. Anyway. Catelyn Stark. Robb Stark. The Whispering Wood. Battle. Here we go.

So, the Starks have prepared to ambush Ser Jaime Lannister and his host, hiding away in the woods. In the previous chapter we saw that Robb had done something strategically sound by sending only half his troops (was it half? I've forgotten) down to face Lord Tywin, saving the rest for Tywin's son Ser Jaime.

As it turns out, the plan to ambush Ser Jaime hinges on a single remark made by Ser Brynden Tully, Catelyn's uncle who came with Cat down from the Eyrie. It is through Brynden's words that we glimpse some information on Ser Jaime the general: *"The Kingslayer is restless and quick to anger,"* and later Brynden adds that Ser Jaime lacks patience. So far, we as the readers are assured that Brynden is right, because we have seen Ser Jaime be restless, quick to anger, and impatient, specifically in that short sequence where he pushed Bran out the window. Catelyn silently prays to the gods for Robb, and it is a heart-wrenching little bit of inner monologue there once you've read the whole series before; she prays for Robb to grow taller, to grow older ... Yeah, it's sad. But she also prays that he will become a father, and *that* door hasn't closed yet, has it?

Before the plot moves along, we are also told a little bit about the size of Ser Jaime's host, and small it ain't—12,000 footmen and between 2,00 and 3,000 cavalry; larger than the host England brought across the channel to France before the siege of Harfleur (according to *Azincourt*). Apparently, Ser Jaime is besieging Riverrun, but won't have the patience to hold the siege, making it easier for Robb to lure him away from the siege to battle. A simple ruse, but it works nicely in the plot, perhaps a little bit jarring how easy the Starks solve the problem, but it doesn't really matter—the military strategies, tactics and logistics have to bow before the power of characterization and not having the story get bogged down in details that would be distracting. Another bannerman of House Stark gets a short introduction, Lord Jason Mallister. Love that character name.

Once we're properly set up with information, the plot begins to move with the characters: *Catelyn watched her son mount up.* Robb Stark rides off to show himself to his men, wanting to do it the same way as his father Lord Eddard.

Cat is at once proud and fearful, and Martin displays those conflicting emotions with quick, effective strokes throughout the chapter. We get a laundry list of characters who follow and protect Robb, some major and many minor—Torrhen and Eddard Karstark, Patrek Mallister, Smalljon Umber, Daryn Hornwood, Theon Greyjoy, five Freys, Ser Wendel Manderly, Robin Flint, and the woman Dacey Mormont. There is a reason for Martin throwing out those names, as we'll see at the end of the chapter.

Suddenly, Catelyn is alone in the woods. Well, alone with thirty guards. You know what I mean. She *feels* alone, and then we get another echo of Tolkien—

They are coming, Catelyn thought.

Can't help but hear Ian McKellen as Gandalf's voice here and it annoys me! *They are coming.* Cause I never imagined Catelyn having a gruff old manly voice. More of an ethereal, edgy and slightly sexy female voice.

What follows is really cool. I believe I mentioned it in the previous post. The contrast. In the previous chapter we had Tyrion smack right in the middle of bloody battle—in this chapter we only *hear* the battle, as Catelyn is safely hidden in the woods, away from the actual fighting. Tyrion fought at dawn, in the light of the morning sun; Catelyn sits still on her horse, in the cold dark night. Lovely contrast, if I were HBO I would have these two battles run simultaneously, cutting between them, though I realize it would be confusing for the viewer with scenes of day and night alternating. But still. Coolness would be mostly assured. Deftly, Martin takes us through the stages of the battle in quick succession, and only by Catelyn's senses. It's so damn well done.

Catelyn *hears* screaming—she does not *see*. Simple and elegant. There's some use of parentheses here which I personally dislike (for some reason it takes me out of the story; and no, you don't need to remind me I use them a lot on this blog). It's like, you know, the author steps forward and winks at you. Anyway, Catelyn hears the clash of swords, cracking lances and all the sounds of battle, but the most interesting sound is that of a wolf—and Catelyn becomes unsure whether she hears one wolf, or several. Is Arya's Nymeria around helping out with some good old-fashioned ripping-throats-out?

When the battle is done, Robb comes back to Catelyn on a different horse. Blunt symbolism of Robb having changed as a character? I think so; having led a battle successfully, he returns not as Robb Stark, the untested son of Lord Eddard, but as Robb Stark, the Heir of Winterfell and worthy. Interestingly, he brings Ser Jaime Lannister with him, as a prisoner. That one I remember came as a shock to me upon my first read. I mean, here we had Ser Jaime, portrayed as one of the baddest asses in the series, and they actually managed to capture him? This early in the story?

With hindsight, the capture is of course but the beginning of the humiliation—and transformation—of Ser Jaime's character. And he is barely brought before Lady Catelyn before he comes with a smart-ass remark that has me laughing.

Funny how Ser Jaime utters his lines with the same droll wit as we've heard (read) from Tyrion. Martin even manages to give relatives similar traits yet still making them distinct. It is nothing but awesome. And the Lannister boys are the awesomest.

Theon Greyjoy wants to see Ser Jaime's head roll, another subtle hint that Theon might just be a tad crazy in the coconut. The bloodlust reminds me of the way he kicked Gared's head after the execution in Bran's first chapter. Best we keep an eye on that Greyjoy boy ...

A tender moment occurs when Robb and Catelyn learn that Lord Rickard Karstark has lost both his sons in the battle to Ser Jaime's sword. Honestly, I feel the scene would be stronger if the characters killed were a tad more familiar to us (say, the Greatjon's son) but then again even these minor characters' deaths will impact the plot later on. This was why Martin offered us a lot of names when Robb rode off—to reinforce this scene where some of them didn't survive the battle (the Hornwood guy also took a permanent time out).

Now to be honest I love this chapter but would have loved it even more if the end had felt less rushed; notice how abrupt the chapter ends, and how cool wouldn't it be with an extended conversation with Ser Jaime; or to go more into the grief of Lord Rickard. Oh well, there's still enough pages left in the series. At least Theon is pleased with the battle, though Catelyn ends off the chapter with reminding him that while they have won a battle, they haven't won the war. I don't know. It's a weak ending compared to many other endings in the series. And so I guess *this* is a weak ending to this post.

See you *soon* with Daenerys Targaryen.

BLOOD SUGAR SEX MAGIK

Red Hot Chili Peppers was never my favorite band, though I understand why many people like them and perhaps especially their classic *"Blood Sugar Sex Magik"* album (or is the album too recent to be called a classic?) Reading this chapter I was reminded of that album simply because it involves Mirri Maz Duur's blood magic. There isn't much about her sugar sex in this chapter though, but what the hell. It's a catchy title. Not a fitting title for a chapter of *A Game of Thrones*, of course, but I've never tried to give these chapters "serious" titles that I honestly believe would be awesome. "Daenerys" is a good enough chapter heading for me. If I *had* to give the chapter a title for future editions of the novel, maybe I'd go with *"The Price of Blood Magic,"* I don't know. It matters not.

Let's see what's going on across the Narrow Sea and in the eastern setting of the novel, the setting that oft reminds me of Robert E. Howard's world of Hyperborea.

Going from not one but two chapters brimming with battles and my favorite Lannister boys back to Daenerys and her Dothraki is a bit of a downer; I do like the character and her story, but it's not as interesting to me personally. I am fonder of the European medieval style than the more oriental (?) style, though Dany's chapters in the later novels become much more interesting. But right here and now, I have returned for the tenth time to a chapter I didn't really grasp the first time around. What was really happening? What was the deal with Mirri Maz Duur and her blood magic stuff? The tenth read should be pretty much an enlightened read so let's see if I can get things straight here.

The above two paragraphs I wrote before actually delving into the chapter—I saved those two paragraphs until I actually found time to read the chapter properly (that is, with a little coffee and my son watching a Disney movie at my side) and lo! and behold! I was really sucked into the chapter and liked it well enough; it works just fine even after those two delicious battle chapters. It feels almost like a denouement done with an entirely different storyline. Martin is taking down the pace, yet the content is pretty dramatic with Daenerys seeming to lose all the control she has gained so far in the story.

Once again, George R.R. Martin is masterful at establishing mood and atmosphere. Throughout the chapter, Martin continually chooses words that relate to heat. Where the previous chapter was cold and dark, this chapter is searing with heat and stinking with rot. So different in style that as a reader, I am immediately torn away from Catelyn's worries and thrust into Daenerys's. The contrast between the two chapters is great, yet somehow, at least now on the tenth re-read, it feels so ... seamless. I guess the switching between Westeros and the east was more jarring the first time around. *A Game of Thrones* is to fantasy what a decent prog rock band or technically competent metal band is to pop music.

The chapter begins ominously with flies buzzing around Khal Drogo as he rides his stallion. Flies buzzing kind of sets off the alarm immediately—the Khal is slowly wasting away, foreshadowing his demise. Martin does not give the glorious Khal a moment of dignity. There is no heroic or honorable, clean death in *his* world; Khal's wounds are festering, he squishes big, fat, purple flies (*bloodflies*, to be more specific) with his fists, it's gross and disturbing in a visceral way. We learn that Khal Drogo has ripped off the bandages Mirri Maz Duur had applied to him, 'cause he doesn't trust her and believes her to be a *maegi*, the word itself close to "mage" and "magician." The cool thing is how Martin has established this relatively magic-free secondary world, so that I for one thought Khal Drogo and his men were merely being superstitious about her: maybe they had heard stories from an earlier age when magic *did* exist or myths and legends that they base their fears for *maegi* on. No, wait: the cool thing is that Martin in this chapter twists it around—Mirri does kind of admit (coming to that in a bit) that she does indeed know the art of magic. I wonder what Khal Drogo would think of the Elves of Rivendell! It would probably be an awkward encounter.

Martin goes on to describe how Drogo deteriorates before Daenerys's eyes, rides half slumped in the saddle, and then he falls off his mount. I had forgotten why this was such a big deal but upon re-reading I remembered that falling off your horse is the same as falling from grace in the Dothraki culture. In other words, he is no longer worthy to be a khal. Say one thing about the Dothraki; they are set in their ways. (Did I sound like Joe Abercrombie now? Where did that come from?) Interestingly, as he lies prone on the ground, Khal Drogo utters *"my horse"*; it reinforces the earlier introduced notion that a Dothraki and his horse are very close, and maybe that he loves his horse more than Daenerys. Personally, I'd probably go for Dany, but only if she'd do the dishes. Oh!

Once down, his bloodriders begin to show their true colors. Sometimes when reading the earlier Daenerys chapters I had a feeling that these Dothraki deferred too easily to Daenerys—even though she was entitled to her power through her marriage with the Khal—but once Drogo drops off his horse, I always feel kind of in agreement with them when they begin to protest and rebel against Daenerys. Like, "you should have seen *that* coming, Silver Lady. Aha!" Know what I mean? Martin doesn't make it easy for her (although I've read claims on the Interwebz that everything falls into her lap); he hasn't forgotten his own established rule, that the Dothraki have little respect for women or for dismounted Khals, and thus their sudden hostility towards Daenerys is all the more believable. It is Qotho who is the most obstinate here, the others kind of struggle with their loyalty but I sense their wish to be as condemning towards her as Qotho is.

Daenerys orders Drogo's tent set up, and the Khal is carried inside, away from the eyes of the host, in an effort to hide the fact that he's fallen off his horse. She makes up an excuse for stopping—that she needs rest because of the baby in her belly—bidding the bloodriders to spread that piece of information. The bloodriders grudgingly do this. When she asks them to fetch Mirri Maz Duur, the bloodriders become even more agitated and one can sense how their anger *flares*, another way of adding the aforementioned heat to the chapter. Like the Khal, they put no trust in Mirri, but Daenerys sees no other way—when she removes the bandages and stuff it is obvious—as Ser Jorah confirms—that the Khal is as good as dead, his wounds black and corrupted.

Remember the poor girl who got gang-raped on a pile of corpses? Apparently she has a name—Eroeh—even on my tenth re-read there are new things to discover. I had completely forgotten she had a name and that she appeared in more than *that* gruesome chapter. She's better off in this chapter. Daenerys slaps her, which I find a bit uncharacteristic of Dany, but then again she's really stressed out about the Khal dying. Everything will collapse, so I kind of understand how she in anger slaps Eroeh when she says Drogo will die. When another handmaiden utters practically the same, Daenerys begins to cry.

Before moving on to the crux of the chapter, I mentioned how this chapter is "searing." A few examples might clarify:

> The sun was high and pitiless ... Heat shimmered ... A thin finger of sweat trickled slowly ... Poppy wine ... Pepper beer ... Brown and dry ... His breath rattled ... The heat of the afternoon sun ... Stifling ... Brazier ... He's so hot... [LOL—that comes out weird when out of context] ... He was a fire in human skin ... Fierce heat ... Skin reddened ... An oath so foul it seared the air ... Dark red ...

All these evocative word choices help give the chapter that quality of searing heat, scorched is perhaps a better word. Martin truly engages the senses with this chapter. I'm sweating as I read about it, guess I hope the next chapter is on the Wall where it's more than a tad colder.

What happens next is what still has me confused after reading it for the tenth time. So Mirri Maz Duur arrives, and Daenerys begs her to save Khal Drogo's life. First Mirri gets a smack in the face, and Qotho suggest the most terrible things to do to Mirri, but Daenerys doesn't want to hear it, angering Qotho further and thus leading up to him going ballistic a little later. He also flat out states that once Drogo is dead, Daenerys is worthless and even suggests to put her on a pile for everyone to rape. Pretty harsh if you ask me. Qotho would certainly benefit from an anger management program of some sort.

And now it gets confusing.

Mirri Maz Duur states that Drogo is *"beyond a healer's skills."* She also states that there is great healing magic in fire. I get it so far. She is basically saying that Drogo shouldn't have taken off her poultices (he took them off 'cause they "burned"), because now his wounds have festered to a point where her healing arts have become useless.

Then Mirri goes on to say *"There is a spell."* Now I am a little confused. There are *spells* in this setting? I mean, did she wake up in the morning, take an hour to memorize a few spells from her spell book? Or should I take the word "spell" as something less Dungeons & Dragons-fantasy type of spell and more of a miracle-type-thing?

She tells us that she learned "the way" in Asshai. Does she mean that particular spell, or the way of casting spells? I am confused—but that little bit about Asshai is tantalizing—so you can learn spells down there (incidentally, "hai" in Norwegian means "shark" and whenever I read Asshai I can't help but think *ass-shark*).

Then, Mirri basically admits that she is a maegi:

"Am I?" Mirri Maz Duur smiled. "Only a maegi can save your rider now, Silver Lady."

So what she's saying is that maegi (which I kind of read as "female mage") have powers to stop death from occurring (or postponing it) and/or have powers to heal mortal wounds (which would be healing magic I guess). Is this the same sort of necromancy practiced by Qyburn later in the series? Or is this more akin to Melisandre's arts?

Mirri now continues by warning Daenerys that there is a price. A ttterrriiblle price. The cost of the spell is a death. What confuses me here is the how and why of this price. Does she draw another being's life energy / soul or something like that (in this case, it would be similar to Melisandre's doings)? And why isn't it Dany's life that must be paid? Because she's the one requesting the spell? Or just because it would kind of stop the story dead? Literally speaking. Or am I just putting too much thought into the "mechanics" of magic as used by Mirri Maz Duur and should rather concentrate on important stuff in life such as American football?

The one thing bothering me with this chapter is that Daenerys doesn't ask Mirri "then *whose* life will you take?" when Mirri tells her it isn't Dany's life. Wouldn't that be the most natural follow-up question in the history of the Targaryen dynasty? (Of course it would ruin the outcome of the story's development).

Mirri is certainly being enigmatic in this chapter.

The Khal's horse is brought forth; Mirri cuts its throat, and lets the blood flow into the bath they've put Drogo in. Then she tells everyone to leave the tent, including Dany, because there will be terrible things. Outside, Dany watches shadows within the tent, the dancing of the dead (?); what the hell is going on in there? And should I read those shadows on the tent wall as kind of similar to the shadows sent by Melisandre?

"This is bloodmagic," Mirri states, and the way she tells the horse's strength to go into Khal's body I have this sense of soul-shifting going on. I want to know more about bloodmagic!

But most of all I wonder—is Mirri really trying to use magic to save Drogo's life, or is she killing him as vengeance for her treatment and the slaughter of her people?

Outside, Qotho finally snaps and we get a rushed, exciting fight, with limbs chopped off and ears cut half off, and in the commotion nobody notices Daenerys goes into labor. Cohollo, another bloodrider, tries to slit her throat; another throws rocks at her; it seems that Dany's rule is over. Fortunately, some of the bloodriders find themselves loyal to her, and she is carried into the tent where Mirri is still busy with her spell. However, Dany *really* doesn't want to go in there after Mirri's warning. And so the chapter ends.

From the number of questions I've put forth, I guess I am indeed more than a little confused about Mirri Maz Duur. There isn't a clear outcome—which bloodriders died here and which were merely wounded? Why didn't anyone throw a rock at Ser Jorah when he lifted Daenerys up to bring her to the tent? Now I admit it's been a good while since last I read *A Game of Thrones* and maybe some or all of my questions are resolved in the next Dany chapter.

While fans mostly assume that the *ice* and *fire* in the saga's title refers to Jon and Daenerys, one could also draw a connection to the plotline beyond the North (cold lands of ice) and the plotline in the east (hot lands of dust), leaving out the plotline that I believe is the most popular, the story in the middle of the conflict, the War of the Five Kings.

But next up is Arya, and I think I remember how that chapter ends.

A Bitter Pigeon To Swallow

A mini-wave in celebration of this blog. This is the 100th post. One hundred posts of waiting for dragons. Though it seems that George R.R. Martin has all but confirmed that only five chapters remain before *A Dance with Dragons* is complete. Could it be? Could he actually finish the thing before I finish my *A Game of Thrones tenth Anniversary Re-read*? Including this Arya chapter, I have eight chapters left to blog. And I don't have the whole day to write. Honestly, I thought I'd be blogging well into *A Feast for Crows* before I saw the next volume of the saga published. Despite what some people may think of me, I am as joyous as the most zealous fan boy over this news; publication may be within half a year's reach, and I will gladly enjoy ripping into the novel. George's miserable PR and hilariously *sad* blog posts are one thing, going back into the world of Westeros is another.

I know when *A Feast for Crows* was published that I, and probably others, found it strange that Arya had only three or so chapters in it. But now that I am thoroughly re-reading *A Game of Thrones* I notice that this is the fifth and final Arya chapter. So she was never very prominent in the first novel either; though I suspect she has more in *A Clash of Kings*. Or does it just feel that way? Her story stretches across the time span of the novels, maybe it just *feels* like such a long story for her. I know I've talked about this earlier, so I'll leave it at that. Anyway. Arya's final chapter. Another character's final moments.

The chapter opens with Arya in King's Landing, chasing down a pigeon. With a few brief descriptions, the author establishes just how hungry and desperate Arya's become since she fled the Red Keep. When she grabs the pigeon by the neck, she efficiently twists the bird's neck until it snaps. A far cry from the court where she was served food—where do her survival skills come from, one might wonder. I'd assume she's had roughly the same upbringing as her posh sister Sansa. Some of it comes from Syrio Forel's training. Arya hunting pigeons in the streets is reminiscent of her chasing cats in the Red Keep. Some of it may be that "wild spirit" she may just have inherited from her aunt Lyanna Stark. Some of it may come from soaking in the rough-and-ready atmosphere at Winterfell and some of it from her especially close relationship with her foster brother Jon Snow. And, of course, the story demands it.

Arya's story is unusual in the fantasy genre, and despite her young age and her somewhat improbable survival skills, I find myself rooting for the character and enjoying following her storyline. It is one of the better ones, in my opinion, but then again I have always had a weak spot for characters travelling through a secondary world, ever since I as a youth by accident discovered *The Two Towers* and read about the travels of Aragorn, Gimli, and Legolas (yes, I know, but I found the copy at a library that for some reason did not have *The Fellowship of the Ring*. I missed a lot of walking and talking, but I figured things out eventually).

When Arya encounters a man pushing a load of tarts, she "hears herself" ask for one. Interesting choice of words, instead of "Arya begged for a tart"; the author tells us that she can't really believe it's *her* begging for food. She offers to trade her recently captured pigeon for a tart, but the man dismisses her— "*The Others take your pigeon*", he says. So even here, far south in Westeros, a common street vendor uses the Others' name as a curse. Or is this subtle foreshadowing of a later scene in which an Other attacks a pigeon? It is not a scene I'd deem necessary to the drama. Ha. Ha. Briefly, Arya considers snatching a tart and make a run for it, but there are members of the city guard nearby, and she can only watch as the tarts disappear down the street.

We learn that there are many rumors out on the streets, which adds to the realistic feel of King's Landing as a setting. It is more credible that Arya hears different stories about the king and her lord father than that she hears the exact truth. The one thing all stories agree on is that the king is dead, and that the bells in the seven towers of the Great Sept of Baelor tolled for a day and a night. (If I had a house nearby the sept I'd be pretty angry with the constant noise; it's hard enough living near a church tolling the bells for a minute every Sunday, but this is admittedly a digression).

We learn that Arya wants to go home, but she's caught within the city walls, hanging out for the most part in Flea Bottom, an area that we get a closer look at than most districts of King's Landing. It's a fascinating, vibrant, living setting George has created in King's Landing—one of my favorite locations in the series. I like how the number seven continually repeats in the city's design (itself based on the seven aspects of the god venerated in the southern portions of Westeros)—seven towers of the sept, and seven city gates, which Arya visits in turn to check out if she can slip out one of them.

There's quite a lot of description of Flea Bottom, actually. Martin avoids making it an exposition, instead showing us through the people living there the character of the district itself:

"Some of them stared at her boots or her cloak, and she knew what they were thinking. With others she could almost feel their eyes crawling under her leathers .... "

A place where the less savory mingle, in other words. Thieves, thugs, rapists, the scum of King's Landing. Not the best place to be for a little girl. Arya descends down a hill towards Flea Bottom, having decided to check out the riverfront. Maybe she can escape by sea, stow away on a ship. Interestingly, this does happen—but much later in the unfolding tale of Arya Stark. Funny though how she thinks of it here. Down on the wharfs, to Arya's surprise, she spies the *Wind Witch*, the very ship her father had planned to take his children home with. Surprised that it is still in King's Landing, and tears coming to her eyes as she sees men in the garb of her family's colors, she immediately becomes overjoyous—and then Syrio Forel's training kicks in, and she decides to *see*—and realizes that these men are strangers, not Stark men. An elaborate hoax, then.

One of the guards asks her what she's doing here, revealing that he thinks Arya is a boy—and she decides to act like a street urchin, pretending to want to sell the pigeon she'd caught. Before, we've read about Arya being boyish, but this I believe (correct me if I'm wrong) is the first instance where she's mistaken for a boy, and it is an important element to her story arc. Thus she manages to get away from the trap (but she loses her pigeon—probably stolen), and returns into the stinking Flea Bottom, when she hears bells chime.

WAITING FOR DRAGONS

Arya stops to listen near a brothel, where a whore and a customer spell out for us that these are not mourning bells—but bells to summon people. Before we know it, Arya overhears that "they" are bringing the Hand of the King to the sept where he is to be executed. The way Martin understates it is absolutely perfect—Arya hears it, but there is no immediate psychological reaction. Instead, she trips in a deep rut, falling and scraping herself bloody. People begin streaming towards the sept as the bells continue to clang, and Arya joins them.

Oh, to read this chapter for the first time again! It is such a bitter chapter, and the first proper taste of just how much pain the author inflicts upon some of the main characters. Arya is alone, hungry, desperate, trapped in the city's bad district, everything is already grim, and then we get the summoning to the sept just to make matters even bleaker. Remembering my first read, I *still* thought Lord Eddard Stark would somehow come out of it a hero—or savior—and that maybe scrawny, quick Arya would be the character to make the difference and somehow—*somehow*—save the noble lord, her father. Squirming through the masses, overhearing people talking about what's happening, Arya comes upon the marble plinth upon which stands the great statue of King Baelor the Blessed, in the middle of the plaza before the Great Sept I guess. She climbs up on the plinth, settling between the Targaryen king's feet. Can't say I remember that little detail—her seating herself there—in plain sight of, well, everybody. From here, she sees Lord Eddard Stark, her father.

Her father speaks to the crowd, confessing treason against King Robert Baratheon. So extremely unlike Lord Eddard Stark, yet upon reading it the first time, I thought, *"Good, he's finally*

303

seen sense. Now, confess and live out your life on the Wall, where you'll be with Jon. That will be a cool story, I'm sure." Or something like that.

Then someone in the crowd throws a stone and hits Lord Eddard.

I *hate* that stone. It's so unfair. Here we have the most honorable man in the Seven Kingdoms, forced to confess a crime he did not commit, while the true culprit is standing close by, and we've just read about just how shitty Arya's life has become, and then some moron hits Ned with a rock. I love to hate this stuff.

Held up by two gold cloaks, Arya sees that her father is as weak as he can be. Okay, so I have read this book *ten* times—and yet I was surprised that Lord Eddard "confessed" his crimes here on the steps of the Great Sept of Baelor. Have I just phased this out? I honestly can't remember he did that. I thought he was stubborn until the end, but there you go, he did in the end—for the love of his children I assume—take the blame for the death of King Robert, his old friend.

Arya prays the gods will save her father. The High Septon, having heard Eddard's confession, turns to Joffrey Baratheon, now the king of the realm, and asks what is to be done with the traitor. And I just *knew* the first time around that Ned would take the black and the story would continue up at the Wall for him, but George surprised me with just how unbelievably nasty Joffrey is (so far in *A Game of Thrones* we've been given hints as to Joffrey's nature, but this is the first *wow!* moment in my case):

"My mother bids me let Lord Eddard take the black, and Lady Sansa has begged mercy for her father."

He looked straight at Sansa then, and smiled, and for a moment Arya thought that the gods had heard her prayer, until Joffrey turned back to the crowd and said,

"But they have the soft hearts of women. So long as I am your king, treason shall never go unpunished. Ser Ilyn, bring me his head!"

A true monster, then. I am looking forward to see how the actor portraying Joffrey in HBO's *Game of Thrones* will play the character. To have that kind of power at such a young age; to be so brutal, so completely bereft of empathy and sympathy—Joffrey Baratheon is the true villain of this novel, no doubts. Things get confusing as Arya ends up in the crowd, with people jostling everywhere, and she catches only glimpses of what happens. We don't actually read Arya seeing her father die, and I wonder why. Did the author just not want to deal with the traumatic sight? Did he not want us, the readers, to be entirely certain of the deed? The whole of King's Landing is watching the execution—there can be no doubt that Eddard is beheaded there on the steps of the Great Sept; yet Martin chooses to not let us see. Arya tries desperately to fight her way through the masses, but it proves impossible. The last thing she sees is Ser Ilyn Payne lift the greatsword—*Ice*, her father's greatsword, the heirloom of House Stark just to rub more salt in them wounds—and then Yoren, one of the brothers of the Night's Watch, grabs her and takes her away.

First time reading it I had forgotten who Yoren was, but it is of course established already in other chapters that the Night's Watch is in King's Landing, and now the encounter flows smoothly. Calling her a *boy*, Yoren seems to want to protect Arya, but the first time reading this I felt really glum. How much tragedy could Martin heap on Arya? This chapter is one downhill ride, that's for sure. On my tenth re-read I know, obviously, that Yoren is Arya's key to escape the city and opens up her story. In fact, Yoren is quite the important character from this chapter and into *A Clash of Kings*, but he isn't recognized (as far as I am aware) as much as other characters, including those with less "screentime." I wonder why? I like the Yoren character. In fact, he's among my favorite non-POVs with Bronn.

The chapter ends with his knife flashing, and this is perhaps the first of many cliffhangers that become more prominent in the later books where you don't really know whether the character is being killed or not (unless you've read it, say, ten times ... sigh). Not sure I like those cliffhangers. I mean, we've been waiting a decade for resolutions to some of the chapters in *A Storm of Swords*, and five years for those in *A Feast for Crows*. I mean, Brienne's been dangling for five years! I do hope the author sees the wisdom in *not* making quite so dramatic cliffhangers in *A Dance with Dragons*, you know, just in case the sixth novel takes a few more years than expected.

Whew, what a chapter. The first half is gloomy and grim, the second half intense and demanding. But this is part of the magic of *A Game of Thrones*. Bitter tears for Arya, and we're glued to the pages, wanting to know what happens next, and what happens after what happens next. This is the chapter where I went from intrigued to fan boy. By *A Storm of Swords*, I had become a rabid, obsessed fan boy.

CRYPTIC AHA!

Noticing that many fans of the series find Bran Stark's character and/or chapters "boring" and "slow" (I'm paraphrasing here), I am somewhat surprised. I do agree that his chapters often do not have the same exciting pace as others—like this one, but he's got some pretty interesting chapters and some of them do have both action and excitement. Take for instance the previously blogged chapter where he is in the woods under attack by those wildlings—action, terror, excitement, something you don't always find in every Tyrion or Jon Snow chapter. My point is I think some people tend to forget that there are many exciting Bran chapters (what about *the things I do for love?* What a tense build-up!). The Bran chapters that *do* seem to move a bit slowly are usually packed with interesting tidbits about the history of Westeros, the mythology of the Others, the Age of Heroes, giving Bran's chapter a heightened sense of epic fantasy. As stated before, his chapters come, at times, close to the atmosphere, the mood and the *wonder*, of J.R.R. Tolkien's *The Lord of the Rings*. The wonder, of course, is enhanced by the fact that we read it through the eyes of young Bran Stark.

We find Bran on the balcony of Maester Luwin's turret. He's still up in the heights, looking down on the world—in this case, the courtyard of Winterfell, watching Ser Rodrik train new recruits to replace those that went south with Lord Eddard Stark. What I find interesting is how Bran, young as he is, still is keen enough to discern the fact that the boys Ser Rodrik is trying to train, aren't very good at fighting. Maester Luwin agrees with Bran, reinforcing the idea that Bran has a good perception, and from the lofty height of the turret, one can perhaps see a foreshadowing of Bran the Lord? Not knowing how the saga ends for Bran, it's hard to call it actual foreshadowing, of course.

Maester Luwin isn't in the turret to watch the training in the courtyard—the author sneaks in a quick note that the aged maester is actually taking notes on *"the comet that hung low in the morning sky."* If I am not mistaken, this is the first mention of the Red Comet, and I just love how understated its first appearance is (considering its importance as an omen later down the line). Bran wistfully reflects on how he'd be able to beat the recruits if only he had his legs. With this, the author once again reminds us of Bran's sad disability, rousing my empathy. When Bran says he could be wielding a pole-axe from Hodor's shoulders, so they can be "knights together", I can *feel* Bran's longing, that he can cling to even such a ridiculous suggestion...or is it? While he doesn't wield a pole-axe, he does end up on Hodor's shoulders on a quest, with Hodor almost functioning like a horse. Maybe we *will* get a scene where Bran fights from Hodor's shoulders. And maybe we will get a scene where Bran, through magical means, regains his ability to walk.

Of all the things one can wish to happen before the series ends, I have "Bran walking again" pretty high up on my list. Once magic seeps back into Westeros, it is not far-fetched that it might happen. The main argument against this, is Martin's reputation for being quite hard on his characters. Lastly, throughout the series Bran becomes more and more adept at certain... other skills that allow him to move, albeit not with his own body; perhaps it simply won't be necessary to give him back the ability to walk, for the sake of the story. I am *very* curious about the further development of Bran Stark's story arc, as it is very different from the other characters' development. To think that if the novels followed our world's timeline ... Bran would be, what, eighteen-nineteen now? Heh.

Luwin tries to discourage Bran from his thoughts about fighting from Hodor's shoulders, which makes Bran bring up another example of a knight no one believed in: Symeon Star-eyes. Luwin dismisses the legend of Symeon as just another fable from the Age of Heroes, but it helps flesh out some of the background history, however distorted it must be (incidentally, the tale of Symeon Star-eyes sounds like some superhero story à la Daredevil, another blind fighter, or that wacky Rutger Hauer-character whose name I can't remember). When Luwin tells Bran he must stop dreaming because it will only hurt him more, we get to a fairly interesting bit, because Bran Stark is reminded of his vivid dreams and tells Maester Luwin he had one about "that crow" again last night.

> "I dreamed about the crow again last night. The one with three eyes. He flew into my bedchamber and told me to come with him, so I did. We went down to the crypts. Father was there, and we talked. He was sad."

Now this is a dream I'd like to witness through Bran's POV directly, but of course, in order to keep his secrets, Martin gives us just a sense of foreboding—and Bran tells Luwin that he talked to Lord Eddard about Jon. Jon Snow, that is. What can we infer from this dream? Is the Lord Eddard in the dream, in truth, the ghost of Eddard (remember, he died in the previous chapter)? Or is it just symbolically? Eddard being in the crypt is obviously an omen of the good lord's demise, but why talk about Jon? Eddard's last thoughts? Or, as a later chapter in the series suggests, is there more between Jon Snow and Bran Stark that we have yet to fully understand (to put it bluntly, do both have abilities connected to the Three-Eyed Crow)? I am both confused and intrigued at the same time by passages like this, that can be analyzed in this way or that, and I guess these tidbits of mystery is part of what keeps us hanging on. *You just keep me hanging on ...*

The discussion about the crow dream also gives us a possible hint that Hodor, simpleton that he is, may just sense bad stuff going on—he doesn't want to go down in the crypts. Does he have some kind of animal sense? Luwin makes a point out of the fact that Hodor is a man and not a mule, but at the same time that is just Luwin's opinion, and the author gives us this idea that Hodor may just sense things others can't. *I see dead people ...*

Since Hodor doesn't want to bring Bran down into the crypts (Bran wants to go down and see if his father is really there—that's how vivid his dream was), Luwin suggests that the wildling captive, Osha, can take Bran down into the crypts. Obviously, Luwin just wants to settle the matter—that Lord Eddard is far away in King's Landing as the Queen's prisoner—but he comes with them.

Osha carries Bran, Luwin leads the way with a torch lighting up the cold darkness beneath the earth. Summer, Bran's wolf, pads along. Interestingly, the direwolf reacts just like Hodor; it stops, doesn't want to go any further into the crypts, snarling—an animal instinct against whatever lurks here. As they pass the tombs of the Kings of Winter, we get a little exposition on some of them, and *that* Middle-earthly feeling wells forth from the page, history and carved figures and tombs and darkness—it is hard *not* to be reminded of Tolkien's Moria, albeit on a smaller scale.

At last they come to the most recent tombs. Bran's grandfather, his uncle Brandon, his aunt Lyanna. Bran tells Osha that Prince Rhaegar Targaryen kidnapped and raped Lyanna, and that Robert Baratheon fought a war to win her back, another piece of the puzzle that is Robert's Rebellion. I love how we are given so little each time we get some back-story, the sense of mystery. Which version of legend comes the closest to the truth? Among fans, the notion that Rhaegar raped Lyanna has long been abandoned; it is believed (based on lots of hints in the books I assume) that she went with him freely. Yet to Bran, Rhaegar Targaryen was a bad, bad boy. Conflicting perspectives: It makes the story so much richer.

Luwin, quite cool and calm, tries to convince Bran that everything's fine, there's nothing here, let's go back and then *wham!* there *is* something in Lord Eddard's tomb, and for a moment the chapter takes on a sense of horror, before we discover that Bran's little (and almost forgotten I have to admit) brother Rickon, and his ferocious direwolf Shaggydog, are hiding out down in the crypts. The mystery only widens when we learn that Rickon has had a dream of their father too, and that he has promised to come home. Finally Maester Luwin begins to show uncertainty about it all, realizing that there is some mysterious (dream) power at play here. The scene gives us our first proper look at Shaggydog's development. Of the direwolves, it is the one we see the least in the story. But it is quite clear that Shaggydog is wilder, more ferocious, than the other direwolves. Maester Luwin is the third man savaged by the wolf, but Bran decides—as the lordling he is—that Shaggydog is not going to be chained. The scene also gives us a glimpse of Rickon's development—it is quite evident from the story that the wolves somewhat resemble the children they belong to (and vice versa); so Rickon is wild and restless, like Shaggydog. Also, Rickon *likes* it down in the cold, dark crypts. What will he become? Some force of darkness? And *where is A Dance With Dragons?*

Bran has decided that the wolves and Rickon can stay in Maester Luwin's turret (it's not clear why Bran chooses the maester's abode, but perhaps it's simply because Bran feels the maester doesn't really try to understand him and his dreams). In the tower, Osha helps clean Luwin's wounds, and we get another bit of exposition, this time on the Children of the Forest. Basically we get two opposing viewpoints, Luwin's and Osha's, with the kids listening in. According to Luwin, the Children of the Forest are long gone, according to Osha they are still around. There's a lot to glean about this mythical people here, so let's sum up some of the more brow-raising bits.

"The children ... live only in dreams."

Could be read as the Children being in Bran (and Rickon's) dreams; could mean the Three-Eyed Crow is a Child of the Forest, possibly in warg-form.

> "Old Nan says the children knew the songs of the trees, that they could fly like birds and swim like fish and talk to the animals."

The Children knew, or know, how to warg into other beings; are the Children teaching Bran his powers?

"And all this they did with magic."

Waiting for Dragons

The Children knew how to wield magic; is Bran turning into a sorcerer character? If yes, will Rickon too? And Jon?

There's a lot more information to digest, about their culture, their appearance, their weaponry, and more. Their "wise men" (shamans? priests?) were called *greenseers* and they carved the faces into the weirwoods. When Men invaded Westeros, they almost wiped out the Children, but the Children used dark magic (which shattered the Arm of Dorne in the process). Their obsidian (dragonglass) was no good in the war against Men, so it is obvious, that they used dragonglass weapons to fight *another* enemy—an enemy we later learn is vulnerable to the material, the Others.

So the Others and the Children are from the Dawn Age. That age ended when Men and Children signed a pact, heralding the Age of Heroes and a long time of peace between the races. Osha claims that the Children went north, beyond the Wall, with the giants and "other old races"; and we know for a fact that there are giants north of the Wall, and Others—so why not Children?

What is obvious from all this myth and legend and tales of the Children of the Forest is that the Starks and the people of the North inherited their "old gods" from the Children, and as such there's at least a spiritual bond between the Stark and Child of the Forest. It seems all but given that Bran Stark is, indeed, under the influence of the Children, who are, as I read it, preparing Bran Stark for the Others. Right? Right?

Summer begins to howl, and Bran is filled with fear. *It's coming.* A raven appears. And Bran's dream—nightmare—comes true. The Three-Eyed Crow had taken him down to the crypts to say farewell to his father, and Maester Luwin, still disbelieving, reads the crumpled note the bird has brought. "What is it?" Bran asks, but Osha gently tells him he already knows. It is clear that Osha is an important character when it comes to knowledge of the Children of the Forest, foresight and green dreams. In fact, she is surprisingly knowledgeable about the stuff, for being a wildling brigand. Do all wildlings know this stuff so well? I am looking forward to see more of Osha (and Rickon) in the story. Let's look at the calendar. Oh, almost eleven years since *A Storm of Swords*. No rush.

I realize this post is mostly reference. I have little to add. It's a bleak, sad chapter, with several mysteries that only deepen; Maester Luwin is almost annoyingly pragmatic (but foreshadows well the general attitude of the maesters of the Citadel); I'd love to read Martin's thoughts on the chapter. Maybe an idea for his next *Not a Blog* post? Arf. Who am I kidding (myself I guess).

It's so tempting to try and unravel all the little mysteries of the Children of the Forest, the three-eyed crow, Bran's prophetic dreams, Rickon's connection, Osha's arsenal of knowledge, but it won't really do good. I am convinced that Bran and the Children of the Forest are linked, and that the crow is a Child, but there are still too many unknowns in the equation to be 100% sure. I dearly hope that *A Dance with Dragons* will shed more light on it all; and I wouldn't mind an Osha chapter either, to be honest. Rumor on the street has it that Martin only has five chapters left of the damn thing, so with some luck he'll find some time off from his vacations to actually finish it.

See you next time, with Sansa's final chapter. I've forgotten her reaction to Lord Eddard's execution, so I am looking forward to it.

WEEPING AND SLEEPING

According to dictionary.com, denouement is "the final resolution of the intricacies of a plot, as of a drama or novel." As I see it, the denouement of *A Game of Thrones* began with Lord Eddard Stark's public execution, and from then on out we get the story's denouement. Not in its truest sense or form—for as we all know, this novel is but the first of four (maybe five one day) novels—but still, there is a form of denouement as each POV character gets a last chapter to round up things, and to set the stage for the second novel in the series, *A Clash of Kings*. In the case of Sansa Stark, author George R.R. Martin doesn't so much set her up as she puts her down ... Hard. Seeing your own father betrayed and beheaded is not enough pain for the young northern damsel, as we will see in this chapter, which reveals that our suspicions about Joffrey Baratheon's true nature are well-founded. Yes, we've known all along that he is despicable, but in this chapter he really shows how terrible he is. Forget Dark Lords and evil sorcerers. True villainy in fantasy literature is when you love to hate characters like Joffrey, or Ser Gregor Clegane, or any of the other scumbags of Westeros.

The chapter opens with a beautifully dark description of both Sansa's emotional state and her lightless surroundings, locked up in Maegor's Holdfast within the Red Keep:

In the tower room at the heart of Maegor's Holdfast, Sansa gave herself to the darkness.

Two probably unrelated things come to mind when reading this. First, I can't help but think of the "heart of darkness," and second I hear Darth Vader's wheezing, sonorous voice asking Luke Skywalker to give himself to the Dark Side. I don't know whether the author intended any nod towards one or the other, but there it is. I love this opening sentence by the way; it really pulls us right into Sansa's distress. Darkness and solitude, sorrow and the absence of hope and light. Who said it was easy being a Stark? Probably Rickon. *He's* had an easy go of it.

We learn that Sansa's sleep is either dreamless, or she dreams of the event on the steps of the Great Sept—she returns to that haunting vision of seeing her father die. What is interesting is how obviously this contrasts with especially her brother Bran, who has "special" dreams. Sansa seems not connected to the more mysterious ways of the world; she remains a girl living superficially, though Joffrey will "help" her connect to her inner self. I guess. Or, as I re-read, and pretending that I do not know how the story progresses, it occurs to me that maybe it is the Hound, Sandor Clegane, who will show her some of the harsh realities of Westeros, as the end of this chapter indicates.

I shouldn't forget the connection between Stark children and their direwolves—Lady is dead, so that could also be seen as a reason as to why Sansa does not have dreams the way the others have. It does not explain why she didn't have dreams like this before Lady died. In Sansa's case, the way that she seems to have thought of Lady as an overgrown lap dog may have contributed to her lack of psychic "rapport" with this huge carnivore.

Honestly, I don't believe GRRM follows a firmly established (self-imposed) rule on the connection between the direwolves and the Stark kids and their dream patterns. More that he uses the effect when it serves the story, and that's it. There is some discussion on this subject on the Internet, but I have not seen any definite conclusions.

After having spent about a page setting Sansa's state of mind (she even considers suicide), we get a small bit where Grand Maester Pycelle visits, has her undress and touches her all over. One would think that a Grand Maester would know that this girl is simply stricken with sorrow, which would give us the information that the man is an old, dirty bastard using his station as an excuse to abuse Sansa. It does not seem that Sansa registers this, but this is what I take from the short paragraph where Pycelle visits. Dirty old bastard.

The chapter kicks into motion when Joffrey Baratheon arrives, with the Hound and two Kingsguard in tow. Yanking off the bed hangings, there is no mercy or compassion in the boy as he simply announces that she has to tidy herself up for a court session later that day. She does not want to, and Joffrey has his Hound—Sandor Clegane—scoop her up from bed. Once again her nakedness is noted (and, I am sorry to say, it is a little bit more disturbing this time around, what with the number of indecent posts about whores and horny moods over at *Not a Blog*). The Hound tells her to obey Joffrey's orders and we get a new glimpse of what we can call the relationship between the Hound and Sansa. Their first interaction was all the way back at the Tourney of the Hand, when Sandor escorted her back to the Red Keep. What we get here is that Sandor is trying to protect Sansa by telling her to do as Joffrey bids, to ease her pain. Sansa finally acts a bit rational towards Joffrey here, finally accusing him of being the bastard he is.

The love she had for Joffrey, imagined or not, is finally gone. It is an important facet of her character development over the series, and a culmination of her arc in *A Game of Thrones*. She has learned the valuable lesson Littlefinger taught her. *"Life is not a song, sweetling."*

Joffrey has her beaten. Ser Meryn Trant does the deed, the same guy who presumably killed Arya's fencing teacher Syrio Forel. What makes Trant different as a villainous character from, say, Joffrey, is that he simply does his job, not caring whether he is being knightly or no. Ser Meryn Trant is the epitome of failed chivalry, which is interesting, since the Hound is considered to be everything a knight should not be, yet it is Sandor who acts the most chivalrous towards Sansa.

The court session is used to establish the new, monstrous rule of King Joffrey Baratheon. Thieves have their hands chopped off right there in the throne room, he orders duels to the death, and not even his lady mother Queen Cersei can sway Joffrey. There's a short glimpse of my main man, Janos Slynt, nodding with approval at everything Joffrey does. Lickspittle that he is, I can understand why nobody loves Janos as a character. I guess that's part of the reason I took his name as my online moniker. Not to be disliked, but for the difference. I guess there are enough Tyrions, Jons, Jaimes and Aryas around. The Hound's words of advice keep coming back to Sansa, so she behaves.

Once the court session is over and done with, and we get the point that things have gone from bad to so much worse in King's Landing with Joffrey on the Iron Throne, and we get to the reason why Joffrey wanted Sansa in attendance.

Sansa is forced to walk with Joffrey to the battlements of the castle, and with dread in her heart she knows he is taking her to where the heads of traitors hang on pikes—the monstrous boy is actually going to show her Lord Eddard's rotting head. And the character of Joffrey Baratheon, a background character for so long, steps forth and becomes the cruel, monstrous, spiteful villain of the piece. Once up on the height of the castle's battlements, Sansa looks away, to the city and the lands beyond, longing for her home, longing for Winterfell. Another cue as to her change—for most of the book she's wanted to get away from Winterfell; she was the one who looked forward to the pageantry of King's Landing; but everything she hoped for has turned to ashes, and now, at the end of her arc in this novel, she just wants to go home.

Joffrey forces her to watch the decapitated, swollen heads; dipped in tar to preserve them longer, the tar also makes them hard to identify. Sansa sees the heads, but she is spared the actual recognition of her father. Having checked out the topic of dipping heads in tar in medieval times, I can confirm that this is truthful; and I believe Martin adds this as a bit of realism rather than hinting at any uncertainty as to Lord Eddard's fate. I've read some arguments that Ned may be alive because we never really "see" him die; Arya doesn't see it as much as hear the sigh of the crowds; and here, we don't get a straight confirmation that it is indeed her father's head Sansa is forced to watch. However, in this same chapter a few pages before we do get Sansa recalling the scene on the steps of the Great Sept. She saw it happen; there is no doubt that Lord Eddard Stark was beheaded by Ser Ilyn Payne.

George R.R. Martin sure likes to rub salt in the wounds (I'm not referring to his blog now); not only does Sansa have to watch her father's tar-dipped head; Joffrey takes her for a walk along the battlements, along rows of decapitated heads, including Septa Mordane's, perhaps the person closest to Sansa for the last few years; and Joffrey explains that he has two spikes ready for his uncles, Stannis and Renly Baratheon (setting up the conflict for the next novel in one simple line of dialogue). Sansa, by being stoic in this terrifying situation, annoys Joffrey even more, showing us just how childish he is. Like a boy who loves ripping wings off flies, but given the power to do it to people. Anyone he wants hurt, he can hurt. When she threatens Joffrey—telling him that Robb will destroy him—pouty Joffrey simply has Ser Meryn Trant beat her again. In the moment that follows, she forces herself to smile so she won't get more beatings, and she thinks that she could shove Joffrey off the parapet, perhaps taking herself with him (suicidal thoughts again), but the Hound steps between them and helps her to her feet and she thanks him.

You may notice that this blog post is more of a reference to the chapter than an in-depth analysis or discussion. The reason is simple. I can't find much to extract here. It is a relatively straight forward development plotwise. We have Sansa's arc coming to an end with her mentality turned around; and a little more development of the relationship between her and Sandor. We get established that Stannis and Renly are still out there, and are Joffrey's enemies. And Joffrey's true nature is finally fully revealed. Oh, and almost lost in the density there's a quick dialogue between Joffrey and Sansa where it is stated that

Cersei thinks Sansa is stupid (and she is because she is surprised to hear it), and that Sansa is still betrothed to Joffrey.

You may remember a post where I discussed the use of violence in the novels. It was a Daenerys chapter, with the Dothraki raping and pillaging and all that. The violence on display in this chapter is of a different kind; it is the more personal kind. It is abuse. Pycelle's touch. Trant's fists. Joffrey's psychological terror. But it does serve the story on many levels; it helps us understand Sansa's mental turnaround. There's a difference between Joffrey's violence and the Dothraki raping a girl on a pile of corpses; the first is used to establish Joffrey's character and make Sansa's living hell believable; the second is more gratuitous than serving the plot.

Still, it is Joffrey's acts that rouse the most emotions. I really hate the character. Martin succeeds in creating a, for the genre, somewhat atypical villain. And we're looking forward to *A Clash of Kings* to see if he's getting his comeuppance. We want more Joffrey Baratheon (or should I start calling him a Lannister now?), but I don't necessarily wait with bated breath on more Dothraki daterape necroparties.

Eeew Dragondew

Lo, and behold! I thought this would be the last Daenerys chapter of *A Game of Thrones*, but my memory played tricks on me. There is no coming alive of the night with music here; quite the opposite in fact, this chapter ends with another major character's death. Not as major as, say, Lord Eddard Stark, but still—Khal Drogo isn't exactly a minor character either, and his death has implications for the plot just as Lord Eddard's. I guess we can call Khal Drogo a secondary character, like other non-POVs that have a lot of influence on the story's progression and/or the POV characters' lives—others would be the Hound, Robb Stark, and Littlefinger to name a few examples.

Reading has been slow these last weeks, and I lay the blame squarely at the feet of *World of Warcraft* (conveniently forgetting to blame myself for re-subscribing to that game). I know I should stay away from digital drugs, but I can't help it. Even though 99% of the people I encounter in the game are, put simply, unashamedly rude and asocial. What is the world coming to when playing a multiplayer game is all about running about the wilds *alone*? But I have digressed again.

Let's hope there will be *Song of Ice and Fire Online* game in the future, which is just as brutal as the novels, where you can actually whack someone when they behave like children (yeah, I know, they *are* children). The effect of *World of Warcraft*—is it the same that keeps me coming back to George R.R. Martin's novels, why I continually check the *Not A Blog* for the tiniest bit of information on *A Dance with Dragons* though I know there's nothing for me there? What part of my brain doesn't understand that I am being ridiculous? I should be washing the car, not hoping that *this* time I'll find a good group for Blackrock Depths; I shouldn't be plowing through a gazillion Martin-related websites looking for the latest info on the farce that is *A Dance with Dragons*.

Daenerys, then (the car will have to wait, although it's getting hard to read the license plate). Before delving into the chapter I tried to remember what the deal with it was, but honestly I couldn't remember much beyond Khal Drogo's death. So it was with some interest I returned to this second-to-last chapter of Daenerys Targaryen, and reading it I realized there were some interesting—forgotten—nuggets in there. Be warned; I may be overanalyzing some of the details present.

The chapter starts off with a typical Martin starter sentence: *"Wings shadowed her fever dreams."* This sentence can be seen as literally a foreshadowing of the dragons coming to life; their presence in her mind being pointed out several times later in the chapter. (I did mention I might be overanalyzing.) The chapter's first segment, which is played out in Dany's mind / dream-world, is fairly surrealistic but knowing that Daenerys' will have some prophetic visions later on, and knowing that other characters have dreams that seem to come true (in some fashion or other), could there be interesting details hidden in her fevered dreams in *this* chapter?

Viserys' catchphrase returns to Dany's mind again and again: *"You don't want to wake the dragon, do you?"* Not sure if I have thought it before, but now I realize how ironic that sentence becomes. After all, waking dragons is exactly what she does! Dreaming of her crappy brother isn't about fearing him; it's about establishing the concept of waking the dragons. Cool beans.

She dreams of Drogo unloading within her, but then the dream becomes disturbing and we can assume that this is the author telling us that, yeah, Drogo is dead. Or good as dead, as we'll see.

"The last dragon", Ser Jorah whispers in Dany's dreams, and then he becomes a wisp, and then is gone. Foreshadowing Ser Jorah deserting Daenerys?

She dreams of the red door—which I have suggested is symbolic for Westeros in an earlier post—and here I become convinced, for she dreams that the red door is so far ahead of her—telling us that there is still a long way to go for Daenerys before she can come to Westeros [a decade by now!]; and then Martin adds the chilling line, *"she could feel the icy breath behind,"* in other words the presence of the Others in Westeros; an interesting nugget right there.

Then she dreams the red door close by, which I take it as a somewhat prophetic dream of what will happen once she is near Westeros, and the cold recedes behind; foreshadowing her driving back the Others? She dreams of seeing Westeros from the sky—foretelling her coming to Westeros on dragonback? I think so; but there is one line in there confusing me:"*... and she flew across the Dothraki sea."* From the rest of the sequence, one can reasonably assume she is dreaming of her return to Westeros, and maybe she will cross the Dothraki Sea by dragon for all I know, but so far it does not seem like she will return to Khal Drogo's lands. Or will she?

Luke Skywalker returns! Dany sees her long gone brother Rhaegar Targaryen, wearing a helmet. When he lifts the visor, Dany sees her own face. Just like the scene where Luke enters the cave on Dagobah in *The Empire Strikes Back*; facing Darth Vader, he chops off his head and when Vader's mask explodes, Luke sees his own face. Just like it is Luke's destiny to become a Jedi like his father, it is Dany's destiny to become the Prince that was Promised, a destiny Rhaegar lost in the Battle of the Trident.

She dreams more of flight; the contrast and similarities with Bran Stark, who also dreams of flight, are interesting. Not that there is much to say about it, at least not at present. Unlike Bran, Daenerys doesn't have an in-flight mentor to steer her on course. Why is that? Because Bran's being helped out by the Children of the Forest who do not exist in Dany's part of the world (is it Essos they call it now)?

When Daenerys wakes up she reflects on her dreams, perhaps egoistically forgetting to think about her husband the Khal and her son, the one she was giving birth to in the previous chapter. It jars a little, but then again her dreams were powerful (though they do not come as forcefully as, say, Bran's dreams—with Bran, you *know* he's in some ethereal place, with Dany you could argue that she's just having nightmares). Or is she simply postponing making the awful truth "official"? When she finds her resolve, she does ask for Khal Drogo and her unborn son Rhaego.

As her dreams indicated, the son is dead. Mirri Maz Duur goes on to tell her that the child was monstrous, some sort of dragon-human breed from the description—but we may never learn the truth of it; other characters do not believe the maegi, but they did see shadows in the tent. As it turns out, Mirri Maz Duur's actions were simple revenge. Revenge for the Dothraki destroying her people and her town. And you know what? I can sympathize with Mirri. Yes, what she does is cruel and twisted, yet she has reason to harbor these feelings of hatred towards Daenerys and the Dothraki. Mirri is the last of the Lamb Men, and what is life worth to her with her people dead?

Turning it around, Khal Drogo is now alive, but a vegetable. What is life worth when you can't eat, see, hear, get an erection? The whole Mirri Maz Duur subplot remains confusing to me, but it's not really a big deal. Maybe the author wasn't sure where he was going with it. He's a gardener, after all. More like a harvester of souls like the creepy überFaceDancers in *Chapterhouse: Dune*.

We learn that Daenerys' host is reduced to a few hundred sick and old Dothraki and a few warriors who chose to remain with her. It seems that all hope is lost ... but for the constant reminders throughout the chapters of the dragon eggs being hot to Dany's touch (and hers alone). In one instance she feels life inside one of the eggs. It's a given then, that the eggs will hatch, and thus—all hope is not lost for Daenerys. Now, returning to strength, Daenerys makes a bold claim and I am curious—will it come to fruition?

Forcefully, she vows to exact revenge on the khals who, among other things, raped Eroeh.

Eroeh, in case you've forgotten, was the daterape necroparty chick. She ended up right where she began, being raped by countless horny Dothraki warriors. The interesting thing is not the author's willingness to so utterly degrade his characters—the interesting part is whether Daenerys will follow up on this promise and how she did not learn a thing about revenge from Mirri Maz Duur; because isn't Drogo's vegetability (yeah that's not a real word) and the death of Rhaego a lesson in eye for an eye?

Although Daenerys is fiery and vengeful, like most teenagers, is there something more to her surprising devotion to justice for Eroeh? Reading between the lines (or not so much, to be honest, it's stated pretty clearly), we find out that Daenerys is now barren and can not have any more children. This will make a nice contrast when she becomes the Mother of Dragons; and gives the character an almost messianic trait, she becomes more than the little frightened red door girl. There is also a hint that she has a moral vision that goes beyond her time and place: an almost modern sense that all victims are owed an equal accounting, regardless of whether they fall into a low-status class.

Facing the loss of Khal Drogo and Rhaego, then, is a defining character moment and though she doesn't learn from Mirri Maz Duur (if you agree that there was a lesson in there), she does seem to settle on a direction and become more resolved. I am sure Khal Drogo, in his tragic vegetative state, isn't thinking *"that which doesn't kill you, only makes you stronger."* But Daenerys ... she will grow stronger, the whole chapter supports this and we who have read the books a zillion times waiting for dragons know it will come to pass: She will become a force to be reckoned with, at least as long as she has those three reptiles now almost ready to hatch.

The chapter ends on a dark note. Khal lies outside, and though he lives, he is lost to her. In a jarring sequence we learn that she tries to get him going, but alas! She finally decides to suffocate him with a cushion. Only death pays for life.

No Time For Mercy

Tyrion's last chapter in *A Game of Thrones* is littered with small details setting up the continuation in the next novel in the series, *A Clash of Kings*, a novel I love dearly. Like a good friend I am looking forward to meet again. Will I manage to blog that book too, before we dance with dragons? I don't believe I'd manage that unless I did five or six chapters a day; by now, *surely* book number five can't be that far away from us in space/time continuum. Himself says he has chapters to go, one of them apparently about krakens (perhaps he's working on a Victarion Greyjoy chapter—or maybe we should take the author's latest vague reference to *A Dance with Dragons* literally and someone, like Euron Crow's Eye, is actually summoning a kraken from the deep).

Anyhow, it is time for Tyrion Lannister, the Imp, to sober up. As a result of the denouement of A Storm of Swords, he spent *A Feast for Crows* drinking his way across the Narrow Sea. In other words, it's been a *decade* since we had a halfway sober halfman.

Fortunately, re-reading *A Game of Thrones* we're not at that point in the story yet. No, Tyrion Lannister is in the riverlands, having survived a battle with part of Robb Stark's host and his future is as of yet unknown. I like to pretend that I don't know how stuff will unfold, as if the book somehow could change its ending *this* time. That's how good this story is (so far); like the blurb on the back of the version I have before me now states:

> "In *A Game of Thrones*, George R.R. Martin has created a genuine masterpiece, bringing together the best the genre has

to offer. Mystery, intrigue, romance and adventure fill the pages of the first volume in an epic series sure to delight fantasy fans everywhere."

Not sure how much actual romance there is to be found, but the rest is pretty accurate (though the creator has gone on to provoke more than delight).

This last Tyrion chapter opens with a line from Lord Tywin Lannister, one of the best realized secondary characters. "They have my son," he says and as if we slip into Tyrion's mind we read how Tyrion feels about his lord father's statement—Tyrion feels that Tywin says "my son" as if he doesn't have a second son, as if Tyrion is worthless and incomparable to his brother Ser Jaime. And in a way, this is the truth of the matter, a painful truth that haunts every verbal confrontation between Lord Tywin and Tyrion.

The characters have returned to the Inn at the Crossroads, and the Lannister bannermen and lords have assembled in the taproom, a fire crackling in the hearth. I mentioned earlier that I wished there was more exposition on these people; the Stark bannermen—Greatjon Umber, Rickard Karstark and Roose Bolton—are vividly characterized, while the Lannister men are given less airtime to convey personalities and styles. However, with this chapter we get a better idea of the Lannister allies, and it is quite interesting to read.

Among the assembled is Ser Harys Swyft, and Tyrion thinks little of the man—a *chinless craven* who has married into the Lannister family; indeed, the character doesn't speak, he *moans*; and Tyrion thinks of him as a lickspittle. Not a match for the hardened men of the North, then. Interestingly, the *craven* Ser Harys dares ask what madness made Ser Jaime split his host—saying this in front of Lord Tywin. So either he isn't entirely craven or he didn't think his words through. I guess it's the latter. Tyrion's uncle Ser Kevan responds and we get a strategic description of Riverrun and how that place would have forced Ser Jaime to split his host into three camps.

Lovely how we get an early description of the location (it features prominently in the next novel) by way of characters being elsewhere; also, it adds to the realism of the story. In many fantasy novels, I feel that battles or important confrontations happen because the story demands it. This is true in *A Game of Thrones* as well, of course, but George R.R. Martin hides this cleverly by coating it with strategic details like this; it doesn't feel as if Ser Jaime was caught in the Whispering Wood because the author wanted him in a dungeon cell so he could end up in Catelyn Stark's hands (moving the plot forward); it feels as if Ser Jaime was caught because of the strategic encumberments of besieging Riverrun and because the Kingslayer is foolhardy and brave. There are many examples of this throughout *A Song of Ice and Fire*; circumstances are woven into the plot in ways that make you forget the storyteller, characters take on lives on their own, every action or reaction has a consequence.

All right, enough gushing. Slynt wants *A Dance with Dragons*. Slynt wants *A Dance with Dragons* bad.

The next bannerman we learn a little bit more about is Ser Gregor Clegane. I was actually surprised on this tenth re-read to find him here in the taproom of the inn. I had forgotten. The effect is cool, though, because he *is* out of place here among the noble lords, and his one line illustrates his character efficiently:

Ser Gregor Clegane is a brute. One hell of a brutish brute. So now we have a lickspittle craven and a brute. It looks as if the mastermind Lord Tywin Lannister's court of allies is full of the wrong people.

Following Ser Gregor's brutal suggestion to the messenger who came to tell the lord Tywin of Ser Jaime's capture, we get another bit of characterization on Lord Tywin. First, he regards Ser Gregor, but Tyrion can't make out whether his father admires the overly large warrior, or loathes him. Then we learn that Lord Tywin prefers to keep quiet during councils, listening to what everyone has to say before saying something himself. So not only is he cruel and disciplined, he is also calculating. Love these little drips of information that flesh out the characters. Ironically, Tyrion thinks of his father's silence during councils as something he himself tries to emulate. Showing us that Tyrion does, after all, look up to his father as a wise warrior lord; also, it is funny because Tyrion usually gets in trouble because he can't keep his mouth shut.

Another bannerman present is Ser Flement Brax; though we get no indication of his personality, we do learn that his father, the lord of House Brax who was with Ser Jaime at the Whispering Wood, according to Tyrion, was a fool for trying to cross a river in full armor. The messenger tries to console Ser Flement by saying his father died gallantly. But as the author, often through Tyrion, likes to remind us—this is Westeros, not Middle-earth. Wear armor and fall off a boat, you sink like a stone and drown. So now we have a lickspittle, a brute, and the son of a fool. See where I'm going with this?

Oh, we also have Ser Kevan, Tywin's brother, who tries hard to be like Tywin but here, at least, seems more like a poor imitation. We hear of Ser Forley Prester whose free riders deserted and became turncloaks. Another sign that all is not well with the forces of the Lannisters. Good thing for the lions that they have plenty of gold and men at their disposal. Ser Addam Marbrand reveals himself to be perhaps a little too vengeful and bloodthirsty and doesn't regard others' emotions. Lord Lefford puts in hope where there is little or none.

Finally, Lord Tywin Lannister breaks the silence—the bannermen are discussing back and forth, and that's how we get those glimpses of these characters—by repeating his opening line. *"They have my son."*

Rising, he bids everyone leave. To his surprise, Tyrion and his uncle Ser Kevan are asked to remain. There's this tiny glimmer of hope here—*waitaminute, is he recognizing me now?* and I know I root for Tyrion to win his father's respect ... and when Tywin says that Tyrion is right that the problem lies with Joffrey Baratheon (because he was responsible for beheading Lord Eddard and thus firing up the North), I can *feel* Tyrion's heart soaring. The author doesn't describe this happening, though, so I can't say whether Tyrion actually feels elation at being recognized for thinking true here.

Anyway, the moment is shattered right away when Tyrion, unfortunately, mentions that Joffrey is young and that Tyrion committed some follies on his own at that age. Tywin immediately retorts that Joffrey at least has not wedded a whore yet. Tyrion wants to fling the cup in his father's face—there's a story here we don't know quite yet—and it turns Tyrion's mood sour (and mine). Just as things were going well.

In a previous post I mentioned how these last remaining chapters form the denouement of *A Game of Thrones*. So far, this chapter has been more backwards, with reflections and discussions regarding the battle in which Ser Jaime was taken captive (but also trying to find out what to do next); but now follows a clear setup for the next novel as Tywin tells his two family members that Renly Baratheon has wed Margaery Tyrell and is raising a host at Highgarden, claiming himself King of Westeros.

Wait, who? Renly? Was that one of the brothers? That's how I thought the first time around. I guess. Renly's been off the scene for a while. Now of course I remember perfectly well Renly offering Lord Eddard an alliance, which Ned rejected, and then Renly, the third Baratheon brother, storming off.

Speaking of Baratheons, have you seen the latest teaser for HBO's *Game of Thrones*? Catelyn pronounces "Baratheon" *so* wrong. What's up with *ba-RA-theon*? That's all wrong to mine ears. It's *bara-THEE-on*. Or was. I guess I'll soon be mouthing it the HBO way. Weird how perception of the novel will change with the TV series. I'm giddy as hell about it, but at the same time it will be *very* strange to see other people's versions of the characters and pronunciations in my head.

Anyway, the setup is obvious now of course. Renly (and Margaery) will be major players come *A Clash of Kings*, but for now the importance of Renly's act remains understated. Though the fact is that with Highgarden backing him, Renly becomes a considerable enemy. Apparently. Tywin tells Tyrion and Ser Kevan that Cersei has commanded him to ride in the defense of King's Landing (which is relatively close to Highgarden), and Tywin scoffs at the gall that a mere daughter of his dares command him. Go away, feminism!

More setup follows as we learn what the *other* brother is up to—Stannis Baratheon, that is. Building ships, hiring sellswords and "bringing a shadowbinder from Asshai." I guess I don't need to elaborate on how this is setup for *A Clash of Kings*, or, as some of us like to call it, *Melisandre's Story*.

Lord Tywin Lannister sums it all up neatly for us: how Ser Jaime has left them in a bad way, what Roose Bolton is up to, where Robb Stark is and so forth. Reading this one can make a map of the various factions and where they are in relation to each other, clearly setting up the next novel while at the same time summing up the military side of things in *A Game of Thrones*. Sweet.

Tywin gives some orders which we'll see come to life in the next novel. Finally, like in a short story, the chapter flips life upside down for Tyrion as he is ordered to go to King's Landing and ... *rule*. Yes, Tyrion is going to be next Hand of the King after Lord Eddard and it as surprising for me as it is for Tyrion.

His main mission: Curb the boy. Stop Joffrey from ruining everything towards Tywin has so patiently worked towards. If Martin had let Joffrey ruin everything instead of waiting to have Cersei do it in *A Feast for Crows*, we may have had no need for the dreadful "split" of volumes 4 and 5, maybe not even the endless wait for both *Feast* and *Dance*.

Tywin does not trust the councilors of the Red Keep—that is, Littlefinger, that "cockless wonder" Varys (had to chuckle at that one) and even Grand Maester Pycelle, whom I so far have thought of as fully under Lannister's influence. (As we learn in *Feast*, the Maesters of the Citadel do have an agenda of their own.)

Tyrion can't help himself and has to ask why Tywin chooses him to do the job instead of one of his bannerman. When Tywin says, "Because you are my son," Tyrion realizes that his father has already given up on Ser Jaime, reinforcing the idea of Tywin being a cold-hearted bastard. *Or is he?*

What is interesting here is that we get the whole scene through Tyrion's eyes. And he just doesn't expect *anything* from his lord father. But what if Tywin now, at this moment, has decided to gamble on Tyrion—after all, he's proven himself in the vanguard in the battle and he came with wise observations in the council. Not too sure about this myself, but I think it *is* a valid observation nonetheless. Or is Tywin merely hedging his bets like a logical Lannister?

As the chapter ends, Tywin warns Tyrion not to bring the whore Shae with him to the Red Keep, but as Tyrion finds his way back to her in his pavilion, he tells her they are going to King's Landing. What a naughty, disobedient son.

Deal Or No Deal

It is the morning of December the 6th; for many people Christmas has arrived early. For tonight start the events surrounding tomorrow's release of *World of Warcraft: Cataclysm*. Thankfully, I have been able to distance myself from the addiction in the last week (we'll see how *that* works out—I pre-ordered the limited edition of *Cataclysm* and both regret it and look forward to it, heaps of money be damned). Not only this, but HBO finally gave us a ten minute look at their upcoming *Game of Thrones* TV series, and it is of course discussed all over the web; at *Westeros* obviously (or so I guess, still being *persona non grata*), but also at *Tower of the Hand*, *Is Winter Coming?*, *SFF World*, and of course *Winter is Coming*, the site dedicated specifically to the TV series.

Generally speaking, it seems that most if not all fans of the books are really looking forward to see HBO's adaptation for television. Myself, I am cautiously optimistic. But then I have been cautiously (albeit somewhat angrily) optimistic about *A Dance with Dragons* being published as well. In this case, however, I am quite confident we *will* see the series, at least season one, and it could well prove successful too—but I am at the same time thinking to myself that it *can't* work for me, for I've read the novels so many times, and each little change they make could be potentially jarring to me as a long-time fan. The trick will be to overlook these minor details and changes, just like I had to do with Peter Jackson's *Fellowship of the Ring*, and see if a TV version can be entertaining in its own right.

Still, upon watching the latest, exciting 10-minute preview for HBO's *Game of Thrones* I can't help but be overwhelmed *and* underwhelmed at the same time. It is a strange feeling. And I've had it before. When *Star Wars: Episode I: The Phantom Menace* was released, it was the same thing. The trailers preceding it both made me excited and overwhelmed by the return of the movies that made such a lasting impression on me and countless other geeks, and underwhelmed by seeing things that to my mind did not feel like *Star Wars*. And now I see things that, to my mind, aren't *A Game of Thrones*, know what I mean?

I see Khal Drogo there in the preview, but it's not *him*. Doesn't look like him, doesn't feel like him. I see Catelyn Stark, but that's not *her*. Not the Catelyn in the novel. So will I be able to get over stuff like this and take it for what it is— "this is the TV Khal Drogo" and "this is the TV Catelyn Stark"? Hearing lines from the characters that don't appear in the books is jarring too, but not as much as the visual element. At the same time, other visual elements are by and large spot-on, and that's I guess what gives me this uneven feeling of both good and bad—simply because those who create the series hit the jackpot on some things, and miss on others. But who am I to criticize a series that has not yet even been aired? Of course, the ever-whining Slynt. aha! Born and raised a critic, but I never realized it until the disappointments from George R.R. Martin began piling up.

But seriously, I will devour this series like a raging mutant gorilla discovering a ripe cluster of bananas dangling innocently from a tree. Jon Snow having what resembles a beard be damned, I tells you.

In the novel, Jon Snow doesn't appear to be bearded. I'll be extra carefully to look for any signs of growth on his face while reading the last of his chapters in *A Game of Thrones*, a novel that will change forever come HBO's version. Will I start seeing Peter Dinklage in my mind's eye? Lena Headey? She can roam around in my brain all she wants. Rrraaarrw!

Anyway, the chapter starts with Jon Snow packing his stuff and leaving Castle Black. Apparently, he's decided to go south and join his half-brother Robb Stark in the war that has erupted between the Houses of Stark and Lannister. It was a surprising twist the first time I read it; I honestly didn't see it coming, and up until this re-read I still think that Jon seemed determined to stay at Castle Black. But of course, the letters coming from the south changed his mind, perhaps abruptly, and that's how this turn of events became a surprise. If GRRM had been leading us up to this point with obvious clues, it wouldn't be as interesting, we'd be waiting for Jon to finally get his ass out of the far north and get home.

Samwell Tarly attempts to dissuade Jon from deserting the Night's Watch, but Jon seems to have set his mind. Remember all the way back to the first proper chapter of the novel? There we learned that the penalty for deserting the Night's Watch is beheading. Especially if you're caught near Winterfell. So, reading this the first time, I thought I knew where Jon's story might be going—he'd be captured, tried, and executed, but since Eddard had already faced that fate he wouldn't be the executioner. Oh no, I thought, that would be Robb, of course, and how would *that* go down?

Oh well, the thought didn't linger too long for by the end of the chapter Jon is back with the brothers at Castle Black, but for a moment one can imagine an entirely different outcome to Jon's storyline. So what does this chapter accomplish? Well, it is the end of Jon's arc and as such it shows us that, in the end, Jon Snow chooses his oath to the Watch over his love for his family by returning to Castle Black.

As Jon Snow flees southward, his thoughts are all about what he is doing, whether it is right or wrong. And, admirably, the author has set Jon up with a pretty hard and difficult choice. It makes Jon a more realistic character than most fantasy heroes, and maybe not that heroic after all. Is he *trying* to be a hero by going after his brother Robb? Is it vengeance for Eddard, or some notion that he can become more than he is—more than a bastard—and that's the real crux of the matter I believe. It is about Jon wanting to be recognized as a Stark, to be recognized as a son of Lord Eddard Stark.

This chapter is pretty straightforward and simple, with most of the "action" taking place in Jon's mind as he flees southward; he ponders his allegiance to the Lord Commander of the Night's Watch, Jeor Mormont, he ponders what Robb will say when they meet again. Jon does realize that maybe Robb won't say that much; poor Jon becomes unsure about his idea, and begins to fantasize about how his life will unfold; always on the run, an outlaw. He reflects that if he had only been from the south, he could have sought (spiritual) guidance from that seven-aspected god of theirs. This, I believe, GRRM puts in as sort of an irony. Because I believe that by having Ghost keeping pace with him down the Kingsroad, he actually has a representative of the Old Gods right there with him.

Jon comes to Mole Town. I like Mole Town. No, not *only* because I'm dirty-minded, but because the location itself is a neat idea. I like "original" locations, be they mighty underground dungeons like Moria, the ensorcelled Wall of the North, the *Planescape*-setting and its weird City of Sigil, the harsh lands of Cimmeria, the Death Star, the Netherstorm region in *World of Warcraft* ... you get the point. Memorable locations that never existed appeal to me. Tolkien did it masterfully, and Martin has some interesting places too. Now, Mole Town in itself can't really compare to, say, Storm's End, King's Landing, or Casterly Rock. But it has a certain something that makes it stand out from other places we visit: There is basically just a shed, and the rest of the town is underground, where the whores await horny Night's Watch members who call them "buried treasures." This is enough to make Mole Town an original place and it would be fun to return to it in a later volume. I am curious and no, not just because of the prostitution. Jon decides to bypass this interesting place altogether, continuing down the road.

As he takes a break to eat some food, he realizes that there are people coming down the Kingsroad behind him; we soon learn that it is Jon's friends who have followed him through the night: Grenn, Pyp, Toad, Halder and three others (Halder? I don't remember any Halder. Even on my tenth). Jon Snow tells them to back off, even drawing his sword, but they won't hear it. *"One against seven?"* Halder asks, as the boys encircle Jon.

Is it coincidence that they are seven? Is George telling us that it matters not whether you pray to the Old or the New Gods? When Jon, as I mentioned earlier, thinks of the gods of the south, I feel that the inclusion of those thoughts come a little bit out of left field; is George connecting it here with seven boys coming after him, or should I go and drink my aftershave?

The seven boys begin reciting the haunting oath of the Night's Watch to remind Jon of his promises. He tries to make them understand that he needs to go for they murdered his father and his brother is fighting in the riverlands; but they manage to force Jon to concede.

And then he says: *"Damn you. Damn you all."* And I can't help but add, *Damn you all to hell!* whenever I read this. Our dear George is a master of dialogue but this one has me chuckle at the cheese if youknowwhatImean.

With dawn one hour off, the eight Night's Watch boys return to Castle Black, before the desertion can be discovered by the Lord Commander. Jon tells himself that he is going to run again, but will bide his time until his friends aren't mindful. Because of Jon's little adventure, there will be no sleep, and Jon returns to the Lord Commander to do his duty as his steward. Mormont then reveals that he knew Jon went away and also says that he knew he would return. The Lord Commander gives Jon a few well-placed words of wisdom which at the same time double for setting up Jon Snow's story in the sequel *A Clash of Kings*: *"Beyond the Wall, the shadows lengthen."* He tells Jon (and us) that Mance Rayder is massing an army of wildlings, the giants are on the move, and finally reveals that the Night's Watch is going to march into the lands beyond the Wall. Mormont, perhaps somewhat bluntly, states that he believes it is Jon's destiny to be at the Wall, and that there is something about Ghost, Jon's direwolf (making me more sure that the whole old gods vs new gods thing planted earlier in the chapter is here kind of confirmed). As the Lord Commander will lead the march himself, in an attempt to find Jon's missing uncle Benjen who's been lost since the beginning of the story, he will need his steward—who also is a squire—at his side and thus he makes Jon vow not to try and run away again.

This made me think of the recent news that HBO have been given some juicy details we are not privy to concerning the story. And I am pretty sure the producers asked Mr. Martin "Will Benjen Stark turn up again? We need to know as we're writing a contract with an actor. Will he be onboard for one episode or two or will we see him in a later season?" I am also pretty convinced Martin replied something along the lines of, "Yes, Benjen Stark returns ... "

THE KING IN THE NORTH

Christmas is descending upon us once again. There's a lot to like about that fact, but there is even more that I despise about this annual tradition. The forced happiness, the expenses, the religious aspect (I tried telling a Christian that the tradition is older than Jesus but he wouldn't have it) which I absolutely abhor, and the fact that yet another Christmas passes by without *A Dance with Dragons* lovingly wrapped in festive paper waiting under the tree that's been dragged into the house and decorated with crap.

Oh well, I'll be reading *Toll the Hounds* by Steven Erikson, knowing that I have timed well my first read of his series; when I am done with the next volume, *Dust of Dreams*, the final volume should be published. And unlike George R.R. Martin, I do actually *trust* Steven Erikson to deliver on time (and if he doesn't, it is far easier to forgive him for missing a date as he is very forthcoming with his readers in a way *Not a Blog* never will be).

And, of course, I will be reading *A Clash of Kings*—with only two chapters left of *A Game of Thrones*, I aim to finish my tenth anniversary re-read this week in time for the holiday when I will be too busy performing several of the seven deadly sins (gluttony foremost). The best part about Christmas—in Norway, at any rate—is food, and lots of it: George R.R. Martin would really love the Norwegian Christmas eve; the fat is positively dripping off the tables as we devour many a fine animal. I usually end up several pounds heavier after a Christmas holiday. There is more to the Christmas holidays than food of course, but this post really was going to be about Catelyn Stark.

Now, where are we? Oh yes. For a while now, we've been gathering the threads and rounding off several character arcs and now we have two characters to go—first we have the last Catelyn chapter, followed by the book's final chapter which belongs to the gorgeous Emily Clarke. I mean, Daenerys Targaryen. Before we get to the hot stuff (literally) we have Catelyn. She is hot on most of the art presented by Fantasy Flight Games, but with HBO's casting she's become ... something else. I will gladly envision Emily Clarke as Dany but I have a hard time seeing the Catelyn in the novel as the actress chosen to play her role in HBO's *Game of Thrones*. She will really have to convince me (and many others, from what I've seen on the various forums I visit but perhaps shouldn't).

For good or for bad, HBO's series is definitely going to change our perception on some or many of the characters in the novels and probably also how we "see" the locations (I never got the impression that King's Landing was even vaguely Mediterranean in its style). Shit, I do ramble on don't I? As you can guess, I am somewhat excited about the TV series *even though* I am pretty sure it won't live up to my wishes for an adaptation of the series.

Catelyn, then. A character whose point of view is very important in the first three novels, as she is witness to many of the great political events that shake Westeros, one of them in this very chapter. At the same time, she is a mother with all the motherly concerns many (nonmothers) find somewhat annoying, that nevertheless serve to ground her as a realistic character. Said it before, saying it again—*A Game of Thrones* wouldn't be as good without Catelyn Stark.

The chapter's first paragraph, while technically correct, always makes me see something I guess the author did not intend: "... and it was across the Tumblestone that they came home now, though the boy wore plate and mail in place of swaddling clothes." As you probably have guessed, the passage makes me see Catelyn trying to carry her son Robb Stark, fully armored. Poor Catelyn's back. Though symbolically, one could argue that the passage evokes the sense of Catelyn Stark carrying the burdens of House Stark on her shoulders. Alternatively, is Robb wearing steel diapers?

Once again I note that the concept of "home" is present, which I have referred to in earlier write-ups. Most characters want to go home but never seem to get there (Arya, Davos, Daenerys), a few get home but it is not to their liking (Theon), a few seek a home they must fashion for themselves (Stannis's "quest" for the Iron Throne) but Catelyn does actually get to come home in this chapter, and though war and suffering surrounds Riverrun, it is one of the few instances where coming home isn't too bad. Oh, all right, her dad's dying and stuff, but still, Riverrun is a nice enough place for the time being.

This is also the chapter where we are properly introduced to Catelyn's family—for she is after all a Tully, and not a Stark, by birth. It is quite interesting how the author manages to flesh out Catelyn; how she is essentially a character defined by her Tully heritage as well as how the environment of Winterfell has shaped her later years. Another point in Catelyn's favor, I have to say. Ever met a woman in fantasy with the same depth?

I didn't think so. Not saying that *all* of Martin's (female) characters are as well constructed, though. (I am looking at you, Arianne Martell.) We have already met Ser Brynden Tully, Catelyn's uncle, but this chapter also gives us our first close-ups of her father, Lord Hoster, and her brother, Ser Edmure. As the Tullys are introduced, *A Game of Thrones* "opens up"; the (fairly) self-contained story of the conflict between House Stark and House Lannister gives way to a larger canvas; House Tully wants to play a larger part in the overall story, and here they are. With *A Clash of Kings*, the story widens even further with the appearance of Stannis Baratheon on the stage, and as we now know, before we get to the end of *A Feast for Crows* the story gives us the perspectives of even more families—the Martells, the Tyrells, the Greyjoys, not to mention all the minor Houses and factions that become involved in the escalating conflict. I am pretty sure Martin never originally intended to let the story grow the way it did; but somehow, somewhere down the road, the fairly simple structure of Stark vs Lannister with the threat of the Others and House Targaryen in the background, changed to a much larger depiction, from more and more points of view, and at the moment I believe we may have been better off if *A Game of Thrones'* final chapters didn't branch off quite so much.

That being said, I can dig the Red Viper or the Queen of Thorns as much as any other fan of the saga. But now it seems that Martin feels the need to capture *all* the essences of medieval history. In *A Game of Thrones* we got a good look at medieval feasts, jousting, and realpolitik. But with each book he seems to want to delve deeper into his main source of inspiration for the series and build and expand and add more. Even as late as in the fourth novel he adds more elements (religion gets an overhaul with pretty clear and direct inspiration from history; naval warfare is given more weight; the need to see the war from the point of view of commoners is added; factions previously thought uninvolved become involved) and yes, most of it is cool and no, it doesn't really help us get *A Dance with Dragons* faster.

I hope this little digression was understandable. Almost stream-of-consciousness writing going on here right now.

Let's get back on track with Catelyn and her coming to Riverrun!

Through Catelyn's eyes we get the first good glimpses at Riverrun, as her boat skids towards the docks. The descriptions are short and effective, and seeing a man drop to his knees in fear of Robb's direwolf Grey Wind is a nice little touch to remind us that the animal is pretty terrifying to people meeting it for the first time. The banners of House Tully are flapping in the wind, but Catelyn is not stirred; her grief for her lost— executed—husband is palpable. She wonders if her heart will ever lift again.

An interesting thought considering her fate in the epilogue of *A Storm of Swords*. I wonder whether this is intentional foreshadowing or coincidence. It can be hard to tell—and the more Mr. Martin treats his readers as idiots the less likely I am to attribute such detail to his talent, instead thinking it luck or coincidence. A shame.

Catelyn notices how people have grown older at Riverrun, which isn't a particularly surprising development, since she's not been there for a while. Ser Edmure Tully, her brother, promises her vengeance for Eddard but she doesn't want to hear it. So raw, the wounds ... she wants to see her father, Lord Hoster, and is brought to his solar. Her brother escorts her, and for a quick moment she reflects back on Brandon Stark and Petyr Baelish dueling for her favor in the courtyard. From here on we'll be fed small details on the past between Catelyn and Petyr, a puzzle much like certain other back-story events throughout the series giving the book a feel of a lived history among the characters, and it works well. Ser Edmure tells Catelyn that their father is dying, and she becomes angry—at herself, for she does see that a lot of the shit going down in central Westeros is *her* mistake, for taking Tyrion captive. Imagine bearing that blame on your shoulder. No wonder Catelyn's character is a bit morose here in her final chapter in *A Game of Thrones*.

In Hoster's solar, she finally meets her father again—and though we haven't met him before, the scene is touchy and realistic. Hoster says he's got crabs pinching him from the inside—is the author suggesting a particular disease? Hoster is happy to see Catelyn again, but sad that Lysa didn't come with her. He loves his daughters. Cat tells him his brother has come too—that would be the Blackfish, Brynden Tully—but once again a tangled back-story shows up—Hoster wanted Brynden to marry, but Brynden disobeyed—the complications of emotion between characters are vividly portrayed by Martin, making me believe all the more in the reality of his fictional setting.

I wonder *why* Brynden couldn't just marry some hot chick, though. Does he prefer to get his tongue brown? Who knows?

Only the Blackfish. Or there is some explanation later on that I've forgotten. (A lot of people seem to think he is gay.)

When her father needs to rest, she leaves him and goes back down from the solar where she has a brief chat with Ser Brynden before going to look for Robb. In the great hall, Theon is enjoying ale and regaling others with the tale of the battle in the Whispering Wood. This is just a quick glimpse to remind us of the character Theon Greyjoy and it's a cool scene to re-read because you see all the personality traits so much clearer in *A Game of Thrones* when you have read his chapters in *A Clash of Kings*.

But Robb is not there; he went to the godswood within the castle walls, and Catelyn reflects that is what Ned would have done too. Here Martin cleverly continues to paint Robb as a "second Ned." Little do we know, on our first re-read, how far Martin is gonna take it. *Heh.*

(See what I did there? I pretended to be Walder Frey. The Lord of the Crossing is cool.)

In the godswood, she finds Robb praying to the Old Gods together with his closest commanders. While she waits for them to finish, her thoughts wander off to her younger days with Petyr Baelish. Being back at Riverrun stirs old memories. Robb tells her that his grandfather Lord Hoster must wait—he must first hold a council, for the news of Renly Baratheon crowning himself king has reached Riverrun too.

The rest of the chapter (roughly half of it) is dedicated to the council and it is surprisingly interesting to read even though it is basically a bunch of guys, a woman, and a direwolf discussing what to do next. It is interesting for several reasons: it sets

351

up the escalating war for *A Clash of Kings*, it further gives us insight into some of the Stark commanders, and the tension between Catelyn and Robb; and the dialogue is good. This can become a great scene in the HBO series (and here I thought I'd be writing a post without mentioning *that* company). Through the heated discussion, Martin tells us the state of the war, the pros and cons of several possible strategies, and I have to say that I am on Catelyn's side in the discussion. But, as the Greatjon says, women have no knowledge of such things, and before the chapter is over he has laid his sword before Robb, and the council and the chapter ends with the magnificent twist—these men will not bend their knees to Joffrey, nor to Renly—but right there and then they swear their fealty to Robb, and proclaim him the *King in the North!*

It's a scene that brings out the goose pimples. In just a few paragraphs, Martin turns the whole Stark plot on its head; there will be no going home to mourn Ned for Catelyn. No, instead Robb and his men choose to go the hard way; and a third king has risen in Westeros and I for one cannot wait to get into *A Clash of Kings* to witness for the tenth time this epic conflict, by far the most interesting part of the whole. The Others and Daenerys? I like it, but I could do without it. But the saga wouldn't be what it is without this central conflict across the seven kingdoms of Westeros.

SUMMING UP

Stranger things have happened. Still, it is strange to have come to the end of the road; the last chapter of *A Game of Thrones*. When I wrote my first post, I had no idea as to whether I would finish the re-read bloggy style. As I stated when I wrote up the prologue, I needed something to do while waiting for *A Dance with Dragons*, and I wanted to do something related to Martin's setting because I love it. Also, I believe I was quite confident Martin would turn out his fifth novel long before I managed to blog seventy-three chapters. Instead, another year rapidly approaching and there is still no sign of that book we're all waiting for (though not longer with bated breath).

Fortunately, in the time it has taken me to blog *A Game of Thrones* (14 months or so), Martin has been very generous with updates on the process, especially around the time HBO greenlit the *Game of Thrones* TV series. Allow me to summarize these updates, these morsels of information which with we've had to do for so long.

- Posts about American football. Sigh.
- Descriptions of George's epic struggles with "Kong." You are one tough dude, George. And stop calling the book "Kong." It's called *A Dance with Dragons*.
- Reports that, having finished a chapter, he now has to rewrite it.
- Cunning allusions to the "Snowy" weather in Santa Fe.
- Endless struggles with the Meerenese knot, written as if he had never heard of the Gordian knot.

- ❖ Cryptic references to "Pat," "Yogi," and "Fred."
- ❖ Whatever you want, George. Just Finish. The Boook.
- ❖ The good news that HBO gave the green light to the Game of Thrones tv series on March 2nd, 2010.
- ❖ PoV chapters for Arianne and Aeron have been moved to *The Winds Of Winter*. An unqualified blessing. Dance became two chapters closer to completion and who knows, maybe he will forget to include the Arianne and Aemon chapters in *Winds* in, oh ... 2045, It's sure to be a winner, stacked up with all the most problematic (and boring) characters from *Dance*.

... And that's what we've been given over in *Not a Blog* the course of 14 months. Maybe one could scan over the entire blog and think that "hey, the man ain't so bad about keeping his fans updated after all." But read closer, and you see that a number of the "updates" can be dismissed out of hand because they contain virtually no useful information.

We got thirteen updates prior to the HBO greenlighting, eleven after. The thirteen prior updates were done within two or three months, and the eleven later updates took seven months. I'd also like to point out that the *Not A Blog* in this time period (November 2009-December 2010) had a total of 301 blog post updates, of which only twenty-four contained any useful information at all.

So, in conclusion, we're a little wiser than we were reading George's message in the back of *A Feast for Crows* back in 2005 (that's in the middle of the previous decade).

I better get on with my re-read. The last chapter of Daenerys' adventures in what now apparently is called "Essos" (terrible name or what?) closes the first novel in the series, and it is an interesting chapter for several reasons I shall delve into in the next update here on my little blog.

Enter The Coal Chamber

And so we come to the final chapter ... the conclusion to *A Game of Thrones*, that novel we all love so much, which has been with us since 1996, the book that kicked off the *A Song of Ice and Fire* series, as well as the long waits for book four and now book five. Can the last chapter of this mighty volume end on a satisfactory note—and will it be enticing enough to lure me into a tenth re-read of *A Clash of Kings*? There's only one way to find out if I am indeed George R.R. Martin's bitch.

I have taken the jump into hyperspace and am reading the last chapter of the novel from my cell phone. Partly to see whether I am able to actually read an entire chapter from the tiny screen of my device. It's a small thing, just a phone using the Android platform, but the text is crisp and clear. I've been living in the future for so long, it's about time I read at least one chapter from some digital source as opposed to my physical books.

Right ... loading up Amazon's Kindle software on my phone ... finding *A Game of Thrones* ... there ... hey, it has the same cover as my Dutch edition in the bookshelf, *Het Spel der Tronen*. Don't ask me why I keep throwing money at the man.

"Daenerys."

It's working, all right. *The land was red and dead and parched, and good wood was hard to come by.* Oh dear, it is perfectly understandable on the smaller screen. Also, it is a description I feel we've had quite a few times in the Dany chapters; the geography surrounding our young heroine is bleak and dismal most of the time, the lush Dothraki Sea excepted.

By the way, I have seen a lot of complaints about the place HBO decided to shoot the wedding scene between Dany and Khal Drogo, because there was sea there (on Malta) and the Dothraki hate the "poison water." Actually, it turns out, *A Game of Throne* does specifically state that Khal Drogo's mansion is close to the sea, so choosing to set the scene near the sea isn't that stoopid after all.

(Sorry for using that Alice Cooper-related word. Must be a subconscious thing, I just learned that Mr. Cooper will support Iron Maiden when they play in Oslo next time. Yes. Good old Iron Maiden. Can't stay home when they are in town. That would be stoopid. Because you know, Iron Maiden rooolz.)

Dany's foragers take the two straightest trees in the woods (do I sense homophobia here), hack off the limbs (again ...), and use the materials to build a pyre. Rhakaro and Aggo kill a horse to be fed to the fires (to accompany Khal Drogo), while Mirri Maz Duur, that tricksy witch, is bound and watches with disquiet. She tells Dany that what she is doing isn't a smart thing to do, but Dany is sick of her and has the maegi whipped. Lord Eddard Stark's words of wisdom came floating up into my consciousness as I read this, in fact. Something like, "A man who hides behind a paid executioner is no man." Yeah I am sure I am phrasing it several kinds of wrong, but you get the point. Daenerys is, at this moment, not a very good ruler because she has someone do the dirty work for her. Will this continue to be a point, and will it mean that once she returns to Westeros (if GRRM ever gets her there ...) she will not rule well—unless she gets some counsel from ... say, Tyrion Lannister or better yet Jon Snow? Only the future-people may know.

When the pyre is finished, the Dothraki heap upon it all of Drogo's stuff. Saddles, vests, even his tent, a bow, a sword, what have you. I am reminded of how the Vikings buried their kings in mounds, with stuff they would need once they came to Valhalla to party with the gods. Ser Jorah Mormont calls Dany "princess," incidentally waking the dragon; Daenerys wants him to call her Queen, for was not her brother Viserys a king? I like that tiny flash of her demanding him to correct himself. She is, after all, a Targaryen, however sweet and innocent she may look in HBO's trailers over which I now have stopped drooling. A well-placed tiny bit of characterization there from our main man, George, back when he was at the top of his game. Of thrones.

Ser Jorah drops to his knees, asking her to not go through with her plans (the specifics to be revealed as you read the chapter). There's a line from the knight where he says he loves Daenerys like he never loved Viserys; one simple line to paint the man as someone whose loyalty changes with the wind, a turncloak. And a hint to us, to be wary of the guy. I never was during my first read. I liked the character and thought him to be completely loyal to Daenerys even though we are told he's working for King Robert Baratheon as a spy. I was always under the impression he was a double-crosser. To put it another way, I love how the author keeps the character and his motivations ambiguous. I also really like the actor they chose for his role in HBO's TV series. At first I thought he didn't match how Ser Jorah should look, but from the shots in the teaser trailers alone, the actor has convinced me he's gonna be a great Mormont knight.

WAITING FOR DRAGONS

We soon learn that Daenerys has planned to climb onto Khal Drogo's pyre once it is aflame. It seems that Ser Jorah believes she wants to die with the Khal, but she swears that it is not her intention. I am still somewhat confused about this scene, even on the tenth read. How and when did Daenerys realize that walking into the flames of the Khal's pyre would not kill her? Answers are welcome.

The sun is setting when the pyre is finalized. She has but a few hundred Dothraki left to her, and she wonders how many Aegon started with (when he conquered Westeros). Funny thing is, if I recall my Westerosi history correctly, that all Aegon really needed was his two sisters and the three dragons they had together ... which of course is why Dany needs to have "three heads for the dragon" (I know, I am getting ahead of myself here). She will need three dragons to subdue Westeros, because that is how the Targaryens did it the last time, where the Field of Fire made it clear the Targaryens were not to be underestimated. Maybe I am reading too much into this little snippet, but hey, gotta have *something* to do while we wait. And wait. And wait.

Dany tells the people remaining to her that they are free, and can choose whether to stay with her or not. That's a better sign of a good leader, I guess. She tells them that *"Today I am a woman. Tomorrow I will be old."* and I must admit I wonder at this particular line. What does she mean? And how many are scratching their heads in confusion when she utters these words? I know I do. Does she know that her walking onto the pyre will change her into a more mature human being or am I totally missing something here? Probably the latter.

359

She then names Aggo, Jhogo and Rakharo her *ko*, but they really don't want to be her bloodriders as she is a chick and it's pretty unconventional for these barbarians to follow a chick. Did I say chick? She's a thirteen-year-old girl. Barely a teenager. I would have refused too, hot as she may be (for her age). Of course, she's going to be a good deal hotter at the end of the chapter ...

Rakharo tells her will ride by her side back to Vaes Dothrak where she is to become a crone of the *dosh kaleen*. Dany nods to this, knowing that things shall turn out differently. Finally she swears to Ser Jorah Mormont that one day she will gift him with a dragon-forged, Valyrian steel longsword. And we have another unresolved detail in Dany's story to look forward to, whether it will have a conclusion or whether ... words are wind. Ser Jorah vows to serve and obey her, even to die for her, whatever may come. Daenerys promises to hold the knight to that oath.

Entering the tent, Daenerys reflects that they all think her mad. A nice nod to the notion that Targaryens have a fifty-fifty chance of being born with madness. She tells herself that if she looks back, she is lost—several times, in fact. She takes a scalding hot bath, and Mr. Martin gets a chance to mention breasts and nipples and pussy and what have you. Quite an unnecessary paragraph right there, though I do like the sexiness of Daenerys's storyline. It's just so obviously filler at times. It is followed by a paragraph about her preparing Khal Drogo for the pyre.

Finally the Khal is carried onto the funeral pyre, and Daenerys commands her handmaids to bring her the dragon eggs.

WAITING FOR DRAGONS

Ser Jorah still doesn't have a clue what she's doing; he believes she wants to send the eggs with Khal to the afterworld. Mirri Maz Duur tells Dany she is mad, and Dany tells Ser Jorah to bind the maegi to the pyre. Ser Jorah doesn't like that idea, but does as she says. Sucks for him that he just swore to obey her whatever may come.

In fact, she's played them all false. But she knows that if her plan works, they will forget about it. As Mirri is bound to the pyre, Dany thanks her (in a sarcastic way I assume) for the lessons. Did Mirri's "lessons" give Dany the insight that leads to this scene? I don't know. One thing is for sure, of all the POVs in the series, Dany's have me confused the most often.

Aha! Here it follows: *"I will,"* Dany said, *"but it is not your screams I want, only your life. I remember what you told me. Only death can pay for life."*

Holy Ramen noodles, I think I finally got it this time around. She is going to use Mirri as payment to bring life to the dragons in the eggs. Mirri dies, the dragons live. But the dragons are three and Mirri, though somewhat rotund, is just one ... so I am still a little confused. But wait! Khal is still alive, in a vegetative state right? That's two. The third is ... Daenerys? But she survives...because she is a Targaryen? For once it seems my brain is with me rather than against me. I feel like having solved a crime. Hope no one objects to my conclusion ... oh wait, they slay a horse to join Khal Drogo. The animal is the third. Makes more sense. Ah, right. Clever, Mr. Martin.

Then we get a short bit where they see the red comet, which they of course take for a sign, and finally we get the astonishing final scene of *A Game of Thrones*. Mirri Maz Duur singing with a shrill voice as the flames take her. Dusk shimmering. The Khal clad in wisps of floating orange silk and tendrils of curling smoke. The odor of burning flesh. Daenerys thinks of it as a wedding as she steps onto the pyre, and the author really manages to convey the sense of *heat* in this scene. I'm feeling warm just reading about it. Also, logs are crackling merrily in the fireplace close to where I sit hunched over my laptop. *Only the fire mattered.*

As the pyre collapses, Dany is showered with ash and cinders and all those around the pyre watching become witnesses to a miracle, but not a nice and clean Catholic type of miracle; no, this one is one of fear and wonder, and it is lovingly described.

When the fire dies down, Ser Jorah Mormont finds Daenerys naked and covered in soot, her hair crisped away, yet she is unhurt. And three dragon whelps are suckling at her breasts. Crazy sight for anyone. Can't *wait* for this scene on TV. People will either totally dig it, or be disgusted depending on how they choose to show it, of course. I wouldn't mind suckling on Emily Clarke myself. It is well known. Shit, how will they do the dragons in the TV series? Surely that must seem an impossible task to the creators? Hope they look nasty and that they do all they can to make the dragons look believably real.

The knight falls to his knees, not believing his own eyes (or, it's been a while since he saw breasts). And like that, the bloodrider boys are convinced there is more to her (how couldn't they) and swear their allegiance. There will be no growing old at Vaes Dothrak for Daenerys. Her story is just beginning. A bit annoying her story begins in the last chapter of the novel, but boy do I want to get it on with *A Clash of Kings* now. The book ends with a favorite line of mine, and probably the favorite of many other fans. In other fantasy novels, dragons are, you know, just dragons. But here, they become something more profound; more *real*. Not terrifying beasts of immense power hiding out in lairs sleeping on hoards of loot, but three distinct beings come to life ... *A Game of Thrones* being such a gritty and quasi-realistic story based on medieval history, the end of the book becomes that much more magical:

> "The other two pulled away from her breasts and added their voices to the call, translucent wings unfolding and stirring the air, and for the first time in hundreds of years, the night came alive with the music of dragons."

Haunting and beautiful. Simple as that. Also, breasts. It is both a closure to Daenerys' story arc in the book and a beginning, for now we are all curious about those dragons, aren't we. Imagine waiting a decade after this chapter. Good things the novels came out at a more tolerable pace back then.

And so it ends.

And ... now it begins ...?